BY THE SAME AUTHOR

NOVELS
The Complete Knowledge of Sally Fry
The Life and Times of Barly Beach

BOATBUILDING
Keeping Nyala in Style

SELF-HELP
Dealing with a Death in the Family
Surviving your Partner

First published 2007 by
S.A. Greenland, 32 Morton Road, Exmouth EX8 1BA

A catalogue record for this book is available from the British Library.
ISBN 978-0-9550512-1-0

Printed and bound by Short Run Press Ltd., Bittern Road, Sowton Industrial Estate, Exeter EX2 7LW

CANDY'S CHILDREN

A Novel by

Sylvia Murphy

Published by S.A. Greenland imprint

To

Marthe Matilde and Peter Jocelyn,

who gave me this story as I was growing up.

CANDY'S CHILDREN

CONTENTS

1
JAFFA

The explosion hit the morning with a blinding flash and a crack of sound, followed almost immediately by the roar of moving air. Pieces of debris hurtled outwards from the epicentre with the velocity of bullets, shattering and splattering everything that stood in the way, turning the busy thoroughfare into a nightmare of death.

The immediate debris was immolated blood and flesh, shattered bone. Unrecognisable pieces of human bodies spread amongst the twisted furniture of the little pavement cafe where the businessmen liked to take their morning coffee. The first to be shredded were the elderly lady in a pale blue linen suit and the young woman in a black *djellabah* who had been hurrying towards her. An instant later two little boys playing football with a tin can in the gutter were ripped open and their viscera splattered against a passing car that was then lifted and hurled into the path of a lorry coming in the opposite direction. The lorry driver slammed on his brakes before he was crushed by a piece of flying masonry. The lorry mounted the car, mutilating its occupants beyond recognition, before hitting the side of a bus that was picking up passengers, showering those inside with shards of glass and bits of twisted metal that acted like daggers. The bus leaned over under the weight of the lorry, tottered on two wheels, then fell on its side, on top of the people who, a moment before, had been crowding around to mount the steps.

The people killed by the flying debris rather than the immediate explosion were dissected more neatly before being hurled through the air. A complete arm here, a head there, a bloody torso wrapped around a lamp post. The ponderous, moustachioed gentleman sitting at a table inside the cafe reading a newspaper froze for an instant before he was flung backwards in his seat and simultaneously decapitated by a piece of metal flying sideways with the force of a falling guillotine. The young waiter bringing him coffee, his mind on fond thoughts of the girl he was to marry next week, was thrown backwards against the counter and overtaken by the plate glass window that cut off both his legs as it crashed around him and left him to bleed to death.

As the front of the cafe disintegrated, the supports of the two upper storeys of the building collapsed and it folded in on itself, burying the cafe proprietor, the chef who had only started work there last week, the grandmother in the upstairs apartment who was sweeping the floor and listening to the chattering of her daughter's infant, left in her care, the young couple on the upper floor who were still learning to live in peace together. The neighbouring buildings were left teetering until a pick-up carrying vegetables from a nearby farm careered out of control as the driver panicked, and buried itself in one of the unstable walls, bringing another building down.

Seconds later the sound of breaking glass came from every quarter as the blast took out windows in an ever-widening circle. Car horns blared as vehicles collided in the spreading chaos.

Then the screaming began.

That evening the BBC's prime-time audience was treated to a jumpy scene filmed by a passer-by on his state-of-the-art cellphone. Hurrying stretcher-bearers and wailing relatives clutched at inert forms discreetly covered by sheets as the newsreader announced, in measured tones, 'A suicide bomber detonated a device this morning in a pavement cafe in Tel Aviv, killing twenty-two people and injuring almost a hundred more. It was believed that the Dowager Countess of Penmore, a distant cousin of the Queen, who was visiting Israel, may be among the dead. No group has yet claimed responsibility for the outrage.'

The twelfth Earl of Penmore folded his newspaper and watched with distaste as his elder half-brother strode across Heathrow's first-class departure lounge towards him. Heads turned, as they always did when Leon was about, and the Earl quivered with embarrassment.

For heaven's sake, would the man never grow up? Surely

those striped Indian shirts with cotton trousers, and the long hair tied back, had gone out of fashion years ago? And that coat – where had he got that canvas coat that swung from his shoulders almost to the ground, like something out of the wild west? Perhaps it was a shade more civilised than the embroidered goatskin he'd been calling an overcoat the last time they met, but it was no less flamboyant. It wasn't as though he couldn't afford to dress properly, so one could only assume that he didn't know any better. The Earl himself was clad in a suit that he considered sombre enough for the occasion, if a little heavy for an April visit to the Middle East. His gabardine raincoat lay folded on the seat beside him together with a neatly zipped flight bag containing a copy of John Major's memoirs and a folder full of the papers and photographs he was going to need when he arrived in Israel.

He stood up as Leon came to a halt in front of him and held out his right hand. Leon's smile looked genuine as he said, 'Jeremy. Nice to see you again.'

The Earl shook the proffered hand and murmured, 'Leon. Long time.' But not long enough. The Earl neither smiled nor said anything about the meeting being nice for him. Not for the first time, he wondered why he found his brother's transatlantic twang so irritating. Then, to cover the awkwardness of the silence that threatened, he added, 'Good of you to come.' It was a lie. There was nothing good about Leon's presence at all. He had demanded to come, wheedled the flight details out of the Earl's secretary so that the two of them could travel together, giving Jeremy the feeling that he wasn't quite trusted.

Jeremy sat down again, clasping his hands across his portly belly as he always did when he was with Leon. How could his brother still be so lean when he was ten years the elder and, from all accounts, led a pretty dissolute life?

'Any more news?' Leon draped himself in the next armchair and Jeremy averted his eyes from the length of sockless hairy leg that appeared between the trouser bottoms and the worn sneakers.

'No.'

'They're sure it's her?'

'Seems they found the remains of a handbag with her passport in it.'

'I always thought her bags looked as though they were armour-plated...'

'Then there were some rings...' How could Leon joke about this? 'That's what I have to identify. I have some of the insurance photographs here.' He patted the flight bag to reassure himself, then looked sideways at Leon and noticed that the profile was tense. Leon turned his face, eyes brimming. 'What the hell was she doing there, Jeremy? Didn't anyone advise her against going on holiday in a war zone?'

Oh God, thought the Earl, he's going to make an emotional picnic of this. How embarrassing! He said, 'I don't remember our mutual mother ever accounting for her actions, do you?' He looked away while Leon took out a large silk handkerchief and blew his nose loudly. Then, because he knew it would puzzle and irritate Leon, he added, 'Of course, she was always talking about going back for a visit.'

'Going back?'

'Yes. She was born there, in Jaffa. Didn't you know?'

The very satisfactory stunned silence that followed was interrupted by a flight manager crossing the carpeted lounge to inform them that their plane to Tel Aviv was ready for boarding. It wasn't until they were comfortably settled in their business-class seats on the plane, seatbelts fastened, and the fluttering of the flight attendants had quietened – not often they had a rock star and a member of the aristocracy on the same flight – that Leon said , 'So tell me, brother, how come Mother was born in Israel? I know she had a seriously weird life but she wasn't Jewish, was she ?'

'Don't you know anything about Middle Eastern Politics? No, why should you? You're American. Up to nineteen forty-eight Israel didn't exist. It was Palestine, ruled by the British. Her father was a British citizen, a fruit broker – used to buy up the citrus fruit crops for a big importer in London. She was born in twenty-four and spent most of her early life there.'

'She told you all this?'

'Some. Under pressure. When my father died the lawyers

needed her birth certificate to set up a trust for her and it was in Arabic. I had the devil of a job getting an English version out of Somerset House. Oh..ho...here we go!' His knuckles tightened on the arm rests as the plane gathered speed along the runway. 'I always hate that bit! They swore the bloody thing didn't exist until I turned up there in person with the Arab version, then they made some excuse about the records being lost in the riots...'

'Riots?'

'The political arrangements were never popular. The period was well punctuated by all the usual atrocities.'

'And yet Mother's family lived there with two young daughters?'

'They and many others. Between the army and the business interests there was quite a flourishing European community. Considered themselves more at home in Palestine than Britain. I think it was only a matter of chance that the family was on leave in England when World War Two broke out and they had to stay here.'

'Otherwise ... the story might have been very different? No you and me for a start?'

'I'm not too sure about that. I suspect England might have been unavoidable even without the war. Things ... happened. They were a very odd family indeed. Not your average respectable colonials.'

'Mother told you more?'

'Not much. But Aunt Netta got very drunk when she came to Granny Hargreaves' funeral, and she spent a whole evening bending my ear about how she'd been done down by Mother – you can imagine the sort of thing – and then Mother realised what was going on and took her out like an exocet and I couldn't help putting some of the home truths together in my head.'

Leon looked at his Rolex. 'We've got the best part of four hours. Why don't you tell me about it, Bro?'

*   *   *

'Wait for me, Candy! Wait for me!'

Candice cringed at the sound of her younger sister's voice. All her life she'd been followed by cries of 'Wait for me!' from Annette, or 'Wait for Netta!' from her mother or their Arab nurse, Leila. There must have been a time when she hadn't been pursued by her responsibility, a blessed thirty-six months when she was her own person before Netta had arrived to plague her, but she couldn't remember it.

It had always been 'Wait for me, Candy!'

Candy quickened her step and left her sister trailing far behind as she widened the distance by stretching her black-stockinged legs beneath her dark blue serge dress. Unladylike, her mother would say. Ladies didn't lope along like horses. But it was difficult not to when your legs were longer than everyone else's. It was only a short walk from the white square of the convent school building through the town to their apartment block but it took them through the teeming Palestinian streets and ever since Candy could remember she had been told never to talk to anyone, never to look too long to right or to left, because terrible things could happen, like being kidnapped and sold into slavery. Whatever that meant.

Whenever she asked Leila the nurse simply shook her head and said 'All of life is slavery for a woman, child.'

'What do you *mean*?'

'You will understand.' Said with that infuriating half-smile that was so often on Leila's surprisingly unlined face, hinting that she had the wisdom of the world at her disposal but wasn't going to part with any of it just yet.

'I want to understand now. I shall ask my mother.'

'Your mother will tell you nothing.'

That was true, for Maddie Hargreaves rarely paused long enough in the company of her daughters to listen to a question, let alone give an answer. She was always doing something that was more important, like dressing in one of her smart silk frocks, or entertaining other wives to tea, or out at a dinner in someone else's apartment, or just lying down in her darkened room recovering from some malady or another. And even when they were together, like out shopping or down at the lido on the beach that the

European families had made into their exclusive club, Maddie had nothing to say beyond giving instructions as to how they should behave in public, how they should keep out of her way, not hang onto her hand or arm, not butt in when she was talking to her friends, not make a noise or stare at people, however strange they looked, and never, never pass a personal remark about anyone. It was a code that Candy knew by heart. Even Netta knew it, though sometimes she forgot and was treated to that dagger of a glare that Maddie did so well and made you want to curl up inside.

Still thinking about the possibility of being sold into slavery, Candy wondered if Netta might one day disappear completely if she was left far enough behind. If only! Then she thought of the trouble she would be in, of the way it would weigh on her soul, imagining Netta's fear and panic as she was bundled into a sack and thrown across the back of a donkey and hurried down to the port to be put in a dark cabin on board one of the many tramp steamers that came and went. And what would Sister Mary Oliver say? Would it count as a mortal sin or would it only be venial, if she hadn't actually arranged for Netta to be kidnapped, just wished it?

She turned the last corner and skipped up the polished stone steps that led into the foyer of the apartment building and hid behind a pillar. She didn't quite dare to be seen to arrive without Netta - that could lead to real punishments like no swimming or no sleeping on the roof – so it was necessary to wait. She knew almost to the second how long it would take her slightly panting and very anxious sister to arrive at the bottom of the steps, lower lip trembling and tears starting to catch at the throat. At the right moment she jumped out, caught Netta's wrist just hard enough for it to give a hint of how much it might hurt if she held any tighter, and shouted angrily, 'There you are, you naughty girl! You've kept me waiting again! Why are you always so slow?'

'I hate you!' Netta twisted her arm against her sister's grasp. 'Mummy said you had to wait for me. She said never to leave me to walk through the *souk* by myself. I shall tell her what a pig you are!'

'And I shall tell her how you dawdle and look into the

shops.'

'She won't believe you. She won't believe you because she loves me best. You know she does. She calls me her pretty darling and you a great gallumphing thing...Ow!'

As rage overcame Candy she flicked up her sister's skirt and delivered a thumping smack onto her navy-blue-knickered bottom. Two passing Arab youths sniggered and she turned and stuck her tongue out at them, which made them laugh even more, then form their mouths into round 'O' shapes and make little whooping noises. Made angrier than ever by their insolence she turned on her heel and flounced up the steps through the big wooden doors that the watchman came forward to open for them. Netta scuttled after her, rubbing her bottom with one hand and her eyes with the other, her big leather satchel bumping against her behind.

The door of their ground-floor apartment was open before they reached it and Leila stood there calm and cool in her faded cotton frock, one finger to her olive-coloured lips. Wisps of greying hair escaped from the pins she used to hold it in a tight little knot at the nape of her neck and the wisps framed her face like fine lace. 'Be quiet there, girls,' she said. 'I could hear you all along the street. My goodness, what do you look like?' She took Candy's satchel off her shoulder and guided her in front of the gilded full-length mirror in the hall.

As soon as she saw her reflection Candy was ashamed of herself. Her cotton dress, gathered at the waist, had ridden up under her satchel, showing too much stocking. Her white starched collar was creased and crooked, two buttons across the front of her slightly rounded bosom were undone, showing a glimpse of her white cotton vest. Her long auburn hair, that had started the day brushed and plaited, was ruffled and sticking out at all angles. And to complete the picture her black stockings were wrinkled and her shoes dusty.

She caught sight of her sister smirking behind her. How did Netta manage to be looking clean and sweet, apart from her tearstained face? It wasn't only her golden curls, there was something about her that made her look like an angel while Candy could only feel gawky and clumsy.

'You go and change right now,' Leila said. 'I've just ironed your blue ginghams. Then we have tea..'

'Where's Mummy?' asked Netta, glancing around with an anxiety Candy recognised because it echoed her own. Where their mother was at any particular time was unpredictable, so was her mood. Yesterday she had found Netta in the bathroom, playing with a long orange rubber tube with a bulb in the middle of it – superb for sucking up water and squirting it down the middle of the plughole – and she had slapped Netta and screamed at Leila for not tidying up properly. The orange rubber toy had disappeared into a cardboard box but not before Candy asked what it was for and her mother snapped 'It's none of your business, child. It's not the sort of thing people talk about.'

So Netta wanted to be sure that she didn't play with the wrong things again. 'Where's Mummy?'

'In her bed with a headache. You mustn't disturb.'

'Oh no!' It was Candy's turn to be threatened by tears. 'She promised she'd take us to the lido today – I have to practise for the swimming sports at the weekend.'

'Not today, Miss. Your mother says homework and piano practice. She will take you out tomorrow.'

Even without the practice it was easy, the following weekend, beating the other girls in the swimming races. None of them could hope to catch her. The very length of her body made sure she was ahead at the moment she hit the water. But beating the girls wasn't enough. The boys' cup was bigger than the girls' and came with more prize money, and she didn't see why she shouldn't be allowed the chance to win it. She told everyone she spoke to, all afternoon, 'I can beat the boys as well as the girls.'

'A girl, race against the boys! It simply isn't done!' said the short, fat club secretary, who couldn't swim at all.

'Be thankful you have your own competition with your own prize,' said the wife of the club president, who thought that such arrogance was only what was to be expected from the daughter of that loose, pushy woman Madeleine Hargreaves.

And Maddie said, 'Really Candice, you do make an exhibition of yourself! It isn't ladylike to be so keen to win.'

So she had to watch Alec Russell, son of the British Consul, who was on holiday from Eton, win the boys' race, when she knew, she just knew she could beat him. It simply wasn't fair. She hated Alec. She had hated him for years, ever since they'd been toddlers together on this very beach and he'd snatched her spade and hit her over the head. Every chance he got he bullied her and laughed at her. Now, at fifteen he was more thickset than she was but no taller and he had the beginnings of a dark down on his chin, in which nestled an ever-changing crop of pimples. But, worst of all, he had an embarrassingly large mound in his groin that was made more prominent by the clinging folds of the wet woollen swimming costume that hung shapelessly from his shoulders. But he was unaware of how grotesque he looked. He thought he was all right because he was a boy. And he thought it was all right to laugh at Candy in front of the other children. 'Just because you're the wrong shape to be a proper girl doesn't mean you have to try to act like a boy!'

'What do you mean by that?'

'Work it out for yourself, beanpole!'

Okay, so she was flat-chested for her age, but that only made her a better swimmer, didn't it? Everyone knew she could swim faster than he could. He was just scared she could beat him over the fifty yard course between the two swimming rafts that were anchored off the beach. 'You're scared to race against me, aren't you.'

'I'm not scared of anything.'

'Show me, then.'

'Okay, tomorrow.'

'No, right now.'

'Now?' He glanced around nervously. It was getting late, evening was setting in. Younger children were being dried and dressed to be taken home. There was a line of smart horse-drawn cabs already waiting at the roadside. White coated Arab boys were tidying the tea cups away and bringing out trays of drinks for the parents of the older children, who could stay later.

'Yes, why not? No one will take any notice once we're in the water. Or are you scared of your parents as well?'

It took them only minutes to swim out to the first raft and she'd been right, nobody took more than a passing interest except for other children such as Esme and Sylvia and two boys who went to the same school as Alec. To their parents they were still children who played together, not deadly rivals, and they were just having a last evening swim after the excitement of the day.

Netta gave one cry of, 'Wait for me!', then stood at the water's edge watching, not quite daring to swim by herself as far as the rafts.

They balanced side by side on the edge of the first raft and, hardly waiting for the boys to shout, 'On your marks! Go!' Candy hurled herself into the warm sea. She surfaced with a splutter, arms already milling into a crawl that drew her swiftly through the water. On the raft behind her she could hear thumping and cheering from the other children. Every time she raised her head to take a breath she could see the second raft where the race would finish, still a distant block on the surface of the water. Somewhere alongside her she could sense rather than hear the churning of the water as Alec Russell powered along the same trajectory. He wasn't behind her yet, but he wasn't ahead of her either. Faster, faster! Candy could feel her heart thudding and her head roaring. The muscles of her arms and shoulders crackled under the strain of moving the endless water aside. And still she wasn't in the lead. She had to give it more.

Half way across Candy could hear Alec grunting and gasping just behind her. He's behind me! He's behind! And, though a moment ago she thought she was swimming as hard as she could, now she thrust forward with even more energy because something told her she wasn't safe until she was out of his reach. She was right. The first time she felt his hand brush her ankle she thought it was a mistake, he was swimming too close. The second time she knew he was doing it on purpose. The third time, only ten yards from the raft, she felt his fingers closing on her heel and her foot being twisted, pulled out of line. Frightened, off her stroke, she kicked out and connected with some part of his head, felt his grasp slip away. She'd been slowed for a moment but she was able to thrust forward again to close the gap of water and grasp the ladder that hung down from the platform of the raft. As she turned, gasping, she saw Alec's face surfacing behind her, his nose streaming blood. She started a grin of triumph but it froze on her lips as his face twisted into a snarl and his eyes flashed pure hatred.

'Cheat!' He spluttered, flicking his hair back out of his eyes with one hand. 'Cow! Cheat!'

'You're the one who cheated!'

'You kicked me in the face! If that's not cheating I don't know what is! Here, take this!'

With his free hand he smacked her round the face as hard as he could in the unsteady environment of the water. Shock ran through her, then fear. She glanced towards the beach but they were too far away for anyone to see clearly what was happening. Alec's eyes glittered with the triumph that comes from using power and strength and Candy knew that she must get away from him. But that wasn't so easy. Desperately she heaved herself upwards onto the lowest rungs of the ladder but Alec wrapped his arms around her legs, twisted and pulled down. For a moment she hung on but it was a choice between keeping her fingers locked on the ladder rungs and dislocating every joint in her body, or giving in and letting go. Still fighting him, she let herself be pulled backwards into the water, then down, down towards the sandy sea bed. She felt Alec shifting his grip to hold her round her waist, then to grasp her body beneath his, wrapping his legs around hers.

He'll let me up in a moment, she thought. Sooner if I don't struggle. And she waited, hating the feel of him so close to her, not believing what she felt him doing as he pulled down the top of her swimsuit and viciously pinched her nipples. Then, as her head began to buzz and her lungs felt as though they would burst, there was a hand between her legs, clutching at her and rubbing back and forth. She tried to struggle free, opened her mouth to gasp. The buzzing in her head turned to a roaring and she blacked out. She came to again lying on the rough brown canvas surface of the raft, coughing and retching. Alec was crouched over her, his hands on her chest, and she rolled away, terrified, remembering. 'Careful,' he muttered, catching hold of her arm to stop her slipping back into the water. 'You nearly drowned.'

Of course she'd nearly drowned! He'd held her under, hadn't he? He'd...oh dear Jesus, what had he done? She had to escape from him. She pushed his arm away and scrambled to her knees and saw that one of the beach canoes was close, paddled by Lieutenant Muldoon, one of the young army officers, the salt water glistening on his spiky ginger moustache. Why was he out there, approaching the raft? Had he seen? Oh, pray God he hadn't seen...

'I shouted for help,' Alec said. 'When you got into difficulties I shouted for help.'

'I didn't get into difficulties!' she hissed. 'I won.'

Alec gripped her arm and thrust his face close to hers. 'No,' he said. 'I won. Remember that.'

Candy rode back to the beach on the front of the canoe, her back to Lieutenant Muldoon, and Alec swam alongside. As the canoe scrunched onto the sand and Candy leapt off she saw her mother coming towards them, holding a big towel in front of her. They met and the towel was wrapped around Candy's shoulders. 'Candice, what have you been doing? How dare you cause all this fuss? Say thank you to Lieutenant Muldoon. And to Alec. If he hadn't raised the alarm you might have drowned.' Bobby Muldoon straightened up from pulling the canoe out of the water and Candy noticed the way her mother's eyes locked onto his for a moment as she said, 'Thank you, Bobby. Sorry to put you to so much trouble.'

And Bobby replied, 'It was nothing, Mrs Hargreaves, nothing at all.'

Without a word Candy gripped the towel tightly around her, and made her way over to the clubhouse to change into her frock. She was aware that Maddie was staring after her, bemused and a little embarrassed at the lack of the correct social responses, but she wasn't at all sure that she could speak at that moment without either shouting in rage or crying in humiliation. Inside the ladies' changing cubicle she stripped off the sagging jade-green cloth of her costume, and began to rub her body, not too vigorously because she was nearly dry already. As she passed the towel between her legs it came away with a streak of blood on it and suddenly her mood changed from anger to terror. Her heart thumped.

What had Alec done to her? Somehow with his rough handling he must have cut her. She felt her face turning crimson with shame. She splayed her legs a little to see where the wound might be but there was nothing. She felt with her hand and her fingers came away with another smear of blood. Where was it coming from?

On the rough wooden wall a small rectangle of mirror hung on a nail and she carefully unhooked it and held it down in front of her so that it showed the top of her thighs and the bright pink folds of the crack between her legs that she knew was private because that was where your body got rid of its dirt. She widened her legs to see further into the crack but it seemed to carry on right inside her and that was where the slight oozing of slimy blood was coming from. Somehow Alec had wounded her deep inside and if anyone was going to be able to make it heal she was going to have to tell them what he had done to her. But she knew she would never do that. Because even though it might lead to him getting into trouble, somehow he would be able to turn it round to being her fault and all the trouble would be on her shoulders. The way it always was. No, she would simply keep her legs as tight together as she could and wait for the bleeding to stop. Bleeding always stopped after a while, didn't it?

'It's the curse,' Leila said, speeding her needle through the cotton lawn they were working on. 'The slavery of being a woman.' Leila did the family laundry and she'd noticed stained knickers. But she didn't talk about it until she was alone with Candy, sitting on the verandah helping her to sew a new white blouse whilst Netta tinkled clumsy scales on the piano inside.

Candy was amazed. 'You mean it happens to all women, all the time?' Even the nuns at the convent school? She found that hard to imagine – the pale, devout sisters, bleeding from between their legs. But no, perhaps not. Perhaps when they became nuns the bleeding stopped if they prayed enough. That made it seem more attractive, being a nun. She was relieved as well, to know that what had happened would have happened anyway on that particular day. It was nothing to do with Alec.

'Does it happen to you, Leila?'

'I told you, to every woman, for all the time she is a real woman. Except when Allah turns it to a blessing.'

'What do you mean by that?'

Leila's needle paused and she regarded Candy with big, soulful eyes. 'The curse of every woman becomes a blessing, but only a man can make it so by giving her children.'

'I still don't understand what you mean.'

'Your mother will tell you in good time.'

'Does she know? About me, I mean?'

Leila inclined her head in a single nod. 'She says she will talk to you after she has had her rest.' Then she held up the gathered sleeve of the blouse against Candy's shoulder. 'Hurry up or you'll have two sleeves to wear to the club tomorrow and no bodice.' Leila sewed beautifully and she did the bits that would show the most while Candy struggled to learn on the tucks and gores that shaped the waistline.

'Does Netta know?'

'Tch! She's too young to be told about these things.'

A quiet knock, on the door that was always closed. Maddie's bedroom door. No reply, so another knock.

Funny, thought Candy, how it was never their bedroom door, only hers, where her father sometimes slept. But, Candy suspected, not always, because there were times when he didn't come home until the morning, or when he was unwell and slept in the spare bedroom. Candy often wondered how someone who looked so ruddy and healthy could be unwell so often.

'Candice. Come in, quietly. Shut the door.'

The room was shadowed, more than it needed to have been at that time of the afternoon. And there was that strange scent, perfume mixed with sweat and something else, something sweet and stale. Maddie was sitting at her dressing table, touching at her hair with a tortoiseshell comb, so that she looked at Candy by way of the triple mirror with the bronzed plaster frame. Candy shifted forward until she could see her mother's face from three different angles. She waited, wondering what to say.

'Leila tells me you've started the curse.'

'Yes. The other day at...'

'Yes, yes. Over there on the bed.' She nodded to the high damask-covered bed. Candy went over and found a rectangular package, something soft in brown paper. For a moment she thought it might be a pair of shoes and she began to open the package. 'Not here, you fool!' snapped Maddie, turning her body so that they faced each other properly. 'It's a packet of ess tees.'

'Ess tees?'

'Yes. To wear. When you've got it. Didn't Leila tell you?'

Leila had given her a white napkin to fold and wear inside her knickers. She'd called it linens, not ess tees. Candy held the package, curious but afraid as well.

'There's a belt there too.' Candy stared at the elastic contraption that also lay on the bed. 'Well go on, child, take it. You'll need it. Next time it happens.'

'What do I do with it?'

'If you can't work it out for yourself Leila will tell you.'

'All right.' She picked up the elastic belt as well and turned towards the door.

'Just a minute.' Maddie's voice stopped her and the comb was waggled threateningly in Candy's direction. 'Just you make sure that you know how to behave now that you're growing up. You must stop playing around with the boys as though you were a child. And you must never mention to anyone anything about having the curse. Do you understand?'

'Come on, child, pay attention! Who is God?'

Candy jumped as Sister Mary Oliver rapped the edge of her desk with her cane. 'God is love,' she repeated automatically, wishing she wasn't so tired.

'And where is God, Candice?'

'God is everywhere, Sister.'

That should mean that love is everywhere, thought Candy. But there had certainly been no love anywhere near her mother and father that weekend. If they'd been in the same room the atmosphere had been like frost and when he'd finally gone out Maddie could be heard weeping in her bedroom. So if love wasn't everywhere, God couldn't be everywhere, therefore there was something very wrong with the catechism they were learning.

'You're still dreaming, Candice!' Sister Mary Oliver was giving out pieces of paper to test them on their Bible learning and Candy's heart thudded. She had tried to do her homework but what with piano practice on Saturday and Maddie taking them to the Major's wife's tea party on Sunday, there hadn't been a lot of time. True, time had been set aside on Sunday morning and Naseem, Leila's youngest son who came sometimes to help his mother and to learn the skills of being a houseboy, had sat down with them to help with their learning. Naseem had been coming to the apartment ever since he was a small child and Candy loved him because he always smiled kindly at her, the only person who ever did that. So when he sat down to test her Bible verses and seemed to be more interested in practising his own reading of English, she encouraged him, and the time passed pleasantly educating Naseem rather than Candy. It didn't matter. Sometimes Sister Mary Oliver forgot about testing them on their homework but when this Monday came, no such luck.

Another proof that God was very far from everywhere.

She sighed, recalling the first few words of the verses they had been told to learn. Perhaps God would be merciful and would slide the words into her head in the right order when she began to write. It wasn't as though Sister Mary Oliver, with her seamed face and her bristling moustache, could make things any worse even if she got it all wrong. She took her wooden pen out of her pencil box, checked the nib, and dipped it into the inkwell on her desk.

'The Lord is.....'

Her mind went blank. All she could remember were Naseem's kind eyes as he smiled at her over the top of the Bible.

Nothing about the words at all. She began to panic, to perspire at the back of her neck. She wrote a few more words, peered sideways, trying to see what Esme was writing beside her. But Esme had her arm curled around her work, keeping it to herself as her pen scratched purposefully across the page.

Sister Mary Oliver swished up and down between the rows of desks and paused just behind Candy. Candy remembered some more phrases and began to write again, bending her head over her work, trying to imitate Esme's secretiveness. But she wasn't sure what order they should go in, and when she re-read them they didn't seem to make sense. Sister Mary Oliver moved on, her cane twitching against the grey folds of her skirt.

'One more minute, girls.'

Candy remembered the last phrase and scribbled hurriedly. As she turned her face she met Esme's eyes, alight with triumph. Esme's work was firmly covered by her blotting paper.

'Time to stop.'

Pens were laid aside, nibs and papers blotted. Sister Mary Oliver's little grey eyes darted around the room, came to rest on Candy. Oh, please choose someone else, Candy prayed. But of course she wouldn't, because this was all a trap to make her look stupid. A trap set by God. As though he hadn't done enough by making her tall and ugly and clumsy.

'Candice. Will you stand and read us what you have written?'

Candy paled and glanced around. If only she could have Esme's or Sylvia's papers in her hand instead of her own. If only Sister Mary Oliver had been kindly disposed towards her and had asked one of the others to read so that Candy could quietly hide her shame. Slowly she fumbled to her feet. Slowly she lifted her paper. Slowly she began to read.

'The Lord is...'

'Yes?'

Candy tried, but she couldn't get a word out. The silence was horrible, like a huge beast hanging in the air above them, waiting to crunch its jaws and devour one of them. 'I...I don't remember the next bit, Sister.'

'And why not?'

'Because...' As she began to speak she remembered something Naseem had said. 'Because God has taken the words out of my mind, Sister.'

Sister Mary Oliver drew in her breath sharply and the class was treated to the sight of her face slowly becoming pink, then red. Then a strange shade of purple began to gather around her twitching mouth. Finally she exploded into something between a bellow and a shriek.

'You wicked, wicked girl! Does your pride know no bounds! You lie and blaspheme in one breath, trying to blame God for your own laziness! Come here!'

Candy stepped forward, cheeks flaming. 'I'm not lazy. I just didn't have time.'

'Why, what were you doing? Attending to the pleasures of your body, no doubt, primping and preening in front of a mirror instead of trying to improve your soul. Your study of the scriptures should be the first thing you do, not the last. To say you didn't have time is to compound your sin! Hold out your hands.'

Candy knew what was coming. Two or three sharp, stinging raps across her palms with the cane, then being kept in at break time to write some lines. But something about what she had said had enraged Sister Mary Oliver beyond the normal and Candy wasn't at all prepared for the ferocious way the cane was brought down. The first blow sliced into her palms, the second broke the skin across the tendons of her wrists, the third broke a thumb. Candy was appalled at the excruciating pain and tears coursed down her cheeks as she stared at her bloody hands. It took several more blows before she had the sense of self preservation to withdraw her hands and hide them behind her back and as the cane swished through space she thought for an instant she was going to be hit across the face.

But the nun stopped, breathing heavily, still red in the face. The silence behind Candy was intense, shocked. Not a shuffle, not a cough. Sister Mary Oliver drew two more deep breaths then said, in a voice that was still shaking, 'Now, go and wait outside Mother Superior's room.'

Out in the corridor, Candy took one look at her smashed and bleeding hands and started to run. Past the niches where the saints stood, staring impotently across their little flickering lamps, past the big brown carved crucifix where the girls and the nuns always stopped to genuflect, past Mother Superior's door which was always ajar so that she could see and hear what was happening outside. Her feet echoed on the flagstones and a novice with frightened eyes came scurrying forward out of Mother's office, hands fluttering to try to stop Candy's headlong flight. But Candy had already passed her, pushed through the fretwork screen into the courtyard, scurried across the stone flags, scattering the chickens, and was trying to pull open the heavy street door with her throbbing hands. Mother Superior followed the novice, puffing and panting because she was overweight, then came Sister Joseph and Sister Aloysius, all excited squeals and flapping garments. Just as Candy managed to pull open the door, Mother Superior reached her and flung her arms around her waist, while Sister Joseph, by far the strongest of them, grabbed Candy's wrists.

'What has happened to you, child?' barked Mother Superior. 'You can't go home like that.'

'I can! I will!' Candy struggled, kicked at Mother Superior's shins and then sank her teeth into one of Sister Joseph's hands. Sister Joseph let go with a yelp and lashed out to slap Candy's face. In the street outside a curious crowd of passers-by was gathering. Mother Superior caught sight of them and she released her grip on Candy and stood aside. 'Sisters, sisters, we are behaving in a manner unbecoming to the followers of Christ. It seems that a devil has come amongst us. We should let Candice go and fight with the evil spirit in her own way. Meanwhile, sound the bell for us all to gather in the chapel and pray for her.'

She watched as Candy forced her way through the watching crowd, shaking her head sadly and sighing heavily. Then she shut the door and left Candy to make her way alone through the streets, trying to hide her hands and her tears from the curious, questioning gazes. When she reached home she fell into Leila's arms, sobbing and choking. Muttering with concern, Leila bathed and bandaged her hands, making them like large white paws. But she asked no questions. It was as though she already knew what must have happened. She gave Candy a bitter-tasting drink that she said would ease the pain and tucked her into bed. 'Sleep a while,' she said, and Candy had no choice as her head swam in time to the slowly revolving ceiling fan, blotting out the awful day.

Some time later she opened her eyes and blinked across the shadowed room where she was lying. She was confused. The heavy shafts of sunlight that crept through the cracks around the shutters, the sounds of people moving in the street beyond the verandah wall, all told her it was late afternoon. So what was she doing in bed? Then she felt the throbbing pain in her bandaged hands and she remembered.

'Can I fetch you anything, Miss Candy?' The soft voice was near the door and Candy lifted her head a little to make sure it was who she thought it was. Naseem, in his white houseboy's uniform and his soft house slippers.

'Is there any lemonade?' Candy struggled to sit up and Naseem came forward to help her. His hands were cool against her hot arms.

'Of course. It's here.' He poured the pale, sticky liquid from a jug on the bedside table and passed her the glass, helping her to raise it to her lips and take a few sips. He said, 'Leila told me to watch over you.'

'Where has she gone?'

'To meet Miss Netta from school.'

'Yes, of course.' School. All sorts of questions flashed into her mind. Would she have to go back? Would Netta be able to carry on going there? What would the nuns say to her parents? What would happen to her if they didn't want her to go back? Perhaps she had already been expelled and would have to have lessons at home. Or perhaps they would send her to school in England. She shuddered. England, where it was always cold and raining.

She felt fresh tears, brushing at them ineffectually with her bandages. 'What's going to happen to me, Naseem?'

He shifted uncomfortably from one foot to the other, eyes full of sympathy. 'What more can happen, Miss Candy? You have already been beaten for whatever you did. That is the end of the matter.'

'I don't mean now, I mean in the future. Nobody loves me – Mother thinks I'm an ugly nuisance and I don't know what Father thinks because he never talks to me. The only things I do well are playing the piano and swimming, and now with these hands I can't even do those. I can never earn my own living and nobody will ever want to marry me...'

His look of sympathy turned to one of distress. He stepped forward and picked up the edge of her sheet, tried to dab away her tears with it. Then he cupped her face in his two hands and began to kiss the tears, the way he had seen Leila do over other upsets. 'There now...' he said softly, sounding like Leila had always sounded when she nursed them. And he kissed her again, this time on her lemonade-sticky lips.

'I'm sorry, Miss Candy.' He dropped his hands and tried to straighten up, but she had caught at his arms with her paws and held him near her, so that he had to sit on the edge of the bed or lose his balance. After the first surprise, his lips felt soft and sweet on her face.

'Nobody has kissed me for such a long time!' And she burst into a fresh flood of tears.

'There, there now...' And he could only kiss her again, then mutter once more, 'I'm sorry. But I can't bear to see you unhappy, Miss Candy.'

Dear Naseem. He'd been around for so long and she still thought of him as a treasured playmate. Now she caught sight of the black hairs on his forearms and the downy beginnings of a moustache on his upper lip and realised he, too had grown up. She thought of the curse and wondered if he knew about it.

'I'm sorry.' It was the third time he'd said it.

'What are you sorry for?'

'I'm sorry that...that I have to be disrespectful to show you that I love you.'

'You love me?'

'Always. Ever since I first watched you turning cartwheels on the lawn.'

Candy giggled, remembering how she'd got into trouble for showing off and for teasing Netta, who hadn't been able to turn cartwheels - still couldn't because she was afraid of falling half way round. Naseem's face was still close to hers and she leaned forward and gave him a kiss on the cheek. 'If you love me, then you won't mind looking after me.'

'Will that make you love me in return?'

'Of course.' She felt much better. It was all so easy. As soon as she had recovered she would become a Muslim and marry Naseem, go and live with him in a little house in the town like Leila's, and have little olive-skinned babies. Of course, Naseem would have to get another job, and probably Leila too – they wouldn't be able to carry on working for her parents after she'd become a part of their family. But there were other jobs in the town, or in the fields. It would all work out.

She reached forward and folded her arms around Naseem in a hug. 'Of course I love you, Naseem.' And in return she felt his arms stealing around her, holding her close. And she felt safe at last.

The front door slammed and Maddie's voice drifted through the house. 'Naseem! Tea!'

Naseem sprang to his feet. They both knew not to be seen together like this, that if it were known how much they loved each other, something awful would happen. There was enough to be dealt with now. Naseem took up the tray with the half-empty lemonade jug, the dirty glass and Candy smoothed her crumpled bedcover. Their eyes said all that was needed as he hurried towards the door.

When he was out in the corridor Candy heard, 'Naseem! Where *are* you?'

'Coming *Memsahib*!' As Candy lay back on her pillows there were lowered voices in the hallway and a moment later the bedroom door burst open and Maddie was standing there, dressed in something pink and flowing, blinking in the half-light as she drew off one white kid glove, then the other.

'What *have* you been doing?' She crossed the room and opened one of the shutters so that the light streamed in.

Candy opened her mouth, then shut it. She didn't know where to begin.

'Naseem says you were sent home from school. Have you had an accident?'

Candy shook her head. She might as well be honest. 'I didn't know my scripture homework. Sister Mary Oliver gave me the cane. I came home early.' That would do. Let her learn the rest from Mother Superior.

'And where is Annette? I don't suppose you thought about your sister, did you?'

'I came home very early. Leila's gone to meet Netta.'

Maddie glared around the room as though looking for someone else to listen to. Then Candy added, 'There might be a letter. I might be expelled.'

'Oh God!' Maddie held one delicate hand over her eyes for a moment, as though trying to shut out the world. 'You stupid girl! As though I haven't got enough troubles already!' And she turned and left the room, the tiny heels of her shoes clack-clacking a steady rhythm on the tiled floor.

Candy watched her go. She listened to the sound of her voice calling Naseem again, and wondered what Maddie's other troubles were, and what God really thought about it all. She wasn't allowed to have any supper and the next morning a messenger arrived at the apartment with a note from the Mother Superior. Leila brought it to them as they sat at breakfast. Her father opened the note and read it, ignored Candy, and passed it on to Maddie, who read it and let it flutter to the floor. With a little choking sob into her napkin, she ran out of the room and slammed her bedroom door.Silently reproachful, Netta picked up the note and read it out loud. It said that Candice could no longer attend the mission school because of the subversive influence of her bad behaviour.

Candy didn't know whether to be pleased or ashamed and as nobody asked her how she felt, it didn't seem to matter. She was left on her own all that day, except for Leila changing her bandages, and she spent the time reading, which was nice and peaceful. At dinner she listened to her parents as they discussed her future with a surprising level of agreement.

'I suppose we could engage a private tutor,' suggested Maddie.

'Terrible expense. What more can the girl need to learn anyway?'

'Precisely. It'll only make it more difficult to find her a husband. No man likes a blue-stocking in his bed.'

I've already found my husband, Candy thought. But they wouldn't have listened even if she'd had the courage to say it. And as she hadn't yet got further with Naseem than talking about love and some furtive kissing and touching, she thought she'd better wait.

'She'll be well enough occupied playing the piano and sewing. As soon as her hands have healed.'

'And she can help Leila around the house.'

'Good idea. Leila has less time now that she has to take Annette back and forth to school.'

'What about her French? A woman who can speak French is an asset.'

'She can study that on her own. She still has her books.You have your French books, Candy? She can content herself with learning verbs and grammar and when we go on leave in the summer she can spend a few weeks in Paris with Tante Marie, practising her conversation.'

'And perhaps finding a husband.'

'At fifteen? She's far too young. Particularly for a Frenchman. No, I'm afraid we're stuck with her for a few years yet. But no harm in letting Marie try to get some fashion sense into her. I'll write to her tomorrow.'

Candy stopped pushing her fish around her plate and laid her knife and fork together, to one side. Maddie gave her a sharp glance, as though realising for the first time that she was there. 'You haven't eaten a thing, Candice. Look at Annette, she's not a fussy eater. Annette, always leave a little on the side of your plate, it's more ladylike.'

But Candy's stomach was churning, she couldn't eat another

mouthful. She hadn't realised it was so close, the summer leave in England. Those three months when the orange harvest was over, when the contracts had been fixed for next year, and there was nothing else to do but swelter in the Mediterranean heat. Then all the European families who were important, and the army officers' wives, would go by train to Port Said and catch a boat to Trieste, or Gibraltar or even all the way to England if they were brave enough to risk seasickness in the Bay of Biscay. Leave always meant at least a month of discussions and arguments about money and about who they were to stay with while they were away. Normally the thought of being in Paris with Tante Marie would have seemed exciting but now...

But now, it would mean being away from Naseem for three whole months. It would be too much to bear. She would have to do something positive. She swallowed hard and said, 'I'd prefer to stay here when you go on leave.'

Maddie and her father and Netta all stared at her. Maddie put down her knife and fork very slowly and her father began to bristle ominously underneath his sun reddened cheeks. Netta giggled, then said, 'You can't stay here all by...'

'Quiet, child!' snapped their father. 'Have you taken leave of your senses, Candice?'

'I think she has,' said Maddie. 'What do you think you're going to do with yourself on your own for three months? Who do you think is going to look after you?'

'I can look after myself. And I can look after the apartment and do the same as you expect me to do all the time anyway. '

'What's the matter with you? You've always been difficult but you're getting worse.'

'It's totally out of the question. You'll come with us as far as Marseilles and we'll put you on the train to Paris and you can join us in London later.'

'What about if there's a war?' She had heard people talking about the ominous rumours of what was happening in Germany and Czechoslovakia.

'There isn't going to be a war,' her father said firmly. 'The British government will see to that. And don't dream up any more difficulties. Naseem! Come and clear these plates!'

As Naseem circled the table Candy caught his eye and she knew he'd been listening outside the door. She gave him a shadow of a smile that was meant to tell him she knew her place was here with him, not in Paris or London. This was the country she'd been born to and the grey facades of northern Europe had nothing to offer in comparison with the red hillsides and the square white buildings. And Naseem. This was where she belonged. She wasn't a child any longer, her body had already told her that. She had the right to make her own decision. She was going to stay, and she was going to make sure there was nothing they could do about it.

'I love you, Naseem.'

'I love you too.'

They lay together on her bed in the shuttered heat of midday, their bodies not quite daring to touch through their thin clothing. The best thing about not going to school was this hour of each day when Leila was walking up to the school to collect Netta, and Maddie was invariably out playing bridge or visiting with the other wives. Then they could kiss and talk and lie together like lovers.

She had been so frightened when Naseem first bared her legs and opened her with his fingers and began to ease his way into her. But he had soothed her and told her that this was what all lovers did, and it was the way to make her a true woman, and when he moved inside her it gave her such pleasure that she begged him to do it again and again. As the days passed it was all she could think of, whiling away the hours until he came to her, when he would stroke her dark hair and kiss her as she had never imagined a person could be kissed.

She told him, 'I want to be here with you for the rest of my life.'

'They will never allow it.'

'They can't stop me if we marry. If I'm your wife they will have to let me stay for ever. I could be a good wife to you in a house like the one you live in now. You would like to be married to me, wouldn't you?'

'You don't understand. Things are going to happen. Bad things. When the British go we are going to have to fight for our country. You wouldn't be safe here.'

'I will be if you look after me. You're not going to fight, are you? You're a houseboy, not a soldier or a policeman.' She didn't notice that he didn't reply to that because at that moment the front door banged open and the sound of Netta's voice came to them. 'I love you, Naseem,' Candy said.

'And I, you.' He only just managed to dress and escape along the passage to the kitchen before Netta burst in, flinging her satchel on the floor. Candy grabbed a book and pretended to be reading, ignoring her sister.

'Have you done your music practice?' Netta demanded. 'Have you?'

'You know very well I can't play yet. My hands ...'

'Mummy says we can go to the Club after tea if I've done mine and finished all my homework.'

'I don't want to go.'

'Well I do. Will you help me with my sums? We're onto long division and I just don't understand it the way Sister Anthony explains it.'

Candy sighed and closed the book she hadn't been reading. 'All right.' She'd always rather enjoyed arithmetic, and never had any problem understanding how to make the answers come out right. And she knew it would be easier to go to the club than to argue. She could swim out to the raft, out of reach of Netta and her mother, and think about Naseem's cool skin and what it would be like to be his wife in a little white Arab house.

Her dreams didn't last long. In fact they began to disintegrate at the first hurdle, a few days later when she was helping Leila to prepare the food for dinner. Eyes aglow she said, 'Leila, I want to tell you something special.'

Leila's hands paused in their task of stripping beans for cooking and Candy looked sideways to catch a glimpse of her face. It was set, frozen with a kind of fear and for the first time a tiny doubt began to creep into Candy's heart. 'It's about Naseem…' she went on, wondering why this was so difficult.

Leila unfroze, sighed and continued her assault on the beans. 'I think Naseem has been saying a lot of things to you that he shouldn't.'

'We love each other.' Her voice faltered a little as she said it out loud to someone else for the first time. It didn't sound quite the way it felt.

'Why should you need to tell me what I can see with my own eyes?'

'You already know?'

'It's hard to avoid when you use every excuse to be here alone together, and your sheets are stained every week. If your mother was more observant...'

'Then you don't mind?'

'You tell me you love my son and ask me if I mind?'

'I thought you'd be angry.'

'Not because you find you love him. But the way of your loving is wrong. There are too many differences between you. Naseem knows that well enough. That is why he loves you in secret, hiding his heart from his family. He knows it has no future. Soon you will be taken away to Europe and when you come back, if they let you come back, you'll be a different person. This love that seems so important now will be dead and forgotten.'

'But Leila...' Candy gently took the paring knife out of the worn, lined hands and grasped both of them her own. 'That's what I'm trying to tell you. I'm not going with them. I've told them already I want to stay here. I refuse to let them take me away.'

'And what will you do here on your own?'

'I won't be alone, will I, Leila? I'll have Naseem, and you. I'll come and live with you.'

Leila gave a short laugh. 'One more mouth at my table? Who has invited you?'

'Naseem, of course. As his wife. We're going to be married, Leila.'

A short silence, then again the short laugh. 'You think they will allow that, your parents? Just because you say you are in love?

You are more of a child than I thought.'

'I know they'll be angry, but they won't be able to stop me because we'll marry in secret and once it's done they won't want me back. It's all arranged. Tomorrow. We run away tomorrow and get married the next day.'

She could tell from the shocked eyes and once-more frozen face that Leila didn't share her excitement. She was shaking. Her face was pale. Tears began to course down her cheeks.

'Oh Miss Candy, you don't know what you're doing!'

'Oh, I do, Leila, I do. I'm making sure they'll let me stay here with you and Naseem.'

Leila said nothing more. A strange, calm mask fell across her face and she stood up and untied her apron, handed it to Candy.

'Where are you going, Leila?'

'To look for my son.'

'You know where he is. He's gone to the market for fish.'

'Which he won't be bringing back here. He must not come back here.'

'But I have to talk to him, make sure he'll be waiting for me tomorrow...'

'He won't be waiting, child. It won't be allowed.' Her eyes softened for a moment. 'Don't you see, once your parents know, he's finished. He'll never get a reference to work, they may even have him arrested...'

'Why? How is it a crime to get married?'

'You think they will forgive him? You think they'll believe you gave yourself to him willingly?' As Candy took in what she was saying, Leila took her black shawl from its hook behind the door and picked up her worn rush basket from its place in the corner.

'But you can't just walk out, Leila? Who'll finish cooking the dinner? Who'll meet Netta from school.'

'You must do it. You must be the servant now.'

'Why are you so angry? I thought you'd be pleased. I thought you loved me.'

'Not so much that I'm ready to sacrifice my son to your

vanity.'

Suddenly Candy saw that life was lurching out of control and the day was changing as it unfolded.

Routine had come to an abrupt end, the hours to come would be played out according to people's feelings, not according to what they were expected to do. As she watched Leila push through the fly screen that covered the back door and start down the steep stone steps, she felt sick with fear. Then she told herself it would be all right. In half an hour Leila would be back with Naseem and everything could return to normal. But in her heart she knew it never could; everything had changed and what had been happy and straightforward had become like a bad dream that she couldn't wake up from.

Brushing the tears out of her eyes, Candy went to the table, took up the paring knife and began to slice the beans that Leila had abandoned.

When Maddie came in she wanted to know why Candy was doing the kitchen work – where had Leila and Naseem gone?

'Leila got angry.'

'Why? What have you done now?'

'Nothing.' She was laying the dining-room table for the evening meal and she avoided looking at her mother. It had been a terrible afternoon – finding a substitute for the fish that Naseem never brought back, rushing along to the school to meet Netta, who had been full of prying questions. And all the time her heart growing heavier and heavier as she wondered whether Naseem would come for her tomorrow or not. It had been so terrible that she didn't want to share the awfulness with anyone, least of all her mother. She just wanted to be left alone with her misery.

But Maddie knew that something serious was wrong. In fifteen years Leila had never let her down; she'd always been there, through storms and sickness, whenever she was needed. It was as though if Leila suddenly wasn't there life might disintegrate. 'You're lying!' she snapped at Candy. Then, when

Candy still didn't look at her, she snatched the tray of cutlery and napkins out of her hands and banged it down on the table, forcing Candy to turn. 'What's happened? What have you done?'

'Leila got angry and left because I told her I was going to marry Naseem.'

'Marry Naseem?' She started back, covering her mouth with a fist, frightened eyes staring at her daughter. Then she whispered, ' What kind of stupid idea is that? He's a native.'

'I love him.'

'Love? What do you know about love? Believe me, it's more than those doe eyes he makes at you – I have noticed, you know, but I thought you'd have more sense than to respond.'

'I love him,' Candy said again. Had they all seen it, without her knowing? She'd thought her feelings were a secret between her and Naseem, now it seemed everyone knew.

'Candy, he's an Arab! This is in your mind, isn't it? You haven't let him...touch you, have you?' She took another turn around the dining room then stopped again in front of Candy, gripping her bony shoulder. 'You're not trying to shield him, are you?'

'What do you mean?'

'He forced himself on you, didn't he? And you're trying to shield him? Yes, of course, that's what happened. You wouldn't understand but these Arabs get funny ideas, they're easily inflamed.' Her hand tightened on Candy's shoulder, began to hurt her. 'That's what happened, wasn't it? He pestered you and assaulted you.'

'No!' She twisted out of her mother's grasp. 'It wasn't like that. I told you, we're going to get married. I want to be his wife.'

Maddie circled the room again, heels clacking on the tiles, skirt swishing. She was shaking her head as though that was enough to make this unpleasant news go away. 'I find it hard to believe, after all we've spent to have you decently educated, that you could behave so badly. We believed you could be trusted. I'll have to tell your father when he gets in. Perhaps we can send you straight to Paris. Now, go to your room and don't you dare try to leave.'

'I can't do that. I have to do the cooking with Leila gone. Unless you want no dinner.'

'Then go to the kitchen and get on with it.'

But in the end nobody ate much. Her father came in an hour later, and spent a long, noisy time in the sitting room with Maddie. Candy could hear them shouting at each other and she dreaded the moment when she would be summoned to give an account of herself. But to her surprise it didn't happen. After the shouting had stopped he went straight out again, banging the doors, and Maddie shut herself in her darkened room from which the sound of weeping came for several hours. Netta appeared and asked in a small voice if she could have some supper and the two sat down to eat a meal in the kitchen. Candy knew that Netta was bursting to know what was going on, but she couldn't bring herself to say a word to her sister. All she was thinking about was whether Naseem would come for her or not.

In the end she wasn't disappointed. Netta was helping her washing the dishes in the stone sink when she heard soft footfalls on the steps leading up to the screened back door. Somehow, above the background noises of the evening she could distinguish the quiet sound from the more distant mingling of voices, music, horses hooves, the creaking wheels of carts and gharries. She went to the door and pushed it open and saw him flinch away, pressing himself against the wall. She put a finger to her lips, then signalled with her hand that he was to stay there.

'What are you doing?' asked Netta. 'Trying to get out of finishing this job?'

'Just taking a breath of air. It's so hot in here.'

'You'll let the insects in and we'll get bitten.'

Candy came back and picked up another plate to dry. 'If you like, I'll finish here and you can go and get on with your homework.' Netta looked at her with suspicion. But she hated washing up. She withdrew her hands from the greasy water and wiped them on the linen cloth Candy was holding. 'As soon as you've finished, will you hear my French verbs?'

'Yes, of course.'

Candy plunged her hands into the sink and drew out

another soiled plate. She rubbed it with the grey dishcloth and laid it carefully on the wooden draining board. Then she went to the door leading to the passage and looked out, checking. She wouldn't have put it past Netta to be standing there, listening, trying to discover what Candy was up to.

But the passage was empty and a light was shining from the living room. A shadow passed back and forth as Netta unpacked her satchel and arranged her books. Candy quietly closed the kitchen door and went over to the outside screen door. Peering out, she saw Naseem sitting on the steps, hunched up with his arms around his knees, head down as though he was afraid of being recognised. He looked up as the door opened and half stood as she came down to him. He put an arm around her and kissed her gently. Then he sat again, drawing her down beside him. With a little sob of relief she leaned against him. All afternoon she'd been so afraid, a little cold worm of doubt creeping further and further into her heart. But he had come to her, and he had waited for her, and he had kissed her, and now he was telling her that he loved her.

'They want to send me away,' she told him.

'Yes, and me. My mother is sending me to my uncle's farm in Hebron. Will you come with me?'

'When?'

'I'm to catch the bus in the morning. From the market square. If you meet me there we can go together.'

'Will it be safe?'

'No. Not if anyone really wants to stop us. But in the morning early, before they are all around, you can slip out and we'll be on the bus before anyone knows.'

'I don't have any money of my own.'

'I have some money saved. Try to find something old to wear and a shawl for your head. Don't turn up with a big suitcase.'

'What do you take me for?'

'My beautiful wife.' He turned and smiled at her, hugging her close. She was swamped by his warmth – he had called her beautiful! She couldn't hold back tears of relief. It was going to be all right. Soon, tomorrow night, they would be in Hebron on his uncle's farm and someone would marry them and then they'd be together all the time, every night, indulging in all those delightful passions that they had discovered together and sleeping close and safe.

'Candy! Where are you?'

They both jumped as Netta's voice echoed through the kitchen above them.

'Out here, cooling off...'

A quick kiss, full of longing, full of the sorrow of farewell. Netta's footsteps, her hand on the door. A parting, another kiss, Candy pushing Naseem away even as Netta opened the door. She came up the top few steps quickly, blocking Netta's view.

'It was so hot in the kitchen.'

'It's hot out here too.'

'But cooler.'

'You don't look cool.'

Candy passed Netta, moving her aside to come back into the kitchen. Netta held open the door, peered curiously, suspiciously into the darkness, but by then there was nobody on the steps or in the courtyard below. In the distance, riding over the sounds of the town in motion, they could hear shouting, the clanging of sticks on metal, some gunshots. Yet another riot, another group of agitators stirring up more hatred. As if there wasn't enough of it around anyway.

Candy went to bed early, leaving Netta doing her homework and her mother weeping in her darkened room. She lay very still beneath the single sheet but she didn't sleep much. She heard Netta going to bed, not trying to be quiet. Then she heard the front door and her father's voice, thick and angry. Maddie met him in the passageway, talking softly. They went into the drawing room together, then there were raised voices, more movements, a cry from Maddie, then stifled sobs. Eventually the apartment settled into night sounds though the town outside was never quiet. Candy wondered what it would be like in the countryside, up in Hebron. She imagined it would be more peaceful. And she would have Naseem at her side. Not long now.

She thought about what she should take with her. Not

much, Naseem had said. What would she need? Clothes – some clean underwear and a clean frock. Her swimsuit? No, there wouldn't be anywhere to swim up in the hills. She'd need her sunhat, her toothbrush, a towel and soap. Would that be enough? Should she take a book, some writing paper? She thought not. Just her clothes would make a bundle big enough to carry down to the bus. Perhaps she should take her birth certificate too, because she would need that to be legally married. She knew her father kept all that sort of thing in his bureau and that it might be locked. But surely she could open it with a knife from the kitchen? It was wrong to break into locked property but once she'd run away she'd be almost a criminal anyway.

She dozed off and woke in the cool early light, as Netta got up and shuffled out to the bathroom. For a moment she lay just savouring the thought that today was the day she would be with Naseem, then she remembered that there was nobody to get breakfast for the family and she might as well do it, and see them all on their way. She couldn't begin packing until they left the apartment. She dressed quickly, choosing a faded cotton shift dress and pushing her feet into her slippers. She would have time to put on stockings and proper shoes later.

Helping Leila the last few weeks had made her competent in preparing the eggs and bread and *yahourt* that they usually had for breakfast. She laid the dining-room table and ate her own breakfast in the kitchen, then while her parents and Netta were eating she went to the bureau in the drawing room. To her surprise it was not only unlocked but open, with some of the papers in disarray. The neat white envelope that said 'Birth Certificates' was still in its place and Candy pulled it out. There were copies of her certificate and Netta's, both issued by the British Consulate and written in Arabic. She picked out hers and stuffed it quickly into her pocket as she heard her father push back his chair. She heard him say, 'Annette, there was trouble in the town last night so you're to stay at home today and help your mother.'

Candy froze with fear. How could she escape if her mother and Netta were in the apartment? But how could she not? She couldn't bear the thought of Naseem waiting for her in the market square, watching the bus fill up, wondering where she was. She had to be there.

In her room she quickly grabbed a set of underwear and a towel and bundled them together into the kitchen. There she tied them into a tablecloth that was waiting to be laundered. Not quite what she'd carefully planned. As she disturbed the pile of dirty laundry one of her father's white shirts fell to the floor spattered with something bright red. She wondered what he'd been up to – was it paint, or something he'd been eating or drinking? Just as well she was leaving or she'd be the one expected to wash it now. She pushed her bundle beneath the sink and began to wash the pan she'd used to prepare the eggs. It would be easy to slip away now but if she went too early they might find her while she was waiting for Naseem in the square. Then she decided to get away while she could, it would be less risky in the square among the crowd waiting for the buses than staying here and then perhaps not being able to get out at all.

Heart pounding, she grasped her bundle and opened the kitchen door and then the fly screen door as quietly as she could.

The air outside was already hot. As she stepped onto the top step she realised she was still wearing her house slippers. She'd have to go back and change her shoes! Then she realised how silly that would be. Most people in the town only wore light slippers or sandals on their feet – it was only the stuffy Europeans who wore socks or stockings and proper outdoor shoes. If she couldn't get to the market square wearing her house slippers she wasn't going to be much use on a farm in the countryside.

Once down in the street she hurried forward, not daring to look back, keeping to the shady side where most people walked. A police truck drove past and Candy felt sure they must notice her. Terrified that her father or one of his friends would drive past, she ducked into one of the narrow side alleys and wound her way through a maze of half-familiar streets. Eventually she came into the square, filled with a bustle of stalls selling fresh produce and baked food that smelled delicious. As she pushed through the crowd she tried to ignore the pathetic animals in their wicker cages, or tethered to the wheels of carts, ready for the butchers' attentions. Soon she was at the side of the square where three ramshackle buses already waited for passengers out into the villages.

'Are you for Hebron?' There were no signs on the buses so she had to ask, using the little Arabic she had learned from Leila. The third bus was the one she wanted and she got on, half-expecting to see Naseem already seated, saving her a place, holding her ticket. But he wasn't there and she got off again, looking all around for him.

'When do you go?' she asked the bus driver.

'Twenty minutes. You need a ticket?'

'I haven't any money.'

'You need money for a ticket.' The driver looked at her as though she was stupid.

'My friend is paying for me. He'll be here in a minute.'

The driver shrugged and Candy went to the side of the road where several people squatted in the shade against a wall. Trying to look inconspicuous, she put down her bundle and joined them, never taking her eyes from the door of the Hebron bus. When Naseem arrived she didn't want to miss him. Another bus drew up and several of the people waiting against the wall heaved themselves to their feet and formed a noisy crowd around the door, as passengers struggled to the ground.

Still no sign of Naseem. With a little flutter of panic starting in her gut she considered what she must do if he was late. She couldn't get on the bus alone because of the money. She would have to hide all day until they could catch tomorrow's bus – if there was one tomorrow. She cursed herself for not trying to bring some money from her father's bureau. It would have been safer to travel alone and wait for Naseem in Hebron than to hang around the town all day and night. She couldn't go to Leila's house - that would be the first place her parents would tell the police to look for her.

The Hebron driver started the engine of his bus as a sign that he was almost ready to go and several people waiting on the pavement took the hint and climbed aboard. The driver looked straight at her and raised a questioning eyebrow. She made a slight inclination of her head and he shrugged. As he crashed the bus into gear and moved forward she saw a knowing smile on his face. She felt angry but he was right, she'd been a fool. She'd believed Naseem's promises last night without realising that he might see things in a very different light today. But perhaps it wasn't his fault. Perhaps he'd had the chance to get a lift to Hebron last night in a car or a truck. There was no way he could have got a message to her. He would be waiting for her and when the bus arrived she wouldn't be on it.

She jumped to her feet, the panic consuming her. She should have got on the bus! Even without the fare she should have got on the bus, persuaded the driver someone would pay for her at the other end. Now there was only one thing to do. She must start walking, in her slippers, with nothing to eat or drink and no money to buy anything.

Perhaps Leila would lend her some money. Leila had worked for years, she must have a little money saved and it would be repaid as soon as things were sorted out. She knew Leila had been angry with her, but Leila loved her really. She'd be sure to help. Taking up her bundle, Candy stared around her for a moment, trying to remember which of the twisted streets led to Leila's house. She'd been there many times while she was growing up, taken illicitly by Leila as she combined her job with running her own household, but the streets changed so often as old buildings were pulled down and new ones built in their place. After a few minutes she was sure she knew which way to go and as she made her way into the maze of alleyways she heard distant shouts and gunfire. She began to hurry her steps and it didn't take long to reach the low block that was Leila's family house.

She paused as she turned into the street, trying to decide what was so strange about it this morning. Then she knew. The street, usually teeming with children and dogs and old people sitting in the shade, was still and empty. All the doors were closed, including the green-painted wooden door of Leila's home. More frightened by the silence than by the sounds of the distant riot, she crept forward and beat a fist against the door. At first there was no reply. Then after a second knock the door inched open and a young girl's face appeared in the crack. The girl looked, but said nothing. Candy thought she was one of Leila's grandchildren, a daughter of the eldest son, but she couldn't remember her name.

In Arabic she said, 'Is Leila home? I need to see Leila.'

'*Imshi!* Go away! Nobody is to come in.'

'I need to see Leila. She'll let *me* in. Go and tell her.'

Then there were footsteps and Leila's face appeared in the space above the child's. It was ugly with crying. The door was pulled wide. 'Yes, come in. Come in and see what you have done.' And she grabbed Candy's wrist and pulled her over the threshold.

The rough handling compounded the strangeness that now engulfed her totally. She'd expected to be able to throw herself into Leila's arms and be hugged, but Leila simply turned away and led her across the tiled entrance room, further into the house. It was dark inside, all the shutters were closed and there was a strange odour; not the usual cooking and laundry smells of a busy home but something sour that told of a lot of people nearby, crammed together in the heat.

But in the room Leila took her to, that Candy thought she remembered as the one Naseem had always shared with his unmarried brothers, there were only two women, and they were bending over something that was stretched out on one of the beds. In the semi-darkness it took Candy a moment to realise that it was a person lying there, being washed by the women, who were sponging blood from the naked limbs and torso. It took her a moment longer to work out, from the way the neck was twisted and the skull smashed, that the person was dead. And then she knew that the bloodied, beaten body was Naseem.

Her heart missed a beat, then another, and her breath tightened in her chest. The room swam around her and she thought she was going to stop breathing altogether and die. The women stopped their work and waited.

She didn't die. Instead she found thoughts tumbling through her head. No wonder he hadn't come to the bus. There'd been an accident and he was dead. Naseem was dead so they could never be married. She turned towards Leila who stood like a statue, face twisted, offering neither comfort nor pity. Then she sank to her knees at the feet of the body and lowered her face to the two broken shin bones that had been so tidily stretched out side by side. She heard a long, low-pitched moan of pain and wondered where it came from, then knew that it came from her own throat. At last Leila moved. She stepped forward and leaned down to take Candy's arm, pulling her to her feet. 'You must go. You have no place here.'

'What happened to him?'

'What does it look like? He was found in the town early this morning, left dead. The dogs were already trying to eat his body.'

'Was he run over?' The accident must have happened soon after he left her on the kitchen steps.

A low hiss escaped Leila's lips. 'You still don't understand what you have done, do you?'

'What do you mean?'

'He was beaten, set upon and beaten to death because of you, because he had the temerity to love a British girl.'

'No, it's not possible! Who would do such a thing?'

'There are thugs who can be bought to fight for anyone. Your father knows where to find them. Your father knows what to do, how to set Jew against Arab so that the police can arrest them and beat them all.'

'My father? He just buys fruit.' He wasn't a kind or loving man, but he wasn't a murderer. Then she remembered the red stains on the shirt in the kitchen and she shuddered.

'Your father may buy fruit but he also deals in lives, and yours will be one of them now.'

'But why?'

'Because he works for British Intelligence – why do you think I have been working in your home all these years? You think I like being a servant? Somebody had to report on what he does.'

Candy shook her head. It was all too confusing. The more Leila told her, the more confusing it became. It simply wasn't fair. Then she remembered that her father had told them not to go out today and what he had said became more sinister. What else was going to happen?

She swayed and put a hand on the door jamb to steady herself. The women continued washing and arranging Naseem's body, a task that should have been hers but she knew she wouldn't be allowed to help even if she asked. Leila wanted her to go, and she knew why. She knew she was in danger here herself, of being taken hostage or even of being murdered in revenge for Naseem's death. With a rush of panic she wondered where Naseem's brothers and cousins were at that moment, why the house had felt so threatening when she came in.

With another glance at the broken, lifeless body on the bed and another deep, shuddering sob, Candy allowed Leila to lead her out of the room, through the house, and push her out through the front door. The sun was now baking down and Candy blinked in the harsh light. As she looked around one of the house shutters moved and she saw the eyes of a man, face swathed in a *galabeah,* glaring at her through a gap. Below his face she could see a dark round tube pointing towards her and she shrank back with terror as she realised it was a gun. She had never imagined anything so serious, so horrific. Keeping close to the wall she set off along the little street, expecting at any moment to hear voices or a shot behind her. But nothing happened. As she turned the corner she passed two men carrying a newly-made coffin. She stopped for a moment to watch its progress, knowing it was for Naseem and longing to go back and hold him in her arms just one more time.

As she walked on there were more rattles of gunfire in the distance and now they seemed more personal to her, not part of someone else's life the way they had been in the past. People in the street were walking quickly, staring at the ground instead of looking around to greet their neighbours. There was a smell of burning in the distance, a column of smoke rose from somewhere the other side of the market square. A big black police car blocked one street that Candy turned into, so she turned aside, into an alley. Suddenly three young Palestinian men ran into the far end of the alley, followed by two British policemen, brandishing guns.

'Psst...psst...' A door opened near to where Candy stood, frozen with terror, and a woman signalled frantically that she should duck inside. As the door closed on them both there was a stutter of machine gun fire, then shouts. Candy tried not to imagine broken, bleeding bodies lying the in the alley.

'Is there another way out?' she asked, and the woman led her through a warren of rooms to a door that opened into another street. Thanking her, Candy hurried on her way, shaking with fear. What was going on? Surely her plan to marry Naseem hadn't caused all this trouble? With an enormous sense of relief she turned the final corner that led her to the apartment block she called home, only to find her way barred by a policeman crouched behind an armoured car. His rifle was trained upwards towards a balcony – the balcony where she had so often sat sewing with Leila. And then she saw that the smoke that had been in the distance was, in fact, pouring out of the windows of her apartment.

A shot cracked out and a split second later a bullet pinged off the side of the car. 'Keep your head down, Miss,' gasped the policeman. 'Better get back where you came from. It ain't safe here.'

'That's where I came from.' Candy nodded towards the apartment block. 'What's happening?'

'Bloody A-rabs is rioting, Miss.'

'Why?'

'Usual stuff. Hate the Limeys, hate the Jews.'

'But why here, in that apartment?'

'Don't ask me. I only do what I'm told.'

'Where are they? The people who live there? Are they...?'

'Nah, Miss, they're okay. Left early this morning. Be on one of them orange boats by now.'

So that was why her father had told them not to go out, why his desk had been open and the papers all strewn around? He'd been arranging for them to escape to one of the fruit boats out on the anchorage. Because he'd known there'd be trouble today, once Naseem had been found. He'd known all along.

Another bullet pinged against the armoured car and the policeman shifted his position. ''Strewth, I wish they'd either let us shoot the buggers or get out of here. Sorry, Miss. Hey, where the hell...'

Candy didn't wait to hear the rest of what he had to say.

She wished she could tell him to give up and go home, there was nothing worth saving in the apartment. She hoped he wouldn't get hurt.

So they'd gone without her. There hadn't been any choice, of course. She hadn't been there and if they'd waited for her, or tried to look for her, they'd probably have had their throats cut. Well, it would serve her father right but she didn't like the thought of Maddie and Netta lying dead in pools of blood. That wouldn't be fair at all.

By now she was exhausted, hungry and thirsty and there was only one place she could think of to go where she had any hope of being given shelter. She hurried through side alleys again, dodging those that were blocked. Joining the groups of frightened people trying to find their way to their homes, she was soon at the side door of the mission school, the door that led straight into the convent. Leaning against the dark stained timber for support she pulled on the bell rope and waited.

2
LONDON

'Are you saying that they buggered off and left her? In the middle of all that blood and mayhem? Are you sure?'

'Well, yes. That's what she told me when I was asking about the birth certificate. She started by saying that it was only a matter of luck that she had it at all, it would have been burnt if she hadn't picked it up that morning, and I said what morning, and she said, the morning they murdered Naseem. And I asked her who murdered him and she said her father had done it.'

'Was he really in the secret service?'

'You know, I was curious about that and as soon as the chance came up under the fifty year rule, I checked. It was true. He sounds as though he was a particularly incompetent agent but he was on their books.'

'But how could they just up and leave her like that? She can't have been more than a kid....'

'Fifteen. She was fifteen.'

'Are you sure?' Leon said again. 'It wasn't one of her flights of Hollywood fancy?'

'I wondered about that too so I asked Aunt Netta about it. She said she could remember that she and her mother and father disguised themselves in *djellabas* and a donkey cart took them to the jetty and they all got into one of the little rowing boats that used to take the crates of oranges out to the steamers and were rowed away. And Mother wasn't with them – she was sure of that. She'd been left behind. Aunt Netta says she was sure about that because she can still remember feeling rather pleased about it.'

'But she did get out later?'

'Well, obviously.'

'How?'

'She never told me that. All a bit of an unsolved mystery. Next thing that's certain is she turned up in the WAAFs in Sussex.'

'Waffs?'

'Women's Auxiliary Air Force. She joined up.'

‘How did she get from a convent in Jaffa to an air force unit in Sussex?’

‘There was a war on. Everyone was expected to do their bit, though I gather that young people regarded it more as an adventure than a sacrifice. She’d have been old enough to volunteer by half way through forty-one.’

‘What did she do in the meantime?’

‘I’ve no idea, old boy. Does it matter?’

Yes, thought Leon. It does. It certainly mattered to her at the time. But that was long ago, perhaps too long ago to find out now that the old lady was dead. And Jeremy obviously wasn’t going to say any more about it just now. He’d tipped his seat back and closed his eyes, as though he’d had enough of talking.

Leon took the hint and closed his eyes as well but he couldn’t doze off, even with the soothing roar of the aircraft engines. She was dead, and that was and end of it; the opportunity to find the answers to all these mysteries about her life had gone for ever and he was already cursing himself for all the times he could have talked to her and asked her questions, and hadn’t thought it important, hadn’t realised she would have anything interesting to say. All the years when there’d been distance and silence between them yawned before him like a chasm filled with regret. How could he have thought it more important to be busy with his own life than to understand hers?

Then he remembered something and he sat bolt upright, startling Jeremy into opening his eyes as well. ‘I know,’ he said, more to himself than to his brother. ‘Pippa was born during the war, wasn’t she?’

‘Yes, I believe she was.’

‘You bloody know she was.’ What it meant was that in a very short space of time their mother had returned to England, joined the WAAF, found a husband and had a baby. That baby. Pippa.

Leon held his tongue and there was a silence between them, neither of them sure where to take the conversation. Then Jeremy said, ‘You haven’t seen Pippa, have you?’

‘Not for more than ... twenty-odd years.’

'You know she'll be at the funeral?'

'I expected as much.' Another pause. 'Where is she now?'

'Technically probably not very far away from us at this moment. But in an aircraft going the other way. On her way to Heathrow, from Australia. '

Another pause and Leon was aware of an increase in his pulse rate as he struggled with emotions he thought were long overcome. 'So she had to go that far, did she?'

Leon was more surprised than Jeremy when they were ushered off the plane by a young man with a shock of red hair who introduced himself as an assistant to the British Consul. He shook their hands, murmured condolences, collected their bags for them and led them through the stifling afternoon heat of Tel Aviv airport and straight to a waiting black car with a police escort and another official from the British Consulate. There was no question of customs or immigration, just a smooth and hasty, air-conditioned ride sheltered from the super-heated landscape by the darkened glass of the car windows. Leon leaned forward in his seat, uneasy at the sight of military vehicles stationed at road junctions. He knew it was all in the name of security but the pervasive military presence hung like a long shadow over the approaches to the town itself. He tried to imagine the same situation back home in the States, in the relaxed and tolerant towns and cities of the Pacific seaboard. Would the National Guard be so stone-faced and formidable-looking as these young soldiers? Probably they would because, Leon very quickly realised, underneath their tanned faces and the heavy equipment that made them look like walking hardware shops, they were all just frightened boys who would rather be almost anywhere else.

'We're obviously very VIPs,' he said as they swept through a road-block without stopping.

'Are you surprised? The last thing they want on their hands is a second embarrassing assassination.'

'Assassination? I thought she was just caught in the

crossfire, so to speak.'

'Maybe. But if not, then we have just walked into a very obvious trap.'

'Why should they want to trap us?'

'Important hostages are always useful in negotiations.'

'And they'd murder a dear old lady just for that?'

Jeremy looked at his brother long and hard. 'This is the Middle East. "They" would murder anyone if it suited them. And never forget this - Mother was not a dear old lady. Emphatically not.'

Leon had to admit that he was a supernumerary on this exercise. Surplus to requirements. When the first emotional urge had come over him, to travel to Israel with Jeremy, he should have listened to his brother, not to his heart. Jeremy had told him all the arrangements were already made, it was only a matter of going through formalities. So it was. The body had to be identified, what was left of it, and a death certificate issued so that it could be taken back to England for burial. In a hot Middle Eastern country it was the custom to arrange these things speedily, even though they now had body freezers just like the rest of the civilised world.

The worst thing was coming face to face with the fact that there was no real body to identify. Pieces of body were all that was left, mostly very small pieces, because their mother had been very close to the seat of the explosion – that was how the Consul put it as he carefully explained it all to them in his office – '...the seat of the explosion...'

'Just a minute,' Leon interrupted. 'What was the so-say seat of this explosion? Where was the bomb?'

The Consul, a heavy, florid man, looked uncomfortably from Leon to Jeremy, raising an eyebrow in a question. He was quite at home in this kind of situation but he was aware that the two men in front of him had probably never dealt with anything like it before. Jeremy gave a half-shake of his head. 'No, I haven't mentioned anything about the actual explosion.'

This made Leon angry. 'Chrissakes Jeremy, she was my

mother too! What are you keeping to yourself?'

It was the Consul who replied. 'The authorities believe...we believe... that the explosion was caused either by a suicide bomber or a device planted under the cafe table. There are surviving eye-witnesses. Your mother was there by prior arrangement, an appointment with a local Palestinian woman, they say. Unusual circumstances...'

'You're telling us that someone purposely arranged to meet Mother in the middle of a crowded pavement cafe when they know a bomb would be detonated – why?'

The Consul raised a hand as if to silence Leon's anger and Jeremy said quietly, 'We don't know why, but there's no doubt about what happened...'

'Why? How can you be sure?'

The Consul continued the story. 'One of the eye-witnesses, a newspaper vendor across the street, was watching the scene because your mother had just bought the air-mail *Times* and he thought it so unusual for an English lady like herself to be on her own in the middle of the town...'

'Well...?'

'He is convinced the Palestinian woman and your mother had an appointment to meet. He said your mother didn't actually sit down at a table. She recognised the woman, they waved to each other, smiled, met, hugged, and then the bomb went off...'

'My God!' Leon felt himself begin to shake.
'You mean...she was deliberately *targeted*?'

'Exactly.' As though through a mist Leon saw Jeremy's face regarding him with an expression he had never seen before, of being totally, coldly in command of an unprecedented situation. Now he understood all the security. He was ashamed that he had to try twice to frame his next question, because his tongue had somehow become stuck to the dry roof of his mouth and he felt as though he might vomit at any minute. 'Do you know...do you know who this woman was?'

'Unfortunately not. It may be possible to make a DNA identification from blood samples but unless some group claims responsibility, which hasn't happened yet, the authorities have very little to go on.'

'But they'll be investigating?'

Again the Consul shifted uncomfortably and glanced at Jeremy, who nodded. 'The bottom line, Leon, is that they've got more to worry about here than identifying one bomber. What this gentleman is trying to say, politely, is that they'd like us to take Mother and her paperwork and get the hell out of their hair as soon as possible.'

The Consul inclined his head in agreement. 'If you gentlemen will accompany me to the morgue, I think we can get all the paperwork through for you to leave with the coffin on tomorrow afternoon's flight.'

Awash with unfamiliar emotions, puzzling about a past to which he had previously given little attention, Leon excused himself early from the dinner table he shared with Jeremy and their minder from the Consulate. The two were providing a model of how to make polite conversation about nothing much in such a way as to convey that what each said was of riveting interest to the other. As much of this centred on mutual acquaintances and a shared attendance at the same school, albeit not at the same time, Leon was sidelined and quickly gave up any pretence of being part of the proceedings. He would have liked to get drunk in order to try to expunge the images of the day, particularly those from the mortuary where all they had been shown of his mother's body was a badly burned claw of a hand with her wedding ring and two mutilated amethyst dress rings still attached to the fingers. There had been other remains carefully laid out beneath a green sheet, he could see the outline quite clearly, but not much above the waist. It was quite clear that Candice, Dowager Countess of Penmore, was no more. But he decided that getting drunk would be a dangerous thing to do in this strange place where forces he didn't understand seemed to be at work. He would have chosen sex instead if a willing woman had been around – and he suspected it wouldn't have been hard to find one in the noisy town outside - but again he was conscious of being a novice caught up in the fringes of a game with rules he could only guess at, and his sense of self-preservation kept him from exploring further.

It seemed that sleep was the only other escape offered to him and he did feel very tired. So he ordered a hefty Scotch on the rocks, excused himself politely, and went up to the hotel room he had been allocated.

But sleep was slow to come. The air-conditioning was noisy and when he turned it off and opened the windows the town was even noisier, with conversations, laughter, music, car engines and horns, all intermingled into a symphony of human sound. It took him back to his early days as an ambitious young singer, touring in one crummy venue after another, having to sleep in the cheapest possible hotels, never being able to get away from the sweat of the stage and the pervasive odour of his companions' unwashed underwear.

He smiled to himself in the darkness. He'd forgotten, hadn't he? Since they'd taken off with that first album and he could afford the best of everything, all the time, memories of how it had been then had faded. Had it been like that for his mother, too? Had she quickly forgotten about the miseries of her adolescence once she'd become famous? Or had she remembered it all and simply kept it away from those she loved?

And she had loved him, he knew that. In the darkness he felt again the pressure of her arms around him, the touch of her lips on his skin, the warmth of her tears as she said goodbye to him on that day his father had come to collect him to take him for a holiday in Hollywood. He'd been so excited to be going with Rupert that he hadn't understood how much it was hurting her to part with him even for a short time. He'd even tried to pull away from her embrace; it was sissy, and there was a taxi waiting outside to take them to the airport, and ...and ...

There was something else there, some underlying pain that he couldn't place. She had just got married to the elderly Earl, who was no match for A-list Rupert in the glamour stakes but who had tried to be kind to him – he saw that later. And she'd been expecting Jeremy, though at ten years old he hadn't understood about that. But there'd been something else, some terrible sadness that had spilled over from her into him and made him feel guilty.

He tried to dig further into his memory, but nothing else came up. Nothing except the excitement of going home – he always thought of it as 'home' – to Hollywood with his father. It was arranged as a visit, he remembered, a couple of months during the school holidays. Had he had any inkling then that it would be far, far, longer? No, he'd been too young, he really hadn't understood, not about Rupert, about Pippa and Danny, about the baby, about the Earl, about Tatton...

He sat up. Tatton? A face drifted in front of him, not very clear, but jolly, laughing. Who was Tatton? Where had he gone? Why remember him now?

Questions, questions...where were the answers? Surely, some must be here, in this dangerous town on the edge of the Mediterranean. Some were lost for ever now but wasn't there anyone who remembered a tall, dark haired English girl who'd been left behind when her family ran away from the riots in thirty-nine?

There was one place, probably not too far away. As he drifted into sleep at last, Leon wondered whether to go alone or to share his thoughts with Jeremy.

He woke late and on the breakfast table found a note from Jeremy saying that he had gone to collect their mother's luggage from the hotel she'd been staying at. So Jeremy was out of the frame for an hour or two and Leon had every excuse to undertake his expedition alone. All he had to do was order a taxi.

The taxi driver didn't hesitate. He knew exactly where the Jaffa mission hospital and the convent were and took less than twenty minutes to get there. 'You want me to wait?' he asked Leon. He was clearly curious about his passenger and Leon wished he looked less conspicuous, less like a rock star and more like an ordinary tourist or businessman. 'Yes, please. I don't know how long I'll be.'

The man shrugged and Leon realised it didn't matter. However long, he would be paying.

He felt distinctly out of place as he rang the bell at the heavy wooden door and waited until a panel was drawn back and a young, anxious woman's face appeared. She said a single word in Arabic, then changed to English. 'Yes?'

'My name is Leon Taylor. May I speak with whoever is in charge?'

'Do you want to make an appointment?'

'Not really. It's an urgent matter.'

'Wait.'

After nearly ten minutes, during which Leon scuffed his feet in the step, looked at the taxi driver, looked away and looked back again in growing uncertainty, the door was slowly opened. Another woman stood there in a modern nun's habit with a short skirt and a neat white wimple on her head. 'Good morning, sir,' she said. 'I am to take you to Mother Agnes, our Mother Superior.'

Leon was led along shadowed corridors where, at intervals, saints stood in their wall niches with little lamps burning at their feet. In her office, Mother Agnes rose from behind her desk and came round to greet him, extending her hand to shake his and indicating a chair for him to sit down. 'It's good of you to see me,' Leon said as she circled the desk again and sat down.

'Not at all. We cannot afford to miss the possibility of a donation to support our work. But I feel sure that is not the main purpose of your visit. You are looking for someone, perhaps? Or for background material for something you are writing or filming?' A slight smile played around her lips as she spoke, not cynical but not openly welcoming either. Plainly, she had heard it all before.

Leon wondered how old she was. It was impossible to tell. Her grey hair was drawn back into her wimple and the backs of her hands were covered with liver marks. The skin of her face had a thin, translucent quality about it but it was completely unlined, like the face of a young girl. It was as though it had been untouched by any emotion over the years; not love, nor anger, nor pity, nor disappointment. Nothing.

'I'm looking for someone.' No, he corrected himself, that's not quite the case. I know where she is. 'I'm looking for information about someone who was here many years ago. Perhaps there's nobody here who can remember back to before World War Two.'

She said, 'Not many. But I came here in nineteen thirty-seven as a novice. From my village in France.'

'And you've been here ever since?' Leon did a quick calculation. This woman must be at least eighty. A lifetime, spent here teaching the young and healing the sick, separated from her own family?

'It is what was expected.'

'So...' He hesitated, almost afraid to ask the question because it would produce an answer and then he would know for sure. 'So do you remember an English girl, Candice Hargreaves? She came to the school here. She would have been about...'

He was sure he didn't imagine the change in her demeanour. Although she struggled to keep her calm wrapped around her it seemed in danger of falling away, leaving her exposed. Two little spots of red appeared on her pale cheeks. Her eyes could no longer meet his, they rested beseechingly on a huge, dark oil painting of Christ on the wall behind his head. Her fingers twisted together on the desk in front of her. She bowed her head and took a deep breath, then looked up again.

'Candice was fifteen when she was expelled from the school. For bad behaviour – irreverence and sloth.'

She paused and he raised an eyebrow, expecting more. 'But...?"

The nun hesitated as another inner struggle overtook her. This time she didn't look up. 'She came back, asked for sanctuary during a riot.'

'And was she allowed to stay?'

'Yes.' It was a whisper. 'She was here for almost a year. She worked in the hospital and the kitchens.' Then, so quietly that Leon could hardly hear her, 'We helped her … deliver her baby.'

'You *what?'* Shaken to the core he pushed to his feet and took a turn around his side of the room before flinging himself down again. A baby? No, the nun had it wrong. After all, it was a long time ago and there may have been other girls…'No, you've got it wrong…'

She shook her head, calmer now in the face of his shock. 'She definitely had a child. A weak little scrap. I remember taking it, trying to hide it from her.'

'It died?'

'It never lived.'

'And …then?' He tried to hide the catch in his voice.

'A few weeks later she ran away. In the middle of the night. I don't know where she went. I never saw her again.'

'Nobody said anything?'

'We were not supposed to talk. But I...it was hard not to say anything to the others. We were told she had been sent back to England and we were not to mention her again.'

A silence fell between them as they both contemplated the ghost they had raised. Leon stared at the Mother Superior and she lowered her eyes, giving him the feeling she was still concealing something. Was she really telling the whole truth? 'She didn't come back to see you last week?'

'No. She was in Jaffa?'

'She was here on a visit. She died the day before yesterday in a bomb explosion.'

The nun raised, wide, horrified eyes to his. She hastily crossed herself, then kissed the crucifix that hung around her neck. 'May God rest her soul. So she did come back. I always feared she would...'

'Feared?'

'She was not a calm soul. She left a long shadow here.'

'What do you mean?'

The composure was returning, the nun was taking control again. 'Let your mother rest in peace.'

'Did I say she was my mother?'

'Your eyes say it for you, my son. Your eyes are as her eyes were, and full of the same pain.'

Now he felt uncomfortable, but he didn't want to leave. He was sure there was more that this woman of God wasn't saying, more that he should know before she, too, took her secrets to her grave. But could he accuse her of lying? All in all, he'd been very lucky to get this far. Then he had an idea.

Out of his wallet he took a business card that gave the addresses of his agents in Hollywood and in London. He said carefully, 'This afternoon my brother and I are taking my mother's body back to England for burial. There may be quite a lot of press interest once the news gets out. If it prompts any more memories, brings any more information to light, I'd be grateful if you would get in touch. And just so that you don't forget, I'd like to make a donation to your mission.' Digging further into his wallet he pulled out a folded book of travellers' cheques. 'Will dollars be all right?'

Mother Superior kept her eyes suitably downcast as she nodded and murmured, 'Dollars will be fine.'

As soon as Leon strode into he hotel foyer, Jeremy leapt to his feet. 'For God's sake! I've been worried sick! Have you no grasp of the security problems they've got here?'

Still swamped by his own fury, Leon ignored his questions and ordered coffee. When it arrived and they were comfortably seated he felt calmer and said, 'I've been to St Joseph's convent – just had a very interesting conversation with the Mother Superior there… did you know?'

'About the child?'

'You do know. Why don't I?'

'What did she tell you?'

'That Mother had a still-born baby while she was still in Palestine – the result of her ill-fated love affair with that Naseem, I suppose? What a tragedy.' As he contemplated the story, Leon suddenly realised that it was no surprise he didn't know – their mother would surely want to have kept such a thing a secret. What was surprising was that Jeremy knew – why and when had he been told?

And why was he staring at Leon now as though he was afraid of what he might say next?

Leon drew breath to ask more questions, but in the same instant the Consul's assistant approached them across the foyer and Jeremy rose to his feet, tapping his wristwatch. 'Time we were off. Have you packed your bag? Settled up?'

And the moment to ask questions had passed.

The news of the death was slipping out of the realm of a private matter and into the public consciousness. A couple of television teams positioned outside the terminal building were filming the aircraft being loaded. Jeremy and Leon were driven out on to the tarmac in the diplomatic car and nobody was allowed near enough to ask any questions. They both knew it would be a different matter once they reached London – they would be besieged by the press. Before they boarded the plane they watched a coffin, wrapped in a plastic cover that bore the warning 'Human Remains' being slid into the cargo hold.

For the second time Candy Hargreaves left Palestine and this time it would be for ever.

* * *

She'd arrived in London in January, the winds colder than anything she'd ever known and certainly too cold for her grey flannel skirt and thin cotton coat. Christmas had been spent at sea, heaving in the Bay of Biscay, because the ship's Captain had refused to dock in Trieste or Marseilles for fear of being impounded by the war that was rumbling and grumbling around Europe, openly declared in some places, just a threat in others. He calculated the bunkers and food on board and reckoned that he could make it to Liverpool with strict rationing and one refuelling stop in Gibraltar.

Candy had spent most of the trip in her cabin, wishing that she was dead, almost wishing she was back in the convent. Almost, but not quite. Every time that thought came to her she remembered that last interview with the Mother Superior. 'I've heard from your father.' That had made her heart lift. It could only mean one thing; her family was back and she was to go home. They'd looked after her as best they could in the convent, nursed her through what had turned into months of illness after Naseem's death, helped her to deliver her sad little baby, but now she was tired of having nothing to do in her spare time except wash laundry and pray, tired of reading about nothing other than the love of God. She wasn't too convinced about that at the moment. God had spared her life, as the sisters kept reminding her, but it didn't seem to her to be a very loving thing to do when she would far rather have died.

'Candice. Your father has made his wishes clear at last. The sisters have been giving me good reports of you. They say you are diligent and obedient, that your work is worthy to be offered to God.'

'Yes, Mother.'

'They agree with me that you may be ready to take your vows.'

Candy stared, thunderstruck. *Take her vows?* Only those who were going to be nuns for the rest of their lives took vows. That didn't apply to her. She was just here to be looked after for a while. She would be going home soon. 'Take my vows, Mother?' she questioned.

'Yes. As a bride of Christ. You will need to choose a new name. Which of the saints to you favour?'

'But...but...that's not what I'm here for, Mother. I shall be going home as soon as my family come back from their leave.'

'Not so, Candice.' Was there a hint of triumph in her eyes? 'Your father wants you to remain with us.'

'But not for ever! He doesn't mean for ever! '

'What makes you think that?'

'He only means until they come back from their leave, I'm sure. '

'Candice, your family will not be coming back to Palestine. They cannot. There have been events. The world is changing beyond these walls.'

'What events? What's happened?'

'Better that you don't know. Better that you remain

ignorant of what you cannot change and accept your future here. It's what your father wishes.'

'He can't do that! I'm a person. He can't just give me away!'

'It has long been the custom with daughters. You are not yet of age under British law.' She paused. 'I see you are not as ready as we supposed, Candice. I suggest you pray for guidance and come back to tell me when you feel you can accept the authority of God.'

Candy had prayed for guidance but only in finding a way past the locked doors of the convent. And in where she should go after she got out. She knew well that she might get into even more serious trouble if she wasn't careful – she hadn't forgotten the stories of the slave traders. But did it matter? She was as good as a slave while she remained here. What would be the difference if she was slave to some Arabian or Numidian? While she raged inwardly and worried, she remembered about the British Consulate. She remembered that it was the job of the Consul to look after British people who got into difficulty, lost their passport, had their money stolen. Her birth certificate had been issued at the Consulate. If she could get there they would have to let her in and protect her, give her a passport and lend her some money, even find her a passage back to England so that she could find her family.

So she knew where to go. All she had to do was look for a chance to slip through the doors, back into the real world. And when she did, she found that her troubles were far from over. But at least the Consul, Peter Russell, Alec's father, listened to her story and seemed genuinely shocked.

'I had no idea,' he blustered. 'I thought you'd gone back with them.' Puffing on a cigarette he stared at her for some minutes as she sat shivering before his desk, her thin shift dress covered by a shawl that his wife had produced from somewhere. Then he said, 'You'll have to go back to UK. We've got instructions to advise all British nationals it's not safe to stay here.'

'Why? What's going on?'

'Don't you know? No, perhaps you wouldn't. We're at war. Have been for a month now. With Germany.'

'Germany?'

'That's right. Over their annexation of Poland.'

'How can that affect us here in Palestine?' She'd have been all right if she'd been allowed to marry Naseem. Living in the hills as part of his family. But now things were different. She remembered the riots, the men with guns in Leila's house. That trouble hadn't disappeared the day she'd gone into the convent.

'Don't worry,' said Russell. 'My wife is booked to leave this week with the two youngest girls. Going on the train to Port Said and catching a steamer. You can travel with her.'

'I don't want to go back to England.'

'You can't stay here. You're in terrible danger here.'

'Danger?'

'Yes, don't you realise? Your name has been linked with the Fahy family who led the riots last year. There are authorities here who would like to question you. I don't recommend that you let them get their hands on you. If the nuns come asking for you, we haven't seen you. I'll give you an emergency passport and you can stay with my wife and me until you leave next week.' And that was all he would say.

She was given a little room in the Consulate, more like a cell really, and Mrs. Russell brought her food and clean clothes and nobody else was allowed to speak until the morning they were hurried into a gharry, together with the two young Russell girls, and taken to the railway station for the long, hot journey into Egypt.

Once they were out of Palestine Mrs Russell seemed to relax a little. She was large and rosy-cheeked, with a few bristling hairs on her upper lip, the very opposite of the neat and elegant Maddie. She was draped in ever-increasing layers of shapeless fabric that were meant to disguise her lack of figure. On the boat she looked in on Candy every day and would sit for a while holding her hand, sighing and shaking her head gently. Candy could tell she didn't know what to do or say and probably wished she didn't have this awkward charge with her, who was constantly being sick.

Soon everything about Candy smelled of vomit, her hair hung like sticky shoelaces, but she couldn't get anywhere to bathe or shower. Every time she stood up her legs crumpled and she had to crawl back to her bunk. Most of the time she slept and every time she woke up she thought about Naseem and wept.

Candy suspected that the Consul's wife thought she was going to die before they ever got to England, which would have been merciful for all of them. But she didn't. For some reason she continued to exist. As though she was being punished for her sins. In a daze, aware that the engines had stopped their endless thrumming, she heard a steward say that they'd arrived in England and she roused herself to look out of the porthole at the slate-coloured sky. She had very little to pack, just a change of underwear and one shapeless green linen frock, bought for her before they left Port Said. Just as well, because the Russell family and the other passengers had mountains of luggage and it took ages to move everything off the ship, then onto a train for London. It took all Candy's concentration to walk along in Mrs. Russell's wake, carrying her little bag, without stumbling. When she found herself on the train, leaning back in a corner of the first class carriage and wondering who had paid for her ticket, she was shaking with fatigue. Half way though the journey she followed blindly to the dining car for lunch but before they got there the smell of the food made her stomach churn again and she muttered an excuse and made her way back to the carriage. Mrs Russell watched her go and shook her head. 'The sooner we get her into the care of her family, the better,' she said firmly to anyone who would listen. 'I can't think what possessed them to leave her behind like that.'

The station in London was all steam and whistles and bustle. Men in military uniform were moving purposefully around with sausage-shaped kit bags on their shoulders. Women and children were gathered in little bunches, some with suitcases and parcels, waiting to travel, others waving and crying. Two elderly porters loaded all the Russell family's luggage onto a trolley and wheeled it out to the taxi-rank. Mrs Russell turned to Candy.

'Where do you want to go, dear?' she asked.

Candy stopped walking, dumbfounded. 'What do you mean?'

'Where does your family live?'

Live? In England? Candy didn't know. They'd been going to stay in a hotel but that was months ago. She hadn't considered where she was to go when they arrived in London. She'd just thought she would be able to follow Mrs Russell wherever she went. She wasn't prepared for making any decision on her own.

'Where...where are you going?'

'Our home's in Berkshire. We'll be staying a couple of nights in London, doing some shopping, then driving down. I expected to deliver you to your parents once we'd got here. Where are they?'

'I don't know.' The station was revolving around Candy at an alarming rate. She suddenly realised that not only did she need somewhere to go, she needed money. What was she going to do?

'You can take one of these taxis,' Mrs Russell was saying, 'But I need to give him an address. Surely you have an address?' They were all standing about, waiting. The taxi drivers were showing signs of impatience.

'Yes.' Candy struggled to remember something. The name of the company her father worked for. Years ago, when she'd been a small child they'd been in London on leave and her mother had taken her to meet him there at the end of the day. She'd been wearing a viyella print dress and neat white socks, with Start-Rite sandals. She remembered a dark, forbidding brick building in a long street of important offices. 'Shannon Carlyon. Fruit Brokers. Something Gate.'

'Bishopsgate,' declared one of the taxi drivers impatiently. 'Fruit's in Bishopsgate. I know where Shannon Carlyon is.'

'There you are!' Mrs Russell beamed and began to usher Candy into the taxi.

'Excuse me, Madam,' said the driver, trying to sound deferential but fixing Mrs Russell with a distinctly non-deferential gaze. 'Excuse me, but has the young lady got the wherewithal to pay her fare?'

Mrs Russell looked annoyed again, opened her handbag and took two half-crowns out of her purse. 'Here you are.' She handed them to Candy through the open window of the taxi. 'Five shillings. That should be enough.'

'I'm sorry,' said Candy. 'I'm afraid I'm being a frightful nuisance, but I'm sure my father will repay you.'

'You don't sound a bit sure, young lady, and I have to agree with you. However, we can only hope. Now, can we proceed with our journey?'

With a cluck of his tongue the taxi driver climbed into his cab and drove away. Candy was quite sure he didn't want her in his taxi. Even in her confused state of mind she knew he would much rather have had one of the passengers with a big pile of leather luggage asking for some top hotel. She was a poor catch by comparison.

After only a few minutes the taxi stopped in front of the building she remembered. 'That wasn't far.' She stood on the pavement and handed one of the half-crowns to the driver.

'No. You could've walked it.'

'I couldn't. I didn't know which way to go. Thank you so much.' She knew that he would expect a tip, like the stewards on the boat and the railway porters, so she picked a sixpence out of her change and handed it to him. He looked at it for a moment while Candy began to stare around her, then leaned across and handed it back to her.

'I think you need this more than I do, Miss.'

'Oh gosh! Did I do it wrong?' Had she offended him?

For the first time she looked properly at his face. It was wide, with a big slash of a mouth, and his skin hung in heavy folds that made him look perpetually sad until he smiled. Then his round blue eyes sparkled and all the folds gathered themselves together and lifted into a moon-like beam. He had beetling slate-grey eyebrows and greasy wisps of grey hair stuck out from his too-small cap. His complexion was pale, specially to someone like Candy, used to being surrounded by suntanned, olive-skinned people. The whole of him, clothing and all, seemed to be covered by a thin layer of greyish grease.

The look he gave Candy was one of pure kindness. 'No, Miss. You didn't do nuffing wrong. Only if that five bob's all you got in the world, I think you may need it all before you're finished.'

'Oh no, it'll be all right. This is the right place. My father works here.'

'You sure?'

'Yes. Look.' She pointed to one of the more ornate brass plates, with flowing copperplate letters inscribing the name *Shannon Carlyon*. 'It says First Floor. I've been here before.'

'Very good, Miss.' He pocketed the sixpence and watched Candy as she made her way up the steps and pushed open the heavy wooden door. It creaked a little as she went through, then swung shut behind her, and she stood in a long, high hallway with a chequered floor leading towards a staircase that coiled around a square lift cage. On a chair outside the lift sat a thin, elderly man in a brown uniform. He was dozing when Candy came in but he watched her approach with a calculating stare. 'Can I help you, Miss?' She guessed he was trying to decide if she was important enough to stand up for.

'I'm going to Shannon Carlyon's office.'

'First floor,' he said with a curt nod. 'You'll be quicker walking.' Evidently he didn't rate her very highly.

But Candy was tired. Her legs were shaking, and she wasn't sure she could walk up a whole flight of those stone steps. Gathering up all the dignity she could muster, knowing she looked like a refugee, she said, 'I'd prefer to use the lift, if you don't mind.'

The man shot her a look of pure hatred and struggled to his feet and she saw then that his hands were stiff with arthritis. Instantly she felt remorse that she was making things difficult for him but it was too late to change her mind. He opened the stiff concertina cage door and she stepped into the clanking lift and stood back while he operated the big lever that caused them to slowly rise towards the next floor. When he let her out she thanked him and tried a smile on him by way of an apology but he continued to glare straight ahead as though she didn't exist.

She remembered the way along the wide corridor towards the front of the building and an ornate door with brass handles and a bevelled glass window. Through the window she could see a woman wearing a black dress, sitting at a tall typewriter. She was sure it was the same woman who'd been there last time she'd visited but she didn't expect to be recognised.

There was a bell outside and she rang it, but then went straight in. The woman looked up. 'Can I help you?'

'I ... I'm looking for Mr. Hargreaves. I'm his daughter.'

'Mr. Hargreaves?'

'Yes...'

Candy was suddenly very uncertain. Memories of their parting came flooding back, memories of their last conversation, of the bloodstained shirt in the kitchen, of the way he'd given her away to the nuns. All the violence and hatred seemed a million miles away from this quiet, dark London office but they had been real, very real. What was he going to say to her? What was she going to say to him?

'I'm sorry, Miss Hargreaves....' The woman's voice was coming from a long way off. Candy had difficulty in concentrating on it.

'...very sorry. Mr. Hargreaves hasn't been based here since before Christmas.'

'He isn't here?'

'Not since soon after war broke out. He's working in Whitehall.'

'Whitehall?'

'That's right. For the government.'

'Do you know where?'

'I'm sorry, we weren't told. Very hush-hush, I understand. We send anything we get for him to his home address. The flat in Tite Street.'

'Oh yes, I know.' She didn't, but she needed to. Number seven, isn't it?' The woman raised an eyebrow. 'You see, I've just got off the boat in Liverpool today and I find I've lost the letter he sent with instructions about where to go.'

'Number twenty-eight. Flat two.'

'Thank you.'

The woman was eyeing her with more curiosity. 'You've come back from America, then?'

'America? No, I've come from Palestine.'

'Funny. I thought you were all in America.'

Wondering where Tite Street was and how she was going to get there, Candy made her way back downstairs, walking this time, and out into the street. As she stood looking up and down, the faint dizziness that had been with her all day grew stronger and she sat down sharply on one of the steps and held her head in her hands. She was aware of someone stopping in front of her.

'You all right, Miss?' She looked up into the worried face of the taxi driver. He'd parked only a few yards further up the road. He'd been waiting for her. She grinned in relief.

'I feel a bit faint.'

'Your father not there then?'

'He works in Whitehall now. I need to get to his flat in Tite Street. Do you know where Tite Street is?'

'Course I do. I'm a cabbie aint I? It's down Chelsea way, near the river.'

'Can I get a bus there?'

'Course you can. You can get a bus anywhere in London. But I fink I better take you.'

'I don't think I can afford it.'

'Don't you worry about that. I can see you ain't well. How'd you like a cup of tea?'

'Candice! My God, girl! What do you look like?'

Candy was too overcome to reply. She didn't know what she'd expected – perhaps open arms, a prickly embrace. Even a shake of the hand, a welcoming smile.

But not this amused guffaw from the man who sat, whisky soda in hand, sprawled on the pink and cream damask settee in this elegant drawing room. She felt a good deal better after the cup of strong tea and the rock cake the taxi driver had bought her at the little cafe near Bishopsgate, but she still wasn't ready for more rejection.

Then she asked herself what she had expected. Love?

'Why aren't you still in that convent? Have you any idea how much I paid them to take you as a novice?'

'You might have asked me first.'

'You chose to go there.' His eyes locked onto someone standing behind Candy, in the doorway, and he smiled. 'Laura, meet my eldest daughter.'

Candy turned and saw the woman who had answered the door and let her into the flat. Candy had thought she must be a maid but clearly she was wrong. When she had opened the door Laura had been wearing a yellow house-robe but now she wore a soft green wool frock with a pearl necklace. She was carrying a glass with what looked like a gin and tonic and she had just lit a Balkan Sobranie cigarette. She smiled a cold smile in Candy's general direction, then crossed the room and perched on the arm of the sofa, behind Leonard Hargreaves' head. 'Darling, this scarecrow can't belong to you.'

Candy was bewildered. Who was this woman who was so comfortable with her father and called him darling? 'Where's Mummy and Netta?' she stammered.

'In America. Ran like scared rabbits as soon as war was declared. Took Tante Marie with them. "Gone with the wind", all of them. Do you want to join them?'

Candy thought of the seasickness of the Bay of Biscay and tried to imagine crossing three thousand miles of Atlantic Ocean. 'Do I have to?'

'Since when does obligation come into your repertoire of behaviour, young lady? I've already made arrangements for your future and then you turn up and tell me they weren't to your liking. What do you want now? Money, I suppose. Just like your mother.'

'I was hoping for somewhere to stay.'

'She can't stay here,' Laura said. Candy noticed that the ash from her cigarette was hanging in a long curve and about to drop onto her father's head. 'We're not having her here.'

Leonard twisted around and patted her hand. 'Don't worry,

darling. Nobody's even suggesting that she stay here. I don't want her, either.'

Candy was suddenly angry. 'In that case, why don't you beat me to death with a stick – then you'd be rid of me.'

Leonard glared. Shrugging Laura aside, he rose from the sofa and confronted Candy, standing close in front of her so that she cold smell the tobacco and alcohol in his breath. His bulk made her feel very small and helpless. 'You useless, meddling little bitch!' Deliberately he drew back his free hand and slapped her across the cheek. She staggered back from the blow, a hand to her face. 'You get yourself involved with a nest of terrorists and then judge me for dealing with them appropriately....you're lucky they didn't bump you off, I can tell you.'

'Terrorists?'

'Of course, terrorists. Why else do you think your precious Leila stayed so long in our household – because she was fond of you? She was a spy, keeping tabs on us and all our friends. And so was her son. They hated us all because that's the way Palestinians see the British.'

Yes. Candy remembered the men at Leila's house. But Naseem – he had loved her. Of that she was sure.

'For God's sake,' muttered Laura. 'What's this all about? I only said I didn't want her here. You didn't have to hit her.'

'I should have thrashed her years ago.' He sank back onto the sofa, then set down his drink and reached into his pocket for his wallet. 'Here...' He withdrew a crisp, white five pound note and thrust it towards Laura. 'Give her that.' As Laura slipped to her feet and passed the money to Candy, he finished up, 'And don't come whining back to ask for more. You won't get any.'

Candy thought of refusing the money but she needed it badly. She'd have to pay for a hotel room and some food. So she snatched it from Laura, picked up her bag and went though the door. The last thing she heard her father say as she opened the front door was, 'Good riddance!'

Down on the street, Candy stuffed the fiver into her pocket and looked right and left. It was already late afternoon, the early dusk was drawing in. Somehow she had to find a hotel room that wasn't too expensive, then think about what she would do next. She had to face the fact that she was alone in the world with nobody to pay for the things she needed. She would have to do what other people did in the circumstances, find a job to support herself.

How do I do that? she thought. She had no idea where to start looking.

She wished that the one person who'd been kind to her, the taxi-driver, was still around. He would know what to do. Then she heard a horn honking further down the street and there he was, sitting in his cab, folding a newspaper. She almost ran towards him. 'You waited!'

'I couldn't go till I was sure. I'd have worried about you all night.'

'I can pay you now.' She pulled out the fiver and showed it to him.

'You found your father then?'

'Yes, but my mother's gone to America and he's living with a lady I don't know.'

'They didn't make you welcome, then?'

'No. I'll have to find somewhere else to live, and get a job. Can you take me to a cheap hotel, please.'

'I think I better take you home with me. My sister Millie, she's a widow and she takes in lodgers, couple of doors up from us. I think she's got a spare place at the moment. Can you sew?'

'Yes. Why?'

'There's jobs going in the clothing factory up the end of the road. Making uniforms. Millie told me yesterday. That suit you?' The flood of relief that engulfed Candy at that moment was so enormous that she burst into tears.

Candy soon began to see that she was out of place, living with Millie Tanner just off Mile End Road, but she couldn't have told anyone exactly what her place should be. Once she'd thought it was Palestine, with the beach club and her music lessons and their smart apartment. But after seeing Naseem dead, after seeing the men with guns in Leila's house, she knew she'd been an outsider, tolerated because her father bought the oranges that brought money into the country. She may have been born there but she'd never properly lived there. She'd been on the edge of the pattern, and when she'd imagined otherwise, tried to get right into it by becoming part of Leila's family, the threads had started to unravel.

So the Mile End Road was as good as anywhere.

She was lucky with Millie Tanner, no doubt about that. The 'spare place' hadn't been a room of her own, as she'd expected, but sharing with Mrs. Tanner's daughter Grace, plus meals, for seven-and-six a week. Grace had emptied a drawer for her in the little chest that stood under the window, showed her how to hang her dress on a coat hanger on the picture rail, showed her the outside toilet and given her a clean towel. Then the next day she'd taken Candy to the clothing factory and handed her over to the foreman.

'She's a rum 'un and no mistake,' rumbled Mrs. Tanner to her brother the next evening. 'Where'd she come from?'

'Don't ask me, love. She just seemed so lost. I couldn't leave her on the pavement all by herself. How'd she get on at the factory?'

''Course they took her on, they'd take anyone they're so short what with all the orders for uniforms. Wouldn't matter if she'd only had thumbs on each hand.'

'I reckon she was born with a silver spoon in her mouth, you mark my words.'

'She can sew, though. Knows what she's doing.'

'Like to know where she comes from, all the same.'

*　　　*　　　*

Leila Fahy paused in her work in the vegetable garden and leaned on her hoe, giving her back a rest. She looked out across the land that belonged to her brother and saw that the recent rains had brought a new greening to the strips between the trees in the orange groves, where the sheep and goats grazed, and that the crops further down on the slope, where the land was flatter, were strong and healthy.

It was hard work keeping the farm with so many of the men in the family hiding in the hills, or training in the army, but it was worthwhile. She was happier here than she'd been all the years living in Jaffa, working as a servant. It had been necessary for someone to watch the British, keep the soldiers informed of their activities, know just how and when they intended to keep their irreconcilable promises to both the Jews and the Palestinians, but she was glad that her part in that particular game was over. Up here on the farm she felt more a part of the reality of a life that went back for thousands of years, since the Assyrians had driven the Israelites out of this land and made it their own. Whatever the politicians and armies thought they had decided, the land belonged to the families who had worked on it for generations, made it productive, earned their living from it.

She saw her young nephews beginning to gather the sheep and goats together to drive them back to the safety of the house for the night and she realised it was time she attended to the meal she was preparing. Quickly she finished the row she was hoeing, then she pulled an armful of plump carrots out of the damp earth and made her away along the path, past the well, and into the kitchen. There, two of her little granddaughters were sharing the tasks of keeping the fire going and watching over a baby that lay gurgling and laughing on a bed in one corner. A kid was already roasting in a pot on the fire and a chicken on the spit. Often they ate only bread and vegetables but tonight the men were coming down for a meeting and so a special meal was being prepared.

Leila laid the carrots on the scrubbed kitchen table and smiled at the girls. 'Nasrat, put another pot on the stove for the vegetables. Asrah, come and clean the carrots.'

'Oh Grandma, I wanted to feed the baby today. I've already warmed the milk.' She pointed to the boat-shaped glass feeding bottle that stood ready on the tiled surround of the stove.

'No. I'll do it.' Leila went across and took up her tiny grandson, smiling down at him and hugging him as she straightened up. She took up the bottle and went over to comfortable chair set near the warmth of the fire. She knew that Nasrat was disappointed but the child would have plenty of opportunity in her life for nursing babies. This one was Leila's prerogative. She needed to hold this child every evening. Giving it her love like this was the only way she could heal her heart, make up for the tragedy she had allowed to happen by not being watchful enough. As she placed the teat of the feeding bottle into the little sucking mouth she looked into the round brown eyes and saw her son Naseem, come to life again. She also saw the child's mother in the full lips and the long, tapering fingers but nobody except her understood the significance of this. As far as the rest of the family were concerned, this child was a foundling, picked up by the night watchman at the convent in Jaffa and brought straight to Leila as he had been instructed to months before the birth. Nobody except Leila knew that money had been paid to induce the sisters to part with their embarrassing burden in a merciful way. Nobody except her knew why she loved this baby so much. But in her heart she knew he wouldn't be hers for long; the Fahy men were not suited to being farmers, accepting the fate that was handed out to them by the politicians.They believed in action, with all the risks that entailed.

Young Naseem didn't remember those early days, of course, after Leila brought him to the farm, but he did remember growing up there, thinking for a long time that his grandmother was his mother. Then when his cousins laughed him out of that belief, pointing out that she was too old to have given birth to him, he decided that perhaps one of his aunts was his mother. When he asked Leila she told him that his father had been her son, and he had died, but would only say that his mother had been a foreigner, not welcome in Palestine.

'So she isn't dead?'

'She is to us.'

* * *

Leon didn't even try to make conversation on the evening flight back to London. He could take the hint that Jeremy was only pretending to read the newspaper he had with him, meaning that he was trying to keep himself to himself. For his own part, he was still preoccupied with his visit to the convent, running through his conversation with the Mother Superior in an endless replay, trying to determine what it was that left him with the feeling that something was being hidden. Like Jeremy, he turned down the dreary food that was set in front of them, but he readily accepted endless free Scotch and soda, hoping they would induce sleep.

He had just become comfortable enough to drift off when Jeremy noisily folded his newspaper and gave him several long, sideways looks. Finally Jeremy said, 'There's something I ought to tell you, Leon.'

From the tone of the voice, Leon gathered it was something important, but all he said was, 'Yes?'

Jeremy tried twice before he could get his next sentence organized. 'That… that…baby. That baby mother had in the convent.'

'Yes?'

'It didn't die. He's still alive.'

3
OBITUARY

The Daily Telegraph

22 April 2004

OBITUARY

The Dowager Countess of Penmore

Candice Jane, Dowager Countess of Penmore, who died last week at the age of 80, will perhaps be better remembered as Candy Price, the sixties film star for whom the term 'legs up to her armpits' was probably invented. Born Candice Hargreaves in 1924, in what was then Palestine, The Dowager Countess appeared to move seamlessly from obscure beginnings through a range of colourful associations to the very highest echelons of society. Her father was engaged in the fruit-importing business and the family was forced by the outbreak of World War 2 to abandon its interest in oranges and flee to England. Instead of following her mother and sister to America for the duration of the war, Candice remained in London, sewing uniforms in an East End sweatshop until she was old enough to join the WAAF. There she distinguished herself by driving a lorry into a parked Blenheim bomber on a darkened airfield. Later she met Flight Lt. Peter Price who became her first husband and the father of her two eldest children.

After the war, and divorce from Peter Price, Candy become a key player in the newly emerging British Film industry, working behind the scenes in the production office at Riverside Studios until she met and married matinee idol Rupert Taylor. After his runaway success in *The Canary Also Sings,* the couple moved to Hollywood with their infant son, Leon (later to become lead singer and songwriter for heavy metal band *The Hounds of Hell*). As a couple they laid the ground rules for many a famous Hollywood marriage to follow, throwing fabulous parties and avowing eternal loyalty to each other whilst apparently frequently playing away. To nobody's surprise the marriage soon foundered and at about the same time someone noticed the appeal of her long legs and large eyes, and decided to put her in front of the cameras. She immediately shot to stardom with such films as *Searchlight, White Moon* and *Carpet of Flowers.* She won her first Oscar for the memorable Cold War drama *The Maribelle Affair.*

Later, Candy returned to England where she lived and worked in London, making several more films and appearing on the London stage in such roles as Blanche in *A Streetcar Named Desire*. It was during this period that she became part of Princess Margaret's 'theatrical' circle and met Tatton, Viscount Northelm. After the Viscount's tragic death in a flying accident, she married the Viscount's widowed father, the Earl of Penmore, who at that time was Lord Chancellor in the Macmillan government. They had a son, Jeremy, who is the current Earl, his father having died in 1984.

There are many who believe the marriage to the elderly Earl was a timely strategic move by a star whose charms were beginning to fade but it will never be clear whether the new Countess abandoned the film industry or it abandoned her. What is known that the Countess devoted the next forty years to her husband, her son and their estates and played no small part in the restoration of Northelm House, where the Queen Mother frequently stayed on her way to Balmoral in the days when she had to make the tedious journey north by road. The comparative obscurity of those years has been brought to a sudden and spectacular end by the manner of her death, in an explosion in Tel Aviv, attributed to a bomb planted by the Palestinian terrorist group Hamas.

She leaves four assorted children: two daughters by her first husband, one of whom lives in Australia and one in a convent in Lincolnshire; Leon Taylor the musician; and Jeremy, twelfth Earl of Penmore.

Jeremy harumphed in annoyance and flung the *Telegraph* aside onto the unoccupied seat next to him as the train gathered speed out of Kings Cross. He drummed his fingers on the arm rest and stared out of the window without really focussing on the passing faceless suburbs, glad of the privacy afforded by the sparsely occupied first class carriage.

Why was he so annoyed? In the past he had enjoyed the particular style of racy obituaries published in his favourite newspaper but now that the snide *double entendres* were directed at his mother, it was different. It wasn't that he had expected her death to go unremarked in the press, but he felt it very unfair that people wanted to remember her by the colourful lifestyle which Jeremy had been born too late to experience and which certainly didn't reflect the hardworking family-orientated woman he had always believed his mother to be.

It annoyed him even though most of what they wrote was the truth – he knew that in his heart. How else had he come by so strange an assortment of brothers and sisters, none of whom ever seemed to speak to one another?

Suddenly overcome by a choking sensation, as though someone had grasped him by the throat, he flung back his head against the linen-covered headrest and closed his eyes tightly. But he was too late to stop the hot tears welling out – one even dribbled down his cheek as far as his lips so that he could taste the salt. Oh God! How embarrassing! When would this stop happening?

He had managed well for the first couple of days after the trip to Israel. Dealing with people was something he did all the time and he knew he did it well. His very competent secretary, Rose Upton, was an expert at making the kind of arrangements needed for a memorial service and a funeral that might be attended by the rich and the royal. He had smoothly pulled the strings that had allowed the shocking remains of his mother to pass quickly from the coroner's jurisdiction to the undertaker's parlour, where, after being re-arranged and subjected to a brief inspection by MI6, they would be sent to Yorkshire in a discreet hearse and arrive at a time of night that would discourage anybody in the family from asking to take a last look at the body. He had accepted gracefully the muted sympathy of everyone who became involved, brushing it aside, thinking that it could not possibly apply to him. Then, as well-oiled wheels transferred the responsibility for making post-funeral arrangements to other people, and his life began to straighten out again like a table cloth that had been rumpled by a careless servant and now needed tidying, he began to realise that this was his mother who had died – his dear, unchanging, infuriating, supportive, charming mother who had been snatched away from him and left a huge, empty hole in the centre of his being. And with his growing awareness of this empty space within him, despite the fact that he had been brought up to the belief that real men didn't cry, he was experiencing these sudden outbreaks of weeping at the most inappropriate moments.

God! Yesterday evening he had even been forced to leave the PM's reception early for fear that he would break down.

As he fished out a crumpled handkerchief and blew his nose angrily, he tried to remember what it had been like when his father died. It had certainly been different. But he had been young then, in his last year at university, already with a carelessly acquired wife and baby, and he had left all the important decisions to his mother. It had been she who had guided the new young Earl and Countess through their obligations and responsibilities. He had felt suitable sorrow, of course, concern, but he hadn't understood the fullness of what had happened, the irrevocability of the life change that had taken place between them. So he had left her with that gaping pit of grief to manage on her own, while he talked to the chaps at Uni in an off-hand manner about his title and his friends coming down for the glorious fourth and how much a year the rents might be bringing in.

Had he really been so shallow?

He felt a worm of self-loathing squirm within him somewhere adjacent to that emptiness around his heart, and he had to admit yes, he had viewed his father's death for what it would bring him. And, what was worse, his mother had watched him, had known what he was, and had forgiven him for it because of the man she wanted him to be.

Had he measured up? What had he done?

He had no idea and only now thought to ask, now that it was too late.

He picked up the *Telegraph* again and shook it flat, turning to the financial pages. Not that they would tell him anything about his investments that he didn't already know from his fund manager's report earlier in the day, but reading what the press thought the pubic would be interested to know gave him a double edge when he was making decisions. And there would be a lot of new decisions to be made once he could wind up his mother's trust and transfer the money. The bulk of it would remain within the Northelm family and he had already taken steps to defeat the Inland Revenue by setting up a new trust for his own children. But he was sure that his siblings would also be due to receive a tidy sum that would come from the Countess's own capital, and that led to him idly wondering what they would do with their share of the money.

Leon was already rich beyond anyone's needs and would probably neither know nor care what to do with any additional money. From what Jeremy knew of him, and that was mostly through the sort of magazines his wife Meggie and her friends read, he was as capable of spending it on an ocean liner, a trip into outer space, or a donation to feed starving Rwandan children. Pippa, his beautiful eldest sister, who dutifully sent a Christmas card from Freemantle every year, might have more need of it, but he didn't know. He hadn't seen her since the rock festival – the first rock festival, the one that had caused all the trouble and put Northelm firmly on the economic map. He assumed that Meggie reciprocated the Christmas card every year, but otherwise all he knew about her was that she had been a lecturer for most of her working life, though he had no idea what subject she specialised in. She must be well over fifty, probably not so beautiful now.

She would surely welcome a share in a small fortune, as would Daniella – the strange and secretive Danny who had spent the last thirty years as a nun in a small convent in Lincolnshire. Jeremy shook his head – poor Danny! He always thought of her as poor, misguided Danny. He had never been able to understand why she had spent her life like that. Surely there were enough opportunities to pray without cutting herself off from the rest of the world to live in a make-believe atmosphere? Still, she would know what to do with money. But she wouldn't talk to anyone about it. She never even sent Christmas cards. When he had telephoned the convent, on that first day when he had heard about the explosion, she had refused to talk to him. He had been forced to leave a message with a secretary and the only response, from the secretary again, had been a request for information about the date and time of the funeral. No 'How dreadful'; no 'Who would have done such a thing?'; no 'Is there anything I can do to help?'

And then there was Naseem. What of Naseem? Undiscovered by the obituary researchers, unknown to Pippa and Danny and Leon, the mysterious fifth sibling. How was he going to fit into the proceedings? Jeremy knew he wasn't in need of money but he was going to figure somewhere in the distribution of assets, wasn't he? Jeremy thought back to the brief meeting with an angry and grief-stricken Naseem in the penthouse offices of Fahy Trading in London earlier in the week. Naseem had sworn he would find out who had been responsible for their mother's death.

'The authorities in Israel and MI6 don't seem capable of doing more than muttering "Hamas",' Jeremy said. 'Individual blame doesn't come into it as far as they're concerned.'

'It does for me,' said Naseem, still barely able to conceal his rage, his dusky skin several shades paler than normal. 'I know people. I will find out.'

'I thought you kept out of all that sort of thing?'

'I deplore violence. But as a member of the Fahy family I still have the means to track down those who perpetrate it.'

'Really?' Jeremy wondered if his government knew that. 'Well, take care, old boy. We don't want another messy situation.'

‘Will your Lordship be having dinner?’ His thoughts were interrupted by a steward who was making his way down the Pullman car with a menu and a note pad. The steward already knew the answer – Jeremy travelled regularly on this train up to Yorkshire and he always had dinner, first sitting. But the formalities had to be observed – one day he might change his mind. He looked at the menu. ‘I’ll have the fish, no starter.’ Easy to resist temptation in these circumstances.

‘Thank you, sir. Half an hour.’ The steward made his way down the carriage to the next passenger.

Half an hour to dinner. They were that far into the journey already and he hadn’t phoned Meggie. With a start of guilt he opened his briefcase and found his cellphone and punched it into life. Meggie only let it ring once before answering; she must have been sitting beside her phone, at the kitchen table, or perhaps on the terrace enjoying her first whisky soda of the evening – no she wouldn’t be doing that, not until she knew whether he wanted her to drive to the station later to meet the train.

‘Darling, it’s me.’ The familiar phrase, stating the obvious.

‘I was just beginning to wonder...’ A warm, semi-rebuke. A scraping back of a chair in the background that told him she was on the flagged terrace, and was probably moving away from her seat because there were other people about. He pictured the familiar scene, the glass-fronted terrace that kept the midges out in summer and the cold out in winter, enabling the view down to the river to be enjoyed all the year round – something his mother had thought out and designed.

‘I’m on the train. I’ll be in at the usual time. Everything all right?’

‘Yes, of course. You want me to meet you?’ He did. It was part of the familiar routine, the express train stopping specially at the tiny estate station, the big four-by waiting almost alongside the platform, the drive home through the dark forest. It was part of the comfort, the unwinding process between his London persona and who he really was. But today? She might already have visitors who needed her attention. Leon might be there – he had been a bit vague when they parted company in the lounge of the Ritz a couple of days ago.

'Is Leon there?'

Did she hesitate just an instant? 'Yes, he arrived yesterday afternoon. Loaded with presents from Harrods. He's been a great help actually, sorting out the ordering for the menus, the wine merchants – things like that.'

Trust Leon to know how to make himself personable. 'And..anyone else?'

'Charlie's back from school – he's finished his exams so they gave him an extra few days. Tatts is coming back from the Uni tomorrow.'

'Have you heard from Pippa?'

'Yes. She phoned. She's still in London but she'll be catching an early train up tomorrow. And guess what – Aunt Netta phoned – she wants to come. How old is she? She must be ancient.'

'A couple of years younger than mother, I guess. I don't see that we can prevent her. I wonder how she'll get there. I just hope she doesn't cause a scene like at Granny Hargreaves' funeral.'.

'I already said it would be lovely to see her.'

'Is that all right? Can you cope?'

'Leon's been making beds as well. Lucky we don't live in a three bed semi. What about HRH Have you heard?'

'Yes. He'll just do the memorial in London next month. It would have been different if Margaret or the QM were still around, but none of the younger lot really knew her and of course it's out of the question for HM without turning it into a circus, though she has sent condolences.'

The train swayed and reminded Jeremy of where he was. He looked up and met the eyes of another City-dressed male passenger across the carriage, who was openly eavesdropping on his conversation with an expression of incredulity on his face. Jeremy had heard stories of people inventing far-fetched telephone conversations on trains simply in order to impress fellow passengers and he felt deeply embarrassed that someone should be thinking that was what he was doing. He averted his eyes and turned towards the window, noticing that a soft mist was creeping over the landscape, punctuated by warm light as the train sped through towns and villages, nearly sweeping away small stations with the turmoil of its passing.

Meggie was still talking, something about one of her horses, and he let her finish, hoping he hadn't missed an expected rejoinder. Then the steward came through, reminding the passengers that the dinner sitting was about to begin, and Meggie heard and said, 'Oh, I expect you want to go. I'll see you later at the station. All right, darling?' And when he was slow to respond, 'All right?'

'Yes. Yes. See you later.' He squeezed the red button on his phone and sat for a moment, aware of the aromas of dinner drifting through the car but more concerned with that continuing emptiness within himself, making as though his usual core of well-being had leaked away without him noticing. What was it going to be like going home for the first time without his mother being there, without being able to see the lights shining in her apartment above the old coach-house, the dowager apartment that had been re-furbished for her soon after his father had died? Sometimes he had hated her being there and had secretly rejoiced when she announced she was going to visit London for a few days, but at the same time he had accepted that she was a non-negotiable part of the estate scene. And, he had to admit, she had achieved a good balance between leaving him and Meggie alone to do as they liked in the big house that had been her home for so many years, and being there to lend support and advice when it was asked for.

What would happen now? What would happen to her apartment? It wouldn't be needed until he died and left Meggie a widow and Tatton inherited the title and brought his own countess to Northelm. Or perhaps if Tatts married before he inherited, they could live in the dowager flat – yes, that was a good idea. He would offer it to the younger generation as they moved up the ladder and knitted themselves into the system.

Hopefully it would be a smooth transition, as his had been after his father had died. Probably better for them, because he had become an Earl at an early age. Tatton was already approaching that age and with luck had many more years to go yet as a viscount.

'Sir...Your dinner...'

He realised the steward was leaning over him , trying to attract his attention without disturbing him unduly – a difficult manoeuvre. Mumbling an apology he picked up his newspaper and briefcase and hurried through to the dining car, wondering if there was any chance he might enjoy his meal.

It was a comfortable and comforting routine. Meggie poured them both whiskies while he took his briefcase through to his study and locked the private papers he carried into the safe. Then he locked the front door and the terrace doors and together they walked up the wide staircase to their bedroom – or suite of bedroom/dressing rooms/bathrooms. They held hands as they walked up, the first physical contact between them other than a brief cheek kiss as he climbed into the four-by at the station. It was very late and the house was quiet, and he was glad he didn't have to face Leon until the morning. Even Meggie was quiet now, and he blessed her unerring instinct that told her he didn't need talk at the moment.

He spent some time showering away the grime of London and by the time he slid into the big bed they still shared she was already there, the familiar perfume of her soaps clinging to her soft skin. He put his arms around her nakedness and buried his face in her neck, feeling the tears threatening again and this time giving way to them.

It wasn't unusual, in what he thought of as his London life, for girls to be made available to him as inducements for financial favours, or for smart, sophisticated women to make it obvious that they would like to add his name to their list of conquests. But, even though many of his friends thought him a fool for it, he was never tempted because he knew he would never be effectively aroused by any other flesh than Meggie's. Since the afternoon when he had first been seduced by her in the little summer house on the other side of the lake, he worrying even then that she reminded him so much of his mother that it was indecent, she had been like a drug to him. All that summer he had been unable to get enough of her, and he still couldn't, after all the years, after her body had filled out and her shock of curly black hair was sprinkled with grey.

Now she held him close, and as he hardened in response to her touch she parted her legs and he slipped inside her, and they copulated in that perfect, matching way that he believed was theirs alone, and he felt whole again.

What he didn't notice was that afterwards she cried herself to sleep, very quietly.

4
NASEEM

The day after his mother's remains had been taken from Tel Aviv back to London, Naseem Fahy found himself making almost the same journey in reverse, both in time and space, and it affected him deeply. As he emerged from the airport into the warm scented air of a Middle Eastern spring a flood of memories washed over him, more than he had ever expected. Of course, things had been very different fifty years ago when he had last been here. There had been no possibility of a smooth transition in a jet plane on that day when his grandmother and uncle had led a weary, footsore family over the hills towards Jimin, away from the only home he had ever known. There had been no passports then, no stern-faced official looking with open doubt from the dark red cover of a British Citizen's passport, to his olive-skinned face, to the information that he had been born in Palestine, which no longer existed. Naseem braced himself for a polite, 'Mr Fahy, would you come this way.' Then, to his surprise, he was waved through, able to retrieve his luggage and walk out to where he knew a car would be waiting for him, driven by a man named Fouad, who was a member of the sprawling Fahy family and therefore nominally his cousin.

He was relieved that he was being met. From the cocooned safety of his quiet office in London he had talked to a lot of people over the last two days, after Jeremy's visit. Coming to Palestine – no, Israel - himself had seemed the obvious solution to the problem of finding out who had killed his mother. But now that he was actually here, his expensive leather footwear at last making contact with the dust of his homeland, he began to feel the foundations of his sense of security crumbling away. After all, although he carried with him papers to show that he was a tourist, and had taken the trouble to dress accordingly in jeans and sports shirt with a well-worn leather jacket, he would soon be meeting with members of what the Israeli, British and United States governments considered to be one of the most dangerous terrorist organisations in the world – Hamas.

He knew he was out of his depth and he was increasingly certain that he would be lucky to get home to London alive. As he sat in the car beside Fouad he recalled the long-forgotten terror of a seven-year-old boy, crouching beside his grandmother behind a fig tree at a farm in the hills.

*   *   *

Jamal had come to help with the ploughing. Jamal did very little work on the farm but nobody in the family complained. They all knew that his real work lay elsewhere, in the alleys of Jerusalem and in the no-man's land between Jaffa and Tel-Aviv. Talking to groups of men, organising the storage and movement of weapons as they came in from Europe on the ships that anchored off the Andromeda rock, waiting to load up with oranges for the return voyage. Arranging small caches of weapons, hidden up and down the country, each known only to a few people. And teaching men and women to use those weapons. Because now that the war in Europe was over, more and more Jewish refugees were making their way to the land that they wanted to call Israel, and the people who owned that land were determined to keep them out.

'The British can't do it,' said Jamal, time and again, in small, closed rooms lit by oil lamps and candles, 'So we must look after what is ours.'

'But Britain is strong,' people said. 'The British have beaten Germany and the Japanese. They can deal with the Jews.'

Jamal shook his head and repeated what he had been told by the men he met when he went to Lebanon. 'Britain was strong once but now she is weak, broken. She is a country in chaos, she can hardly hold herself together, let alone keep promises she has made to look after Palestine. She only won her wars with the help of the Americans, and now the Americans want to let Jews into Palestine. You'll see, Britain will give in. Very soon. And we will have a war on our hands.' People believed him. He was so sure. They made ready. An army preparing to fight for Palestine as soon as the British gave it to the Jews. And the younger, wilder men believed him so passionately that they weren't prepared to wait. They took the guns and grenades that they were supposed to be looking after and attacked Jewish settlements. And some of them attacked British soldiers and police units and blamed the murder and carnage on the Jewish Irgun terrorists.

As time passed Leila grew more and more afraid. Not for herself but for her ageing brother and his wife, for the girls that Jamal and Hanif had married and brought to the farm with their babies. For her nephew's daughters, Nasrat and Asrah, now beautiful teenagers. And for seven year old Naseem, who followed his uncles everywhere whenever they visited, and who could already hit a moving rabbit at fifty paces with a sling and stone. Although there were no weapons hidden at the farm, Jamal and Hanif and men who worked with them needed to hide from time to time and they had enlarged a cave that ran into the hillside behind the house from under the spreading branches of an old fig tree. They had made space enough for a dozen people and they'd bored a hole down into the back of the cave from the pine wood at the top of the hill, with a dizzying rope ladder to climb, so that the cave would never be a trap. It was as safe as it could be but not safe enough. Leila pretended that she thought it would protect them but in her heart she knew that every time the men came up the hill from the village they might be followed. By police, by soldiers, by other people who could earn large sums of money by betraying the young leaders of the Palestine Freedom Fighters.

It made Leila jumpy and wary. Not that any of Jamal's militiamen would ever be turned away. But on the day when trouble finally became personal, there was a great deal to lose.

'Grandma!' She heard the piping voice before she saw Naseem, running down the slope from the look-out point above the road to the village, where he took the sheep and goats to graze every morning. 'Grandma!' He burst out of the orange grove, breathless, as she ran forwards to catch him in her arms, quieten his voice a little.

'What is it?'

'Grandma!' There were tears in the boy's eyes. 'There are jeeps, coming this way. Three of them.'

'How far?'

'They have just come out of the village.'

Two miles. They had ten or fifteen minutes. It could be the British police but they came in pairs and they didn't drive jeeps, they had big black cars. A single jeep could have been any kind of visitor, to be treated with caution but not feared. But three jeeps together meant strength, which could only mean a threat. And it wouldn't be an accidental threat. Not with Jamal ploughing the cornfield further up the valley on the new tractor. Somebody knew he was there.

Leila's legs were getting too old for serious running but she covered the distance to the farmhouse fast enough that Naseem couldn't keep up with her. She pulled at the rope that swung at one corner of the porch and a bell rang out clanging a warning that everyone in the family would recognise as being more urgent than the summons to a meal. With the wind blowing up the valley Jamal might hear it above the engine of the tractor but Leila needed to be sure.

Letting go of the bell rope, she grasped Naseem by the shoulders. 'Get on your bicycle and go up to the cornfield, quick as you can. Tell Jamal what's happening, then go with him. Don't come back here whatever you do. Go!' She gave Naseem a little push. 'Your uncle's life depends on you.'

The boy didn't hesitate. She stood a moment, watching him pulling his small cycle out from under the porch and setting off up the track beside the stream. A lump came to her throat. She wanted to keep him beside her because of all the family he was the one she loved the most, but he had to learn to play his part. And he did it well – he was a brave boy, he already knew the meaning of loyalty and responsibility.

Now she went into the house and quickly raked out the smoldering wood fire in the cooking range. With any luck the unwelcome visitors would believe the whole family had gone to market and they would leave once they'd had a good look around, perhaps ransacked the place. Then she took up her niece's baby that was sleeping in a cot in the corner of the room and hurried out of the house and pushed into the overhanging branches of the fig tree. As she scrambled into the cleft behind the tree she was followed by the baby's young mother. Then her brother and her nephew Rashid joined them along the path from the vegetable plot where they'd been planting beans and cabbages. Leila looked around at the family, settling themselves to wait by the dim light that filtered through the fig leaves.

Where was Hanif's wife?

'Nuria?' she asked. 'And Petra?' Rashid's wife, mother of the teenage girls.

'They were working further up the valley,' Hanif said. 'I saw them running into the woods. What about Naseem and Jamal?'

'They'll go the other way.' Leila looked around at the frightened faces and she could see that they were all shaking as she told them what was happening. Then they began to hear the sounds of engines growling slowly up the stony road. Her nephew sighed with relief. 'It's nothing, then. You've brought us from our work just for an army patrol.'

'We can't be sure,' Leila insisted. 'If they were coming up the road from the village they must have been headed here. So what do they want?'

'We know what they want,' said Rashid. 'They want Jamal. And if they find him they will kill us all. Who has gone down to warn the girls to stay in the village when they come out of school?'

'They'll go away before that,' Leila said. It was a long time until school finished. She was more anxious about Jamal and Naseem – surely they would have made their way through the other entrance by now, further up the valley? If only Jamal would be content to hide, not start fighting.

Then they were there, the boy and his uncle, coming from the back of the cave after climbing down the rope ladder, Jamal carrying a Sten gun. Leila immediately began to tell Jamal what was happening but he cut her short. 'I have seen them.You did right to call us in. They are Irgun.' He spat out the name, then he went close to the entrance where he could watch through the veil of fig leaves as the three jeeps drew up in a wide circle in front of the house. Leila stood beside him, her fear growing as men in grey hoods came out of the jeeps and made a ring around the house, holding machine guns. One of them shouted, they heard the name Jamal Fahy, then there was a brief moment's silence. Suddenly, at a signal from the man who had done the shouting they raked the house with bullets, then stood waiting again. Leila let out a sob of anger and stuffed a fist over her mouth. The baby began to whimper and Jamal signaled urgently to its mother to keep it quiet. The girl gazed at him with big, frightened eyes as she opened her shirt and thrust a nipple into the baby's mouth.

The men were moving into the house and into the surrounding sheds, kicking open doors and smashing windows and fly screens with the barrels of their guns. One man went over to where their little cow stood in her paddock, gazing impassively at the scene. He put the muzzle of his gun to her neck and pulled the trigger. The cow's head fell sideways in a shower of blood and her knees crumpled.

Leila was aware that Jamal was shaking with anger. 'Somebody has talked,' he muttered. 'Someone has told them I come here.'

Rashid came to stand beside Jamal, pushing Leila to one side. 'You should have stopped long ago. I told you to stop. I told you that you were putting us all in danger for your dirty war.'

'It's your war too, Rashid. You think all you have to do is continue to dig your fields and pay your taxes to whoever is the government? Don't you believe it. You think the British have been unjust? You wait until the Jews take over.'

'The Jews are terrorists. They will never govern Palestine.'

Jamal nodded towards what was happening outside. 'They already do, in all but name. And that will soon come. You haven't read their latest representation to the United Nations. I have.'

An explosion sounded outside and Jamal cursed. Angry at finding nobody hiding in the building, one of the masked men had dropped a grenade down the well. A shower of stone and dirt flew into the air, almost in slow motion, followed by a geyser of water.

Rashid thumped a fist against the earth wall of the cave and tears of rage came to his eyes.

'Look what they've done!' he hissed. 'It will be months before we can repair that!'

'You will never repair it,' said Jamal. 'It will never be safe for any of you to live here again.'

'But it's our farm, our land....'

'In ten years' time there will be a Jewish settlement here and it will be Jewish land. I tell you, you are speaking of stopping the flood of a tide, stopping the turning of the earth.'

Down below, some of the men were climbing into their vehicles. Engines started and for a moment Leila thought they were moving out. But her hopes were quickly dashed. The drivers manoeuvered their vehicles round to face the road, one behind the house perilously close to the old fig tree, one where the track led off up to the cornfield, one beside the last bend in the road. The leader positioned himself on the porch of the house, slouched in Leila's rocking chair, and lit a cheroot. He had to pull up his mask to smoke it. Other men began to fling themselves down under the shade of trees and pull water bottles and food out of their pouches. One man pissed through the broken window of the girls' bedroom. Then he went back to his companions and they all settled to wait as the hot air pressed in on all sides.

'What are we going to do,' whispered Leila.

'We'll wait until it gets dark,' said Jamal, 'Then go out through the tunnel. We can cross the hill from there without coming near here.'

'Suppose they catch us?' said Rashid quietly. 'Suppose they already know about our tunnel?'

'If they did, they would be here already. But to be certain, I will go first.'

Leila felt Naseem pulling at her hand. 'I'm not afraid,' he whispered. 'I can go first if you want me to. They won't catch me.'

'You must wait,' said Leila. 'You must be a man before you can take your turn for your country.'

'Rashid...Rashid....' Jamal and Rashid turned at the sound of Petra's voice. 'What about the girls?' Her eyes were wide in the semi light.

'Where are the girls?' asked Jamal.

Rashid replied. 'At the school in the village.'

'Who went to warn them?'

'Nobody.' It was Leila who spoke. 'I thought this would end quickly. I thought they'd just look around then go away.'

'They must stay in the village,' Jamal said. 'Somebody has to go and tell them.'

'Perhaps it should be you,' said Rashid.

'It could be me, but can you lead the whole family over the hills in the darkness?'

Rashid stared for a moment and Leila saw that he was clenching and unclenching his hand as though he wanted to hit Jamal. 'Very well,' he said. 'I will go. Be so good as to help me out up the ladder.' As the two disappeared into the darkness towards the back of the cave Leila heard Jamal saying softly, 'When you have them, hide in the village until nightfall, then make your way north until you are in Jimin. The blacksmith there will...' And their voices faded away.

When Jamal came back Leila asked, 'Where have you arranged for us to go?' She didn't doubt that he had an escape route set up.

He said briskly, 'Lebanon. We have people working there. The blacksmith in Jimin is called Jamal Eban. He will get you to the frontier and tell you who to contact in Beirut.' He nodded over his shoulder to the rest of the family behind them. 'You are the only one who knows this.' Leila understood. The fewer people who knew the names of contact people the less likely they could be betrayed. The fact that Jamal had told her meant that he had serious worries for their immediate future.

The men outside lounged, every now and again one of them moving around to piss or to cadge a cigarette light from one of the others. Heat pressed in on all sides. Crickets sawed, flies buzzed around the corpse of the cow. A little tabby cat, looking for a meal, wandered out of the bushes at the side of the road. One of the men took a pot shot at it and it dived back the way it had come. Inside the cave they sat, dozed, took it in turns to cradle the baby, waited for time to pass.

Suddenly the tension was broken by the sound of another jeep coming up the road, engine racing as its tyres spun on the loose surface. The men around the house immediately came to their feet and grabbed their weapons, went for cover where they could. Except for the leader who stayed where he was on Leila's chair on the porch. He only stood up when the fourth jeep came into sight, bristling with more armed men, and three other people huddled in the back restrained by handcuffs.

As soon as the vehicle came to a halt the armed men half pushed, half pulled the three prisoners out of the back, sending them sprawling onto the dust of the yard. Jamal swore as he recognised Rashid and his two daughters. Even from a distance he could see they were terrified and one of the girls already had the top of her school dress ripped to show one pale, half grown breast.

The Irgun leader pushed himself to his feet and came forward quickly, smiling. He spoke quickly to the newcomers, then raised his gun and stared around him at the hills and bushes. 'Now if you are hiding there, Fahy, come out! I know these girls are innocent. Give yourself up and we shall spare them, return them to the village with their father.'

'Damn!' muttered Jamal again. 'Why did we not think they would be watching the village too?'

Leila was beside him, a hand on his arm. She gripped him hard, feeling the strength of his muscles beneath the dark skin. Her son, the soldier. The one who always knew what to do. But did he know now? 'Jamal...think carefully before you do anything. Think who needs you most.'

She was trying to tell him to save himself above his family, but would he listen?

The leader was dragging one of the girls to her feet, the eldest, Nasrat. She screamed and he lifted her off the ground and held her close to his face, then signaled to two of the men standing near. They came forward, grinning, and took her arms and half lifted her, half dragged her towards the nearest jeep, then spread her across the bonnet. She screamed again as one of the men roughly ripped her dress.

With a whimper her mother leapt foward to the front of the cave, only to be held in an iron grip by Jamal, his hand over her mouth. Rashid elbowed himself up from where he lay and hurled himself forward at the feet of the men who were handling his daughter. The leader casually raised his gun and shot Rashid in the legs. He fell back howling with pain and screamed, 'There is nobody here, I tell you! Nobody will come out because nobody is hiding!'

'In that case,' said the leader, 'Only these girls are of further use to us.' And he shot Rashid again, this time in the stomach and chest. As her father died Nasrat screamed and struggled but this only served to make the man standing in front of her hit her across the face before opening his trousers to continue his assault in the most basic way he knew. Another man came forward and picked up a sobbing Asrah from the ground and threw her bodily into the back of the jeep, then climbed in after her. As her screams began to rend the air Leila felt Jamal coiling beside her. Flinging his better judgment to one side he leapt forward with a roar, through the cave entrance, through the branches of the fig tree, and was half way across the open space towards the house, his gun blazing, before the terrorists saw him coming. He killed three of them as they left the girls and scattered, diving for cover behind jeeps and buildings. But he couldn't shoot as widely as he wanted to because his instinct wouldn't let him risk killing his nieces and so the leader was able to raise his gun and aim deliberately at Jamal's chest, felling him as though he'd hit him with an axe. As Jamal fell, spouting blood, the leader grabbed Nasrat's hand and pulled her forward.

'Who is this man?' he asked.

The girl stared in shocked silence as Jamal's body stopped twitching.

The man shook Nasrat and clubbed the side of her head with the barrel of his gun. 'I asked you, who is it?'

'It's...my uncle...Uncle Jamal....'

'Jamal Fahy?'

Nasrat gulped, then nodded.

'Good.' Still holding her, the leader took a pistol from his holster, put it to her head and pulled the trigger. Then he carried her to the back of the jeep where her sister was and heaved her body inside, firing a shot into the younger girl in the same motion.

Gesticulating, shouting, he ordered his men to load up Rashid's and Jamal's bodies, firing some extra bullets into both of them as they did so. Then as though finally to make sure that the family would understand the message, they took out petrol cans, poured some down the well and sprayed the rest over the house and the outbuildings. A few matches sent the place up like a bomb, finally driving the shaking Leila and the sobbing Nuria to the safety of the back of the cave. As she moved, Leila saw that little Naseem had been crouched close to her at the entrance and he had seen everything. The full horror of conflict was indelibly etched on his young mind and he never forgot what it meant.

* * *

Naseem never knew exactly where Fouad took him on that journey. They drove along main roads and side roads, past military checkpoints, at one point alongside the sea for several miles. At the start he tried to ask a few questions, hoping Fouad might be communicative. At first he spoke in English, then in Arabic, the language he hadn't spoken since he was a teenager in Beirut, but Fouad shook his head, not keen to talk. As Naseem's tongue stumbled over the unfamiliar syllables that he couldn't be sure were even comprehensible to his cousin, he began to realise just how far he had grown apart from this country he had once called home. I can't speak Arabic clearly any more, he thought, and yet I know I still have an accent when I speak English. Leila was right, I don't belong anywhere.

Leila, his daughter. He used to think of her as a rude and rebellious teenager, then an opinionated young woman, but now he wished he had listened more carefully to what she was saying. Or if he couldn't listen to her properly he should have listened to his mother when she had tried to tell him what it was that was making Leila unhappy. If he had listened he would at least know where she was now.

It was dusk when the cab finally drew to a standstill in the courtyard of a two-storey house on the edge of a town. As Fouad cut the engine and flung open the driver's door, Naseem could hear the craking of crickets and he saw that the edges of the courtyard were planted with oleanders. Insects swarmed in the shafts of light that came from the open, netted windows of the house.

Naseem climbed stiffly out of the car and followed Fouad up some shallow stone steps to where a door was already opening to admit them. The man who opened the door exchanged a few words with Fouad, that Naseem grasped were meant as a greeting and a query about the difficulty of the journey. Then he came forward, shook Naseem by the hand and said, 'Come in, come in. Welcome to Gaza.' As Naseem followed him inside he noticed that the man wore a holstered hand gun at his hip.

They showed him to a washroom, then took him into a room that contained a long conference table and an assortment of chairs, and brought him sweet lemon tea and baklava, which were welcome – since the plane landed he had only had bottled water. He sat for some time at the table, then grew uncomfortable and began to walk up and down the room. As he did this he paused to look at some maps tacked to the wall and when he did this he was ushered back into a chair. He was never left alone. Men came and went, some wearing military fatigues, some wearing a variety of civilian clothes, all with their faces half hidden by hastily flung *kuffiahs*. Every now and again a cellphone would ring and one of them would answer, listen, then bark a few words in reply. They brought him more tea, more cakes. They seemed to be waiting for someone, though not certain when he was expected. This was another thing that Naseem realized he had forgotten about Arab life – patience. Time meant nothing and nobody apologised.

Eventually they were moved to comparative action by the sound of engines outside and the room was invaded by half a dozen suited men who arranged themselves around the conference table, inviting Naseem to sit amongst them. The man who took the seat at the head of the table, grey haired and, Naseem thought, about the same age as himself, took a sheaf of papers out of an inner pocket and laid them on the table.

'*Salaam aleikum,*' he said in a quiet voice. 'Good evening. You are Naseem Fahy?'

'I am. Who…'

'I am Jamal Gerady Fahy. I understand we are cousins. I am pleased to meet you, though sorry about the nature of our business.'

Naseem sighed, leaned forward and covered his face with his hands for a moment. He was very tired. In the strangeness of the situation he had almost forgotten the object of this extraordinary journey. He had almost begun to believe that his hosts had instigated this visit, not that he had demanded, from the smoothly run interior of his offices in London, that they make themselves available to him to answer his questions. And yet here he was, against all the odds, in a room with a group of people half of the world's spymasters would give a small fortune to meet, being treated deferentially and civilly. And probably all because of his name.

He looked up, straight into Jamal Gerady Fahy's dark inscrutable eyes. Was this the infant that Jamal's wife had been nursing on that long ago day when the Irgun had paid their murderous visit to the farm? If so, did he know what had happened that day? Had he been told the story?

'You were enquiring about your mother, the English Countess,' Jamal prompted gently.

'I am. I'm sure you know the circumstances of her death. The British news reported that Hamas claimed responsibility for the bomb.'

'Don't they always? Isn't Hamas the only scapegoat they know about?'

'Can we be straightforward? I want to find out why my mother was killed and to receive your assurance that the murderer can be brought to justice.'

There was a pause. Then Jamal said, 'I can see that the realities of life here have not penetrated your world. Why should justice matter for her when every week scores of innocents die?'

'Surely, it should matter for everyone? Surely it only loses its value when you accept this violence without doing anything about it?' Naseem watched Jamal carefully, saw how his eyes darkened as he tried to control a tide of anger that was rising within him. He wondered how far he could go in provoking that anger further. Wondered, too, if Jamal had any inkling of his own growing inner rage at the attitude that one person more or less didn't much matter in the struggle to build an autonomous nation.

'Come, cousin,' Jamal almost hissed. 'You may be a smart businessman but you really don't know anything about our politics, do you? Allow me to educate you a little. Which faction in our struggle would benefit most from the publicity caused by the violent death of a seemingly innocent but socially prominent old lady?'

'None, that I can see. The British press has already devoted an inordinate amount of air-time to the matter. Theories spread like wildfire. Any organisation that can be blamed is castigated as being a den of monsters. Specially if it can be shown to be an organisation connected with the Palestinian Authority.' As Naseem spoke he noted that Jamal was punctuating his remarks with increasingly vehement nods, accompanied by a small, cynical smile.

'So,' said Jamal. 'You still don't get it? Who regularly goes out of their way to make the Palestinian Authority look like a den of monsters?'

When the answer came to Naseem he couldn't believe he had been so slow. 'The government? The Israeli government?' Arranging a prominent murder to discredit their enemies? 'Do they often do that?' Jamal continued to nod and Naseem continued, 'And why would they think the world will believe them?'

'Because someone knows the truth about her connections with you, and through you with us? Think, Naseem. Anyone who knows the whole story – and I mean the whole story, and the way you ran out on your family all those years ago - could well see your mother's murder as the legitimate trigger to another explosion of violence. And to the outside world, wouldn't it look like Palestinians fighting amongst themselves.'

Naseem felt crushed. He hated being reminded of how he had disobeyed his uncle Hanif and gone to England, and steadfastly refused to return. He hated being reminded that he had turned his back on Palestine and taken his life into his own hands, for reasons that had seemed sound enough at the time but which he had since realised were purely selfish. Hesitantly, he tried to keep his mind focused on their conversation, a kind of conversation that seemed to be run of the mill for Jamal but which for him made him feel as though he was dreaming. 'So...a couple of days ago someone here assured me that you could give me the name of whoever killed my mother. What you are saying now it that it isn't possible. Nobody can bring a whole government to justice.'

Jamal smiled once more and spread his hands. 'We try. It is often like trying to pack an octopus into a paper bag.'

'It's hopeless. Even I can see that.' Naseem broached a new subject, one that he wouldn't have had to bring up at all if Leila had been there to meet him as he had hoped. 'And my daughter, Leila. Last year she came to Israel via Beirut to work for you and she has disappeared. '

'Disappeared? Even here, disappearing is hard to do.'

'Then let us say I haven't heard from her. Do you know where she is?'

Another pause. Naseem noticed that the men around the table were exchanging glances, none of them looking at him. Staring hard at the papers in front of him, Jamal said, 'Your daughter did work for us, here and in Ramallah. She was a headstrong young woman, not easy to control once she had an idea in her head, and her ideas clashed with much of what we try to do here. But she was a lawyer, very good at what she did. Only sometimes she forgot we are trying to form a government here.'

'Was? Did?' Naseem looked from one to the other. 'You mean she has gone?'

'Unfortunately yes. Unexpectedly, we have lost her. It's a pity you didn't keep in better touch with her. If you had, what I am going to tell you now wouldn't come as such a shock.'

5
PIPPA

Pippa Price strode down Knightsbridge in the bright afternoon sunshine, losing no opportunity to catch a glimpse of herself in the shop windows she passed. She knew she looked good in her new white trouser suit with a deep pink silk blouse, and a pair of heels that had cost more than she had ever spent on shoes before. The natural grey of her heavy, shoulder length hair had been expertly streaked and tinted into a slightly lighter shade than its original auburn. She wore just enough make-up to make it obvious that she didn't need very much and that her sixty year old complexion still had the peaches-and-cream glow of many women half her age. Her satisfaction with herself was rounded off by the knowledge that she hadn't increased a single dress size since she was last in London, twenty-five years ago.

It was mid-afternoon and the pulse of traffic was slowing down, gathering itself for the evening rush hour. Pippa carried several more new outfits in a collection of bags that swung heavily against her legs as she walked, but her hotel was only a few hundred yards beyond Harrods so she didn't need a taxi. She had plenty of time to change, have something to eat, and get herself to the West End for the theatre she had booked.

She was happy. It had been a thoroughly wonderful day, a bit like the days she had spent shopping in London with her mother when she had been a budding teenager. It had the same feeling of being stolen time. She knew that Meggie had expected her to go straight to Northelm when she arrived from Fremantle and had been a little bit put out when she had phoned two evenings ago and said she was staying in London for a couple of days.

'We were expecting you to come straight up here,' Meggie had complained. 'There's a lot to do, getting ready for …'

'I want to buy some new clothes. I haven't anything suitable for a funeral.'

'You could have borrowed something from your mother's stuff. She's got rooms full of clothes. But perhaps…'

'No.'

And I want to get the feel of London again, she had thought. And I want, I want so much, to see Leon. But she didn't dare say that. She knew he was in London because she had seen the photographs in the paper of him and Jeremy arriving back from Tel Aviv with the coffin. She could easily ask Meggie now where he was. But supposing he didn't want to see her? Pippa couldn't quite face that possibility – better to hide than be ignored. So she deliberately hadn't say where she was staying, just promised to arrive in good time for the funeral. She intended to catch an early train and Meggie had said there would be cars to meet people at the station.

As she unpacked her shopping in the hotel, Pippa wondered how it would be meeting her sister Danny after so long. They were so different. Any sisterly affinity had been steadily eroded over the years as she grew more like their mother and their father's mean-spiritedness took over Danny's nature. Not for the first time she asked herself how two such ill-matched people as their father and mother had ever got together. She had never asked, and now it was too late.

*　　　　*　　　　*

Every time a bomb exploded a fresh shower of dust was sprinkled over the four people who sat huddled beneath the table in the middle of the Ladies Waiting Room on Guildford station. Two WAAFs, one tall and auburn-haired, one blonde and petite, tried desperately to shield their newly-permed hair and freshly pressed uniforms. Leaning back to back with them, two young Flying Officers sat as still as they could, hardly able to believe their luck at being so neatly stranded by the raid with the two girls, all waiting for a train back to their base.

'One each,' Flying Officer Fisher had muttered as they ran for cover after the alarm sounded.

'But we don't know them,' said Flying Officer Price as

he held open the door to the first waiting room they'd come to.

'That'll soon change.'

Now, huddled beneath the table, feeling the back of the tall thin WAAF shifting against his every few minutes, or stiffening with each fresh explosion, Peter Price had to admit that his companion had been right. The whole situation had become really chummy.

'What d'you think they're bombing?' asked the tall WAAF. She seemed the more serious of the two, the one least put out by this interruption to their journey.

'Us,' said the small WAAF with a nervous giggle.

'I should think it's the railway they're after,' said Fisher. 'Just think of the problems moving stuff around if they cut all the main lines out of London.'

'Just think of the problems we're going to have if they cut this one tonight. How will we get back to the south coast?'

'We won't.'

'We can't be late back from leave. What will they say?'

'What can they say if we're being bombed? You worry too much about doing the right thing. Suppose the next one drops on us. We'll be more than late then.'

'That'll be different.'

There was a sniffle from the small WAAF and the tall one said, 'I wish you two would shut up if you can't think of something cheerful to talk about. Excuse me...' and she shifted her weight from supporting the young man's back so that she could put an arm around her companion. 'It's all right, Grace,' she murmured. Peter Price became aware that she had a strange accent, something he couldn't place, sort of upper class but with a foreign twang. Slightly French, perhaps. Not at all like the broad Cockney of the little blonde girl. 'It's all right. They're making a lot of noise but I don't think they are very close to us.'

'It ain't us I'm scared about,' said Grace through her sniffles. 'It's me Mum. I wish she'd move away, go to America or something like your Mum done.'

''She'll be all right. If they're bombing us here they won't be bombing Mile End Road.'

'I'm sure she'll be all right.' Seeing his chance, Jack Fisher turned round and pulled a clean white handkerchief out of his pocket, offering it to Grace to dry her eyes. 'More likely she's worrying about you, you know.'

'My mother lives in Taunton,' said Peter. 'That's safe enough.' He missed her dreadfully since he'd joined up but he didn't dare to say to. It sounded so wet.

The tall WAAF fished something out of her bag and Peter heard a faint rustling sound and smelled peppermint. 'Here, I forgot about these.' In the almost total darkness he could just make out that she was pushing a crumpled little bag of humbugs towards him.

'Oh, I couldn't. That's your sweet ration.'

'That's okay. I don't eat many sweets. Anyway, if we're bombed it's better to have eaten them than have them in my pocket.' She thrust the bag at him again so they all took one in turn and sat sucking in companionable silence until the next bomb dropped and Grace sniffled again and muttered, 'Wish we was in the tube station.'

'They do say,' said Fisher, 'that you're no safer underground than up top if you get a direct hit.'

'I'll give you a direct hit if you don't shut up,' said the tall WAAF, which surprised Peter because he was beginning to think of her as the kind of person who didn't answer back, rather like himself.

The droning of heavy engines overhead began to fade. They knew the signs and they'd already begun to move out from under the table, stretching and dusting themselves down, when the steady note of the all-clear siren sounded over the town. Out on the platform they stood together, staring helplessly up and down the tracks. The only light came from some distant blazes caused by the bombing. Peter had the feeling he and Jack should know what to do next, being officers, but he had no idea. He looked at Jack beside him and wondered if he had any ideas himself, then decided Jack must feel pretty much the way he did. Thing was, were they going to admit it?

'What's the time?' asked Grace.

'Don't know,' said Peter. 'Cant read my watch.'

'I've got a torch,' said the tall WAAF, fishing a tiny metal tube out of her regulation shoulder bag. 'Be careful, keep it pointed downwards.'

'We're not stupid,' said Jack contemptuously as he shone the faint beam on Peter's wristwatch. For a brief moment it lit up the anxious ring of young faces. 'Ten-fifteen. More or less.' A short silence. 'My guess is, the train won't come now. We're stuck here till the morning.'

'We'll have to sleep in the waiting room,' said Grace.

'Perhaps not,' Jack said, nudging Peter. 'There must be a hotel in the town. They may be able to put us up.'

'At this hour? It's hardly respectable to turn up with two girls at this hour looking for a room.'

'But this war time. There's been a raid. And we won't be looking for 'a' room. We'll be asking for one for us and one for the young ladies.'

'A hotel?' Grace giggled. 'I ain't never stayed in a hotel. It'll cost a packet, won't it?'

'Nothing we can't afford, said the other girl. 'Don't forget, the government's paying us for wearing these uniforms.'

'Long as nobody's offering to pay us for taking them off.'

'We'll take that as a warning,' said Jack, sounding a good deal more composed than Peter felt, as though he really did know what to do after all. 'So that's settled, is it? We go into town and look for a hotel. I'll lead the way. Can I borrow your torch again, Miss...What *is* your name?'

'Candy,' said the tall WAAF. 'Candy Hargreaves. And this is my friend Grace Tanner.'

Stumbling a little on the darkened pavements they set off, a little group huddling together. They passed other people, walking singly or in pairs, hunched into their overcoats, making their way back home after the raid. Jack asked the way of the first man they met and he pointed over his shoulder. 'Try the "Crown". They do rooms there.'

Before they'd gone very far they seemed to have split

into two pairs and Candy found herself walking beside Peter. Ahead of them Grace and Jack had linked arms.

After watching them in silence for a few steps, Candy heard Peter clear his throat awkwardly. 'I think Jack's hoping we'll pair off.'

'Looks as though we have,' said Candy, peering down at where she was putting her feet. The last thing she wanted to do was slip over in the dark and make a mess of her uniform.

'No, I mean for the night.'

Candy was silent for a moment, fighting down a mixture of anger and amusement. It was the same as always. Ever since she joined up she'd been aware of it. At one level it was all just saucy banter between the girls and a bit of making eyes and waggling of hips in the general direction of anything in trousers that wasn't a senior officer. At another level it made every personal relationship seem slimy and dirty. It meant that every time a fellow saw a girl in uniform he just assumed that she was going to want to throw herself at him.

At first it had upset Candy, made her go hot and cold all over to hear the way the girls in the barracks talked and to feel intrusive male eyes wandering over her uniform. It brought back memories of Alex in the swimming race, and then Naseem, and she realised now just how little she had known in those days that seemed a lifetime ago. What had she been thinking about, imagining that love had anything to do with what happened between men and women? It took a while before she could put away her disgust with all the other feelings that she kept safely locked up, out of reach of anyone. The only time now that she became angry was when a hand strayed onto her shoulder or her backside as she worked in the typing pool.

And she knew that Grace felt exactly the same as she did. Grace might have a Cockney accent, and she certainly had a more friendly nature than Candy, but she wasn't going to give herself to a chap she'd just met on a railway station because of an air-raid. Candy was sure about that because she knew Grace rather well by now, after two years of working together in the clothing factory and sharing a bedroom, then joining up and going through their basic training together.

She said firmly, 'I think Grace will be expecting to share a room with me. She's a respectable girl.'

Another silence. Then 'And what about you, WAAF Hargreaves? Are you a respectable girl as well?'

'Very much so.'

'In that case, would you let me take you out to dinner next week?'

Candy hesitated. She quite liked this quiet young man who seemed to be suitably respectful. But that was all. She didn't actually care if she saw him again or not. But going out to dinner would relieve the boredom of the camp evenings, and would certainly make a change from the terrible diet of potatoes and cabbage and bully beef. 'All right,' she said as she watched Grace pulling away from Jack, squeaking in offence at something he'd whispered in her ear.

'Candy...I...'

Peter Price gazed at Candy across the sturdy square restaurant table, laid with starched white cloth and solid EPNS cutlery. It wasn't the first time he'd felt completely tongue-tied in her presence, it happened quite often in fact. It completely unnerved him, the way she would stare directly at him with those grey-green eyes and slightly raise one eyebrow when he began to speak. This evening he'd been meaning to tell her that he loved her – it must be love because he could think of nothing else but her face through every hour of every day – but his nerve failed him. 'You look absolutely beautiful tonight,' he finished lamely.

Then, encouraged by her slow smile, he reached across the expanse of table-cloth and closed his hand over hers. 'Candy, I've got a few days' leave coming up. I planned to go down to Taunton to see my mother. Would you...could you...come with me? I'd so like you to meet her.'

Candy gently withdrew her hand and dabbed at her lips with her starched white table napkin. She took a sip of water, trying to remove the clinging flavour of parsley sauce from her teeth and at the same time considering carefully how to reply. This was the third time she'd been out for an evening with Peter. As far as the other girls in her unit were concerned, they were a couple, though many of them thought it strange that the tall, gawky, least glamorous amongst them had been the first to land an officer. But they didn't hold a grudge. They gladly lent her their frocks to wear so that he never saw her in the same thing twice, and they shared their precious Max Factor and silk stockings with her.

It would have been churlish to tell them her true feelings, or lack of them. Besides, it was fun, being taken out like this, away from the camp.

But going with him to visit his mother was something else altogether.

She knew from listening to the girls talk that meeting a mother was considered to be a major step in a relationship with a young man. Once he asked you to meet his mother you had him in the bag, he was seriously thinking about popping the question. And if that was in his mind, so was the other thing.

And the other thing worried Candy.

Not that she minded the idea of letting him do it. After all, it was nothing new for her. If she liked him and it made him happy, and he didn't hurt her, it would be part of being married, and in return he would look after her. Being looked after was a very appealing idea. When the war was over, in that golden time to come that everyone talked about longingly, she wouldn't be needed in the WAAF. She would have to earn her living doing something else, and remembering the long hours and pressure of the work in the clothing factory, the thought of being looked after was very appealing indeed.

But would he know?

Would he know as soon as they got into bed that she'd done it before? There was no doubt in her mind that if he knew, he would be angry, because she'd already discovered the great conspiracy amongst the girls for each to present herself as totally pure, never touched above the wrists by male hands. Every chap wanted to be the first.

'Well?'

Candy looked at Peter and smiled again. 'Thank you,' she said. 'I'd love to come to meet your mother. I'll arrange some leave.'

The sturdy detached house that hid behind the high laurel hedge was indistinguishable from the others in the street. They shared the same colour schemes of drab green or brown paint and the inside of the windows were all draped in variations of cream net curtains. As though, thought Candy, anything going on in any of these houses would be interesting enough for anyone to want to peer inside and watch. They had caught the train up from Sussex, changing at Guildford station, and when they arrived at Taunton they discovered that there were no taxis, due to the petrol rationing. So they walked hand in hand through the town, the collars of their greatcoats pulled up against a heavy drizzle, and only as they turned into this street did Peter deliberately drop her hand and begin to walk half a step in front of her, as though it was necessary to lead the way.

He led her up the little flagged path to the front door, the laurel hedge giving off a sharply acid scent. As they approached the front door Candy was sure she saw the curtain to her right twitching, as though the person inside the house had been looking out for them for hours, but when Peter rang the bell it took a full minute or more before the door was cautiously opened by a middle aged woman, sturdily built, with a flushed face, wearing a brushed cotton print frock, lisle stockings and flat brown shoes.

'There you are, dear boy! I thought you'd never get here.' The woman smiled up at Peter and turned her cheek for a kiss, but didn't offer to kiss him in return.

'Mother! Lovely to see you!' Peter's kiss was no more than a duty peck as he pulled off his gloves and stood back to usher Candy ahead of him through the narrow doorway.

'Mother, this is Candice Hargreaves.'

'Welcome,' Evadne Price said formally, shaking the offered hand while Candy murmured, 'Pleased to meet you, Mrs Price.' She assumed that Evadne did have the capacity to smile warmly when she was more relaxed, and that the rictus that settled across her lips at that moment was simply an attempt to be polite in a situation that made them all nervous.

Evadne said, 'Peter, take your young lady's coat and I'll show you up to your rooms. I do hope you like pork, Candice. I managed to get a lovely joint from the butcher yesterday. Not a very big one, but a good lean leg fillet. It does pay to have long-standing connections with the local tradesmen. Did you bring your emergency cards with you?'

Candy gasped as a searing pain shot up her vagina and into her womb, replacing the swift pulses of excitement she had felt when Peter was stroking her thighs and working his penis against her clitoris. She moved her hips, hoping to find a position that didn't hurt, and that made Peter thrust himself more firmly into her, then start to rock in and out, hurting her even more.

'Oh, Candy!' he moaned. 'Candy, my darling, this is...this is...'

Candy grasped his shoulders and held on tight, gasping and sobbing. When he ejaculated, then collapsed on top of her, the pain stopped, and she went limp beside him.

'Oh Candy, darling,' he sobbed, 'That was wonderful! Wasn't it wonderful? Oh, thank you, thank you so much!' Then he moved to gaze at her face in the light of the single twenty-five watt bulb that hung from the ceiling of the small, uncomfortable hotel room. As he moved they both became aware of the mess of semen and blood where they had joined, with a torn, wrinkled, condom poised on the end of his penis.

'Look, you're bleeding. That shows it was the first time, doesn't it? I'll confess to you Candy, it was my first time too, and I was quite worried whether I'd be able to do it right. But it was good, wasn't it?'

Candy knew she was expected to agree. And she couldn't think of any reason not to. Her pain wasn't his fault. She could have looked at it as a punishment for sinning again but she took it more as a reminder that she didn't care for Peter the way he cared for her. But she hadn't been able to say no to him, not when she got the letter from Newcastle telling her that he was being posted overseas and asking her to meet him for the weekend.

What had just happened between them was only to be expected in the circumstances, but it had brought to an end the innocent stage of the relationship, when it might have been on or might have been off, and no harm done either way. Now they were lovers, and when he came back from wherever he was going, he would expect her to be waiting for him.

That won't be hard, she thought as she took the handkerchief he offered her and wiped the sticky mess from between her legs. I won't be tempted by anyone else if it's going to hurt this much.

'It was beautiful, wasn't it, Candy darling?'

'Yes, of course it was.' She looked up into his anxious blue-grey eyes. She had never lain so close to him before, never seen him naked, and she was surprised at how pale his skin was, almost dead white where the sun had never reached him. Not like Naseem's firm brown flesh, she thought, then quickly told herself it was unfair to make comparisons.

'Candy, if...if I don't come back will you go and see my mother, help her to get over it?'

'I thought nobody talked about not coming back.'

'I know, but I can't help thinking about it. And if I do come back...'

'When you come back ....'

'When I come back, when the war's over, will you marry me and have my children?'

'Yes, of course.' It was so easy to say. Knowing the survival rate for pilots, she wasn't taking much of a chance of committing the rest of her life to him.

He raised himself onto one elbow and kissed her gently, almost reverently. His free hand began to stray over her large, brown nipples, standing hard on her tiny breasts. His thighs stirred against hers.

Oh God, she thought, he wants to do it again! How can I stop him?

'Candy darling...I want to tell you something...'

'Yes...?'

'I could never tell anyone else but you. Promise you'll keep this between us two, for ever...'

'What?'

He paused, then blurted out, 'I'm frightened. I know that makes me a terrible coward, but I'm frightened. Not of dying, that would be easy, but of being shot down in flames, of being burnt, or terribly injured. I'm frightened of how much it will hurt. I don't think I'm very good at suffering.'

'Is anybody?' She had a sudden picture of Naseem, bloody and screaming, being hit again and again, trying to scramble up and run away on broken legs. Nobody had given him a choice about pain. He must have died in agony. Was that the fate of every man she made love with?

'Do you think I'm a terrible coward? Can you still love me?'

'It's not being afraid that makes you a coward, it's what you do when you're afraid. Are you going to run away, not go and fight?'

'Of course not.'

'Then you're not a coward.' She reached up her arms and wound them around his neck. 'And of course I still love you.'

He turned onto his back and reached for another condom from the bedside table. She watched him unrolling it over his hardening penis. When he had it in place he turned back towards her and began to kiss her again, his hands moving hesitantly over her shoulders and her breasts, down across her flat stomach. As he touched her she felt the excitement awakening between her legs once more and wished that it could lead to the convulsions of pleasure she had once known. Perhaps it could happen with someone else. Perhaps this time...

Unable to judge whether she was ready for him or not, Peter stopped his perfunctory caresses and rolled on top of her, pushing her legs apart and stabbing at her to find his way inside. Her anticipation evaporated as soon as he was half way in and the pain hit her again. She sobbed with the shock of it and he murmured, 'My darling! You feel it too! You are wonderful!' Then his lips closed on hers, clamping her beneath him as he began his frenzy of uncontrolled thrusting.

Candy dug her nails into his back and tried not to scream.

It'll soon be over, she told herself, soon be over.

Candy stared at the letter. Her heart was beating overtime and a harsh pain had started to throb in her right temple.

'What's up?' Grace's question came from the next bunk. Grace was leafing though her own letter from her mother and had turned towards Candy to tell her that Millie sent her love. She always did.

Candy sat up slowly, trying to still the waves of sickness flooding through her. 'It's Peter. This is from his mother. He's missing...'

Up and down the hut, girls heard what she said and slowly sat up. It was always as though it hadn't happened before, always that wave of raw sympathy.

'Missing isn't dead...'

'He was in Java...'

'I thought they'd been sent to North Africa.'

'Seems they were sent to Java. She's been told missing, presumed shot down in action.'

'It's been totally chaotic there,' said one of the girls and another nodded.

'Yeah, nobody knows what's happened to anyone. '

'Japs have over-run everything...'

‘I heard lots of them escaped to Australia...’

‘One whole squadron taken prisoner....’

Grace’s arms were round Candy’s shoulders. ‘There’s still hope, Cand. Keep your spirits up.’ Grace was warm and her plump arms were comforting. But they didn’t make the shock or the sickness go away. If anything, she felt worse, with shame and fear and guilt wrapped up in the same package. ‘I’ll have to go to Taunton to see Evadne – I promised I would if anything happened.’

‘It ain’t like he’s been reported killed. Give it time.’

But Candy knew she didn’t have time. She’d been pulling the waistband of her skirt higher and higher, hoping against hope that Peter would soon be back to keep his promise and marry her. Now he might never be back and she couldn’t keep her secret much longer. He’d promised to be careful and she’d trusted him. If only she’d realised he’d never had sex before, let alone used a French letter... Now she was going to end up with a baby.

She still couldn’t believe it.

At first she tried to ignore it but common sense told her it wouldn’t go away by itself. If she wanted to get rid of it she would have to do something about it. But she knew in her heart that what seemed like the easy way out for some of the girls wasn’t really easy at all. She couldn’t ignore the whispered stories that circulated, stories about sisters, aunts, cousins who had bled to death, or contracted septicaemia. Anyway, even though her life in Palestine and being loved by Naseem were something that might as well have happened to someone else in another lifetime, the thought of another dead baby was hard to take, even when she felt most depressed about the situation. Somehow she would have to organise her life so that she could have her baby and look after it, and the first step along that path was to apply for a compassionate discharge.

The interview with the WAAF Welfare Officer didn't go well. The woman listened in stony silence to Candy's explanation of her condition, then said, 'Well, WAAF Hargreaves, I don't suppose you want your family to know about this, do you? I can arrange for a compassionate posting to a welfare home, then you can have the child adopted.'

'You don't understand, Peter's going to marry me when he comes back.'

The Officer's expression said that she'd heard it all before. Without any attempt to be gentle she said, 'You have to recognise that even if he does come back, which is doubtful from what I hear, he may change his mind once he knows you're pregnant. Far better to have the child adopted and start afresh when the war's over.'

'No. I want to keep my baby. Even if Peter's dead I won't have it adopted.'

The Officer softened her tone and leaned forward slightly. 'You must think of what's best for the child, WAAF Hargreaves. Adoption will give it a stable home which you may have difficulty providing.'

Candy noticed that her eyes were cold and hard. I'm just another statistic to her, she thought. She's just telling me what she knows she has to tell me. She pushed back her chair and stood to attention. 'Permission to apply for a discharge, Ma'am?' she said.

Grace burst into tears when Candy told her what was happening. 'You poor darling,' she sobbed. 'I thought you looked a bit peaky. I saw you was putting on weight but then we all are, aren't we, with these ruddy endless potatoes. Listen, why don't you go to my Mum's? She'll look after you.'

'I may do that. But I have to see Mrs. Price first. I promised Peter.'

'Peter? You don't owe him nothing, darling. You got to look after yourself now.'

In less than a week Candy was wearing civvies and walking alone up the dreary road in Taunton. She'd sent a telegram to say she was coming on a short visit but she wasn't sure whether she was welcome. As she walked up the path she saw the net curtain twitch to her left but this time the door was quickly answered. She'd only just put out a hand to ring the bell when the door opened and Evadne was standing there, a pale shadow of the Evadne she'd met a few months ago, with grey hair awry and dark rings under her eyes. Without a word, Mrs Price stepped out and put her arms around Candy. She smelled of sweat and lavender water and Candy was sure she could hear her corsets creaking as she moved. Candy returned the hug with the hand that wasn't carrying her bag and murmured words about being sorry.

Evadne drew her inside the dark polished hall. 'Thank you for much for coming,' she said, her voice breaking. 'I haven't known what to do with myself since I heard. How long can you stay?'

All through their supper of tasteless vegetable soup and sardines on toast Candy listened to stories of Peter when he was a baby, Peter going to boarding school, Peter passing his examinations, Peter studying to be an accountant. I never knew Peter was to be an accountant, she thought as she struggled with the watery and unseasoned soup that provided little nourishment. The sardines, that might have been more filling, were so strong-smelling that it was all she could do to swallow one down without feeling nauseous.

After supper Evadne brought out three photograph albums with padded paper covers held together by beige tassels. She began to share a lifetime of crumpled black and white snapshots.

'He was such a lovely boy.' It was the twentieth time she'd said it. 'I miss him so much.' But now she was dry-eyed.

'More than when he joined up?'

'It was different then. I knew he was coming back and it was like he was going to boarding school again.'

'But he's only missing, isn't he? You haven't given up hope have you?'

Evadne closed the photograph album with a little sigh. 'What's the point of hoping? We've all heard what happened in Singapore.'

'But...'

'Listen, Candy dear...' A pat on the hand... 'He's better dead than being taken prisoner by the Japs. Don't forget, he was missing in action. That means he was flying, shot down. You of all people know what happens to those little planes when they crash.' She paused a moment, looked at Candy with eyes that were dead and despairing. A lump came to Candy's throat as she remembered one of the hurricanes crashing on the airfield only last month, trying to land with the flaps shot away. It had cartwheeled across the runway and they'd all watched in horror as it broke up like matchwood, smashing up the pilot at the same time. Grace had been driving the ambulance that was the first to reach the crashed plane. She'd sat in silence watching the attendants picking up pieces of body from the grass alongside the runway, then cried for hours afterwards.

'No,' Evadne sighed. 'He's dead and there's an end of it.'

They sat together in silence for a moment and Candy had the feeling that Evadne wanted to say more, but didn't know how to. Twice she drew a shaking breath, then changed her mind and let it out as a sigh. Then the third time she looked very directly at Candy. 'I don't suppose...' She trailed off.

'What?'

'I know he was in love with you. I know I shouldn't even think this of you. But I don't suppose...'

'What?'

'I don't suppose you and Peter slept together?'

Candy lowered her eyes. How would Evadne take the truth? She seemed such a very conventional person.

‘I don’t suppose there’s any chance some of that weight you’ve put on could be a baby?’

Silence. Candy still didn’t know what to say.

‘Because if it is, I’m grateful to you for having the courage to come here, Candy. A lot of girls wouldn’t have. I know what Peter would have wanted in the circumstances and for myself, I can’t bear the thought that I might never have known my grandchild.’

Candy put her hands in Evadne’s and gave them a squeeze. ‘You’re an angel.’ she said softly and she meant it. A great weight lifted from her heart, as though the gates of heaven had just opened in front of her. ‘You already know the answer, don’t you?’

‘In that case, my dear, I expect you’d like to stay here with me and let me look after you.’

So the next morning, with the aid of Peter’s grandmother’s gold wedding ring retrieved from its tissue-paper wrapping in the bottom of an old rosewood jewellery box, Candy became Mrs Candice Price, Peter’s widow, and began to learn how to be a respectable suburban housewife.

Grace’s eyes filled with tears.

‘I’n’t she lovely!’

She snuggled the baby’s soft forehead into her neck, a dreamy look in her eyes. Candy watched from her perch on the window seat, where she was darning a stocking. The baby snuffled contentedly and a little dribble of half-curdled milk slipped out of the corner of her bow-shaped mouth and onto the collar of Grace’s uniform shirt. This was the first time Grace had ventured to visit since Candy had unceremoniously discharged herself from the WAAF, and she had brought the collective best wishes of all the other girls in the unit, all those who were left anyway. Several had gone the same way as Candy.

‘Perhaps it’s time to put her down,’ ventured Candy. ‘While she’s still got that full feeling in her tummy.’

But Grace still hugged the baby. 'I can hardly believe it.'

'Me neither.' The past months of being told she needn't worry about a thing still seemed too like a dream to be real. Nothing like that had ever happened to her before. Always in the past she'd had to worry about her clothes, what she said, who she spoke to, how long she spent doing her homework, whether her parents were going out or not. Then in the factory she'd had to worry about doing her best work, making sure she completed her quota every day, taking care of the machinery. It had been better in the WAAF but still there'd been that feeling of being constantly on her best behaviour, of the people above her always wanting her to do things that little bit better than she could actually manage.

Evadne told her she was fine, she mustn't do too much. So while Evadne cleaned and shopped and cooked, Candy sewed for the baby and read books and played the piano every day. She used the music books she found in a cupboard, Bach and Beethoven pieces that Peter's father had played but Peter had never been advanced enough to tackle. She was getting quite good again, though she would never be able to stretch her damaged hand to the arpeggios and chords in the same way as before.

Evadne had been overjoyed when the baby had arrived and it was a small sacrifice on Candy's part to agree to call her Philippa, in memory of Peter's father, Philip. Candy would have liked Rosebud because the baby reminded her of a tiny, perfect rosebud, her small fingers and tiny eyebrows looking like the first delicate petals peeling back as they opened. But she knew in her heart that Rosebud was a childish name, the sort of name you gave a doll. So they agreed on Philippa Rose.

'Philippa Rose,' cooed Grace, adjusting the baby in her arms and walking around the cot in a small circle. 'Sounds lovely, don't it. Philippa Rose Price.'

'Apparently I can't officially call her Price. She's Hargreaves. The Registrar says it's not possible to put a father's name on the birth certificate unless he's there to sign it himself, if you're not properly married. If he was still alive and we could get married, we could re-register her as his after the wedding. As it is...' her voice faltered here, remembering how upset Evadne had been. 'As it is she'll always be illegitimate.'

'Poor little bugger.' Grace sighed, looking down into the baby's eyes, now wide open. 'Never mind eh, she won't be the first. You'll rise above it darling, won't you?'

Philippa Rose screwed her face into a tight grimace and gave a little whimper. The sound of a small eruption came from the region of her nappy and Grace quickly stopped the cuddling and held the small body at arms' length. 'Oh no!' she squealed, 'She's doing something! Here, you take her Candy!'

Laughing, Candy dropped her sewing and rushed forward to help. She scooped the now wet and smelly bundle into her arms and laid it on an armchair. Philippa Rose began to wail as Candy unwrapped her and removed the offending nappy. Grace watched as Candy, still clumsy handling the child, carried her over to the washbasin the corner, washed her bright pink back end, then laid her down again and powdered her and pinned on another nappy.

'Do you like doing all that?'

Candy thought for a moment. 'I don't exactly like that bit but the poor little thing can't do it for herself, can she?' She picked up the clean baby who began whimpering and snuffling her mouth against Candy's clothes. 'She's hungry again, now she's got rid of that lot out of the other end.'

'Blooming eating machine!' Grace watched as Candy sat down again on the window seat and unbuttoned her dress and fiddled with a flap on her monstrous-looking brassiere. As soon as a breast was bared the baby latched onto it. She sucked greedily for a few minutes, then lapsed once more into sleep. 'What does that feel like?'

'It's nice.' That was an inadequate way of describing the sensation of total abandonment that stole through her body whenever she fed the child, but she couldn't think how to put it into words that Grace would understand. It was beautiful, the same kind of all-consuming feeling that she'd shared with Naseem on those long gone afternoons.

But Grace would only know about that if she'd done it with someone she loved and she'd never said anything to Candy about that. Candy was sure Grace must have been to bed with Jack sometime but it Jack mightn't have been any better at it than Peter had been. It mightn't have been much fun at all for her, either.

She leaned forward and kissed the soft top of her baby's head. 'It's a beautiful feeling,' she said. And not for the first time, she let herself imagine that the child she was holding wasn't Peter's but Naseem's, born of some seed that had somehow lain in her body unused for the intervening years.

From inside the butcher's shop Candy could see the little knot of women, shopping baskets on their arms, who were gathered around the pram she had left parked outside, like sparrows around carelessly dropped crumbs. Phillipa Rose was sitting up, safely strapped in by means of a pink leather harness with little bells attached. She was smiling and gurgling at the ring of faces, but they weren't smiling back. Because the early summer day was warm and the shop door was open, Candy could hear what they were saying.

'She may call herself Price and wear a wedding ring but her ration book says she's Hargreaves, and her baby too. She's registered in Liptons, where my daughter works.'

'Shouldn't be allowed, deceiving people like that!'

'His father would turn in his grave, that's for certain. Respectable, he was. We all looked up to him.'

'I'm surprised at Mrs Price letting it happen. Should have thrown the hussy out, not given her a home.'

A couple of the women moved on, two came into the shop and watched balefully as Candy bought four thin, gristly sausages. Thanking the butcher with her best smile, Candy manoeuvered herself and her shopping basket through the shop door. Mr Ellis had slipped her a whole tin of spam without the other women being able to see. Evadne would be pleased;

keeping all three of them fed on their ever decreasing rations was a constant worry. There'd been quite a bit of spam around since the Americans moved in to the nearby air base but not everyone got it, only the people Mr Ellis liked.

As Candy came out onto the pavement the group round the pram turned and smiled. 'Good morning, Mrs Price,' said one woman.

'How's little Philippa?' asked another.

'Very well, as you can see,' Candy replied briskly, trying to hide her anger as she placed her basket in the pram and kicked off the brake. She didn't care what these women thought about her. They weren't her friends, not like Grace or Evadne were. But what was going to happen when Pippa was a little older, when she wanted to play with other children in the park, when she had birthdays and wanted to have a party? When she could understand what the people around her were saying? She was a bright little child, not yet two years old and she would sit on Candy's knee in front of the piano and let her little fat fingers be guided up and down the keyboard to make the tune of "Baa Baa Black Sheep".

Not for the first time, Candy thought about moving, taking her baby somewhere else where nobody knew about Peter, and starting again. But what would Evadne say? Would she want to move as well? After all, she had lived here for most of her married life and if she didn't want to go, how could she be left behind when her whole life was now wrapped up in this baby?

She thought and thought about the problem. It nagged at her as she walked down the street to the shops or the park, it nagged at her as she lay in bed at night listening to the wind in the trees or the distant rumble of aircraft overhead. And the more she thought about it, the more she began to hate Taunton, with its dark brick houses, its rain and its gossip. And as she thought, a plan began to grow in her mind.

'We must go away,' she said to Evadne one afternoon as they shared the washing up.

Evadne was so surprised that she dropped the teaspoon

she was drying. 'Why? What are you talking about?'

'We must go and live where I can have a better chance of pretending to be a widow.'

'But why?' Again.

'Isn't it obvious?' Without turning to face Evadne, Candy angrily swished her hands around in the cold, greasy water that remained in the enamel washing-up bowl, fishing out two forks.

'What do you mean? Aren't you happy here?'

'Are you?'

'What do you mean?'

'What have we got here that we can't have somewhere else but without all the gossips who know that I never had the chance to marry Peter.'

Evadne was silent a moment, then she moved over to one of the kitchen chairs and sat down heavily. When she turned at last to look at her, Candy could see that her eyes were brimming with tears.

'I thought we were getting on all right,' she sniffed. 'Now you say you want to leave, take Pippa away... please don't...I couldn't...'

Candy dried her red hands and went over to put an arm around Evadne's shoulders. 'I meant all of us to go together. You too.'

'But what's the point? Wherever we go they'll see you're single when they look at your ration book.'

'No. We'll be cleverer than that.' Her plan was very simple. 'We'll go and live near London, on a train route somewhere. I'll get a job in London and we'll register our ration books near where I work, so I can collect the groceries every week on my way home. That way nobody near to where we live knows anything about us.'

Evadne shook her head. 'It all depends on you getting a job. What can you do that anyone would pay you for?'

'Listen, the WAAF taught me shorthand typing. I can get a job in London, easy as anything....'

'But you've got Pippa...'

'You can look after Pippa while I work in the West End. I can earn enough to support us all.'

Evadne shook her head doubtfully. It was hard to think in new patterns all of a sudden. 'But isn't London dangerous? What about the doodle bugs?'

'We won't be living right in London, remember? Where we live will be safe enough. Loads of people live around London – it hasn't emptied just because of the war.'

'I don't know. Selling up? I've lived here for so long.'

'You don't have to sell up. Rent this house out and we'll rent somewhere near to town.'

Evadne looked up, not exactly smiling but not finding difficulties any more. 'Let me think about it.'

'Don't think for too long. And for heaven's sake don't talk to anyone about it.'

'When would you want to do this?'

'Soon. Very soon. Listen...' Now that she had broached the subject, she was keen to act quickly. 'I'll go up to London tomorrow – no, the day after – I'll need to wash my hair and my clothes. I'll see what kind of a job I can get and find out about houses. I can stay a few days with Grace's Mum...' Suddenly she felt elated; a new sense of freedom began to creep into her heart. Making her plan had been one thing but talking to Evadne about it had brought it to life. Now that there was a way to escape, she had to admit that the prospect of living here for the rest of her life had chilled her. She'd put it aside because of Evadne and Pippa, thinking that being here was best for them. But that wasn't true any more.

In the end it took her several days to get herself organised but eventually one afternoon she was on a train that lumbered into Paddington after ambling far and wide over the countryside to avoid places where the lines were out of order. Once, after a long wait in an anonymous station they were passed by a long train full of tight-faced men in khaki uniforms and somebody muttered that they were on their way to France.

'No, Germany,' said another. 'They're fighting in Germany now. That's where they'll be going.'

‘Or Burma,’ said another. ‘Java. The Japs.’

Heads nodded wisely and Candy thought of Peter. Crashed in the jungle somewhere, nearly three years ago now. She knew that jungles grew quickly and covered up what they consumed. His name would still be written in some records somewhere but he’d never be found. Poor Peter. If only he’d been more clever about things, not left her with an illegitimate child to look after. Then she tried to imagine life without Pippa. Given the chance, would she put the child back, not have her?

Would she? She thought of what each morning would be like now if she didn’t wake up to Pippa’s gurgling and chatting in the cot across the room, if she couldn’t feel those chubby arms closing around her neck and those great squashy kisses that were followed by ‘Love ‘oo Mummy.’ No, of course she wouldn’t be without Pippa now, whatever it had cost to come by her.

By the time the train arrived in London it was far too late to begin job and house hunting. She’d sent a telegram to warn Millie Tanner she was coming but she couldn’t be sure Millie would have got it. It didn’t matter, she knew she would be made welcome whether they were expecting her or not. Candy was shocked as she walked down the gap-toothed streets near Mile End and saw for herself the mess the war had made of London. They’d heard about it on the wireless, of course, and they’d read reports in the newspapers. But this wholesale maiming of a city had to be seen to be believed and it made her realise what a quiet sheltered time she’d had for the past three years.

As she turned the final corner she saw that half the street was missing, exposing the naked ribs of the gas storage tanks on the edge of Bow Common. She wondered how Millie had the nerve to stay there after that, wondering every day when she went to work whether her house would still be there when she got home, going to bed every night knowing she might not wake up in the morning. She wondered if it was such a good idea, bringing Pippa and Evadne to live close by. But everyone said the Germans were on the run, the blitz was just about over. Surely they would be safe enough, somewhere in the suburbs?

Nobody answered the bell but the door opened when Candy tried the knob and she let herself in. It was expected here, though it would have been unthinkable in Taunton. Memories came flooding back as soon as she was inside, setting her little overnight bag down on the floor of the tiny passageway, going into the kitchen and filling the kettle, fumbling around for matches to light the gas cooker. Nothing had changed except that the lino was more worn and scruffy than before, and blackout curtains hung at the window. The single light bulb hanging over the table still had no shade, still had its adaptor for the iron to be plugged into the same fitting.

The tea caddy was almost empty and Candy realised that there might not be any more in the house. She hadn't brought an emergency card for just one or two nights, but she had brought some rations with her. She went back into the passageway to fetch the tea and sugar, margarine and bacon and two tins of spam that Evadne had so carefully packed for her. She would have liked to bring some cheese too but they'd run out till the beginning of next month. And milk, but she couldn't carry that and anyway Pippa had most of the milk that Evadne could lay her hands on.

Back in the kitchen, Candy spooned a few leaves of tea into a mug and poured the boiling water on. No sense in making a whole pot when she didn't know when Millie would be home, or anyone else for that matter. Just as she sat down to drink the tea the front door opened and closed. Candy jumped to her feet again just as Millie lumbered into the kitchen. She set down her string bag with a few carrots and onions and a turnip poking out through the holes, flung her arms around Candy and burst into tears.

Selma Lee spent some minutes examining the results of Candy's shorthand and typing test. It only took her a moment to see that this young woman was as competent as she'd claimed to be on her application form but she needed a few minutes to try to assess the whole picture. Why was this girl looking for work? Was she really a widow? Was she running away from something? Selma sighed inwardly – whether she'd ever been married or not, did it make any difference? Wasn't she just one of many who were going to end up without a man to support her and her family because of this awful war?

Candy waited. She knew she hadn't made many mistakes. She'd always been good at Pitman's and she'd practised every day the week before, taking down the BBC news and then reading it back to Evadne. Even allowing for being out of practice, and having had one or two drinks too many with Millie and Ted in the pub the night before, she couldn't have done that badly.

While she waited, she stared around the small office. Papers were piled up in wooden trays, on top of a filing cabinet and on half of the desk that Mrs Lee was sitting at. On a smaller desk beside the wall there was a big typewriter, where she'd done the typing part of her test. The brocade curtains that hung crookedly on each side of the big sash window were torn and filthy. Candy longed to wash and mend them. In fact she longed to put the whole office in order. Why was it in such a mess? If the agency couldn't keep their own place in order, how did they manage to serve the employers who came to them looking for staff?

Mrs Lee herself was tidy enough, though her once-smart green tailor-made suit was out of shape, cuffs beginning to fray. Her auburn hair, pulled behind her head in a French pleat, was obviously dyed and she was carefully made up, with bright red lipstick and long red finger nails. Perhaps she spent all her spare time on her nails and her face and didn't have time for the office.

'Mrs Price....' Candy snapped her attention back. 'You've done a good test here. Where did you say you come from?'

'Taunton. My mother-in-law and I thought we'd move up here now that things are better so that I can work and she can look after my little girl.'

'Your husband....' She looked down at the application

form on the desk in front of her. 'Ah yes, I'm sorry. Well, people are crying out for good secretaries just at the moment, as you can imagine. I can offer you a choice of jobs but I wonder - would you like to come and work here?'

'Here?' Candy stared round the office once more. It wasn't very glamorous, but it was close to Oxford Street and to the tube station.

'There's a lot to do, as you can see. The trouble is, I can't keep staff because as soon as a really plum job comes in they take it for themselves.'

'Why should I be any different?'

'I'll pay you thirty bob a week. That's as much as you'll get anywhere else.'

'When do you want me to start?'

'Tomorrow?'

Candy laughed outright. 'That's not possible, I'm afraid. I have to find a house to rent, move my family up – it could take a month.'

'Where do you want to live?' Last evening Millie had thought Chelmsford would be a good idea; she had relatives there and knew of a couple of empty houses to rent. But that would mean traveling right across London every day. Mrs Lee was going on, not waiting for an answer. 'Because my sister lives in Gerrards Cross, nice country area, lovely for your little girl, and it's only a short train journey out of town. There's a house to rent in her road, people going back up north. I could....'

'That's very kind of you. I'd be most grateful. In that case, I'd love to come and work for you, Mrs Lee.'

By the time she caught the train back to Taunton the next day, Candy had signed the lease of a nice detached house in a leafy suburb with fields at the end of the road and a ten-minute walk to the railway station, and had managed to persuade Mrs Lee to pay her thirty-seven and six a week after the first month's trial period.

The following night a doodlebug flattened all the remaining houses in Millie's road.

Candy didn't know about this until the day they were

doing their final packing up to move, when a pale and exhausted Grace walked up the garden path and collapsed sobbing into her arms as she opened the door.

'We can't go to live up there,' said Evadne flatly as they sat in the midst of their suitcases eating a lunch of cold sausages. 'I don't know how I could have agreed to put the child in so much danger.'

'It's not the same place, Evadne,' said Candy. 'The East End is miles from Gerrards Cross.'

'Just the same, I won't feel safe. I want to stay here.'

'We have to go now. You've let this house and everything's fixed up at the other end.' Candy felt desperate. In a way she knew Evadne was right, it was more dangerous everywhere near London, of course it was, but now that she had managed to open up an alternative there was no way she was going to spend any more time living the sort of life they lived here. But she couldn't go alone. She needed Evadne. Without her to look after Pippa, her new life as a working mother would be very difficult indeed. She thought that Evadne would go along with what she wanted rather than losing Pippa, but she couldn't be sure and she didn't care to put it to the test. She got up and put an arm around Evadne's shoulders. 'I know it's hard for you to move after all this time, but we'll be all right, I promise you. I'll look after you.'

'But who'll look after me?' Grace whimpered. 'I'm on compassionate leave but ain't got nowhere to go any more.'

Candy put an arm around her shoulders too. 'You'd better come with us,' she said as Evadne pursed her lips and hugged Pippa more closely to her big chest.

* * *

Gerrards Cross was nice, Pippa remembered as she rode in her taxi to the theatre. They could go for walks in the field and pick blackberries, and she'd gone to a little nursery school where she learned her letters. As soon as the woman she remembered as Auntie Grace was de-mobbed from the WAAF she came to live with them permanently and Candy found her a job as secretary to one of the directors of Peter Jones department store. Her mother and Grace used to set off for work together every morning and Pippa would love waiting for them to come home in the evenings and talk about all the things they'd been doing during the day. It had been such a happy time. How had all that happiness suddenly faded away? She paused for a moment, hunting in her bag for change for the taxi, quite surprised to find that tears were pricking at her eyelids and she had a lump in her throat. Something had changed, something had gone wrong that she had been too young to understand.

* * *

It was teatime, Saturday, already dark outside, the four of them in a tight female knot around the veneered table in the dining room. The table had a special cloth to spread over it when it was being used, to save the surface. It hadn't taken Evadne long to decide that it was safer to leave the cloth on all the time, just in case, what with Pippa always bouncing around, and Grace apt to leave cigarettes burning on the edge of saucers. She'd felt guilty about this because she could see she was lowering her standards, but it wasn't their table, was it? And what was a standard or two when it meant she didn't have to worry about Pippa spreading out her drawing book or her dolls' tea set? Candy and Grace didn't care. She'd told them, the first week, to leave the cloth out because it was easier and they'd just said, 'Yes, good idea,' and she didn't bother them with it again. She was conscious that they were slipping into a different world, a world of making decisions and discussing things that she knew nothing about, and they shouldn't be having to think about domestic things. It was as though they were men, though they weren't of course, they were women in that world that had always been meant for men. The woman's world was what Evadne did in the quiet house all day, looking after Pippa, taking her to school, making sure she got her rest, making sure she put her toys away when she'd finished with them, reading to her, taking her for walks, doing the washing and ironing, eking out the rations, trying to put by enough to make a decent Christmas cake.

Rations were a headache all of their own. Like everyone else, Evadne had imagined that the end of war would mean an immediate return to the way things had been before, but it wasn't like that at all. Instead of having more, everyone had to make do with less. Not for long, they were promised. Just until everything got back on its feet again.

Whenever that might be.

Sitting round the table that Saturday afternoon they were talking about making the Christmas cake together on Sunday morning, trying to remember all the things that should go into it because Evadne had left her recipe book in Taunton. They were poring over an emergency recipe in a magazine Grace had been given by one of the girls where she worked. They had dried egg and flour and some margarine, though it would mean dry toast for breakfast all next week. They had some evaporated milk, nearly enough sugar, some carrots to grate up and a small lump of suet the butcher had spared. But the recipe called for half a pound of dried fruit and there was only half that in the pantry. And they needed one orange, both the squeezed juice and the grated rind...

Oh, if only! Candy sighed inwardly. None of them had seen an orange for years. She closed her eyes for and moment and saw golden hillsides covered with ranks of dark green trees heavy with fruit.

'There's that tin of peaches I've been saving,' Evadne said suddenly. 'Do you think they'd do?'

'Why not?' Grace said. 'Sort of thing my Mum would've done. Make up for the missing sugar...' The doorbell pealed, breaking into their circle like a shock wave. Grace pushed back her chair. 'Okay, I'll get it...'

'Okay,' echoed Pippa, pulling the magazine away from her grandmother so that she could feast her eyes on the photograph of the finished cake.

'Don't say "okay",' muttered Evadne. 'It's not nice.'

Pippa pursed her lips and looked from Evadne to Candy. She had already learned that they didn't always tell her the same things about what to do and what not to do. 'Okay,' she said with a mischievous grin. Evadne coloured a little and opened her mouth to speak. The door opened and Grace came back in, a funny look on her face. Evadne looked past her into the hallway and her face went white. She gave a funny little cry and a hand flew to her mouth. A man pushed past Grace and caught his mother in his arms just as she fainted.

Candy stared, frozen in disbelief. 'Peter?'

Between them Grace and Peter half-dragged, half-carried Evadne out of the kitchen and into the lounge to lay her down on the beige tweed sofa. Candy sat as though attached to her chair, heart thudding, telling herself that this wasn't happening.

It couldn't be, could it? It was some emaciated ex-POW who looked a bit like Peter – for heavens sake, how many men must there be in the forces who were light skinned, with straight blond hair, five foot eight or nine, slight build? This man had probably met Peter, brought back some of his things to give Evadne.

Peter was dead, had been for years. How could he be alive, walk back into their lives when they had it all organised to do without him?

But if it wasn't Peter, why had Evadne fainted? Surely a mother must know her own son?

Pippa shuffled her plate on the table top and Candy became aware of her wide eyes, brimming with tears. 'Granny's not dead, is she?'

'No, no. I think she's...ill. Stay there.'

Candy rose unsteadily and made her way through to the drawing room. Grace was standing, grinning nervously, by the tiled fireplace, watching while Eavdne and Peter clung to each other, both openly sobbing.

Candy heard a sound behind her and saw that Pippa was here, using her skirts as a shield to see what was going on. 'Mummy,' she whispered. 'Who is that man?'

Candy turned and picked her up. 'He's your daddy, darling.'

The expression of interest in Pippa's eyes deepened. 'I haven't got a daddy,' she said.

'You have now.'

At the sound of the child's voice, Peter turned to look at them. He seemed to take some time to register what he was seeing and, still holding one of Evadne's hands, he came to his feet.

'Candy?' He sounded doubtful, as though he didn't really remember what she looked like.

As he let fall Evadne's hand and came towards her, Candy took stock of his emaciated body, his lank hair, his unshaven chin, the lost look in his eyes. She couldn't help herself as she shrank back a step, delaying the moment when she would feel his arms close around her. The truth was that there was nothing familiar about this person at all, and nothing even remotely attractive. Yet she knew that she was going to have to marry him or Pippa would remain a bastard for the rest of her life.

Peter stayed until after Christmas. He slept on a makeshift bed in the drawing room because Evadne, Candy and Grace each had one of the other three bedrooms, Pippa sharing with her mother. His presence seemed to fill the whole household, dominating everything they did. The cosy female atmosphere disintegrated and instead they were each wrapped up in their own concerns, wondering what changes were coming, how to deal with the ones that had already overtaken them. Instead of one big happy family they were a group of individuals, talking to each other in private corners. Evadne said to Peter, 'When are you going to get married to Candy? The sooner you can share a room the easier it'll be for us all to fit into this house.'

'I must go back to my squadron after Christmas and wait for a proper discharge. I can't get married now. I haven't any papers.'

'You could set a date. The poor girl's had to put up with enough, being left to face the music like she was. You should never...'

Peter didn't want to be reproached by his mother. He wanted to be looked after by her. He wasn't at all sure that he wanted Candy and Pippa to be part of the picture at all. The child wouldn't talk to him and every time he tried to play with her she threw a tantrum. 'Give me time,' he said testily. 'I'm not at all sure about anything at the moment. I must get a job. Then I'll decide.'

'You don't have a choice,' Evadne said firmly. 'If you don't marry Candy and legitimise my granddaughter, I'll never speak to you again.'

Candy had been afraid that sex would hurt again but this time she didn't feel a thing, not a thing.

Well, that wasn't quite true. She felt Peter's timid hands touching her, felt his body closing over hers, pressing into her. But she felt neither the pain she had feared nor the excitement she had hoped for. She lay in the cold bed in the hotel room, staring at the flaking paint on the ceiling, waiting for him to stop pounding at her, wondering whether Pippa was asleep yet and wishing the child hadn't cried so much when she held Evadne's hand and waved goodbye as Peter whisked Candy away from the wedding reception in the sports car he had bought as soon as he had been discharged.

When it was over for him, Peter pulled away and lay beside her with a huge sigh and turned his face from her. A moment later she realised that his shoulders were trembling. He was sobbing quietly into the pillow. She felt awful. Here she was worrying about herself and about Pippa, and Peter was the one who had really been suffering all this time. She raised herself on one elbow and put a hand on his back.

'Peter, Darling....' The word came out quite easily, though she'd been afraid to say it all through dinner. 'Darling, what's the matter?'

He turned his face towards her in the dark. 'You've no idea, Candy, how much I've been longing to do that to you – all those years – nothing except heat and dirt and insects while you've been living in comfort. You've just no idea. No idea how wonderful it is to do it at last. I know it's different for women. I know you're not supposed to feel it like men do. But I'd like it to mean something to you as well.'

She was silent. Her hand moved to his shoulder. Would he ever know that it hadn't been wonderful at all, that there was no spark between them to make it wonderful?

Probably not, if she didn't tell him.

But one day, one day when this marriage between them was growing stale, surely he would meet some woman who could make magic for him? Then he would know. Then he would understand that this was a sham, that she had betrayed him right from the very start, just by being there and pretending. But not now. Now there was still time to try to make it up to him. And she did want to make him happy if she could. If for nothing else, she was grateful to him for giving her Pippa, whose new birth certificate now lay in his wallet alongside their marriage certificate.

Yes, she could love him for that, if for nothing else.

She moved closer and put her arms around him. 'Of course it means something to me,' she murmured. 'You're my husband now, and Pippa's daddy.'

'And as soon as we can get mother's house back we're going to be a proper family. They're still holding my job open at the accountants in Taunton. In fact as soon as we get back next week you can give in your notice and start being a proper wife and mother. Oh Candy, it's all going to be so lovely!'

Tears forgotten, he began to smother her with kisses but she found it hard to respond. Her tenderness had vanished as quickly as she'd conjured it up, swept away in the cold shower of his expectations.

She drew away from him. 'I'm sorry, Peter, but I am rather tired. It's been a long day... Perhaps in the morning.'

He stopped. 'Of course. I'm sorry darling. I didn't think. But this is our wedding night.' And then he carried on, climbing on top of her as though she'd never spoken and pushing himself between her legs.

You will have to think, Peter, she thought, closing in on herself again and letting the little seed of dislike begin to grow in her heart. You'll have to start thinking very soon. Very carefully. Because I'm not giving up my job, and I'm not going to be an accountant's wife in Taunton for the rest of my life.

6
DANNY

Sister Mary James had spent all night on her knees in the sparsely furbished grey chapel, praying for her mother's soul. By the time the fingers of the dawn were beginning to paint in the colours of the window above the altar, her knees ached and her head throbbed. The residue of stale incense on the air made her cough from time to time. But she knew she had to carry on to the end of the penance because if she didn't do it nobody else would. They might write reams about her mother, about the glamorous life she had led, resurrecting wild speculations about her wealth and her success, but nobody else would think to pray for her soul. Nobody else would understand the gap between the fable and the catalogue of mortal sins the old lady had committed and left unconfessed.

It was a long time since Sister Mary James had been little Danny Price – a shortening of Daniella that she thoroughly hated. The fact that she never had the power to resist the nickname was an indication to her of the lowly status she had always occupied in her mother's affections and still caused her a surge of rage whenever she consciously thought about it, even now, after she had spent thirty years as Sister Mary James in the calm seclusion of the Carmelite convent. The fact that she was the only person who had ever thought it mattered only added to her feelings of self-pity.

It pleased Sister Mary James to think that she alone might have the power of heaven or hell over her dead mother. It was an idea that came to her slowly, as the night wore on, as she peeled back the layers of her mother's life and mentally prepared herself for her journey to Yorkshire for the funeral, for her first foray into the outside world in thirty years.

Her first response to Jeremy's telephone message, handed to her on a folded scrap of paper in the refectory, had been that there was no question of her going. Why should she go? It was years since she had any contact with her brothers and sister, mainly because she steadfastly refused to respond to any of their letters, telephone calls or Christmas cards, and in the face of that apparent rejection they all, one by one, gave up on her. At least, Pippa and Jeremy gave up. Leon never even tried to make contact but then that was Leon, selfish, not to be trusted, even from afar. She read about him in the newspapers that sometimes made their way into the convent wrapped around groceries. He seemed to be driven by lust and greed, and he even made jokes sometimes about having a sister who was a nun. As though it was impossible to understand how a sister of his should end up in a convent. Not too difficult, though, when one remembered what he had done to Pippa, practically stolen her soul. If there was any one point that had driven Sister Mary James into the arms of the Lord, that was it.

And if her mother had regularly sent gifts of money and small luxuries every Christmas, these had been conscience gifts, not true gifts in the spirit of Our Lord's love. Sister Mary James had given the money to her Mother Superior to distribute to needy Africans and thrown away the talcum powder, soap, embroidered handkerchiefs that her mother had imagined she might welcome. The accompanying cards and letters she stored, unopened, in a leather-bound travelling letter-writing box her father had given her that time he'd brought her and Pippa back from America. He'd bought them lots of things then because they were frightened and cried a lot, missing their mother and believing she had sold them to him without telling them because she wanted to get rid of them and live just with Rupert and their new baby, Leon. Pippa said no, Daddy had stolen them, Mummy wouldn't give them away, let alone sell them, and she loved them as much as she loved Leon, but Sister Mary James had known the truth. The gifts had dried up as life had settled down to the grey, cold monotony of life at Brisewood School, where their father seemed to be in charge. After a while they had stopped crying themselves to sleep at night, quietly so that Daddy wouldn't hear, but Sister Mary James had never stopped crying in her heart, crying for the terrible sin Mummy had committed in fornicating with Rupert and so bringing Leon into the world, an event that had caused nothing but disaster.

* * *

Candy had known she was pregnant with Danny a bare month after she married Peter and at the time she'd been angry with him. One accident could be put down to over-enthusiasm or lack of experience, two were sheer incompetence. So she thought at time. Later she hadn't been so sure, when he'd started sulking and making scenes about going back to Taunton, drawing Evadne into endless rows about their future. He tried to make her give up her lovely new administration job at the film studio that she had grabbed for herself as soon as it came into Selma's agency. The more he bullied her the less she looked forward to coming home in the evenings, but he didn't seem to realise that. It was only after Daniella was born and she went almost straight back to work that he saw she was serious about staying near London. So he found himself a job in a bank in Gerrards Cross, where he could have been working for the last six months instead of relying on her to support him. And then he'd almost insisted on being included in the social goings-on at the studio – the wrap parties, the premiers, the jaunts to location. And he'd sulked again about being an outsider at these events, tried to isolate Candy from the crowd when he knew that the success of her job depended on her being right in the thick of things.

It had all been very tiresome. But then Rupert had come on the scene and there had been no point in carrying on the pretence that she loved Peter.

Rupert Taylor was one of an illustrious group of matinee idols who emerged in the British cinema during the post-war years. With his dark hair and melting brown eyes, framed by long black eyelashes, he captivated the hearts of a million women with no effort at all. When he smiled, straight white teeth flashed behind full lips, his eyes twinkled, and a dimple appeared on each cheek. He was lean and muscular, kept that way by a punishing routine of weight lifting, and his arms and chest were covered with thick back hairs that Candy loved to stroke. She was his adoring slave from the moment he first came into the production office to ask if anyone could post a letter for him. She blushed helplessly as she noticed that he gave her a double take.

'Dreamy!' murmured the typist who sat at the desk in the corner. 'Wonder if he's married?' As far as Candy was concerned, it was irrelevant. Everything was irrelevant as she felt her hand shake and her guts curl up inside her with a feeling she had never thought would come her way again.

Even looking at his photograph before they'd started work on the film she recognised that his dark good looks reminded her of something buried in her past. Feeling his larger than life presence in the tiny production office, the overpowering scent of his skin and the flash of his dark eyes, took her all the way, brought memories flooding back of a love that felt as though it had happened in another lifetime. His smiles and touches soon moved on to stolen kisses, excuses for her not to catch her usual train home so that they could spend an hour or two drinking together, then clinging together in his car at the entrance to the train station. And very quickly after that she was in his bed in a little, shabby flat near the studio where she laid on his rumpled sheets looking at the torn net curtains and the cracked plaster and – oh blessed happiness – enjoyed sex without pain for he first time for years.

Their partnership was soon known and accepted by the entire production team which meant that Peter got to hear of it and it was only a short step from there to a divorce, liberally laced with bitter rows, and Peter and Evadne moving back to Taunton at last. Candy didn't care about Peter's misery and bitterness. She was in love with Rupert, she was expecting his child, and he had promised to marry her as soon as the film was finished.

And so he did. On a bright spring day Candy stepped out of the door of Caxton Hall Registry Office as Mrs Rupert Taylor, on her way to Hollywood where Rupert was contracted to make his next film. People waiting on the pavement cheered. She put up hand to the crown of her hat as the wind caught it, then turned and smiled happily down at Pippa and Danny as they followed her out onto the steps. Not for the first time that day she felt proud to have such a pretty pair of little girls; in their matching floral-print dresses and white socks with pale blue strap shoes they looked like the royal princesses. One of the photographers waiting on the pavement stepped forward and grabbed a shot of them, even before he snapped Candy and Rupert. Other people poured out around them and Candy drew the children close, afraid they might get knocked down the steps.

Pippa laughed, happy, and she fished in the little handbag she held slung over her arm and producing a bag of confetti. Danny gasped with horror. 'We mustn't. They said no litter on the pavement.' At five years old the world was very black and white, and to flout the clear instructions of authority was very dangerous.

'But you can't have a wedding without confetti.' Pippa bent forward to help Danny whose small fingers weren't as nimble as her big sister's, and anyway she was clinging hard to the confetti bag, still fearful to be disobedient which might easily result in her being carted off to prison instead of going to Rupert and Candy's wedding party. As her lower lip began to tremble she stuffed the confetti back into her bag and stared, saucer-eyed, at the crowd on the pavement, people who didn't know her and Pippa, waving and shouting just because their mother was marrying a film star.

More and more people were crowding out of the doors of the registry office behind them and pushing forwards. Rupert put a protective hand around Candy's waist. 'Come on, honey, time to go.' Candy could see the line of limousines waiting beside the wide pavement, protected from the crowd by three smiling policemen.

'Chuck us yer bouquet, Candy!' yelled a girl in the crowd.

'God bless yer, darling!' yelled another. Candy smiled and simpered one more time, then she raised her hand and flung her posy of roses into the crowd. More photographs and a mad scramble of flailing arms ended in two girls punching each other on the nose but Candy didn't see that as Rupert ushered her towards the white Rolls-Royce. The crowd opened to let them through and now Rupert led Candy by the hand, making sure the girls were safely ahead of them. Candy felt safe. He was protective and caring, which was one of the many reasons why she loved him. And the fact that half the women in the western world would have given anything to be in her shoes that day only added to her sense that the long struggle was over. At last, she was going to be allowed to be happy.

She wasn't disappointed. The months whirled by, mainly filled with shopping, parties and glorious sex, and soon after Leon was born in a clinic in London, they were off to Hollywood. It didn't take Candy long to transplant her little family to a rambling white villa in Beverly Hills where her girls could play and go to school in the sunshine, and Evadne and Grace could visit whenever they wanted. The only shadow that lay over this idyllic life, and one they mentioned as little as possible, was Peter. When Candy had married Rupert she had hoped he would lose interest in being father to Pippa and Danny, and quietly melt out of their lives. But he was too angry for that, and he insisted on flying to California and taking the girls away on holiday, with Evadne's help.

Lying beside her swimming pool, wearing one of the daring new style bikinis, one delicate hand balancing the ashtray that was resting on her flat belly, the other holding a burning cigarette, Candy was trying to pretend to herself that his second such visit next week wasn't going to happen. She was dreading having to drive Evadne and the girls down the coast to the hotel in San Diego that Peter had booked, and leaving them there with him.

She watched Pippa and Daniella playing in the shallow end of the pool with little Leon, holding his hands carefully and jiggling him up and down so that bright droplets of water splashed into his face. Every now and again they would duck him quickly beneath the surface and each time he came up spluttering and laughing. She wondered whether it was really a good thing for a baby not yet a year old to be ducked like that but he seemed quite happy about it so she said nothing. Evadne, stretched out in a lounger close by, also said nothing, though Candy noticed that she was watching the children closely over the top of the copy of *Vogue* she was reading.

Leon was a lovely baby, always either asleep or smiling. Pippa and Danny had been pretty children but Danny had been a fractious baby, as though she knew that she was unwelcome and caused her mother pain and inconvenience. She had kept them all awake through the long nights of her first year of life with a succession of colics, tummy aches and teething problems. Not so with Leon. He shone non-stop like this lovely California sun. Dreamily, Candy watched the children and the sparkles of sunlight on the water. If she turned her head the other way she could see the waving branches of bougainvillea and beyond that the pine-clad hills with other big white villas dotted amongst the folds of rosy earth. The light and colours nagged at the back of her mind as she tried not to understand how strongly it all reminded her of Palestine.

There was a squeal and a splash from the pool. Danny had lost her footing and they had all disappeared under the water. Both Evadne and Candy leapt forward but before they could reach the pool, Pippa had recovered Leon and was jiggling him up and down as though the accident had been part of the game. Danny wasn't so easily mollified and Candy waded into the water up to her knees and pulled Danny towards her, folding her arms around the child and comforting her.

'Come on,' she murmured, 'Let's get a soda pop.' She would once have called it lemonade but she was learning to say things the American way.

Danny pushed her away. 'You're cold.'

'I don't think so! But if you are, here's a towel.' Candy wrapped the child in a big, fluffy yellow towel and led her over to Evadne for a cuddle. She tried not to feel slighted by the fact that since Leon's birth, Danny seemed to prefer the cuddles of her granny or the nanny, a competent Mexican woman called Isabella. She told herself it was simply a phase, a stage in the process of sibling rivalry, so she gave in to her and didn't try to press her affection on the child because she liked to keep the peace and Danny was becoming very good at disturbing it. It amazed her how easily the family mood could be destroyed by one sulking child especially late in the afternoon when Rupert was expected home. So if Danny didn't want to be cuddled, Danny didn't get cuddled, and Candy gave more and more of the physical affection that was generated by her wonderful sexual relationship with Rupert, to Pippa and Leon.

Half an hour later Rupert was there, sweeping up the drive in his white convertible, braking in a flurry of gravel, leaping out of the car with his usual energy, plus a dose of good humour which told Candy and Evadne that he'd had a good day's filming, with no nasty surprises, only the expected number of minor disasters and irritations. He bounded up the steps and somehow managed to pick up Leon in one arm and field the two girls with the other as they hurled themselves at him, squealing with excitement. Candy came forward too and his eyes met hers with a warm exchange that didn't need to be spoken as he leaned across the children's heads and kissed her on the lips. Then he allowed the children to pull him towards the pool and, after pretending to teeter helplessly on the edge, they all overbalanced into the water in one laughing mass of arms and legs. Both Candy and Evadne rushed forward to lift Leon from Rupert's arms and leave him free to keep Danny afloat.

Evadne turned from drying Leon, poured herself another of those long refreshing concoctions of bourbon and lemonade that she was becoming so fond of, and settled back in her lounger. The shadows were lengthening and she'd soon have to go in to shower and change, but she did so enjoy being able to watch her granddaughters as they played in the pool with their stepfather. Rupert had stripped off his soaking outer garments and was down to his jockey shorts, standing waist deep in the water, trying to coax the nervous Danny into swimming. She knew she ought to resent the fact that the girls seemed to love Rupert so much, and didn't miss Peter one bit, but she couldn't. Even being Peter's mother didn't cloud her acceptance of the fact that Rupert was a much better father than Peter had ever been. She couldn't imagine him tolerating being dragged into the pool with all his clothes on as soon as he got home from work, couldn't imagine him spending time trying to teach one of them how to swim, or ride a bicycle as had happened yesterday, or play a tune on the piano, as she'd seen at the weekend.

The truth was that everyone liked Rupert and Evadne was no exception. She only wished that she could stay here for ever instead of just visiting. She didn't look forward one bit to next week when Peter would be arriving and would take her and the girls to the hotel in San Diego for his access visit. Evadne sighed. It would be a difficult week. Somehow Peter would see to that, manage to make a misery of the lovely surroundings so that the girls would be nervy and anxious and as often as not would be in tears of frustration by bedtime because nothing they did ever seemed to please their father.

She knew that long before the end of the week she would be wanting to interfere instead of placidly sitting and listening to her son needling, undermining Candy and Rupert in the children's affections. Last time she had told him to shut up, in front of the girls, then spent days trying to restore their sense of security.

It was all so unfair, specially as it was Candy who paid Peter's fare for the visit.

'Granny, I'm getting tired. Will you come up with me?' Pippa was standing beside her, dripping onto the glossy cover of Vogue.

Evadne set her glass aside. 'Where's your towel?'

'Don't know.' Pippa looked around her. 'Somewhere. Very wet.'

Evadne scrambled to her feet. 'Never mind, Isabella will find it in the morning.' Then she laughed at herself. She'd been so disapproving the first time she'd heard Candy say that. It was easy to get into the habit of knowing that someone else would pick up after you.

In the nursery Candy held Leon on her lap, sweet-smelling and powdered from his bath, and fed him warm milk and biscuit for his supper. In the next room she could hear Evadne talking to Pippa as she ran a bath for the child. A few minutes later there was Danny's voice too as Rupert brought her in and led her through to join the bathing ritual.

Isabella came in with an armful of freshly ironed clothes which she stacked in a cupboard in the corner. Then she turned to Candy. 'You want me to help you, Madam, or help Mrs Price with the girls?'

'Go and give Mrs Price a hand, will you? I'll see Leon into bed.'

Leon dipped his fingers into the milky bowl and reached them out towards Candy's face. 'Mama eat. Good girl.' Or at least that's what Candy thought he was trying to say. She laughed and he chuckled back at her, then his beam widened as Rupert came into the room.

Candy smiled too and felt her stomach muscles contracting as he locked his eyes on hers. His thin wet shorts did nothing to hide the arousal that Candy knew had been there from the moment he came home. He always came back from a day's filming in a high state of excitement. It seemed to be part of what he did.

He came across the room to lean over them and wrap his arms around both of them, burying his face in each of their necks in turn. One hand strayed further round and splayed out over the bare skin between Candy's shorts and her top. She quivered and turned her face up to his and his kiss found her mouth.

He stood and gently wiped the excess milk off Leon's face, then took the child in his arms and reached down to take Candy's hand. They crossed the room to the cot that stood in one corner and Rupert kissed the child, laid him down and gave him a loving caress before covering him with a light blanket. Candy leaned over to kiss the little face and felt Rupert come close behind her, his hands covering her breasts, then his fingers feeling their way inside the cotton of her halter top. Her nipples stiffened under his touch and he moved his hardness against her, then began to caress the back of her neck with his tongue.

She stopped him. 'Not here...' They'd made love in a lot of strange places in and around their house but never in the children's room, never with other people doing normal things within earshot.

'Why not?' His hands came away from her breasts and unhooked the fastening of her top.

'It's not right....' At the sound of their voices Leon opened his eyes and gazed up at them.

Rupert cupped her bare breasts in his hands and began to knead them gently. 'It feels very right to me. We are his parents, and we are married.'

Candy leaned over to give Leon another kiss, then followed Rupert through to the master bedroom. He was already in the shower and she followed him in and wrapped her arms around him, feeling hungry for sex now that he'd aroused her. But he laughed and pushed her away. 'Oh, so you're ready for me now, are you?' he grinned. 'You'll have to wait. It's time to dress for dinner. Anyway, what kind of a wanton hussy has sex on her mind when her ex-mother-in-law's in the next room putting her children to bed?'

But he did make love to her, as she'd known he would. In the shower it was quick and urgent but later in the evening, when they finally went to bed and the house was sleeping, it was less driven, more sweet and complete, until he finally fell asleep in her arms, the sweat-soaked sheets wrapped around them.

As soon as she was sure he was asleep, Candy slithered gently out from beside him and crept through to the nursery to listen to the quiet breathing of the children. She straightened their covers and kissed them, then crept back beside Rupert. As she drifted off to sleep she told herself that for the first time in her life she was experiencing something like happiness. She had Rupert, she had a beautiful home in a setting that reminded her of Palestine, she had servants, she had all the lovely clothes she wanted. It should be enough, but sometimes she felt as though it was some kind of consolation prize for a little white house on a hillside covered with orange trees, and a family of olive skinned babies to cook for.

Peter Price gazed out of the aeroplane window as they circled to land at Los Angeles. Because he'd been a pilot himself he tried to pretend that he was calm about the whole process of flying as a passenger but he failed miserably. The fact was that he was terrified. He mentally followed the pilot through all the processes of lining up, reducing airspeed, lowering the flaps and undercarriage, levelling out. Damn it, why did they always have to leave every manoeuvre just those few seconds longer than he'd have done if he'd been in their place? It tore his nerves to shreds and it was all he could to stop himself screaming instructions, unbuckling his seatbelt and running forward to do the job himself.

He wished he'd never learned to fly. What ever had made him think he wanted to be a hero? Why hadn't he joined something safe and sensible like the catering corps? If he hadn't joined the RAF he would never have met Candy, he would have gone home after it was all over and found his mother safe and grateful in Taunton and he would have taken up his old job and married one of those nice girls who used to go to the Grammar School.

Instead of which he was in a DC6 landing in an exotic American city to spend a week with his daughters in the name of paternal access, while his ex-wife languished in the arms of a film star. Not the sort of thing that happened to decent, ordinary chaps.

The plane landed with a thump and as it taxied along the runway Peter began to look forward to stretching his legs. He was very tired. The journey was long and tedious with a number of stop-overs in god-forsaken places. He was looking forward to his hotel room, to showering and resting before Candy arrived with the children and Evadne in the afternoon.

The immigration official flicked through his navy blue, gold-embossed passport and his visa document and raised his eyes to compare the photograph with the face in front of him. 'Your daughters not traveling with you this trip, Mr. Price?'

For a moment Peter's mind stumbled. How did the man know he had daughters? Then he realised – their names were right there in the passport. 'Er, no. Not this trip.'

'Only it's uncommon for kids to travel on their father's passport. Usually it's the mother.'

'Their mother and I are divorced.'

'Uh-huh. Okay.' The man flicked through the rest of the passport, then stamped in the date of entry and smiled as he handed it up to Peter. 'Have a nice holiday, Mr Price.'

'Thank you.' Peter had the sense not to convey that he was going to hate every moment on US soil, wouldn't be able to get away fast enough. This was the second time he'd been forced to go through this farcical procedure and it was twice too much. But this time he was going to do something about it. This time would be the last.

The car jerked forward as Candy slammed her foot on the accelerator to pull away from the front of the hotel. Her throat was tight and she was half blinded by welling tears, yet she couldn't bear to stay there a moment longer. What if the children came running out, crying, begging her to take them with her back home? She wouldn't be able to tell them they must stay with their father, and that Evadne was there to mediate for them, make sure they were taken proper care of. She would have to let them bundle into the car and come back with her.

She'd tried to make the journey fun, stopping for hot dogs and soda and ice creams, even having a swim in the sea at lunchtime. But all day her heart had been heavy, now it was fit to break. The only way she could restore herself was to get back to Rupert and Leon and her heart softened at the thought of Leon's sunny face. Cuddling him wouldn't make the separation okay but it would make it bearable.

Meanwhile she could still feel Pippa's tears on her neck and the pressure of Evadne's last hug as she whispered in her ear, 'Don't worry, Candy. I'll see they come to no harm.'

Harm? How could they come to harm? The point wasn't that they might come to harm but that she was going to miss them like hell and there wasn't a thing she could do about it.

Danny rubbed her eyes and came awake as Peter leaned across and fastened her seat belt. For a moment she couldn't remember where she was or why she was in an aeroplane. Then she remembered that it was part of her holiday with Daddy and she felt a curious little ache of doubt and fear in the pit of her stomach. This trip to Mexico was supposed to be a secret from Mummy and Granny, that was what Daddy had said, and it didn't feel right at all. Exciting in a way, but very naughty. What would Mummy say when she found out?

Danny was terrible at keeping secrets, she would be sure to let it all out when they got back home next week, then everyone would be angry with her.

She saw that her Daddy was waking up Pippa in the seat on the other side of the aisle. She felt very thirsty and wondered if she could have a drink before they landed but when she saw how busy the uniformed stewardess was with the other passengers she decided not to ask. Instead she started to cry and said she wanted to go home. She didn't mean to cry, she knew it would make Daddy angry, but she suddenly just couldn't help the tears coming out.

'Don't be a silly child,' Peter said briskly. 'Once we've landed we'll have a lovely day.'

'I wanted Granny to come with us.'

'She couldn't. She had some shopping to do.'

Danny looked across at Pippa with a pleading expression on her face but Pippa only frowned. It would be better if they both behaved themselves, then Daddy wouldn't get cross and they'd all have a more enjoyable time. Otherwise there'd be shouting and spankings and Daddy would go on about how they were being spoiled and had no idea of loyalty, and needed to be sent to a sensible English boarding school to be taught some proper manners.

It had all happened before, in England soon after the divorce and last time Daddy came to America to have a holiday with them. The same words, the same threats, and one day they would come true.

It wasn't until they were in the airport building, holding tightly onto Peter's hands and staring round fearfully at the strange looking people, that Danny noticed how uncomfortable Pippa was looking and she began to suspect that something was very wrong. She'd expected them to go straight outside and take a taxi to whatever hotel they were staying at. Instead, Peter led them to another check-in desk and began talking to the clerk about a connection to London.

She thought, London? We can't be going to London. Peter had let their hands go to take tickets and a passport out of his jacket pocket and she reached round his legs and tweaked at Pippa's cardigan. 'Did you hear that?'

Pippa craned her neck to see what was going on as Peter settled their travel arrangements over the tops of their heads. When he seemed to have finished he looked down into their faces and said, 'Right, let's get something to eat while we wait.'

'What are we waiting for?'

He didn't answer at once. He took their hands and led them away towards the door marked *Restaurante*. Only when they'd found seats did he say, 'I've got a great surprise for you. I'm taking you back to London with me. California is no place for two nice little English girls to grow up so you're coming to live with me and go to school in England.'

Pippa gasped and said, 'Oh no!' The horrible empty feeling spread from Danny's stomach right through her chest. 'Boarding school?' she said in a tiny, faltering voice.

'Eventually, yes, when you're old enough. But at first you can live with me and we'll find you a new mummy who'll look after you properly.'

'We don't need a new mummy,' said Danny, looking anxiously from Pippa to Peter and back again trying to ignore the lump growing in her throat which would inevitably lead to more tears.

Pippa tried to keep her voice polite and steady as she said, 'Pardon me, Daddy, but we don't want to go to London. Mummy and Granny will be very upset. We want to go home, please.'

'London is your home.'

'No, we want to go home to Beverly Hills, please.'

Danny was frightened to see that her daddy's face was going all hard as Pippa spoke to him. He glared at her for a moment, then said, 'You don't have a choice in the matter. You are my daughters and we shall shortly be on a flight to London.'

Something snapped in Danny's chest as she realised that they might never get home again to Beverly Hills, might never see her mother and Rupert again. She felt desolate tears rushing into her eyes and streaming down her face. 'No! Please no, Daddy! Please take us home!'

She saw Pippa's face crumple up as she, too, began to cry.

Faces turned towards them and one or two dark-eyed women began to click their tongues with disapproval. Peter reached out his hands and grasped each of them by a wrist, so tightly that it hurt. 'You will be quiet and behave yourselves,' he hissed. 'If you don't, I will carry on to London by myself and leave you all alone here. You will become lost children and have to live on the streets and be beggars.'

Danny drew a sobbing breath, trying to control herself, knowing that being left alone would be worse than being forced to go with him. Perhaps after a little while in England they would be allowed to go back to Mummy in California.

He went on, 'I am your father and I do have the right to have you living with me. You are too young to know what's good for you. I have arranged this with your mother and she is in complete agreement that I take you with me. I should tell you that she was only too pleased to be rid of you. She certainly doesn't want you with her any longer.'

Danny opened her mouth to shout that it wasn't true, Mummy did want them, Mummy and Rupert loved them. But a tiny voice inside her asked if her Daddy might not be right, if perhaps they were nothing but a terrible nuisance and Mummy really only loved Rupert and Leon.

She closed her lips tightly and stared in blank misery across the table to where Pippa was rubbing her eyes and whispering, 'I want my Mummy!' over and over again.

'I just don't know!' Evadne sobbed into the telephone. 'They've been gone all day and I thought he'd taken them for an early morning swim but now it's well past their bed time and they haven't come back and I'm so worried....'

Candy's voice was strained and hollow. 'What about the police? Could they have been involved in an accident?'

'I've called them. They don't know anything but they're sending someone round to the hotel. But I thought you should....' Cold panic swept over Evadne for the umpteenth time that day as she considered what might have happened to her son and the little girls. Mugged, drowned in the sea. Terrible scenes flashed before her eyes.

'Yes, of course I should know. What about the hospitals?'

'I'll give them a try. Candy, I'm so sorry. I feel so responsible....'

'It's not your fault. Hang on...'

Evadne blew her nose as she heard a conversation in the background. Then Candy said, 'We're driving down. Rupert and I.'

'What about the filming?'

'Bugger the filming, Evadne. We want to know where the children are.'

It didn't take the two police officers very long to find out from the desk clerk that Peter had ordered a taxi at six in the morning. The clerk knew who the taxi driver was and that led them to the airport and the flight to Mexico City. At that they shrugged their shoulders and told Evadne their hands were tied.

'Sorry Ma'am, nothing we can do. If he'd landed in another US City he could have been stopped. Mexico's out of our jurisdiction, even if he's still there. Chances are your son's used it as a stopover to get a plane to London. Best go home, Ma'am and take it up with him there.'

Evadne was stunned. Unbelieving. Devastated.

She sank down in a chair in the hotel foyer and buried her face in her hands. She'd trusted Peter. He'd always been a good son. Perhaps not quite such a good husband but the circumstances had been against him. And she'd brought him up to be a gentleman, not to break his word and take the law into his own hands. A long sigh escaped her. Was this her fault? She'd tried not to take sides because though she felt sorry for Peter over the divorce and she'd been angry with Candy when she brought the girls over to the States, she loved Candy and could see things from her point of view. Now she had a keen sense of what Candy would go through when she and Rupert walked through the door in an hour or so and learned what had happened.

Could she have done anything to make any difference?

'Are you all right, Ma'am?' The police officers were still hovering. Evadne had told them the children's mother was on her way.

'She'll kill him,' Evadne muttered. She really believed it was a possibility. Either Candy or Rupert.

The officers both pricked up their ears. 'That would be a serious felony, Ma'am.'

'I wonder...' Evadne raised a blotched and tear-stained face.... 'I wonder if you could wait until they arrive and lend your weight to my account of what's happened?'

Rupert stood with his arms around Candy, his cheek against the top of her head, trying to still her paroxysms of sobbing. They were back in their home after hours spent in Los Angeles telephoning airlines and consuls and embassies and judges. Everyone gave the same response – once Peter was out of US jurisdiction there was nothing that could be done from this end. The only progress they made was when they called Rupert's London solicitor, Bob Stevenson, who had very discreetly handled Candy's divorce from Peter. He had promised to get an injunction to arrest Peter as soon as he landed with the children. 'That is, if he hasn't already got here and disappeared with them. You should have called me first.' But they hadn't thought of it first, he was their last resort. And there was no guarantee that a British judge wouldn't decide that it was better for the girls to live in England with their father than in Hollywood with their mother.

Candy had sobbed all the way home, in the back of the car with Evadne's arms around her. She had sobbed while cuddling Leon, making him cry so that Rupert signaled to Isabella to take the child away from her. She had sobbed instead of eating the meal that the maid prepared for them. She had sobbed through Grace's voice on the telephone from London trying to soothe her and tell her it would be all right.

Now Rupert was stroking her hair, wondering whether he should call a doctor and get her a sedative. Frustration and despair welled up inside his heart. He wished he had a script to tell him what to do next, what he should be feeling. So the little girls had been snatched away but there was no mystery about it. It wasn't as though they'd been kidnapped or murdered.

He ran a hand through his hair, looked down at her. 'Candy, I love you darling. And I love those little girls. I don't want this to happen.'

'But it has... I hate him! I hate him!' She flung down onto one of the red leather sofas, covered her face with her hands.

He went to her side, knelt and took her hands. 'Darling. Calm down. You know they're safe. It's not as though they're dead...'

At that, Candy did stop crying. She stopped doing everything, as though she'd had an electric shock. The face she turned up towards him was white and drained of blood, the eyes huge and haunted, as though they were looking right through him instead of at him. 'What do you know about dead children?' she asked in a whisper. 'What do you know? What do you know?' And she shook her head slowly.

Just as Rupert was wondering whether Candy was losing her senses and he really ought to call the doctor, Evadne came down the stairs carrying a suitcase. Thankful for something to distract him, Rupert hurried forward to help her.

'You're not going?' He was relying on her to help him look after Candy. Without her there he wasn't sure he would be able to get away to work. 'Please, you don't have to go. Let the lawyers sort it out.'

'Yes, I do. Peter's not very good with those children. It's best I go back, help out, stabilise things while all this goes on....' She sniffed and a big tear rolled down her cheek. 'Remember, it's my family. There's a flight this evening. I'll call a cab in a little while.'

'I'll drive you...'

'No, you stay here with Candy.'

But Candy was struggling to her feet, swaying a little. 'I'm coming with you.'

Rupert rushed across to steady her. 'You're not fit to travel, darling.'

'I can't do anything here. I'm going with Evadne. I'm going to look for them. '

Rupert felt cold panic clutching at his heart. He was hearing her say she was going to England, leaving him on his own. It would be bad enough getting by without the little girls, what would he do without her and Leon? It might be weeks before she came back. She knew he couldn't just drop the picture and come with her, he had at least two months of filming left. How could he make her wait until they could go together?

'No, please. I need you here, you and Leon.'

'And what about what I need?'

'You need rest and care, not a long plane trip and an emotional search...'

'I need to find my daughters. And I believe I'm the best person to do that. I'm not going to take Leon. I can't search and look after a small child, and there's no time to get a visa to take Isabella.'

'Candy!'

She sounded so cool. Now she was the one in control and he was the one bordering on unreasonable hysteria. 'You can't just leave Leon. He needs his mother.'

'He'll have you. He's better here than being dragged around strange places. Honestly, I wont be away long. It shouldn't take more than a few days to find them, should it? We'll be back inside a fortnight.' She moved him gently aside from her and looked towards Evadne as a wave of helplessness swept over him. 'What time did you say that plane goes?'

'Six.'

'Right. You call the airport and book me a seat. I'll see Isabella and Leon.' She paused and sat down and put her arms around Rupert. He could tell they were meant to be comforting arms but he didn't feel any comfort, only rejection and frustration. 'I will be back very soon,' she promised. 'Take care of Leon for me.'

As the plane took off and banked over the sea, turning to climb over the hills in the evening light, the lump in Candy's throat had nothing to do with leaving Rupert and Leon, leaving this beautiful dream where she'd been happy. She was transported back to another sea, other hills, another departure. Then her life had been ragged and uncertain, almost destroyed, but she had fought back, pulled it together again. Now a gaping hole had been torn in the fabric she had so carefully woven around herself and through it the blackness and despair of the past could be clearly seen, lurking, ready to erupt and swallow her.

She had to find the girls and then get back to California to Leon. She had to have her children with her. Rupert didn't seem to understand any more than Peter the enormity of what had been done. None of them could begin to know what her children meant to her, could they? Not Rupert, not Grace, not Evadne. Nobody knew. Nobody had any reason to know.

The house in Taunton, where Peter and Evadne had returned after the divorce, was cold and empty even though it was a warm afternoon. The lawn was unkempt, the flowerbeds overgrown with the remains of tangled golden rod and phlox. Evadne had been so sure that Peter would be there with the children that by the time the taxi turned into the hedge -lined road she had almost managed to convince Candy that they would all soon be together again. But as they drew up the empty windows told their own story and once inside it was obvious that neither Peter nor the girls had been there. As they paid the taxi and took their luggage inside, curtains twitched behind the privet hedge across the road.

Without even taking off her jacket Candy strode around the house, checking everything, finding nothing. Then she slumped down on what had been her chair at what had once been a familiar kitchen table and watched while Evadne put on the kettle for a cup of tea, and struggled to light the Ideal boiler to make some hot water for them to take a bath. When the tea was made they had to have it without milk because there hadn't been time to let the milkman know they were on their way home. The only cake had gone mouldy in its tin, the Marie biscuits were soggy in their brown paper bag. Candy listened dispassionately to Evadne's running commentary as she gazed around her. Why had she never noticed that the paint was beginning to flake in the corners, that the enamel was chipped on the boiler? How had they ever managed to keep house without a Frigidaire and electric water heating?

The grey silence of the house was broken by the telephone. Evadne pushed back her chair and went to answer it and Candy heard her say, 'Yes, speaking.....Oh yes......Yes......Yes.......all right.......one-thirty's fine. Thank you.'

She came back and said, 'That was Bob Stevenson. There's an emergency court hearing tomorrow at two. We're to meet him at one-thirty in the court office.'

Candy stared into her ugly dark brown tea. 'It won't

bring them back, will it?'

Evadne stared at her. 'It will put Peter firmly in the wrong.'

'But that won't matter if we don't know where they are.'

'He can't just disappear with two little girls. He has to have money. In a minute I'll phone the bank where he works.'

'They'll just say he's on holiday.'

'He may have left some clues.'

He had. The assistant who answered the telephone told Evadne that Mr Price had resigned his job the week before last and drawn out all his money from his savings account. She was surprised they didn't know and she couldn't tell them where he had moved to.

Evadne had tried so hard to keep her feelings under control, to remain calm for Candy's sake. Now she came and sat down again across the table and began to cry, quietly and hopelessly. Peter had obviously planned this very carefully and he had used her, deceived her. She felt a great surge of anger towards him – no, it was stronger than anger, it was sheer hatred. She wished she'd never given birth to him.

Then she felt ashamed. How could any mother wish she'd never had her child? That made her some kind of monster, didn't it?

Candy reached out an elegant, well manicured hand and covered hers for a moment. 'Have you any idea where he might have gone?'

'I've been wondering about that. I wondered if he took them back to Gerrards Cross?' He would be able to get a job there without difficulty and find someone to look after the girls.

Candy shook her head. 'No. Too obvious. Let's see if he's left any real clues.'

Together they went to the writing desk and sifted through every piece of paper they could find. Then upstairs, they went through Peter's wardrobe, his tallboy, looked under the bed, everywhere they could think. All they discovered was that he'd taken most of his clothes and left nothing by way of correspondence, papers or financial records.

Sitting amongst the scattered remains of her son's possessions, Evadne's heart tightened around the painful truth. Peter had simply quietly packed up and moved out. Without telling her. Whilst she was visiting in California.

'Wards of court?' Candy echoed as they stood in the dark paneled foyer of the county court building. 'What does that mean?' Her voice was sharp, high pitched and angry. Bob Stevenson placed a cupped hand beneath her elbow and guided her to a seat in an alcove, away from curious ears. Bewildered, Evadne followed them.

'It means that the Court can decide who looks after them, where they live, and they mustn't be taken out of the Court's jurisdiction without permission.'

'The Court's jurisdiction?'

'The boundaries of the United Kingdom. The Judge wasn't too pleased that you took them to the States in the first place.'

'I had custody. Nobody said I had to ask permission.'

'You did have to allow Peter access and by taking them overseas without his permission you made it very difficult for them to see him. I'm afraid the Judge took that into account.'

'What I don't understand,' said Evadne quickly before Candy could raise her voice again, 'is how this helps us to find them.'

'There's an injunction. Peter has to return them to the care of the Court for a decision to be made about where they're to live.'

'That's senseless,' Candy said. 'What difference will an injunction make if nobody can find Peter to tell him about it?'

Bob Stevenson shifted uncomfortably. 'Until he complies with it, he's breaking the law. That means he's likely to be arrested when he is found and the girls will be taken into care.'

'Taken into care? Why? Surely they'll be returned to me?'

'Not if you're living in California.'

'What's wrong with California?'

'It isn't in Great Britain.'

Candy sat very still and her face was white. 'You are telling me that I either have to abandon my husband in California or lose my two daughters?'

'That just about sums it up.'

'What kind of a lawyer do you call yourself, to get me into a situation like that?'

'It's only temporary, isn't it? Rupert will be coming back to England when he's finished his film?'

'How do I know?' Candy covered her face with her hands. Anything might happen. Rupert saw his career as being in Hollywood now, and anyway, she didn't relish the idea of living in England for years to come, with the rain and the rationing. It wasn't as though she'd ever thought of it as home. The best thing she could do was find Pippa and Danny herself and do exactly what Peter had done, spirit them away without a by-your-leave from some crusty judge. Her heart ached as she thought of them now, how frightened they must be, wondering why she'd let their father take them away, wondering whether she still loved them.

'One thing you mustn't do,' said Bob, watching her carefully, 'Is take matters into your own hands. If you try to snatch them back you will end up in prison yourself and then you won't be able to look after any of your children.'

'But what am I going to do?'

'I suggest you go back to your husband and son in

California and wait until you hear from me.'

'But...'

'Surely it will be easier to wait with them than over here with nothing to do?'

'Will I have to wait long, do you think?'

Danny sat staring at her porridge, feeling a sick little lump forming somewhere in her tummy. She knew that the lump would go on growing until it somehow came up into her throat, with a choky feeling that made it hard to swallow. Then it would go into her head and make her eyes want to cry.

She looked across the table at the newspaper that hid her father and listened to him crunching toast and marmalade. She often wondered how he could hold the paper up like that and be reading the pages, yet at the same time be eating his breakfast. Beside her, Pippa was spooning the disgusting, salty porridge into her mouth, staring straight ahead, her eyes glazed. She knew by those eyes that Pippa was pretending, thinking of being back at home with Mummy and eating waffles and honey for breakfast. It was something they often talked about when they were alone in the dark, after Daddy had put them to bed. Home with Mummy, in the sunshine, eating waffles and honey.

Danny closed her eyes tight, trying to remember what the warm honey smelled like. It was easy to forget when there were so many other smells to get used to – the smell of damp leaves, of mansion polish, of disinfectant and boys' sweaty underwear. Smells of this place where they lived now. Lincolnshire, they called it. Smells of the boarding school where her Daddy worked in the office all day, counting the money. Danny imagined him like the picture in her nursery-rhyme book, the bit where it said 'The king was in his counting house, counting out his money.' Only she knew he didn't actually sit counting pennies and half-crowns because she'd been in there lots of times and seen him adding things up in a big book, and not a bit of money in sight.

Daddy rattled the newspaper in that particular way which told Danny he was about to fold it up and put it down and ask if they'd finished their breakfast. Perhaps...perhaps it meant he'd stop teasing now and give her a big hug and say 'What's the matter, Danny? Why haven't you eaten your porridge? Are you feeling ill?'

Danny couldn't contain herself any longer. He really had forgotten! Tears began to roll down her cheeks. Daddy turned to Pippa. 'What's the matter?'

Pippa deliberately gave her plate a last scrape with her spoon and ran the spoon between her lips, then placed it in the bowl. She looked steadily at their Daddy and said, 'You've forgotten, haven't you? It's her birthday today.'

'Of course I haven't forgotten.' He rattled the paper testily as he folded it into a narrow column. 'But breakfast time, when we're all in a hurry, isn't the time to be giving out cards and presents. I was leaving it all until teatime, then we can have a cake and enjoy ourselves a bit.'

'She would have liked a party.'

'How can we have a party out here, miles from any other children. Miles from any other little girls, that is.'

'Some of the boys could come.'

'I've told you before, you mustn't mix with the boys.'

'You don't mind us having lessons with them.'

Danny didn't care about the party, a cake would be all right. She slipped from her chair and went round to where her father sat and reached up her arms to him. He bent forward and she hugged him around the neck and planted a kiss on his cheek. She knew Pippa would say afterwards, 'I don't know how you can kiss him, he's so horrible to us.' But she thought that perhaps a kiss would make the cake a little nicer, something she really liked, pink icing, perhaps. She noticed that he pulled away before she'd finished the kiss, moving her aside as he got to his feet.

'You're going to school without your breakfast then,

are you?' He was beginning to pile the dishes onto a tray to take them through to the kitchen. Just then the letter box rattled and Danny remembered why she hadn't felt like eating her porridge. She was waiting for the postman. Waiting for the card that would surely arrive today, perhaps even a parcel, from Mummy.

She ran into the hall and picked up the two envelopes that had fallen onto the mat. One long and brown with a wndow in the front, one white with a typed address. Both were for her father. She looked around again, even moving the doormat to make sure.

Nothing else.

She took both envelopes through to the kitchen and handed them to Pippa, who was folding up the table-cloth. Pippa raised her eyebrows in a question. 'Nothing?'

Danny shook her head. 'Nothing.' Then the awfulness of it swept over her and, though she tried not to let it, she felt her lip quivering and the tears coming.

'What do you mean, nothing?' Her daddy snatched the envelopes as though she was trying to keep them to herself. 'There's one here from Granny. I expect she's sent you a postal order.'

Pippa put an arm around Danny's shoulders as she spoke. 'Mummy hasn't sent anything. It's her birthday and Mummy hasn't sent a card.'

Through her tears Danny saw a blurred vision of her father's face screwing up in anger.

'Mummy?' he shouted. 'Mummy? After all I do to look after you, is that all you care about? It's time you two realised she isn't going to write, she isn't going to send you anything! It's time you understood that she doesn't care one little bit what happens to you.'

Eleanor McCrae, Matron of Brisewood Preparatory School for Boys, stood by the tall window of the school sanatorium and watched the new bursar as he walked across the playing field from the lodge where he lived to the main school building. With him were his two little girls, one on each side of him, holding his hands. They looked regular and orderly, dressed in grey tweed coats and dark red pixie hoods, the same colours as the school uniform the little boys wore, but adapted for girls. Their father wore a brown tweed coat with a checked Horne Brothers scarf at the neck and a checked deerstalker hat – an odd combination but it looked well on him.

As she watched she noted that the little girls walked almost unnaturally, dragging their feet through the damp leaves as though there was something very heavy in their Start-Rite shoes. They seemed not in the least tempted to run or skip. Just getting to school was enough for them.

But of course, poor wee lambs, what else would they do, so recently bereaved of their mother? Eleanor's heart went out to them, and to the young widower who was so bravely trying to start a new life away from his memories.

She'd been doubtful when Mr Walsingham, the Headmaster, had told the staff that he had engaged a widower with two small girls as the new bursar. Never mind that he had excellent references and was undoubtedly very suitable in a professional way, two little girls might find it difficult to settle in a boys school, and part of the meagre salary for all the staff included having their children attend the school as day pupils free of charge. But they seemed to be getting along all right in Class 1 and when the boys played games she took them out for a walk or sat with them, teaching them embroidery. They were amenable children, if sad, and they never mentioned their mother.

Yes, it was all working out rather well, thought Eleanor. Mr Price was neither too young nor too old and she felt sure that before long she would be getting to know the little girls well enough to come close to him. A favour here or there, a piece of advice, and he would begin to rely on her feminine knowledge. When the holidays came and the big school building was empty there would be opportunities for walks and perhaps even excursions to Skegness or Lincoln in his little car, invitations to share tea around the coal fire in her sitting room.

The trio gained the main entrance to the school just as the first car delivering day boys turned into the drive. Eleanor wondered whether to continue with her usual task of tidying the dormitories or whether to nip downstairs and help Mr Price take the girls' hats and coats off. She only hesitated for a moment. It was never too early to start making herself useful. She hurried to the top of the main stairs, then slowed her pace as she walked down, a beaming smile on her face.

'Good morning, Mr Price. Good morning, Philippa, Daniella. Let me help you with your coats, girls.'

'Good morning, Miss McCrae,' said Pippa politely.

'Good morning,' said Danny, as Eleanor began to unbutton her coat for her. 'Do you know, it's my birthday today. I'm six.'

'Your birthday? No, I didn't know. Many happy returns.'

'And my Mummy hasn't sent me a card or a present.'

Poor little lass, thought Eleanor. She still doesn't understand, does she? 'Well, she wouldn't, would she?' she said soothingly. Then with a nod to Peter, she said, 'Come along, girls, I'll take you to your class.'

*   *   *

Sister Mary James rested her head on her arms, fighting the cloak of desolation that had settled about her. She tried to push away the memories that threatened to curl up her heart and choke her with tears, even after all this time. That birthday had emptied her soul of joy for ever, even after she'd known what had really happened. By that time her father and Eleanor had married, she belonged in their word, in the secure atmosphere of the little school. Visits with their mother had been fraught with danger, strewn with opportunities to be sinful and disloyal, and she couldn't quite make herself follow the example of Pippa and actually enjoy herself when they were finally allowed to go to London or Yorkshire.

A door creaked at the back of the chapel and Sister Bernadette shuffled in, quietly, genuflecting as she drew level with the altar. Sister Mary James looked up, questioning.

'Good morning, Sister. Mother Superior sent me to make sure you knew the time. A taxi will be here soon and she is anxious that you might miss your train.'

'Thank you, sister.' Sister Mary James pulled herself painfully to her feet, swayed for a moment, then clutched the pew end to steady herself. She genuflected and crossed herself quickly - Father, Son and Holy Ghost – then turned and made her way out of the chapel to wash and change her black clothes. As she prepared for her journey, the old, fierce hatred boiled up within her and she did nothing to try to subdue it. Rather, she allowed it to fill her heart. It gave her strength and determination to face the day and the people who had pushed her out of their lives so long ago.

7
LEON

Leon woke early. Before he was fully conscious he reached out a hand to feel the pillow beside him and, finding it empty, was prodded towards wakefulness by a surge of disappointment. Then he remembered he was in Yorkshire, not California or even London, and it was the day of his mother's funeral, and a deep gloom descended on his spirit. He lay still for a while and let the sound of birdsong clear the fuddle in his head caused by too many, too stiff single-malt whiskies the night before. The half empty bottle was still on the table beside the window, the almost full bottle of spring water beside it testament to how little he had diluted the spirits. A mistake, but last night after he had retired, leaving Meggie to meet Jeremy off the train and go through her domestic routines undisturbed, he had needed a prop, something to soften the memories brought back to him by this place he had once sworn never to visit again. He would have used a line or two of cocaine if he had had the choice, but he had thought better of taking the risk of travelling through international airports with anything incriminating in his bags, and during the last three days in London he had been too busy with shopping and business to seek out a reliable supplier. But he would need something to ward off the pain that he knew would hit him today, when there would finally be no escape from seeing her, from seeing Pippa again. Pippa, whose life they said he had ruined – how could loving someone ruin their life? Surely it was the lack of love that did the ruining?

When he had finally struggled awake he showered and shaved and dressed, not in the formal dark suit that hung, newly pressed, against the wardrobe, but in jeans and a sweater, both of which had cost a minor fortune in California but now looked as though he had been swimming in them. He made his way downstairs through a house that still seemed to be sleeping and remembered that Jeremy and Meggie must have been very late to bed. Anyway, he was glad not to bump into Meggie yet. He had spent most of the previous day helping her prepare her house for the visitors who would be arriving for the funeral, and as the day passed he had caught her looking at him several times in a longing, deeply interested way that he had long ago learned meant trouble. He didn't want to hurt her, but he didn't want her, either. Hell – even if she hadn't been his brother's wife, he didn't really go for that middle aged English Rose look.

He went through the kitchens to a scruffy cloakroom that Meggie called the gun room, though there were no guns in it that he could see, and found an old green Barbour jacket that fitted him, hanging among many. Two Golden Labrador dogs roused themselves from a heap of rugs in one corner and raised hopeful eyes, so he whistled them to follow him and let himself out into the expectant morning.

Once out of the yard that had at one time been part of the stables, and across a small fenced meadow, he turned back to look at the vista of the house and its once-formal garden looking out over the home park, saw it slowly stir just before the sun hit it. He blinked for a moment at a vision of tents and flags and colour that had been there last time he stood in this spot, many years ago. He had to pause then, admit the memory he had been trying to push away ever since he had arrived, the memory of the last time he had been here, the weekend of the rock concert. Or, as it had been billed, the *Modern Music Festival.* It had been the first of its kind, had sealed the name of his band amongst the top ten performers of the seventies and, so he'd been told, saved this mildewing stately home estate from bankruptcy.

The word had gone out that it would be gig of the year and the whole park had been filled with a moving patchwork of people in bright clothing. The main set had been by the Stones and to Leon, making music with his first professional band, it had seemed a godsend of an opportunity when heard about it. At first he was resentful that they hadn't told him personally, but perhaps they would have done if he'd ever kept in regular touch with his mother and her new family. The whole thing had been the teenage Jeremy's idea and the ageing Earl had indulged him with a sort of juvenile excitement. Leon and his band had arrived at the last minute, short of money, unbooked, hoping to play a few support numbers, and they had been instantly swept into the inevitable juggernaut of experience that the occasion generated. Music, girls, and what by today's standards seemed a very mild array of drugs. And then, on the last night, *the* girl, the one he had fallen in love with, who had changed everything.

Leon hunkered down and shook his head slowly as a lump gripped his throat and a mist of tears blinded him. Bored with waiting for him the dogs made off on their own, leaving him to his memories of bright auburn hair and soft white skin and sex that had been more magical than anything before or after. As he watched her sleeping beside him, replete and softened by hours of loving, he had told himself, 'When she wakes up I shall tell her I want to spend the rest of our life together.' But when she did awaken, the first thing he had asked her was who she was, and their world together had fallen apart.

He shook his head to lay the ghosts, and smiled ruefully. The last time he'd been here, the last time he'd seen her, any of them...

He opened his eyes again and rose to his feet, unbending his ageing legs slowly. Now he was unsure of which way he should go, but the dogs seemed to know he might be lost and they circled back for him. He followed them along a narrow track that wound upwards from the back of the house and onto a tree-clad hill. Half way up the hillside the track divided, one way continuing up towards the moorland and the other levelling down into thicker woodland, and again Leon hesitated. Then he heard the dogs yapping down on the lower path and he turned that way, wondering belatedly if he should have taken them out at all, specially without leads, and not wanting to lose them.

He needn't have worried. He found them waiting beside the small river that ran round the base of the hill. Each had found a stick and they sat hopefully beside the water where a deep pool carried the sparkling, limestone-filtered water from one set of shallows to another. He guessed he was supposed to throw the sticks into the water for the dogs to retrieve and sure enough, they hurled themselves into the pool after their sticks and brought them back to him, again and again. Gradually the sticks disintegrated and the dogs began to tire, and when Leon sat himself on a log and began to listen intently to the sounds around him, they lolled at his feet, panting.

As the sun came up and began to spread shadows through the woods, small eddies of breeze stirred the branches, making a soft backing sound to the insistent, higher-pitched melodies made by the water as it plunged around the stones. Beneath these melodies he began to hear bass notes, made by the water on the edges of the pool as it beat upwards into small hollows carved into the rocks at the level of the flow. Patterns began to form in Leon's mind and he felt desperately in the pocket of the Barbour and was relieved when he pulled out a stub of pencil and the remains of a packet of cigarettes. Unwrapping the cigarettes he stuffed them back into the pocket, then spread out the outer wrappers on a stone he found by the path, and began to make notes. As he worked on the sounds, words began to tumble after them and he knew that here was the theme for his next album, the one they had been pressing him to start on for months now, the one that was to mark the final stage of his transition from a rock musician to a fully-fledged modern composer.

By the time he got to his feet again, prodded by the dogs, he even had the name for it – *The Yorkshire House.* It would be about his own interpretations of what he could hear in the air around him, and of course it would turn into a series of love songs. He would rent a place nearby somewhere and stay for a few months, taking in changes of season. There would be plenty of opportunities to do concerts in London during that period. It would be a rest from California and the frantic life he lived there.

Love songs – words began to arrange themselves in his brain and with them came the familiar vision of a willowy young woman with auburn hair and pale skin.

'If I had known I loved you, when first I saw your face, I would have turned and walked away, from yo.u.u.ur embrace...'

Yet again he wondered what she would look like now

and that brought the all too familiar choking sensation.

Leon's head began to throb and before the pain took over too completely he blew his nose angrily through his fingers, got to his feet, and told himself, as he had done a thousand times over the years, that it was ridiculous to imagine that he could have been faithful to one woman, and that if she had defied her mother and come back to the States with him, her life would have been ruined for ever. He would have used her, then broken her heart – wasn't that the way the story went? It was what he had done with everyone else so what would have been special about her?

He turned his back on the stream and took the path back to the house, where doubtless breakfast would be well on its way by now. Crossing the yard, he raised his eyes to the top windows of the stable apartments and remembered Meggie telling him that these had been his mother's rooms for the last years of her life. Almost without making a conscious decision, he turned his feet towards the stairway that led to the front door of these apartments. The door was unlocked – nobody seemed to lock anything around here – and he opened it quietly and tiptoed inside, as deferential as when he had been a small boy, which was the only other time he had been here except for the one momentous occasion of the rock concert. He stood still in the half-light, absorbing the feel of the place, thinking again in terms of music. It could all be incorporated, the delicate pieces of Sheraton furniture, the modern paintings that had the look of California – no, Palestine – about them, the richly patterned Shiraz and Bohkara rugs, the faint aura of an expensive perfume that would hang in the air here for years to come.

Moving forward into the main room that stretched the length of the one-time stables below, he stood before a portrait that hung on the wall, facing the window. He knew it was her, but unable to see it properly he stepped back and drew the curtain away from the window, letting in the pale morning light. He thought it must have been painted soon after she married the Earl because it showed her to Leon as he remembered her, not as the grey-haired stranger who graced photographs in the house itself. In this picture she stood, leaning against an anonymous piece of furniture, wearing a flare-skirted evening gown of peacock blue shot silk that nipped in at the waist, caressed the curves of her breasts and swept around her creamy shoulders in a wide halter. The simplicity of the dress belied the expert cut and perfect fit. As was the fashion at the time, the gown was mid-calf length so that her pretty legs were exposed, crossed at the ankles, her feet looking almost delicate in shiny blue court shoes of the same material as the dress. Above the dress, dominating it with the intensity of her gaze, her face was a perfect oval. Her high cheekbones and the faint hint of a smile on her full lips suggested mystery. Her thick auburn hair was bobbed, parted on one side, falling to just the level of her chin, looking for all the world as though she had just tossed her head at the artist over some shared joke. The artist had caught all the reflected lights from the blue silk so that even on this dull morning it shimmered just as Leon remembered it.

It took him a moment to realise that there was something odd in his remembering that particular dress so vividly that he knew if she turned around there would be a rose of matching material attached to the back of the skirt. He had seen her wearing that dress, and his memory also threw up a picture of Aunt Netta wearing it, and arguing bitterly with his mother, and of Jeremy being there – no that wasn't possible, Jeremy wouldn't have been born then, let alone be a grown man. But there was someone very like Jeremy. Who...?

At that moment Leon decided that his *Yorkshire House* album would dedicated to his mother, the mystery Countess, and like everything else he had ever written it would be a sure-fire smash hit.

His train of thought was broken by a step behind him and he turned to see Jeremy coming through the door. He nodded his head towards his brother, half annoyed to be disturbed from his reverie, half pleased to have someone to share his thoughts with. Jeremy smiled, anxiously, and fixed his gaze on the portrait. 'It's lovely, isn't it? But I have to say, I don't remember her looking like that.'

'It's how I remember her best,' Leon said. 'The middle-aged lady in twin-sets and brogues and skirts from Harrogate doesn't register for me at all.' Half her lifetime, and he didn't know anything about it.

*   *   *

'Mummy's coming home!' Rupert burst into the nursery and plucked the half-asleep Leon from his cot, dancing around the room with the child on his arm. When Isabella came in to see what was happening he ignored her remonstrations of 'Senor, I have just put him down!' and put his free arm around her waist, dancing perilously with both of them so that they shared his laughter.

'She's coming home! She's just called from the stop-over in Gander, she'll be landing at first light. Do you think I could take Leon with me to meet her?'

'Of course you could, Senor.' Isabella took the child from him gently. 'But the Senora will be tired. Surely it would be better to meet her alone, then bring her back to a happy child who had started his day with familiar routine?'

'Yes. Yes, you're right.' Rupert gave the child a fond hug and kiss, then relinquished him to Isabella. 'We must have a party, tomorrow evening. Can you organise some eats, Isabella?'

'Yes, of course.' He didn't expect her to say anything else. Isabella could always do everything that was asked of her. As she laid Leon back in his cot she asked, almost as an afterthought, 'She has the girls with her?'

'No. She's alone.'

The eyes Isabella turned towards him were full of doubt. 'Then are you are she will want to party?'

'She's coming home, isn't she? Home to us. That's got to be worth a celebration.'

Isabella just nodded. 'For sure, Senor.' But her eyes met his and said far, far more.

He wondered, did she know? He had only screwed with Della Rees a couple of times while Candy was away and it wasn't serious. Surely it was understandable when he spent half his days playing tender love scenes with her in front of the camera, and he had nobody at home to take the resulting ache from his well-aroused senses. He had to put his monstrous hard-on somewhere or he couldn't sleep, and Della was only too willing, as she had made clear from the start of the filming. He thought they had been discreet but there was always someone who noticed. But Della knew the score. Della knew he was married to Candy, who had given him his lovely son, and that came first. Hell, he was still in love with Candy, with her big grey-green eyes and long legs. Della was only a convenient lay, a tart. If it hadn't been her it would have been someone else plucked at random from the set.

He remembered that they'd arranged to meet this evening, at a restaurant in the hills. He must phone her, put her off, tell her about Candy's return. Then he wondered if it was a good idea to ask her to the party tomorrow; then he told himself it would be pretty obvious if she wasn't there, and someone might drop a hint to Candy. The last thing he wanted was to upset Candy. He wasn't at all sure how understanding she would be.

But when he saw her he knew it was all right. When she came staggering through the barrier with all the other bleary-eyed passengers he called her name and took a few quick steps forward and folded her in his arms. They clung together there, ignoring the people milling around with silly smiles on their faces. He buried his face in her silky hair, whispering to quiet her sobs, rocking from one foot to the other as her perfume enveloped him. Oh, how he had missed her! He didn't know how much until he had her there and felt himself hardening against her flat stomach. It didn't matter that she was alone, that she had failed to find her girls. She was here with him and there would be other babies to take their place.

Luigi Farlesi, film director, shrugged out of his linen jacket and laid it carefully over the back of his chair. He said in measured tones, 'We have two weeks' more shooting to do on this film, Rupert. I'm over budget already. I'm more than pleased that dear Candy is back. Just keep her away from the set is all I ask.'

Rupert was puzzled. Okay, so this morning he had arrived nearer to lunchtime than breakfast, short of sleep and utterly drained from making wild love to Candy several times between meeting her at the airport and finally abandoning her to Leon beside their pool. But when did Candy ever hang around the set? And if she did, why would she be unwelcome?

Luigi saw his puzzlement and put an arm around Rupert's shoulder. The contrast between the short, compact Italian and the tall, spare Englishman was almost ludicrous, and Luigi had to reach upwards to speak discreetly in Rupert's ear. 'You don't realise, do you, what is very obvious to most of us on this crew...?'

'What? What?' Rupert, tired and impatient, almost shouted the question, though he thought he knew the answer already and he resented Luigi's interference.

Luigi nodded towards the make-up cabin where Della had just emerged, freshly invented for the next scene, flashing her Max Factor smile at everyone. 'Della has a lovely nose and I don't want it put out of joint.'

'I wouldn't dream...'

'Wouldn't dream of upsetting her? So you are able to continue to conduct an affair with her while you keep your wife well-fucked at home? I don't think so, Rupert. Not even you could rise to that challenge. But I see you are going to try. All I ask is that you keep them apart. And keep Candy away from the crew because someone is sure to feel they have to enlighten her.'

Rupert shrugged and walked across to have his own make-up done. As he passed close to where Della was sitting studying her script she looked up and her smile changed from the publicly composed, formal upturn of her painted lips to something more like a private caress. As he responded with a tight, anxious smile and a nod of the head the look in her eyes turned to a question, a question Luigi had just asked him not to answer.

And when he thought about it, he knew why. This morning they had to play their last passionate love scene, a very daring scene in a bedroom, a scene that would lead to a murder. Tomorrow they were to fight, the first of several sequences where their underlying lust led to them spitting hatred and frustration at each other. On previous evenings he had lain helpless in her arms for hours, his senses bewitched by her touch, by the scent of her perfume mingled with the sweat that soaked her sheets. Tonight he would have Candy in his arms once more and Della would be alone. It was bound to affect the chemistry between them, wasn't it?

Yet surely it was what Della had expected. He'd never told her he loved her. She'd known their affair was only while Candy was away, hadn't she? Something to satiate his arousal at the end of each day's work? She knew when she issued the invitation into her bed that he would be using her. Didn't she?

Della got up and followed him back into the make-up cabin and arranged herself so that she could talk to him from behind, through the mirror. The make-up girl was accustomed to conversations like this between the actors and actresses and she began to work on Rupert's eyebrows as though she existed only in another dimension.

'What's going on, lover boy?' Della pouted. 'Get a letter from wifey this morning?'

Rupert hesitated. What was he to do? His instinct was to tell her now rather than try to keep his news to himself or hide his feelings about it. He was unlikely to be successful on either count, several people had heard him tell Luigi that Candy was home. Supposing Della heard it from one of them?

'No, no letter. A phone call.' He gave Della what he thought was a disarming grin through the mirror. 'She got home this morning.'

Even the make-up girl hesitated for the next beat, while Della's expression froze, then unfroze again.

'So I'm afraid dinner's off this evening.'

Della said silkily, 'That's all right, darling. It's only natural that you should want to welcome her back. So, when do I get to see you again?'

'Tomorrow, on the set. But not in private. That has to end now. You must know that was part of the deal.'

Della gave a strange little laugh. 'Deal? What deal? We have this beautiful thing going between us and you call it a deal? We are lovers, you and I. We are married in the eyes of God. I am only waiting for this film to end to start making beautiful babies with you.'

Rupert went cold and it had nothing to do with the panstick being massaged into his jawline. 'Don't be foolish, Della. Candy's my wife and I love her. If I have any more children it will be with her. You must have known that's how things are. Everything that's happened between us off the set is nothing.' He wasn't sure if he believed that, or even wanted to believe it. But he had to say it because otherwise things were too complicated.

He braced himself for the explosion but it didn't come. In fact, to his surprise, Della never stopped smiling. She leaned forward, meeting his eyes squarely in the mirror. 'Isn't it you who's being a little foolish, darling? Do you really believe Candy will accept that what we have done together is nothing?'

'She'll have to, because I shall tell her so. Anything else will be studio gossip.'

'Studio gossip...' Della said it slowly, as though tasting the words. Then she placed one of her delicate hands on Rupert's jaw and turned his face towards her. He couldn't help himself tingling at her touch and he was afraid she would know it. Leaning forward, she kissed him slowly, running the tip of her tongue round the inside of his lips. Then she drew back and looked at him again in the mirror. 'We shall see, lover boy. We shall see.'

And she turned and left.

As the make-up girl made herself busy with tissues, looking anywhere but into his face in the mirror, it began to dawn on Rupert that he might be in serious trouble.

That afternoon Luigi's cameras caught the most sex-charged love scene yet between his two stars.

'I knew I was right,' he muttered to his assistant. 'That was stupendous. But it would have collapsed if he'd told her it was over between them.'

The assistant nodded. He was Luigi's nephew and he found it politic to agree with everything his uncle and mentor said. Otherwise he might be dismissed as being incompetent, which wasn't true, and sent back home to Umbria, which was a place he hoped never to see again. 'But she is going to know sometime, isn't she? What will happen then?'

'What indeed, Carlo? Sometimes I wonder why we pay good money for film scripts when real life is so much more interesting.'

Luigi got his way and peace reigned on his set, but they had barely finished the film before the gossips pounced in print. Della's thickening waistline, which she did nothing to hide, was attributed to Candy's 'long' absence in Europe during the filming and there were even suggestions that Candy's trip had been to meet up with some un-named lover in London. At first Rupert tried to deny everything. He was quoted as saying that Della was known to have had several affairs during the last few months. Della stuck to her story that her child was Rupert's and he had promised to marry her as soon as he got rid of his boring little wife without it costing him too much. Hollywood loved it.

Candy, already struggling to recover from the loss of the girls, sank into a trough of grief that made her daily more desperate and unattractive and it was this that finally drove Rupert to pack his bags and move in with Della. His last words to Candy were 'It's plain you're not a good mother in the state you're in. I'm going to have custody of that boy and I'm taking out an injunction to prevent you removing him from the country.' That was the final blow to Candy's self-confidence. She had no idea then what to do and where to go.

It was Luigi who came to her rescue. In the semi-darkness of the curtained room where she had lain helpless for days, hoping to die soon, he sat down on the bed and told her to stop spoiling her lovely face and to stop behaving like a little shorthand typist who couldn't look after herself.

'What do you know?' She sobbed. 'You think I'm fooled by your sympathy? If you want to sleep with me, go ahead, stick it in and enjoy yourself, you don't have to pretend it's because you want to help me. As you say, I'm just a stupid little jumped-up secretary who didn't even have any decent clothes before she met the great Rupert Taylor.'

'Is that what he told you?'

'It's obvious, isn't it? I can't compete.'

'You have done very well so far. I have been watching you carefully, even before this fiasco with Della. I know you think you can't act, and your dress-sense can do with improvement, and you are feeling very sorry for yourself at the moment, but all that will change if you do as I ask. I will put you in front of a camera and the camera will see you as I want it to, and you will be beautiful and sexy and, eventually, very rich.'

She stopped crying then and peered at him through wet lashes. Did he mean it or was he just spinning her a yarn? What did he really want with her? Perhaps there was only one way to find out and that would be easy enough now. It wasn't as though it was her first time.

'Okay,' she said. 'I'm ready. Show me what you can do for me.'

She expected him to make love to her and when he just leaned over and kissed her cheek before getting to his feet, she felt almost slighted. 'Is that all you want?' she asked, sniffling into a handkerchief.

'Be at the studio at six tomorrow morning and I will begin to show you what I want of you.'

In the weeks that followed Candy could hardly believe how that new relationship with Luigi had transformed her from a pathetic, deserted wife with nobody to support her, into an enormously competent actress. He did make love to her, in such a way as to make her feel she was worth a million dollars, and that gave her power over herself. He showed her that sex was a mutual satisfaction of the senses, not tied up with sentimental emotions like love. That it was something they could have together or give to other people as they liked. And, best of all, she learned that the more she was able to enjoy the things that the ugly little Italian maestro did to her body in private, the more beautiful she became in public.

She'd been terrified at first. Terrified of the slick, professional people on the set, terrified of letting down Luigi, most of all terrified of the huge, unforgiving eye of the camera pointed at her. How could she, failed mother, failed wife, learn to dominate them all and make them believe she was powerful and beautiful and talented and desirable? Then, as the camera began to turn and she followed Luigi's directions, she realised the truth. That the camera, coupled with Luigi's faith, made her into whatever she wanted to be. As his voice told her to smile she lifted her face and looked into the camera as though she saw there everything she had ever wanted. As he told her to be angry she thought of Peter kidnapping the girls and something crackled through her and seemed to twist her emotions and project them out towards those who were watching. And when he told her to cry she thought of Rupert's betrayal and her eyes flooded as she turned her face towards the ground and allowed a single tear to course down each cheek.

As her first film came together for Luigi, Hollywood was spell bound. By the time they were coming to the end of the third one, Candy had achieved the status of a minor goddess. None of the tough, cynical crew on the set ever forgot the afternoon when, hardly daring to breathe, they watched as Candy surrendered to the passionate kiss of the leading man, winding her arms around his neck, feeling his hands on her buttocks clutching her against his growing erection. She started to uncurl her arms, pull away from him. Her mouth only an inch away from his she shook her head. 'This mustn't happen,' she said.

'You know it's the only thing that matters.' He tried to find her mouth again but she strained back and slowly he released her, though their eyes remained locked together.

For a long, painful moment they gazed in silence, then she said, 'No more.' She turned and took up a little clutch bag and a wrap from a table top and walked with carefully measured steps towards the door. She knew that the outline of her figure was impeccable in the sculpted, beaded sheath dress that she had been literally sewn into that morning. It revealed just enough of her flawless shoulders and the curve of her breasts, just enough of her legs to hint at scandal while still giving the impression of moral respectability. Across two continents women would be trying to imitate the way she looked today, most of them with little success.

Half way to the door she paused, swung on her toes to look over her shoulder at the man who stood, devastated, holding out his arms to her. Her glance was a mixture of longing and of triumph. Then she tossed her sleek, auburn hair and turned her back for the last time, opening the door to pass through but not closing it behind her, so that he was forced to watch her all the way down the long paneled hallway.

She didn't stop walking until she heard Luigi's voice. 'And cut!' A pause. 'Belissima! That was something else!'

There was silence on the set. One or two handkerchiefs came out of pockets and surreptitiously dabbed at tear-filled eyes. Luigi came from his place behind a camera, arms outstretched, and he almost bounced along the set towards her. His huge hug lifted her feet from the ground, even though she was taller than him in her high heels. 'Belissima Candissima!' he shouted, whirling her around. She heard the beginnings of a ripple of applause from the crew. 'You have surpassed yourself! We have a hit here, a huge, huge hit. It deserves a great party.'

'And a big bonus,' muttered Craig, the leading man. 'I nearly split my trousers that time.'

Candy smiled. 'You're going to have to get used to the difference between fantasy and reality, isn't he, Luigi?'

'As far as I'm concerned there is no difference,' Luigi said. He gave Craig an encouraging clap on the shoulder. 'Okay everyone, rushes at five, party at eight.' Candy kissed him fondly on the cheek and as she turned towards her dressing room she heard Luigi add to Craig, 'And I should bring your own woman. You may have fallen in love with that one but you must know by now that she has nothing but hatred for men, particularly film stars.'

It didn't take them long to wipe off her make-up and cut her out of her dress and Candy was soon focused on going home. She sat back in the big white studio limousine, unseeing eyes fixed on the backs of the heads of the chauffeur and the security guard who rode beside him. She was still charged with emotion about what they'd achieved today. On schedule and with only three retakes they had the last, most controversial, sequence of what might prove to be Luigi's greatest film to date, a sequence she was sure people would be talking about for years to come. As the car sped up into the hills she unwound inside, came back from being Candy Price the film star to Candy the ex Mrs Rupert Taylor, single mother. She wished she didn't have to go to the party this evening. The only person in the world she really wanted to spend time with would be waiting for her already, her beautiful little son Leon, and she didn't have to dress up for him and pretend she was someone she would rather not be.

She could hardly believe it but as the months stretched into years and her success put her name on the lips of everyone who really mattered in the film world, her grief over losing the girls slowly faded, together with her anger and humiliation when Rupert had told her he was leaving her. It all began to meld together into that other time, before Luigi had come to her and given her a new box to re-pack her life. Dear Luigi. She knew their relationship couldn't last. He was renowned for only keeping his leading ladies for three or four films and she was pushing her luck expecting him to sign her again next year. She had no intention of letting herself join the ranks of ageing Hollywood stars fighting over new scripts and glamorous young men to escort them to other people's premieres. She should pack up and go, while she was still getting offers to play the stages in New York and London. California was lovely but it wasn't her real home and she would like to live somewhere she didn't have to hire security guards to keep Leon from his father.

That was a daily battle she could do without but how could she forget it after the threats Rupert had made when they were getting divorced? Now, every time she came home from work the studio limo had to stop at the gates of her mansion while a security guard unlocked them, then locked them again behind her. And Leon wasn't allowed to go anywhere on his own. She hated it but how could she stop herself from dreaming, time after time, that Rupert had snatched Leon from her and hidden him away? No matter that her lawyers assured her it would count as kidnapping, a federal offence that would land him in jail for years. That didn't make her feel in the least bit secure. Peter had committed a crime when he had snatched the girls but that hadn't brought them back, it had only made him hide them all the more cleverly so that they would never be found. She wasn't sure that Rupert would have the wit to do the same, but she didn't want to find out. Better, surely, just to put as much distance as possible between their lives?

She thought about it every time she went through the homecoming ritual of sitting with Leon on the pool terrace, sipping at the glasses of fresh orange juice Isabella brought out, talking about what they had done that day. It was beginning to spoil their time together as she waited for the moment when Leon fixed his wistful brown eyes on hers and said, 'Daddy was outside the school again today.' Then he would catch sight of the expression on her face and continue quickly, 'But he didn't try to talk to me, Mom. He just sat in his car and watched while Carlo took me into the limo.'

'Did you tell Carlo?'

'Carlo saw him. It was okay.' Leon sipped his juice and Candy drew breath to ask him what he'd learned in school today. But before she could get to the words, Leon said, 'Mom, I wish Daddy would talk to me. Or give me a wave. But he just sits there.'

What could she say? That he'd be in danger of having his precious face smashed in by Carlo if he approached his son? 'He comes to watch you whenever he can because he loves you.'

'But why can't I talk to him properly, go visit with him?'

Because I don't trust him. 'Because we don't live together any more. We're not a family any more.'

'Steven's Mom and Pop don't live together any more and now he has two Moms and two Pops, one set in each house.'

'Yes, that's very nice for them all but Steven's parents haven't had the same kind of arguments that we have.' She paused, still wondering if it had been worth it. She had salvaged her pride but at what expense? Words spoken that could never be taken back, accusations that clouded all memory of the early, happy days.

'Daddy lives with another mommy, doesn't he?'

'He lives with Della. She's Francine's mummy.'

'She could be mine if I went to live with them.'

'I'm your mummy and you live here.'

'And are you going to find me a new Daddy?'

'It's not something I'm planning on.' They always seemed to cause trouble.

'I wish you would.'

'You don't need a daddy when you've got me and Isabella and all the people here who look after you.'

Leon paused a moment, then drained his glass. As he set it down he gave her a look that told her he didn't agree with what she'd said, didn't believe her. It was a disturbing look from a kid of five, going on six. He was growing up too fast, the last of the baby plumpness had left him already, one of his milk teeth was loose. And the baby joy had left him, his eyes held a doubt, a resigned sadness that shouldn't be there.

It was all her fault. She had tried to protect him and it hadn't worked. To save herself, her independence and her dignity, she had removed his father from his life. That hadn't been fair. And she was about to do more.

'Leon darling, how would you like to go to England?'

His eyes lit up. 'A trip to London? See the Queen?'

‘A longish trip. They want me to work in England for a bit.’ For quite a while, in fact. Now that the end of her contracts with Luigi was in sight she had decided to talk with the London agent who had been calling her on and off for months. Luigi was positively encouraging and she knew he had found fresh talent he wanted time to nurture in his own inimitable way, though he hadn’t even hinted to her that he wanted her to move on. But she knew, and she pretended it was time to develop the kind of roles she could play. The money would be less to begin with but she’d be working with some interesting people. They’d mentioned James Mason and Stewart Grainger. The first film they wanted her to work on offered a months’ location in India. From Hollywood the furthest she’d been was the San Fernando Valley.

Leon’s face creased with worry. ‘If you’re working, what will I do all day?’

‘For a start, you’ll go to school.’ A good English prep school where he’d get rid of that American accent that was beginning to irritate her. ‘And we’ll take Isabella and Carlo if they want to come. They can look after you when you’re not at school.’

‘And Daddy?’ Then the eagerness and interest was wiped out of his face and his shoulders slumped. ‘Daddy won’t be coming, will he?’

‘Not with us.’ That was the best part of it. Rupert was firmly entrenched in the Hollywood scene at the moment. London would be out of his reach.

Pippa almost missed her mouth with the porridge as her eyes fixed onto the outside of Eleanor’s newspaper. Breakfasts were still silent, except for the regular clink of spoon in bowl and the intermittent rattle of paper being shaken into shape as pages were turned behind the phalanxes of print at each end of the table. But they had been more interesting since Eleanor had got married to Daddy last year, because Eleanor read the *Daily Express* and the best news was on the front page. Not like

Daddy's *Times,* which presented the most boring outside to anyone sitting on the wrong side of it. This morning's news in the *Express* was more interesting than usual, to Pippa anyway. She read the headline carefully, studied the photograph of a film star arriving at Claridge's Hotel, then gently kicked Danny under the table and nodded her head towards it. She couldn't stop the glow of excitement that began to spread up through her chest.

Danny read carefully, then gave a slow nod. She didn't smile, her eyes looked frightened. They couldn't talk about it now but there wasn't much to say. At last Mummy was back in England, and it was time to put Pippa's plan into action.

A little later, on the bus that took them to the Girls' High School in the town, Pippa dug out of her satchel the list she'd been carrying around with her for two years. It wasn't the self-same list that she and Danny had started when they first began to discuss the plan. It had been copied and re-copied a dozen times, as the seams worn by folding and unfolding had caused the sheet of exercise book paper to fall apart. The handwriting had changed, too, since the list was started. The rounded ten year old hand had developed with the writing of hundreds of pages of study notes and essays, and the mastery of English grammar, and now it reflected the budding confidence of a clever fourteen year old. There were some things Pippa hated about growing up, like breasts and periods, but she loved having beautiful, distinctive handwriting.

The list that they studied on the bus was in two parts. The first part consisted of things they must remember to take with them – telephone numbers, the cash they had saved and their post-office books. Balancing the paper on the back of her satchel Pippa added, 'picture from the Express'. Below that was a list of clothing, not too much because they would have to pack it into their satchels. They couldn't possibly risk taking suitcases out of the attic room where Peter and Eleanor kept that sort of thing. They'd already practised and knew they could get a spare pair of knickers, a change of socks, an extra cardigan and a nightdress into a satchel, together with a toothbrush and a hairbrush. The towels, the clean blouses, the dressing gowns they would have liked to take were still on the bed as they struggled to do up the straps.

'It doesn't matter, does it?' Danny said. 'Mummy will buy us what we need when we find her.'

'If she wants to see us.'

'I wish we knew for certain. Couldn't we ring up that hotel in London?'

'We could try. In the dinner hour. From the box in the square.' Pippa wasn't sure, though. What if it was true and Mummy really didn't want to see them? After all, she had Leon, and perhaps other children by now. What if she didn't even want to talk to them? That would be the end of it, no more point in dreaming about escaping from Brisewood, nothing to look forward to but her O Levels and then choosing a course at college. The headmistress at the High School had already asked her what career she was thinking about. The only thing she'd been able to think about as sounding worthy was training to be a nurse. The Headmistress had smiled and nodded and made a note on the paper in front of her and Pippa had thought that was settled. The rest of her life accounted for, unless she met someone nice to fall in love with and get married. She'd told Eleanor that was what she wanted to do. Eleanor had told Daddy and Daddy had got cross and said she'd be better occupied working for him at Brisewood now that he was headmaster. She'd be able to choose, teach the younger boys or work in the office, learn to do the typing and the accounts. So there was another good reason for running away. She'd done a bit of the office work already, in the holidays, and she hadn't been paid for it. When she'd asked he'd flown into a rage – a rage worse than just being grumpy and cross – and told her, not for the first time, that she was ungrateful and did she realise how much it cost him every year just to keep her in clothes and school books, and pay her school fees?

Two more stops to go and Pippa looked at the second part of the list. A timetable. 9.30, finish prep and go to bed, 12.30 get up and pack, 1am, out by the kitchen door, bikes from the bike shed, 4am arrive in Spalding. 6.30 am train to London.

They'd checked the time it would take them for the cycle ride several times that summer, when Eleanor had packed them a picnic and told them to get out from under her feet. 'I'll ring up and double check the bus and train times today,' Pippa said, folding the list and putting it away. She stood up and steadied herself as she reached for the request stop bell. Several other girls in the green High School uniform were moving out of their seats. The conductor smiled at them all as they made their way onto the platform as the bus drew to a halt. Danny smiled back but Pippa was wondering if it wouldn't have been better to have brought their money and to go straight to the station and get on the first London train instead of going to school .

But no. As soon as the register was called, someone would ask questions if they weren't there. The other girls would say they'd seen them on the bus. The Headmistress would phone Daddy. He might call the police and they'd be taken off the train at the first stop. The way they'd planned it they could be nearly in London before anyone started to look for them.

She felt a little thrill of excitement.

This was more than being naughty, more than flaring up and being rude to the grown-ups the way they sometimes were. This was a big adventure, once they started there would be no turning back. If they were caught it wouldn't just be a matter of getting the cane, having their pocket money stopped, being made to do the washing up for a week. This time the police would be involved, lawyers. She knew they wouldn't be actually arrested because they didn't arrest children, but they might be taken to a police station. Daddy might get into trouble for not looking after them properly. He might even get into trouble for taking them away from Mummy on that holiday years ago, when he wasn't supposed to keep them.

Suddenly she wondered if he might get arrested. And she wasn't sure if she wanted that to happen. For sure it would mean that he couldn't keep them but supposing it was true that Mummy didn't want them either. What would happen to them then? Where would they go? Would granny Price look after them? They hadn't heard from her for ages.

As she thought about all this her knees went wobbly. It was all going to be much more serious and complicated than she'd realised. Perhaps it would be better not to do anything, to accept that they lived with Daddy and Eleanor and couldn't see Mummy any more. Perhaps they should give in. But she couldn't say anything to Danny because they were going through the school gates surrounded by other girls, laughing and talking about their ponies and their homework. And by breaktime, when they could talk, she had put thought of failure from her mind, decided that giving up was a cowardly thing to do. It would be taking the easy way out, which wasn't what people did who were worth anything. Or so they had been teaching her at the High School.

The easy way out seemed very appealing in the early hours of the morning when she and Pippa were toiling along the road to Spalding on their bicycles and it began to rain. They were wearing their gabardine macs but these didn't keep their feet and legs dry. As the stinging drops blew into their faces, each of them in turn thought of giving up and going back home, but kept on going so as not to let the other down. They had been planning this for so long. They had talked about finding Mummy for so many dark, miserable nights after days when Daddy had been particularly cross and critical, or Eleanor had called them little madams for wanting their own way about what they ate or what kind of clothes they wore. She did that a lot, usually starting with 'If only you knew....'

But she never did tell them what it was that would be sure to change the way they behaved if only they knew about it. Remembering all this they couldn't possibly give up just because it had started to rain while they were on their way to catch the train.

As they came near to the town a big rattling lorry overtook them, loaded with sacks of something. It screeched to a stop behind Danny, hooted, then pulled out and the spray splashed their clothes. Pippa wobbled frantically as it whooshed past them, then put a foot on the ground to steady herself, waiting for Danny to catch up. Ahead of them on the road the lorry pulled up and the driver jumped down from the cab.

'All right?' Pippa asked Danny.

'Yes.' There was the hint of a choke in Danny's voice. Pippa felt her stomach churning as the man walked back towards them along the dark stretch of road. What was going to happen now?

She gathered her courage. 'It's okay,' she called out. 'We're perfectly all right, thank you.'

'I didn't see your lights.' The man's voice sounded kindly, concerned as he came into the faint beam of their front lights. 'Very faint, they are, in this rain. I was afraid I'd knocked one of you off.'

'No, we're all right, really we are.'

He stood for a moment, staring at them, at their expensive gabardine coats and the bulging satchels stuffed into their bicycle baskets. His face was quite young. 'If you don't mind my saying so, how can you be all right when you're cycling along a dark road in the rain in the middle of the night? Who's supposed to be looking after you?'

'I'm fifteen,' lied Pippa. 'I can look after myself, and my sister.'

'Seems irregular to me. My mum would go spare if she thought my sisters were out in this on their own.'

Pippa was worried that the driver might take it into his head to tell the police they were wandering around by themselves. How could she persuade him that what they were doing was allowed? She wondered if the truth would do the trick. 'Actually, it's our mother we're on our way to see. She lives in London and we have to catch the early train from Spalding. It's all been arranged.'

He hesitated another moment, then shrugged, deciding it was none of his business. All right then. Take care.' To Pippa's relief he began to walk away. Pippa leaned forward and adjusted her light. It was getting very dim. The battery must be running out. Danny swung her pedals round and pushed off, then she wobbled and stopped, leaned forward and poked at her front tyre.

'I've got a puncture,' she said in a small, defeated voice.

'Oh damn!' Pippa thought quickly. The driver was about to climb back into his lorry. 'Hey!' she shouted, speeding forward on her bike.

He stopped, waited for her, and her heart flooded with relief as she braked beside him. 'Excuse me,' she said, 'But my sister's got a puncture. You couldn't give us a lift to the railway station, could you?'

He looked surprised, then nodded. 'Yeh. Alright. Get in.' Enormously relieved, Pippa called to Danny, 'It's all right, he'll give us a lift.'

Danny began to wheel her bike forward. Pippa unstrapped her satchel from her basket and the driver clutched her bike in his two enormous hands, carried it round to the back of the lorry and threw it inside over the tailboard. Then he took Danny's bike and did the same after she'd extricated her satchel.

Inside the warm dry cab of the lorry Pippa somehow felt safe as it began to rattle and bump its way along the road, the big engine roaring in front of them. She knew they weren't really safe at all – in adventure stories chance meetings like this sometimes wrecked a whole carefully-laid plot, and their situation was no different. But for a few miles someone else was in charge of things.

'We really are most terribly grateful,' she said to the driver.

'Oh-ar?' he said. 'I were right worried about leaving you there in the rain.'

'What's your name?' she asked.

'Robert.'

'We're pleased to meet you. My name's Pippa and my sister is Danny.'

'Danny?' said Robert. 'That's a boy's name.'

'Short for Daniella,' said Danny. 'I don't know why. Mummy said it seemed like a good name at the time.'

'That's your ma you're going to meet in London.'

'That's right. She staying at Claridge's. We haven't seen her for a long time. She's been living in America.' At that, Pippa gave Danny a little tap with her foot so that she wouldn't give any more away. Robert probably wouldn't believe them anyway.

'Seems funny, sending you off like that in the middle of the night to catch a train. Tell you what, why don't I give you a lift all the way?'

'All the way to London? Is that where you're going?'

'Yup. I'm taking these spuds to Covent Garden. Should be there by six.'

Pippa glanced at Danny in the light of the dashboard and could see the big, hopeful pleading eyes turned in her direction. It would certainly be easier and more comfortable just to stay where they were.

'It's very kind of you, Robert.' she said. 'We could pay you something towards it. We have our rail fares with us.'

'Don't worry about that. It's nice to have some company. You can entertain me with more fairy tales on the way. I bet I know the real truth. You've been sent to some posh boarding school and they're feeding you on bread and water and you want to escape. Is that it?'

It was raining in London too. Candy looked out of the heavily curtained window and remembered the Californian sunshine. Why had this ever seemed like a good idea? London was bright and exciting enough at night, with the lights of the West End never far away, but during the day it was drab and uninviting. And frightening too, as she'd learned yesterday.

She listened to a man talking on the phone. Rick was one of the security team she'd hired through an agency, mainly to protect Leon from Rupert. Candy wasn't at all sure how good any of them were at their job. They hadn't stopped the reporters taking photographs when she'd arrived at the airport, and printing reports of where she was staying. And where had Rick been when she came out of Harrods yesterday with Isabella and

Leon and those press reporters and photographers swooped on them while they were waiting for a taxi? She'd immediately screamed and dragged Leon away inside the store again and asked the doorman to call the police. They'd all accused her of over-reacting but they had no idea of how terrified she was of losing Leon. It had taken an hour to calm her down and to reunite her with Isabella and Rick, who swore he'd only been standing feet away from her. The studio publicity people weren't very helpful either. Candy had nearly hit the young woman who'd come round to the hotel in the evening and insisted that she shouldn't keep her whereabouts a secret from her fans, because it was good for the picture if they knew all about what she was doing.

'The only thing that's good for the picture is to make it well, so that everyone wants to come and see it,' she snapped.

'Even a good picture won't make much money if the fans aren't interested. We have to encourage them.'

'Not to snoop on my private life or put my son in danger.'

The woman had shaken her head, a pitying look in her eyes, implying that Candy just didn't understand the situation. Candy remembered back to the days working the production office at Shepperton and decided that she understood only too well. Which was why Rick was on the phone at this moment, making reservations in another, less conspicuous hotel, and Isabella was in the adjoining room packing Leon's things. Leon stood beside Candy, looking gloomily at the wet street and the streams of dark-clad people getting on and off the red buses. Her arm was on his shoulder. 'Does it always rain here?' he asked.

'No, of course not. It can be absolutely beautiful.' But she wasn't sure any more. Was that really true? Had she just remembered it wrong?

Leon was silent for a moment, staring at the rain on the window pane. Clearly he wasn't sure whether to believe her or not. Then he complained, 'I hate living in hotels, Mom. You didn't tell me we'd be in a hotel all the time.'

'We've only been here a few days. I intend to buy us a house.' As soon as she could safely leave him with Isabella without risk of reporters or autograph hunters bothering them, she would start looking. She'd already contacted a number of estate agents. There were plenty of suitable houses she could afford once she'd made up her mind whether they would be better off living in town or the country.

'Can I help you choose it?'

'Sure. And your new school when we decide where we're going to be.'

'School? Ugh!'

Rick put down the phone and Candy turned. 'That's all arranged, Madam,' he said, sounding certain and efficient. 'Bookings at White's and a car will be here at twelve, at the side entrance.'

'Nothing conspicuous?'

'No, a green Rover. We'll take your bags separately. Shall I notify the studio people?'

'Not yet. Leave that till we're settled in. But tell the desk to stall any autograph hunters until we've gone. Not to tell them we're going, just to ask them to wait until after we've left.'

'Very well. And I've arranged for two of us to be on duty, just to be on the safe side. Terry will be here at eleven. He's an ex-Royal Marine.'

'Are you sure this is the place?'

Satchels slung over their shoulders, leaning on the handlebars of their bikes, Pippa and Danny stared up at the front edifice of Claridge's Hotel. The uniformed doorman who stood on the pavement immediately in front of the entrance regarded them with suspicion out of the corner of his eye as he greeted guests and signaled to taxis. They didn't look like hotel guests, with their lumpy clothes and flat lace-up shoes, and particularly with those bicycles. Nobody who had any right of entry arrived at Claridge's on a bicycle. But they didn't look like office girls either, the type who hung around to catch a glimpse of the famous, rush forward and stick autograph books under their noses.

After some minutes of hesitation the girls made up their minds. They wheeled their cycles to one side of the big entrance door and leaned them carefully against the facade, then turned towards the door.

The doorman barred their way. 'I'm sorry Miss,' he said, trying to sound respectful just in case they turned out to be somebody important, 'But you can't leave those there.'

'Where can we leave them?'

'Do you have business in the hotel?'

A moment's hesitation. 'Yes, we have to meet our mother.'

Ah, that seemed reasonable. Now he could place them. Boarding school girls. They might well have parents who were guests in the hotel. Better be nice to them.

'You can put them a little more out of the way, Miss, around the corner there.'

'All right. Thank you.'

He turned his attention to a taxi pulling up at the kerb, but still half-watched as they re-parked their bikes and made their way through the door, the bigger girl ushering the little one in front of her. There was something about them that didn't quite fit in. They looked vaguely bedraggled, like those cartoon schoolgirls. Still, even if he'd got it wrong and should have kept them out, it wasn't as though they could do any harm, like assassins or kidnappers.

Pippa marched up to the reception desk with as much confidence as she could muster. She felt dreadfully tired after the long, uncomfortable journey. The bacon sandwiches and cup of tea in Covent Garden had revived them after Robert helped them to repair Danny's puncture but after that the cycle ride through the dismal early morning rain had been nerve-wracking. Cars and taxis and buses had left them little room and a constant stream of spray had been splashed in their faces. It felt so dangerous that after a few streets they had walked most of the way, pushing their bikes. It had taken hours. Now that they were actually at the hotel, actually close to finding Mummy at last, they were both ready to collapse.

But they had to keep going just a bit longer. Just a little bit longer.

'Can I help you?' asked the bespectacled, black-suited, middle-aged receptionist with the hair drawn back into a tight bun.

'Yes. We want to see Candy Price. Can you tell us her room number, please?'

The receptionist glanced sideways at the morning-coated man who stood beside her. Then she looked Pippa up and down slowly, with what felt to Pippa like contempt. 'Is she expecting you?'

'Oh yes,' Pippa lied, smiling as brightly as she could. 'She said just to ask for her when we arrived.'

'Yes. Very well. If you'll wait in that lounge through there, I'll tell her you're waiting for her. What name shall I say?'

'Tell her Pippa and Danny are here.'

'Very well. Over there, please.'

Wearily, feet dragging a little, they trailed off to the side lounge. There were a few other people sitting around there, and a pile of newspapers on a table. Pippa picked up two of them and passed one to Danny. 'See if there's anything about us in them,' she hissed. 'I expect Daddy's called the police by now.' They looked, shuffling as best they could through the large pages, but they couldn't find anything about two missing schoolgirls.

'I expect it's too early,' suggested Danny. 'He wouldn't have known till breakfast time.'

Pippa refolded the newspapers and put them back on the table. 'She taking a long time.' Expectant excitement was mingling with a strong sense of disappointment. She had thought they could go straight up in the lift, knock on the door of Mummy's room, fling themselves into her waiting arms, at last be looked after by someone who cared about them.

'Perhaps they've forgotten about us,' Danny said in a small voice. Pippa could see that she was feeling the disappointment too. Her lip was trembling.

'I'll go and ask again.' Pippa got up and went to the reception desk. The woman with the glasses wasn't there but the same man stood at the desk dealing with a guest, a tall woman wearing a full length fur coat. When she had finished her business and turned away Pippa said, 'Excuse me, but have you told Candy Price that we're here?'

'Yes, Miss. She knows. There are several people waiting to see her.'

'But we're special. We're....'

His lip curled in a supercilious smile. 'They're all special, Miss.'

Pippa's disappointment mounted. She went back to Danny and sat down. 'Don't worry,' she said, trying to sound confident. 'We will see her soon.'

'The car's here.' Rick put down the phone. 'Everyone ready?'

Candy picked up her coat. Isabella helped Leon to shrug into his bomber jacket, then put on her own coat, a new Harris tweed from Harrods. Rick and Terry picked up black Hombergs and umbrellas and cast their professional eyes over their charges.

'You have checked, haven't you?' Candy asked anxiously.

'Yes Madam,' Terry said. 'I was down there a few moments ago. There are a couple of reporters and a few autograph hunters but they're all sitting in a side lounge. You'll be past them before they know you're out of the lift.'

Rick opened the door, glanced up and down the corridor, then led the way along to the main lifts. Candy followed him, then came Isabella holding Leon's hand, then Terry at the rear. As the lift doors swished shut, Candy found that her knees were trembling. The scene the day before outside Harrods had shaken her more than she'd realised at the time. It wasn't that she minded being gawped at, that was part of the job. It was simply that when people rushed at them she couldn't tell who was who,

who meant harm and who was just being friendly. In the lift she smiled nervously at Isabella, then grasped Leon's other hand. The lift trundled down, the doors opened, Rick stepped out. He looked around quickly, then motioned Candy to follow him and set out across the wide entrance foyer, umbrella at the ready.

'There she is!'

The exclamation came from somewhere to their left, from the side lounge. A dozen or more people came quickly to their feet and hurried forward, faces alight with recognition. Candy glanced wide-eyed in their direction, then hurried towards the door as Rick and Terry closed ranks, umbrellas held at waist height as weapons, already prodding people back. A hall porter jumped forward to open the side door and a moment later the film star, her son, his nurse and their bodyguards were outside and bundling into a large green Rover car that was parked beside the pavement, engine running.

'I'm sorry, Isabella.' Candy gasped as the engine purred and they pulled away. 'I promise it won't always be like this. We'll soon get settled and when I start work the novelty will wear off.'

Isabella shrugged and smiled. As far as she was concerned, it was all part of the excitement of working for a film star. She had long ago accepted that strange things were going to happen. She stared out of the window at the shop fronts going past and wondered if Candy had noticed. Probably not. Better not to mention it, because it had only been a fleeting glimpse, a face amongst the many that had pushed forward, a child who had reminded Isabella of the little girl Pippa. But it wouldn't be Pippa because Pippa would be a teenager by now, almost a young woman, not a little girl. She wouldn't look anything like Isabella remembered. It had been years. In fact, it was quite likely that even Candy wouldn't recognise her own children any more.

When all the fuss had died down, Pippa and Danny sat at separate ends of the large settee and sobbed into their handkerchiefs, each of them sunk in her own private pit of misery. Nobody took any notice of them, nobody listened. Eyes were politely averted, though one or two embarrassed glances were exchanged.

She looked right at us! Pippa thought to herself, over and over again. She looked at us and walked past and let those men push us away with their umbrellas! She felt ugly and crumpled and rejected. The safety net in her world had fallen away and left her with nothing to hope for or look forward to. She knew that Danny was hurting as much as she was but she couldn't bear to move along and comfort her, she couldn't bear Danny to know how awful she felt. She was the one who'd planned all this, she'd been so sure it would work out, now Danny would accuse her of getting them both into trouble, and Danny would be right. She'd been a fool, led her little sister astray. And, worst of all, Danny might ask her what they were going to do next, and she didn't know.

Her misery was so raw that she no longer noticed her surroundings and she didn't see the couple who came through the door and went to the reception desk, then wandered across the foyer towards the side lounge. She didn't even notice when they stopped in front of the settee, looking down at her and Danny. It took several more heaving sobs for her to be aware of them standing there, and for her swollen eyes to focus on their legs, his in grey flannels with well-polished brown brogues, cut with patterns of little holes, hers with lisle stockings and medium-heeled, navy blue lace-up shoes.

Feet she knew so well.

She raised her face slowly and met the mocking look in her father's grey eyes.

'Hello, Pippa,' he said, in a voice that sent a chill through her because she knew now that there was no escape from it. 'We thought we might find you here. I take it you've had a disappointment. Are you both ready to come back home with us?'

'It's gone!' Pippa was sitting on the floor of their shared bedroom surrounded by the contents of her private cupboard, where she kept her diary, her book of poems – and her scrapbook of *Picture Show* cuttings about Candy.

Which wasn't there any more.

She was weeping quietly, but she'd hardly stopped all the way back in the train, sitting opposite Daddy and Eleanor who'd buried themselves behind their newspapers and said nothing. Now she turned and looked over her shoulder at Danny who was carefully taking off her dirty socks.

'It's all your fault,' Danny said. 'What will we do without our pocket money for a whole year?'

'What does that matter? They've been through my things and taken my scrapbook. It's not fair!'

'Were you going to keep it after she didn't want to see us?'

'Yes, of course.'

'I can't see why. What's the point?'

'The point is...' Pippa paused. What was the point? Daddy had been right all along. Mummy didn't want them, she didn't love them and she would never talk to them again. But without the scrapbook there weren't even any pictures to look at, to remind herself. There was nothing, just an empty space at the bottom of her life.

And if they'd been through her things and found the scrapbook, they must have looked at her diary and her poems. Must have read it all.

Pippa blanched, first with embarrassment because she knew the poetry wasn't very good. It was all about her feelings and some of it didn't even rhyme. The diary wasn't so bad because it was mostly about books she'd been reading. But after the embarrassment came a fierce shame. They had looked into her most private places and judged her. And they had confiscated a part of her life. It made her feel dirty in a way she'd never experienced before.

* * *

In an apartment in Beirut where the Fahy family had lived in comparative safety ever since they had left Palestine, a grey-haired Leila Fahy was turning over the pages of some English newspapers she had been hoarding for several days. In each newspaper she came across photographs and news reports that made her smile with satisfaction as she wielded her large pair of dressmaking scissors and clipped round the items she wanted. When she was sure there was nothing more of interest in the papers she laid them to one side and drew a chair from the table to stand alongside a heavy teak dresser that stood against the wall. Balancing precariously on the chair she reached down a battered grey cardboard box from the very top of the dresser and laid it on the table. Inside the box was a collection consisting of several brown envelopes, and half a dozen bulging and mis-shapen school exercise books that were full of scraps of newspaper reports, and dated passages hand-written in Arabic, as though they were a diary, though there was no continuity between the dates. Leila lifted all these out, selected one of the exercise books, and began to glue onto its pages the pieces she had just cut out of the newspapers. She smoothed them down, then dated each entry, then peered closely at the photographs that were attached to the news reports, running a forefinger across the features of Candy Price and trying to still a knot of regret that always gathered in her heart when she looked in this box.

Poor child!

She hadn't been a bad girl and what happened hadn't been her fault. She had been caught up in events that were too big for her, as they all had. Leila wondered, did she still think of Naseem, the one she had loved? Or had she loved too many others since? What would she do now if she knew about the other Naseem, the young man who was her true first-born son?

She let the thoughts sit in her mind for a few minutes, then she shook her head and took out her pen and wrote across the top of the last page she had used, *CANDY THE FILM STAR COMES BACK TO LONDON – May 1957.* Then while she waited for the glue to dry properly, she checked the contents of the envelopes – a death certificate and a birth certificate, both in the name of Naseem Fahy, but the dates made it obvious they weren't for the same person because the oldest of the two had died before the youngest was born – a bit of basic arithmetic showed that the dead man must have been the father of the younger one, but to be sure that nobody missed the point, Leila had explained it in detail in the first of the exercise books.

She was just putting the books back into the box when her brother Hanif came bustling into the room and before she could hide what she was doing, he was looking over her shoulder, flicking through the pages of one of the books. Laying a gentle hand on her shoulder he said, 'I don't know why you keep all that rubbish, sister. What good can it do?'

She turned away and continued to pack the box. 'You know what I have said. He may need to know one day, and that day may be when neither of us is around any longer to explain to him the truth.'

'Will it matter? '

'It will to him. Think, he will be of age within two years and he has a right to know who brought him into this world and why.' The box was packed now and Leila laid her hands on it and waited for Hanif to offer to return it to its perch for her. He picked it up, gave her another exasperated look and climbed laboriously onto the chair, still grumbling.

When he got down to floor level again, Leila looked him steadily in the eye. 'Don't forget, Hanif. I know you Fahy men. You seem so respectable but all the while you are hatching other plans. But Naseem may not want to spend his life as a soldier or an exiled person with no state. He should know that he has a choice. You promised me. You promised years ago that when I have gone he will have the box. Before you make him do anything else he will have the whole truth, so that he has a past to guide his future. Promise me again?'

'Of course, I promise.' He smiled at her then,

indulgently, and kissed her cheek before putting the chair back in its place by the table. Of course he would carry out her wishes. He just didn't see that it would make any difference to Naseem's life here in Beirut. 'Anyway, sister, I will probably go before you do.'

He was wrong. Only a few months later Leila was in her coffin. Struggling up the stairs with her shopping once too often, her stout heart finally gave out. She might have been saved if someone had attended to her right away but she lay on the steps for two hours before Hanif came home and found her, and by then it was too late.

Hanif didn't forget about the box and his promise to Leila, but it took him weeks before he could sufficiently overcome his grief to sit down with his great nephew and tell him the truth about his mother. Naseem was bewildered, wondering why nobody had told him this before, when he was a small boy and had asked why he lived with his grandmother. He thanked his uncle politely and took the box away and began to study its contents bit by bit each evening. Leila's notes were easy enough to decipher but the cuttings from English newspapers were a challenge because English wasn't his first language and he had never been keen to study it at school. The story that emerged was, in his mind, too strange to be true, yet why would they lie to him? And even if it was true, what difference should it make to him now that he knew about it? He would soon be enrolling at the university because he knew the family hoped he would become an engineer or a teacher. Sometimes, when they all sat around the big table on the terrace after the evening meal, they talked about going back to Palestine, but it all sounded very insecure and Naseem believed he would probably spend the rest of his life as an exile in Beirut. So why had Leila taken so much trouble, assembling the evidence about his mother? What use could it possibly be?

It took a while for him to realise that perhaps Leila wanted him to go to England one day to find his mother. Even then, he wasn't sure why.

*   *   *

Leon hated London. He hated the cold and the rain, the dirty streets, the noisy traffic, the kind of clothes his mother made him wear, the stuffy school she sent him to, and most of he hated the fact that his father wasn't there.

He hated, too, the big house his mother had bought in London. She'd said he could help her choose it but when it came to the point he just tagged along with Isabella after his mother had already made up her mind. She took no notice of his protests that it had too many stairs, just seemed to go up and up instead of spreading out across the hillside like their house in Beverly Hills. And it had no swimming pool and no basketball pitch. She just kept saying that this was London and they couldn't expect it to be the same as California. This was where they belonged and he'd soon get used to it.

8
JEREMY

Conscious of the fact that today his public role as Earl of Penmore was about as important as it could be, Jeremy sat upright, his shoulders held rigidly back, in the front pew of Northelm Church. Beside him sat Meggie, hair immaculately topped by a small black straw hat - he was thankful she hadn't chosen one of those silly plumed things that women seemed to be wearing these days. On the far side of Meggie sat his sons, Tatton and Charles, both looking very proper and not at all the rebellious younger generation he had been afraid they might want to play at being today. They were stern-faced, dry-eyed. They had known their grandmother well, she had been a part of their growing up, but they didn't seem able to connect the old lady to the remains they were burying today. Jeremy reminded himself that when their grandmother Hargreaves had died they had been deemed too young to attend a funeral so this was the first family funeral they had experienced and they must be feeling very unsure of themselves.

Jeremy risked a glance to his left, to the plain oak coffin that stood on a trolley before the altar, totally covered by a huge, tasteful spray of lilies, carnations and cream roses. The coffin was full size – he had insisted on that – even though it didn't actually contain a body, as such, just a jigsaw arrangement of limbs and pieces of clothing. Everyone had been very understanding about this. The only person who had been insensitive enough to ask to see their mother's body had been the stern-faced little fat nun who had arrived on the mid morning train and who had appeared to have difficulty understanding what a body might look like that had caught the full blast of an explosion. When she finally grasped what he was saying, she asked, 'How do you know you haven't got bits of other people in there as well?'

It was a long time since he had seen the younger of his two sisters. He was acutely aware of her sitting in the pew behind him, smelling of a mixture of camphor and unwashed underwear, murmuring to herself as she passed a rosary endlessly through her fingers. When had they last met? He had probably been no more than a toddler. She certainly hadn't been at the rock concert, which was the last time he had seen Pippa. Or Leon for that matter.

Pippa sat at the far end of the same pew as the nun. Jeremy hadn't missed the way Danny drew away from Pippa's arm when they greeted each other outside the church, as though to be touched by her sister might contaminate her soul. There was no sign of Leon, who had said he would walk down from the house and was probably swanning around somewhere outside, signing autographs, avoiding seeing Pippa until the very last moment. And what about Naseem? Jeremy was expecting him to turn up but he had no idea of the outcome of that trip he had made to Israel.

A sudden commotion at the church door forced Jeremy to look around, and over the heads of the assembled villagers and county dignitaries he caught a glimpse of Leon's head, long hair scraped back into a bunch at the nape of his neck, as he bent to help an old lady who was hobbling on very high heels, wearing a mink coat over an unsuitable and ill-fitting blue shot-silk evening dress. Her slurred, querulous voice was clearly audible over the soft organ music. 'All I ask, dear boy, is that you show me to a seat where I've got a good *view!*'

'My God!' muttered Jeremy, 'Isn't that...?'

'Aunt Netta! I hoped she'd given up the idea of coming. How the hell did she get here?'

* * *

Emerging from her taxi outside the house in Curzon Street after yet another mammoth expedition through Selfridges shopping for her new home, Candy was surprised to see another taxi in the road outside the house, just waiting. There was something menacing about it because she couldn't see who was inside. As she came closer, the passenger door opened and two women got out, one about her own age, one older. There was something familiar about the older woman but Candy couldn't place her. Someone she'd met working in London before she married Rupert?

A husky voice drifted towards her as the older woman came forward. 'There you are! It *is* Candy, isn't it? My goodness, it's been hard to find you.' An outstretched hand clutched at Candy's arm.

Candy drew back, hesitating, half-recognising the tones of the voice, half unable to comprehend what she was hearing.

The voice became more insistent. 'Candy! It's me! Surely you recognise your own mother!'

'Mummy?' Something cold was clutching at Candy's heart. She turned her face towards the younger woman. 'Netta?'

'Yes, darling, it's us. Aren't you pleased to se us?' And then, as the front door of the taxi opened and the driver clambered out, 'Can you pay this taxi for us, darling? And then what about a cup of tea?'

In a daze, still not fully grasping what was happening, Candy did as she was bidden and let them all into the house, leading the way into the newly-decorated drawing room, its tall windows overlooking the street. Maddie lit a cigarette and settled back in a pale brocade armchair, gazing critically around her. Netta perched on the edge of another chair. She wasn't at all comfortable, her eyes darting around and not meeting Candy's, as though she wished she were anywhere else but here in the home of this stranger who had once been her sister. Their clothes were shabby; they both wore out-of-date tailor-made navy blue tweed suits, though Maddie had made the effort of pinning a bunch of artificial cherries to the lapel of her jacket.

'I'll get some tea,' Candy muttered, wondering whether it was a good idea to make any welcoming gesture. She was still stunned. What nightmare had these two come from, transporting her back into another time when she was another person, bullied, unsure of herself, frightened? She wanted to know what they were doing here but most of all she wanted to know when they would be going and how she could make sure they never visited her again.

'It wasn't easy to track you down, I can tell you,' Maddie was saying. 'We saw those pictures in the paper about you coming back to England and I just knew it was you. I said to Netta, didn't I darling, I said, that looks just like your sister Candy. We must find her and make sure she's all right. Didn't I, darling...?' Netta stared at the ceiling, then out of the window, then at the pale blue carpet. 'But you've no idea how difficult it was to get your address out of that film studio. So stubborn, they are, those offices, but finally I persuaded some little secretary to tell me...'

Wait till I find out who, thought Candy.

'...and aren't you pleased to see us darling?'

No, not at all pleased. Why was that? Slowly, accusingly, Candy said, 'You left me all alone.'

'Nonsense, darling. We left you in the care of the nuns. It was the only thing we could do in the circumstances. I see you've risen above it all now.'

'You meant me to stay there. For the rest of my life.'

'Not at all. We were coming back for you after our leave. It wasn't my fault a war broke out.'

'Father meant me to stay there. He sent a letter.'

Maddie waved a hand in a vague gesture of negated responsibility. 'What your father did was nothing to do with me. He behaved abominably. He refused to pay our fares back from the States after the war and he filed for divorce for desertion in my absence. I couldn't defend myself, or ask for maintenance. When I got back I found him married to some floozie and completely unrepentant about leaving us penniless.'

Candy remembered the woman who'd been with her father in Tite Street. Was she the one he'd married, or one of many he hadn't? She glanced at Netta and saw a rich crimson blush stealing up her sister's neck. Suddenly she felt sympathy for Netta, wondering if she might tell events in a different way. Maddie's gaze was going around the room as she shied away from the subject. 'Anyway, darling, you've got a nice big house here. How many bedrooms?'

'You can't stay here.' Candy had thought she was shocked enough but this was worse.

'Oh, darling, I didn't mean that. We have a nice little flat in Earl's Court, don't we, Netta? But since you're obviously so well off, we could do with some help with the rent.'

Candy glanced at Netta again but her sister was still looking at the floor. She hadn't spoken a word except please and thank you since she'd come into the house. Candy went to her handbag, that she'd put on the window seat when they came in. She took out her cheque book and a fountain pen, sat down at the little mahogany bureau.

'How much?' she asked. 'How much do you need to go away and look after yourselves somewhere else?'

A spark of hope came into Netta's eyes as she looked up but once again it was Maddie who spoke. 'Darling, how crude! Well, yes, don't let me stop you writing out a cheque – how about a thousand? But that's not the idea. The reason I've brought Netta here is for you to find her a husband. You must have so many smart contacts. Didn't I see a photograph of you with Princess Margaret in some magazine? Perhaps you could take Netta under your wing and introduce her around.'

'What?'

'She's looked after me ever since she left school, never had any social training, no chance to find a decent husband. But you're well-connected now, you know people with money, don't you? You can make sure she meets the right sort.'

Netta raised her eyes and spoke for the first time. Her voice had a slight American twang. 'Mummy...I...I told you. This isn't necessary.'

'Nor is it possible.' What did Maddie think she could do? Introduce Netta to some of the Hollywood jetset? Had she any idea what happened to young girls with stars in their eyes who competed for the attention of the rich and famous? Stars between their legs was all they got. And Netta wasn't even pretty, thought she did have a frailty about her that some men might find attractive.

Maddie sank back into the armchair, a hand on her chest.

Her face was pale. 'It has to be, darlings. I've done all I can for her but I have to hand over to you, Candy. You see, I've got a heart problem. I might go at any time. The last doctor I saw gave me six months...'

'It's true,' said Netta as Candy glanced from one to another in disbelief, her pen still poised above her cheque book. 'She's had a couple of heart attacks already. It was pretty frightening.'

Candy sighed, signing the cheque and handing it to Maddie. Once she would have given in to this emotional blackmail but she no longer saw herself as to blame for everything that went wrong for the people around her. The girl they had left in Palestine was just that – someone left behind. She was able to ask herself what Maddie had ever done for her and the honest answer was nothing. Nothing at all.

Nor had Netta, of course, but Netta could at least benefit from some help. She could make an effort for Netta. Give her a means of escaping from the drudgery of being Maddie's permanent companion.

'Listen, Netta. What I can do for you is to pay for you to go to a secretarial college for a few months so you can get a decent job. How about it?'

'You mean go out to work in some dreary office?' Indignation made her come to life.

'That's exactly what I mean. Don't you realise, dreary offices are usually full of men?'

'You selfish cow!' Netta's face turned a different kind of red this time as she stamped a foot and practically spat at Candy. 'You've got all this…' with a sweep of her hand '…and all you can think of for me is to be some bloke's secretary for ten quid a week!'

'Take it or leave it. It's more than I started with when I got back here during the war...'

With a cold panic closing around her, Candy could hear *Wait for me!* echoing in her ears once more. She struggled with the dislike that was rapidly growing in her heart. When she'd been a child she hadn't cared for Netta's enforced company very much but then she had known it was her fault; sisters were supposed to love and look after each other and if she couldn't love Netta it was because she was being a selfish big sister. Now that it was happening all over again, she couldn't see that she should be in any way to blame for the fact that Netta didn't know how to earn her living.

'There you go, feeling sorry for yourself,' murmured Maddie. 'You don't know how lucky you've been, Candy. I think you should share what you've got with your sister.'

'Candy, Candy darling, there you are! Can I borrow this dress?'

Candy shrank at the sound of Netta's voice, accosting her even before she came through the front door. It was becoming regular practice for Netta to stop over at the Curzon Street House on her way home from her Foreign Office secretarial job and get changed for her evening out. Candy endured it with good grace. How would she have felt if she'd been forced to have young men picking her up at the shabby bedsitter that was what the 'flat in Earl's Court' turned out to be? Far more impressive to give out the Curzon Street address, and more economical to shower here and use Candy's soap and perfume.

But tonight Candy was very tired and as she took her keys out of the Yale lock and glanced up to the top of the stairs where Netta was standing, striking a pose like a model, encased in deep blue shot silk, something snapped.

'That's my Balmain! You've no right!' It was too much! Netta must have spent ages rifling through her wardrobe.

'You've only worn it once. It's not as though you ever go anywhere. Nobody will know!'

'Take it off at once!' Candy dropped her bags on the floor and started up the stairs at speed. She loved that frock. She would rather rip it up than see Netta wearing it to one of her diplomatic receptions. How did she get invited to them anyway, the smug little cow? She was only a shorthand typist yet she seemed to go to all the important places. Last weekend she'd been to some do at some big house in the country. There was only one answer that Candy could see and she was trying not to make a judgment. Netta must be sleeping around. But she wasn't going to do it in Candy's Balmain gown that she'd bought for the premier last month. She wasn't going to be fondled and felt up through that neckline, she wasn't going to have her knickers pulled down and somebody's sticky cock pushed into her under that lovely, expensive, hand-stitched skirt.

'Okay, okay you shirty cow!' Netta turned and ran into the spare bedroom she usually used to change in. She slammed the door and by the time Candy had reached it and pushed it open again her sister had already unzipped herself and shrugged out of the dress. It lay in crumpled folds around her on the floor. She stepped out of it and gathered it up and flung it at Candy.

'You are selfish!' she shrieked. 'You can easily afford another one. I've got nothing to wear!'

'I can see that.' Under the dress she had on only stockings and a suspender belt, confirming Candy's suspicions about the main objective of the evening.

'Haven't you anything you can lend me? It's an important reception. I can't let Tatton down.'

'Who's Tatton?'

'Oh, some viscount or other. I never can get it straight, they have so many different names. We're going to the Lebanese Embassy. His friend is aide to the ambassador. Come on, Candy, it was you who suggested I get to mix with the right people.'

'No it wasn't. I suggested you learn how to earn yourself a living. Mixing was mother's idea and I'm not sure she meant you to be so free about it. Here.' Candy relented and passed the frock back. It was true she could afford another model next time she needed one and she didn't think she'd feel like wearing it again after this scene.

'Oh thanks! I'll take care of it, I promise.' Netta grabbed the dress and stepped into it, turning her back so that Candy could help her to hook it up. 'You're wrong about Mother disapproving, you know. She doesn't care what I do as long as I do it with the right people. And you can't get more right than the heir to an earldom.'

'Take my advice and put some knickers on,' Candy said as she turned away. 'You might catch cold.'

'Don't be so old-fashioned, Candy. This is London in the sixties. Everyone's doing it. Except you, of course.'

The last remark followed Candy as she stepped out into the passageway and closed the door just as Leon came hurtling up the stairs.

'Hey Mum, you're back! I thought I heard you. You didn't come and say hi to me first.'

'I'm sorry.' She swept him into her arms and kissed him before he remembered that the other chaps at school thought that nine-going-on-ten was too old to be kissed by your mother. As he pulled away she said, 'How's your prep going? Is supper ready? I'm starved.'

'I've done my prep. Honest, I have. It was Geography about North America and I already knew it. I did a good map, though. Want to see it?'

'Sure. Where is it? In your room? Hey, did you get in the football team for the weekend?'

'We don't know yet.' Together they climbed another flight of stairs to the floor where they both had study-bedrooms and she looked over his map, not only accurately drawn but enlivened with colourful illustrations of mountains and forests. He loved to draw pictures but she didn't make too much of it because she couldn't see a lot of future in being an artist. She wanted him to think about something straightforward and secure, like running a business. Being creative would do for his spare time.

While she was there with him she sat down and looked over his maths and English books – he had good marks in both. The only part of his school life he got poor reports for was games. Once, out shopping on a day she had no studio call, Candy had seen the crocodile of little boys in football shorts walking from the anonymous red brick school building in Hans Crescent towards Hyde Park. Curious, she had followed at a distance and watched for a while as they reached the park and changed into the leather boots they carried slung around their neck by the laces, then played a ragged game of rugby football under the direction of a rosy-faced young woman in a linen tunic and an elderly lady with strap shoes and a bun and a pleated tweed skirt. They both had whistles which they blew at random, with little relationship to the rules of the game as Candy understood them. Two or three of the boys who did seem to know the rules, repeatedly ignored the whistle and told the others what to do. The overall effect was genteel chaos.

As she watched, Candy reflected that she was paying quite a lot for this inexpert tuition. But she'd already known when she chose the school that it had no playing fields of its own and didn't concentrate much on sport. What she needed was a school that was convenient, within walking distance of where she'd bought her house, so that Isabella could easily take him and fetch him, and where he would have the experience of mixing with little boys who were going to grow up to be Englishmen. Soon, though, she would have to seriously consider sending him to a boarding school and there'd be plenty of time there for him to learn the rules of rugger.

She smiled up at him in the light of the Anglepoise lamp, then reached up a hand and ran her fingers through his tousled, golden brown hair. 'You're doing great.'

He leaned towards her. 'I just wish...'

'Wish what?'

'I try hard to remember to speak properly but they still tease me about my accent.'

'I thought we talked about all that. About how there's nothing wrong with being different.'

'Yeah, but I don't want to be different. When are we going home, Mom...Mummy?'

'Leon, darling, this is our home.'

'No it's not.' He shook his head and turned his face away, and she could see he was trying to hide tears that welled in his eyes. 'Home's back ...home...in Beverly Hills. I want to go back there. D'you realise, Mom, I haven't been swimming for ages?'

She put a finger against his cheek and turned his face towards her. She knew what he meant - the yearning for the sun, the red earth, the bright flowers. She'd known what expect when they came back to London and for her there were compensations. This house, for instance. How she'd loved buying and refurbishing it, lavishing money on it after the ravages of war, followed by years of neglect, had loosened its tiles and let in the damp and rotted the window frames. And the people she worked with – there was a buzz of creativity, of excitement, of faith in the future, as thought London had finally flung off the drab cloak of the war and decided to dance again. And she was part of it. But of course, Leon didn't have any of that. Leon was a young boy who found himself different from the other boys around him, who missed his Dad and missed his home in the sun.

'Leon, this is home. We're both English, not American. We had a wonderful time for a while in the States and sure, we may go back there when my contract here runs out, but for now this isn't a holiday. This is where we live.'

'Why is it so important, your contract? Why can't we go where we like?'

'Because I have to work to earn money to pay for so many things. Nobody else helps. It's all down to me, our clothes and food and your schooling and Isabella and Carlo's wages, and Granny and her flat - it all costs a lot of money. If I don't have contracts to go and film where people want me to, they'll find someone else to do the work and we'll have nothing.'

'Nothing?' Leon looked a little frightened and Candy's heart ached for him. He went on slowly, 'Most chaps at school have fathers who go to work and mothers who stay at home to look after them. Why can't we be the same?'

'Darling, why do you want to be the same as everyone else? You're different, special. Your parents are film stars and you've had the good fortune to spend the first years of your life in California. You'll never be the same as everyone else you meet. Why should you be? I love you the way you are. Learn to make the most of it.'

There were steps on the stairs and Isabella appeared at the door. 'You want to eat now or leave it till breakfast time?' she asked sharply, but laughing at the same time.

'I'm sorry.' Candy got to her feet. 'We got talking about Leon's school work. I'll just pick up my bags and wash, then I'll be with you.'

'I picked up your stuff off the stairs. I dish up in two minutes. Come and help me, Leon?'

She took the boy's hand and they went downstairs, easy in each other's company. Candy went through to her bathroom and washed, changed quickly from her worsted suit into slacks and a Viyella shirt, and started down the stairs. As she reached the last flight the front door bell rang and Netta came quickly out of the drawing room and opened it. She was wearing the Balmain dress and a short fur jacket that Candy had never seen before. She noticed Candy standing there, blushed, then said to the person standing on the doorstep, 'Hello, Tatts. You're bang on time. I'm all ready.'

Curious, Candy said, 'Why don't you ask Tatton in for a drink, Netta?'

'Oh, I don't think we've got time....'

'That's very civil of you,' the young man said. He stepped over the doorstep and looked from one sister to the other, raising a quizzical eyebrow that invited an introduction.

'If you're sure...' Netta hurriedly closed the door behind him. 'Candy, this is Tatton, or perhaps I should say, Lord Tatton Thingummy, Thingummy, Viscount North-something. Tatts, this is my sister, Candy Price.'

Candy found herself looking down into an adoring pair of blue eyes set in a round, fleshy face topped by unruly golden curls. 'I'm...I'm...I'm charmed to meet you,' he stammered, bowing his head slightly as she came down the stairs towards him.

Candy heard Netta mutter, 'I'll bet you are,' as she swept back into the drawing room.

'G and T, or Scotch?' As Tatton stood aside to let her

precede him, Candy smiled slowly into those blue eyes and saw him begin to blush. She knew exactly the effect she was having on him but she was enjoying getting her own back for the frock. Netta was about to learn that it wasn't couture clothes that mattered, but who was inside them. Even wearing Balmain she was no match for Candy in her C & A slacks and shirt.

Netta flounced into an armchair and Tatton stood in front of the fireplace, watching Candy's every move as she poured the drinks. She deliberately touched his fingers as she passed him his glass, then seated herself opposite Netta so that he had to choose which one of them he looked at.

'Netta tells me your friend is aide to the British ambassador in Lebanon.'

'She exaggerates a little. He's something very junior in the diplomatic service and they've attached him to Lebanon to learn about the political situation in the Middle East. I understand you used to live there.'

'Before the war. And what do you do, Tatton?'

'Oh, I don't have a proper job. I'm the heir, coerced into learning to run a rather threadbare estate on the edge of the Yorkshire moors. All past and no future.'

'Sounds like a proper job to me. Pretty important. I don't envy you the responsibility of having the future of Britain's heritage in your hands.' She noted with satisfaction that Netta was beginning to seethe.

He gave a nervous little laugh. 'I must say, I never saw it like that. I'd rather be involved in something creative, like you are. It must be so exciting, working on a film set every day.'

Pretty humdrum, really, but if he wanted to think so... 'Perhaps you'd like to come over and see what goes on.'

'Oh really, could I?'

'Of course. Just give me a ring one day and I'll arrange it.'

There came a knock on the door and Leon came in without waiting for an invitation. 'Isabella says....'

'Yes, I can imagine.' Candy sprang to her feet and set down her drink unfinished. 'I'm so sorry, they're waiting for me for supper. It's been a pleasure meeting you.' She smiled into Tatton's eyes, then went across and shook his hand, just to make sure she left her touch on him for the rest of the evening. Over her shoulder she said to Netta, 'Have a lovely evening, darling. Do be careful of my frock, won't you.' Then she swept out, an arm around Leon's shoulders, satisfied that she had ruined not only Netta's evening, but her entire relationship with Viscount Northelm.

Candy's next film was a wartime romance set in England. The first few weeks' shooting were done in Riverside Studio, alongside the Thames in London, then the whole crew set off for a couple of weeks on location near to Taunton and Candy began to struggle with a strong sense of *deja vu*, the feeling that she had been here before and done all this already, of a past life sneaking up and short-circuiting into the present. It unsettled her, made her want to glance over her shoulder all the time to see who was following her, spying on her.

She knew there was no mystery about it. The reason she had the strong impression that she'd been there before was precisely because she had, but that didn't make it any the less disturbing to be filming on the banks of the river where once she had walked hand in hand with Peter and he had told her that he loved her. At the end of every scene she looked guiltily towards the little knot of spectators that inevitably gathered to watch what they were doing, expecting that she might see Evadne watching them, yet knowing that she probably wouldn't, because Evadne hadn't been in touch at all since the girls had disappeared, as though she had found the conflict of loyalties too much. Yet Candy felt a yearning to talk to her friend again, to sit down over a cup of tea and have a good laugh about something.

She kept telling herself she didn't have the time. During the day she was in almost every scene they were rehearsing or filming and the pace was frantic, trying to take advantage of a spell of fine weather, packing as much as possible into every hour of daylight. They were staying at the Castle Hotel in the middle of town and once they'd got through the long-drawn out ritual of dinner in a private dining room there was precious little time to go upstairs, study her script, and get herself into bed so that she could be sure of eight hours' sleep before the six o'clock call the next morning. It was a hard schedule and she was mighty glad they were only here for a month, with weekends at home in between. There certainly wasn't time for looking up old friends.

Then the weather broke and for a rain-soaked afternoon there was nothing else to do. Candy took it as a sign from the heavens and without thinking about it further she threw on an old Gannex raincoat, borrowed an umbrella from one of the drivers, and set off to trace her steps through the once-familiar streets to Evadne's house.

There was nothing familiar about the place as she approached it. Somebody had obviously been working hard to make what they imagined to be improvements. The privet hedge had been grubbed out and replaced by posts and a black-painted chain. The green wooden gate had been replaced by wrought iron, the whole of the front garden had been concreted over and tubs of ill-kempt hydrangeas and pansies stood around uncomfortably. There were no lace curtains at the windows, the woodwork had been painted white and the porch had been enclosed with glass panels.

It all looked so unfamiliar that Candy wasn't a bit surprised when a strange woman answered the door and snapped, 'Yes?'

'Oh, I...uh...I was looking for Evadne...'

'Who?' The woman's eyes filled with suspicion. A hand reached down and began twisting in the folds of a print pinafore she was wearing over her linen skirt and cardigan. She had an ageing, dried-up look that showed in the frown lines on her forehead and the down-turned corners of her mouth.

'Evadne Price. I thought she...'

'You mean the old dear? She was taken off years ago.'

'Taken off?' Candy's heart missed a beat. 'You mean

she...died?'

'No.' A pause while the woman obviously considered whether to tell her more, whether this stranger on the doorstep might go away quietly when she'd been told what she wanted to know, or whether she might invade the wall of privacy that began on the doorstep. She seemed to come to a decision and drew a pained breath. 'She had a stroke and her son put her into a home and sold the house.'

'A home? Where?'

'Blowed if I can remember. It was years ago and I didn't live here then. Yes, I know, I remember Mrs Evans across the road saying what a disgrace it was. He put her into that County old people's home place in the town. The Haven, I think they call it.' '

'And she's still there?'

'How would I know? It's none of my business, is it? Now, if you don't mind, I've got ironing to finish.'

'No. I don't mind. Thanks...for your help.' Candy turned away, fighting the umbrella as it was buffeted by wind from a different direction.

She took the few steps down the path and as she opened and closed the gate she turned back and looked over the front of the house once more. A substantial house. It must have sold for quite a lot of money. She could understand that Evadne wouldn't be able to look after it if she was unwell, but surely she could afford a private nursing home out of the proceeds? Yet the woman had said she was in a county welfare home. That would mean one of those run by the council for people who couldn't afford anything else.

It didn't add up.

Candy never even considered leaving it there, not taking the next step to find out what had happened. She walked to the end of the street where she remembered there was a telephone box and she looked up the address she wanted in the telephone directory that hung inside. The street name was familiar but she had to think hard to recall which part of town it was in. When she remembered she caught a bus that took her through the town centre and out into a district of small, red brick terrace council houses. A big Victorian house that occupied a corner block had a painted notice that declared it to be *The Haven County Welfare Home for the Elderly*. As Candy crossed the road towards it she noted that it looked clean and well-kept but there was no garden, it opened straight onto the road.

The doorbell pealed into an echoing silence and it was some minutes before Candy heard footsteps and the door was opened by a young woman in a blue nurse's uniform. 'It isn't a visiting day,' the woman said, and began to close the door again without even asking what she wanted.

Candy stuck her half-furled umbrella into the gap. Once she would just have turned around and gone away but not any more. 'I want to see Mrs Price.'

'I've just told you, it isn't a visiting day.'

'Unfortunately it's the only day I have. Please can you take me to see whoever is in charge.'

'It's not worth it anyway. She won't know you.'

'I'll be the judge of that.' If Evadne recognised anyone it would be her, Candy. 'May I come in?'

The nurse hesitated another moment, then stood back and led Candy into a long, narrow hall where she left her sitting on a straight-backed chair against one wall and went off through a solid, mortice-locked door.

A dismal silence hung over the place. There were no sounds of people talking or moving about, of food being prepared in some distant kitchen, of anyone playing a gramophone, of feet on the stairs. The mingled odours of urine and disinfectant hovered on the air. As she sat there, Candy felt as though a dark shadow was slowly stealing over her spirit. Fancy being brought to this place and knowing you were never going to be able to get out again!

After what seemed a very long time she heard footsteps on the stairs and a white-clad figure pushed open the fire door. A crisply-starched nurse stood in front of her, towering, scowling.

Without preamble, she said, 'This isn't a visiting day.'

'I can't come on a visiting day. I want to see Mrs Price.'

'There's no point. Didn't they tell you? She had a stroke. She can't speak.'

'Nobody told me anything. She's my friend and I've only just found out she's here.' And she won't be here much longer if I have anything to do with it.

'I'm sorry, I can't allow...'

Candy stood up, straightened to her full height, and the nurse figure took a step back.

'Who are you, to allow or not? Your pay comes out of the taxes of people like me and Mrs Price. You are a public servant, and I am the public, asking for a service. Are you really refusing me?'

The nurse's eyes widened and she swallowed hard. Then she said 'Wait here,' and turned and banged through the fire door. Candy wondered if she'd gone too far – perhaps the next move was to send for a policeman to throw her out. Then the door opened again and the woman who'd answered the door came back and said, 'This way, please.'

Candy's heart lifted – she'd won! She followed the woman along a corridor, past the open door of a big room with a wide circle of armchairs. In each chair sat an old person in some stage of decrepitude, staring into the space immediately in front of them. None of them was speaking or relating to anyone else in the room.

With a little shudder, Candy walked on quickly, following to the end of the corridor and up a narrow flight of back stairs to the first floor. They turned a sharp corner into a corridor lined with cream-painted doors. The woman opened the first one they came to and said, 'Mrs Price is in here.'

Candy had to sidle past her to get into the room and she stood for a moment, unable to take in what she saw. The room was tiny. A bed, a small closet and a threadbare chair with wooden arms next to the window took up all the available space. Sitting in the chair, wearing a rose-pink candlewick dressing gown with a crust of vomit down the front, was Evadne.

Or rather, an effigy of what Evadne used to be.

She was thin, the flesh that had once been smooth and ruddy hung in folds below her shadowed eyes and her whole face was twisted, like a child who had pulled a rude face that had stuck when the wind changed. One eyebrow was higher than another, her mouth hung permanently open, wider on one side than the other, and a little dribble of spittle drooled out as her head dropped slightly forwards. Her shoulders were hunched and crooked and her hands were crabbed rigid on her lap. Yet as she saw Candy a change came over her. Her sunken eyes lit up, and one of her forearms began to twitch, moving her hand in spasms in her lap.

Candy knew that her shock had shown in her face. The woman who had brought her here stood in the doorway, arms crossed and an expression on her face that said 'I told you so.' Candy went forward and sat on the edge of the bed and took the twitching hand in hers. Immediately the feeble fingers closed on hers. With her free arm she hugged Evadne to her chest. Then she became acutely aware of the dreadful state of her gown – the vomit wasn't fresh and there was more than one stain.

She turned to the woman in the door. 'Will you fetch Mrs Price something clean to wear?'

'I can't do that. Saturday's changing day.'

'Go and fetch the woman who's in charge – the matron.'

'She's having her tea.'

'Go and fetch her, or I shall go out and come back with the Council Welfare Officer and a reporter.'

'You're a right troublemaker!' muttered the woman as she went off, leaving the door open.

Tears were welling in Candy's eyes at the state Evadne was in. She wanted to ask all kinds of questions about when and why she'd had the stroke, what medical care she was getting, why the house had been sold, where Peter was. But Evadne could give her no answers. Could she even hear?

'Can you hear me, Evadne?'

The hand that still lay in hers gave a small squeeze, then it was repeated urgently and Evadne's eyes took on a fearful, appealing expression.

'Don't worry, I won't leave you here. Don't worry.'

The hand squeezed hers again and Candy began to run her mind over what she must do. Nothing would be too much for this woman who'd taken her in when she most needed help and who'd cared for her in a way her mother never had. Evadne needed medical care, that was obvious, but more than that she needed love and reassurance. There had to be a bed available in a private nursing home near by as a temporary stop-gap – Candy remembered the Greenfield where she'd had Pippa amid bright chintz and clean efficiency. There must be a specialist in London who would understand her case and be able to do something to help her.

The matron appeared at the door and glared at them. Candy didn't miss the fear in Evadne's eyes. She just said, 'I'm moving Mrs Price.'

'Today?'

'Yes, today.'

'She's in no fit state to be moved. Can't you see?'

'I can see she'd in no fit state to be left here.'

'It could kill her. You'll have to take responsibility.'

Candy thought grimly about who was really responsible for Evadne's condition. Peter?

'I want you phone the Greenfield Nursing Home for a bed for her, and notify her doctor, then call an ambulance.'

'The Greenfield? Do you know how much they charge?'

'Of course I do. Tell them I'll be coming in with Mrs Price and I'll pay when we arrive.'

She could afford to pay so she could afford to be high handed and demanding. For a moment she wondered what it would be like if here was no money, if she had to leave Evadne here. She thought of the people she'd seen in the lounge downstairs who had no choice and she felt a shiver of guilt. The matron gave her one final glare of what was, by then, pure hatred, and left the room. As Candy detached her hand from Evadne's and began to look around the room for any personal possessions to pack, she saw big tears running down the slack face.

'Mom! You're home!'

Leon ran down the stairs and into her arms before she even had time to close the front door. Laughing, she pulled him towards her and hugged him. Then Carlo appeared at the double from the basement, closely followed by Isabella, both anxious. They relaxed when they saw it was her.

'What a surprise!' Isabella exclaimed. 'We didn't expect you back until the weekend.' She beamed widely, always pleased to see Candy home even if it did seem as though she'd been caught out.

And Carlo, ever concerned about security, said, 'You should have told us you were coming back. It is dangerous to become complacent.'

'Yes, sorry.' She kept an arm around Leon's shoulders as she spoke. 'This is only a flying visit – I have to go back tomorrow.' The director had already screamed down the phone at her several times that day. But what she'd been doing was more important than his filming schedule, though she'd avoided telling him that outright.

'You want supper?'

'Yes, of course. I'll eat with you all downstairs. Oh, Isabella, I can't keep it to myself – I've found out where Pippa and Danny are!'

Isabella's face went through a series of emotions - shock, happiness, concern - then it crumpled into tears. She came forward and put her arms round Candy and hugged her. 'It's been so long!'

'Eight years.'

'How...'

'It's a long story, but I found Evadne – you remember her? – and among her things she had Peter's address. Some school somewhere in Lincolnshire...' Then she caught sight of Leon's puzzled face, glancing anxiously from one to the other. He'd only been a baby when his sisters had been kidnapped. He wouldn't even remember them.

Isabella understood that she must wait to hear the whole story and she turned away. Candy turned to Leon. 'Come with me. We're going to do a tour of the whole house. Count the rooms again.' They hadn't done that since they'd moved in, while the renovations were being done. It had been fun, climbing through all five floors, allocating bedrooms and study rooms and a bathroom each. Now Candy wanted to reorganise her thoughts, allocate two of the rooms on the second floor for the girls instead of a workroom for herself and a guest bedroom. There would still be room for Netta on the first floor, though Netta hadn't taken advantage of her hospitality nearly as freely since the incident with the Viscount and the Balmain frock.

The following Monday morning, back on the set, Candy wasn't made so welcome.

'Next time I give you the afternoon off because of the rain I expect you back on the set the next day, not a week later!' Candy couldn't blame Marcel for being angry with her because the delay had cost money. But he didn't have to bawl her out in front of the whole crew. It had been four days, not a week, and she'd already apologised profusely. Still, she was in the wrong. So she apologised again and turned on the charm and began to work through the scenes she'd been studying on the train.

It was hard to concentrate, though. Her mind was on conversations with the specialist at the Harley Street clinic where she'd left Evadne, conversations with Isabella, conversations with Bob, her lawyer. She had wanted to catch the next train to Lincolnshire and burst in on Peter and the girls but Bob had advised caution, approaching Peter by means of a summons and then arranging for the girls to come to visit her with the full weight of the law backing up her claim.

'Visit me? They'll be coming back to live with me, won't they?'

A pause. 'Not necessarily. You must remember that they're considerably older than they were when you last saw them. The judge will want to consider their welfare, their preferences and their educational arrangements too.'

'But they'll want to come back to me! And I can afford the best education in London for them.'

'I'm sure that's true. But Candy, they've had a different

life for years now, a life you know nothing about, over which you have had no influence. They're different children.'

'You're saying they'll have been brainwashed, aren't you?'

'That's one way of putting it. I'm just trying to warn you, Candy, things may not go entirely your way. Be prepared for disappointment.'

She couldn't get that out of her mind. She'd never even considered that the girls wouldn't be overjoyed to see her, to be taken back to live with her. They'd been such a happy family in California. Why wouldn't they want to be with her again?

'Cut!' She looked up. 'Candy darling, concentrate! You're supposed to react when he points the gun at you, not look as though he's offering you a sponge cake!'

'I'm sorry. I didn't know we'd got to that bit.'

'Where did you think we were? What's got into you? You fallen in love or something? Why don't you share it with us? Who's the lucky man? Who're you lining up as husband number three?'

Candy tossed her head. As though! The last thing she needed in her life was another husband!

Peter Price, headmaster and owner of Brisewood Preparatory School, gazed apprehensively at the document that lay before him on his desk. He disliked the document itself, summoning him to appear before a judge in the Family Division of the High Court, and he didn't like the way it had been delivered. The man who had appeared on the doorstep and asked for him in person looked worn around the edges, an impression not wholly due to his threadbare alpaca coat and down-at-heel shoes but certainly enhanced by them. His wide moustache, a greying ginger colour, badly needed a trim and reminded Peter uncomfortably of his wartime Squadron Leader. It wasn't him, of course, but it was probably somebody's one-time wartime officer, reduced to earning his living by serving summonses. After he'd signed for the package, in his office away from the curious eyes of his secretary, Peter watched him through the window as he departed, and noted that he didn't even seem to have his own car. He must have come by train from London and walked out from the station.

It made Peter painfully aware that he could have found himself in such a situation, like so many ex-service officers and men. He'd been lucky – lucky to have a good qualification, lucky to have found Brisewood, lucky to have met Eleanor who shared his single-minded pursuit of security and respectability.

Decent, that was Eleanor. Decent and hard-working. She had never expected him even to begin to fabricate the illusion that he was in love with her any more than he expected her to pretend anything so puerile. He understand that he was the man she had been waiting for, but only because he could provide her with an unassailable position, a job to do and a roof over her head for life. For that she was willing to help him take responsibility for the upbringing of his two rather awkward daughters – whose conception he freely admitted had been a terrible mistake – and to make herself available from time to time in the secret darkness of their twin-bedded room for him to make use of the body that she held rigid throughout the short duration of the intimate act.

But this document – it threatened everything. He had managed to get rid of the messenger without arousing too much suspicion and he could take himself off to London to the court without asking anyone's permission, but what then?

He had to face three facts. Firstly he had acted illegally in taking his daughters away from their mother in the first place. He, Peter Price, had broken the law. It hadn't seemed such a dangerous thing to do at the time. But now, years later, it put at risk everything he'd been working towards. He was even afraid that if he didn't co-operate now, he might end up in prison. He could hardly believe that he'd done anything so stupid as snatch the girls just to get even with Candy. At the time it had seemed like a triumph. But what had it brought him? Two sulky daughters who cost him money and the possibility of public disgrace.

And, secondly, the press were unlikely to ignore a court case that involved Candy, not now that she was a glamorous film star - how had she managed that? How had the mousy little WAAF risen to the upper echelons of show business? Only one way that he could see and she was good at that, putting herself about to get what she wanted. Wasn't that how she'd trapped him in the first place?

Finally, the wretched woman seemed to have taken it into her head to kidnap his mother, to arrange for expensive private treatment for a condition he had been assured was incurable. He hoped he wasn't going to be expected to pay for it – all the capital he had accrued from selling her home had gone into buying Brisewood and the only way to get it back would be to mortgage the school. To be sure, he did sometimes have twinges of conscience about the way he had dealt with Evadne but Eleanor had persuaded him it was only what the old lady would have wanted if she could have talked to them, and anyway she was as good as dead already.

How could he get through this? A business like a school could collapse under even a small amount of negative publicity. A few parents withdrawing their children could mean that difference between profit and bankruptcy. The more he thought about it, the more the hairs stood up on the back of his neck and his stomach churned. And the more he hated Candy.

Why couldn't she just let it go after all this time?

He had to face up to it. It wasn't a nightmare he would wake up from if he sat here long enough staring at the summons. It was reality, and he had to deal with it. He picked up the phone and dialed the number of his solicitor in Spalding to make an appointment. He had already decided that appeasement would be the best tactic, but he wanted to do it through formal channels. He couldn't bear the thought of actually speaking to Candy.

'They're coming!' Candy cried excitedly. 'No fuss or bother, they're coming at the end of term.'

'For keeps?' Netta looked puzzled. She wasn't really involved in this, she just happened to be sitting close by when Candy put down the phone that afternoon. They had been talking about Maddie while Netta varnished her long nails a slightly too racy shade of red.

'I hope so. There's some proviso about letting the girls choose which parents they want to live with, they have to go before a judge next month, but basically I've got them back, as long as I can show I can give them a good home.' She knew she was letting her excitement get the better of the caveats and cautions that Bob had hedged around his message. She knew in her mind that the case was far from over but in her heart she was getting her children back again. She never even began to consider that they might no longer be the delightful little girls she had last seen.

'I don't know how you can be so ungrateful,' Eleanor said, with a well-practised pained expression on her face. 'After all your father has done for you.'

'She is our mother,' Pippa pointed out, reasonably.

'She also abandoned you,' said Peter, hardly looking up from his desk where he was signing a pile of school reports. 'And now she thinks she can just come back into your lives and take you over because it suits her.'

'I'd still like to see her,' Pippa said. 'Whatever she's done.' There was a little corner of her heart that still went all tight whenever she remembered the special scent and feeling of Candy bending over her, kissing her goodnight. Something buried there told her that whatever Daddy and Eleanor said or did, Mummy loved her in a way that they never could.

Eleanor spoke to Peter over their heads. 'She's sure to be a bad influence. I don't know what to think...'

Peter shook his head. 'We just have to accept that she

does have the right to see them.'

Danny said, 'I don't want to go.' Her voice wavered and she avoided Pippa's contemptuous glance. Pippa wasn't surprised. Ever since they'd run away to London Danny had refused to talk about their mother or to listen to anything about her. Pippa knew it was because Danny wanted to be in Daddy and Eleanor's good books, wanted them to love her, and believed that would only happen if she told them that she didn't love Mummy any more. Pippa saw it as a betrayal. Danny might have forgotten, but she could still remember her terror in Mexico City when she realised what was happening to them, that they weren't going to be able to go home. That hadn't been Mummy's fault, had it? Surely not? She would rather have bread and water every day for supper than admit that Daddy could be right and Mummy wrong.

Into the triumphant silence Danny added, 'I want to stay here for the holidays with you, Daddy.'

A little smile played around Peter's lips as he said, 'I'm pleased to hear that, Danny, but you don't have a choice. You have to go. The law says so. If you don't, I shall get into trouble.'

Danny's face was stricken. 'But I don't want to go!'

'You have to,' Eleanor repeated. 'But of course when you go to the court next month you can tell the judge you didn't like her and you want to live with us.'

Danny looked happier. But Pippa thought to herself, I won't. I'll tell him that I want to live with Mummy because I know she loves me best.

But it wasn't as easy as that. Once they were actually in the court, it didn't seem to be about what any of them really wanted at all. As the judge's voice droned on, and Pippa looked more and more unhappy, Candy's rage grew in her heart until she thought it would explode. She held herself rigid on the hard bench, knees and feet together, hands clasping and unclasping in her sensibly-skirted lap.

'I have to take into account, above all, the welfare of the children. This, you understand, comes over and above the wishes of either party or any perceived faults on either side…'

Candy bit at her lip to remind herself not to try to speak, and stared straight ahead so that her eyes wouldn't slide sideways to where Peter and Eleanor flanked Pippa and Danny. She couldn't bear the looks on any of their faces. Peter and Eleanor both had small, smug smiles playing around the corners of their lips and at the end of every phrase they exchanged a satisfied glance.

'The points I have taken into account are these…'

The girls both wore neatly pressed school blazers over cotton frocks and they sat with their white-socked ankles crossed, every now and again scuffing their plain black shoes against the rails of their chairs. Pippa's pretty hair had been scraped back into two tight bunches that stuck out from behind her ears making her look younger than her seventeen years. But it was their faces that Candy most wanted to avoid seeing. Danny was pale with the dark rings around her eyes that told Candy she had been crying. She kept her eyes lowered, her gaze fixed on the floor. Pippa, on the other hand, was constantly looking up, trying to catch Candy's eye. Whenever she managed it the look of pleading was almost too much to bear. As the outcome became more apparent to them all, her lower lip began to tremble and several times she had to raise a sleeve to brush away tears.

'…the stable marriage of the defendants, the home they can provide and the responsible guidance they have already given to these girls over the years…'

Beside Candy, Bob sat making notes but other than him, she was alone. She wished now that she hadn't told Tatton not to come – the solicitor had told her it would look better if she was on her own. But they didn't take into account how it would feel. They didn't know how much she had come to depend on Tatton in the past weeks. They didn't know that she was already carrying his child from that first ill-advised, excited, unprotected coupling and that he had asked her to marry him. And if anyone did know all that, what sort of a difference would it really make? Would the judge be prepared to take into account her impending marriage to a viscount?

Anyway, he wasn't here. He had taken Leon to the zoo instead.

'On the other hand, whilst I recognise that the plaintiff has sufficient wealth to provide every comfort and buy every advantage for her children, she is currently a single woman with two failed marriages behind her, and this can only lead to emotional imbalance in a household with no father figure…'

There – she should have asked Bob to tell the judge about Tatton. He'd hardly have been able to say there'd be no father figure if he'd known about that.

'…the nature of her professional commitments must mean long spells away from home, leaving her children in the hands of paid employees…'

But they'd known Isabella almost all their lives…

'And finally, I don't believe that the circles in which the plaintiff moves in her professional and social life can provide the right sort of moral atmosphere for two growing girls…'

Candy shook with rage and she felt Bob's warning hand on her arm. She pulled a freshly ironed white handkerchief out of her bag and crumpled it in her fingers.

'Therefore I have no option but to award custody of these two girls to Mr and Mrs Price until they each attain the age of eighteen, when the case must be reviewed in the light of plans for their future. However, it is important that they grow up knowing their mother, so I am granting access one weekend every half school term, and one week during each school holiday. Any plans for them to travel out of the country during this period must be referred to the court.'

'Mummy!' Pippa sprang to her feet but she was clutched from behind by Peter and Eleanor together whose combined weight served to pin her into her seat. It was Candy who strode across the room and flung her arms around her daughter. As they sobbed on each others' shoulders the judge ordered that the court be cleared and ushers came forward to pull them apart. 'Darlings, I won't let this rest. I'll appeal. And anyway I'll see you soon for a weekend…'

Candy instinctively reached out an arm towards Danny to give her a farewell hug but Danny had already turned her back.

'Darling, don't be so hard on yourself.'

Tatton was sitting on the edge of her bed in the darkened room and Candy heard his words through a mist of tears and heartache. Dear Tatts, what could he do? He'd sat there for hours now, and she knew she was hurting him, knew she should be thinking more about his child growing inside her, giving her attention with good grace to their forthcoming wedding , but she couldn't. Every time she made up her mind to get up, bathe, put on her makeup, she thought of Pippa's stricken face and Danny's cold indifference and she started to weep afresh.

'Darling, you're doing nobody any good like this. What about our trip to meet Father?'

The Earl? They'd planned to fly north next weekend, Tatton proudly piloting them in his little private plane, to break the news that the only heir was about to marry a twice-divorced actress. It had to be done gently. With charm. Not by a tearstained woman who could barely muster a smile, actress or no. The Earl would have to wait. She couldn't see anyone important while she was in this state.

A knock at the door brought Isabella with a tray of supper and Leon close behind. While Isabella came in and set down the tray on the bedside table, Tatton took the boy by the hand and led him to the bedside. 'Your dear mother's not very well,' he murmured. 'Just give her a little kiss.'

Leon leaned over obediently, then his lip trembled. 'She's not...not going to die, is she?'

Candy heard the small voice and felt a shaft of guilt. How could she be so self-indulgent as to let Leon suffer for a moment? She turned on her pillow towards the child and held out her arms. 'No, of course I'm not going to die. I'm just very tired.' The arms closed around him in a hug.

'But you will die one day, won't you?'

'Not until you're an old man.' She kissed him warmly, several times on the forehead and both cheeks. 'Now, run along with Isabella – you too, Tatts. I'm going to get up.'

'I say, Darling, you look absolutely sumptuous in that...'

'You really think so? You don't think the colour makes me look sallow...?'

'Nothing could make you look sallow...' Candy was up and about again and they were in a Hardy Amies' fitting room, surrounded by a level of luxury that she had come to take for granted. She was having the final fitting of some outfits that studio was buying for her new film. The studio was footing the bill only because she was playing the sort of woman who would be dressed by Amies, on the understanding that she would then buy them herself at a reduced price, and so save both the studio and herself the full cost of the clothes. In fact, Candy hadn't yet decided that she wanted to have the clothes for herself, she was only going along with the plan because it was the easiest course to take. But Tatton's enthusiasm was making her think the outfits might well be worth having.

Her mind wasn't entirely on the clothes as she stood still and let the fitter pin her hem straight. They were arguing about Leon.

'You didn't promise him?'

'Well, sort of…'

'You should have asked me first.'

'I know that now, but I'm not very experienced at this father thing.'

'I really can't come until tomorrow. They've scheduled more scenes for this afternoon.'

'But you said...'

'I know I *said*, but I didn't know they'd changed the schedule until this morning. Why can't you put off going till tomorrow.'

Tatton shifted unhappily. 'Accountants. First thing in the morning. Hate the damn creatures but Father insists I'm there...'

'In that case you'll have to fly up by yourself this afternoon and we'll follow on the train tomorrow morning.'

'I could take Leon with me...'

'Suppose he's sick again?' She suddenly looked down at the fitter's grey head below her and her voice took on a sharp edge. 'What's the matter? Do be careful of my nylons.'

'I'm sorry, Madam.' The woman kept her head down, eyes on the space between Candy's elegant knees and the floor, where the soft material of the dress swung with every movement. The trouble was that the skirt wasn't hanging quite as straight as it had on the first fitting a couple of weeks ago, it was straining over the hips because Madam had put on a little weight. Not much, but enough to spoil the line of the dress. And it wasn't the sort of weight that was going to go away with a couple of days' dieting. The seamstress had done the same job for thirty years and she had seen this happen before. She wondered quietly how Madam was going to get into these clothes in six weeks' time, when she would be wearing them in the film.

'He won't be.' Tatton's attention was still focused on Leon.

'I don't know. I'll think about it.' She knew Leon got on well enough with his stepfather to be, and he was certainly jumping with excitement about the flight, but after that he would have to spend the night at Northelm House without her. How would he feel in a strange country house, a huge place full of twists and turns and shadows, amongst people he didn't know? He would surely be frightened, wouldn't he? And for what? Just because Tatton had carelessly promised him a flight in the plane? He'd get his flight later, on the way home at the end of the weekend. So better to keep him with her. But she said nothing. She hated to disappoint him, be the breaker of promises. Perhaps she would let him go after all, ask him how he felt about it. 'How much longer?' to the greying head still bent over her hemline.

'Finished, Madam.'

Candy turned to the long mirror and inspected herself critically. She couldn't detect the rounding of her hips that had been bothering the fitter because the woman had done her job well. But she knew her body was changing and she was a little afraid of what they would say at the studio. Thankfully they'd already shot more than half her scenes so they were unlikely to go to the expense of cancelling her contract and re-shooting. But what about her next film, already scheduled to follow on from this one? By then she would be safely married to Tatton but all the same she would be breaking a contract and that could be expensive. There were already too many calls on her income.

She smiled at her reflection in the mirror, her face giving away none of her worries. With a little swagger she turned to Tatton. 'How do I look?'

'Perfect, of course.' His smile, flooding across his whole face and crinkling the corners of his eyes, was open and loving. 'Isn't she?' he finished, turning to the fitter.

'Madam is very beautiful.' The fitter smiled too, wondering which of the pair was the luckiest; the Viscount for sharing the bed of this fabulous creature from Hollywood, or the film star for being loved by this handsome young aristocrat.

Out in the street, hand tucked in Tatton's arm as they waited for a taxi to take her back to the studio, Candy made up her mind. 'All right, he can go with you.' Why spoil the boy's fun? He would be fine with Tatts. When I get back to the studio I'll phone Isabella and get Carlo to pick him up from school and drive him to the airfield. '

'No, just tell her to pack his bag. I'll pick him up – it'll be quicker. I need to take off by three at the latest to get there before dark. And I'll see to your train reservation for tomorrow. I'll get Thomas Cook to deliver the ticket to your house.'

She squeezed his arm as he hailed a taxi. How good it felt to be looked after. She knew it would be all right, he wouldn't let anything go wrong. He kissed her as he handed her into the taxi. 'Take care, darling. I'll be waiting at Northelm station tomorrow afternoon.' He slammed the door. 'Riverside

Studios,' he told the driver, 'at Shepherd's Bush.'

'Cut!' For the fourth time in ten minutes the director's voice rang out in exasperation. 'What exactly do you think you're doing, Edgar?' The director had leapt to his feet and across the set in two strides, and he grasped the leading man by his lapels and shook him so hard his teeth rattled. Two production assistants jumped forward to drag him away before he could injure the precious star. Candy, looking ravishing as a French resistance fighter fresh from battle, ripped blouse barely concealing her breasts and skirt split to her hip, laughed outright. She had been finding it hard to concentrate on her role with Edgar ad-libbing new lines whenever he forgot what he should be saying.

Freed from the director's grasp, Edgar brushed down his rough jacket and, red in the face, screamed, I'm only acting – you do know about acting, don't you? Going with the emotion? You have heard of the Method, haven't you? For Chrissake, this woman is telling me she just shot my fiancee for collaborating with the Germans. I need to emote, not speak wooden lines...'

'Keep your fancy theories to yourself. There's no place for that kind of acting on my set. The lines are only wooden because you say them that way. You say what is written, the way I told you, or you may find an early firing squad written into the script.'

Edgar continued to harrumph and shake himself but he said no more. The director turned to Candy. 'I do apologise, darling. Are you ready for another take? If we get it right this time we can break for tea.'

'Tea? It's nearly five.'

'Martinis, then. Anything to perk you up, darling. Just think, we have two more scenes on the schedule, and you have a day off tomorrow.'

Am I wilting? thought Candy as she let the make-up girls and hairdresser rough up her appearance a little more. She couldn't afford to look tired, there was too much to do.

Edgar got the message and managed to remember most of his lines and moves by the third take. And by five to six Candy was in the dressing room having her make-up removed and her hair combed. The girls were chattering and there was a radio on in the background, the BBC Home Service churning out the weather forecast before the pips for the six o'clock news. But Candy was wrapped up in her own thoughts, not really listening. Her thoughts were on Tatton and Leon; they would be landing soon and she could expect a phone call early evening. She wished she'd been able to go with them.

Suddenly she was aware that the chatter in the room was silenced and everyone was listening intently to the radio and staring at her strangely.

'What's the matter...'

'Shhh..listen...'

'...wreckage exploded when it hit the ground and no survivors have been found. The Viscount was an experienced pilot and the authorities are initially attributing the accident to engine failure rather than navigational error. The Queen is said to be...'

Candy leapt to her feet. 'Leon!' Then her brain seemed to explode and she blacked out. She was caught by the hairdresser as she slid to the floor. At the same moment the director came into the room, a script in his hand. He moved forward to help, grasping her legs as they carried her to a couch.

'What...?'

'Careful with her,' cautioned the make-up girl. 'She's pregnant.'

'What!' He yelled it this time, dropping Candy's legs as though they had scorched him. 'Pregnant? She can't be, we have a film to finish. She can't keep fainting whenever we do a little overtime.'

'That's not why she's fainted.' The hairdresser was weeping now. 'Poor darling, we just heard on the radio that the child's father has killed himself in a plane crash.'

'Who? That soppy milord? Thank goodness for that.

Now she can have an abortion and we can get on with our film.'

Candy soon recovered from her faint but only to be overtaken by a pall of weeping. As she wept she ran and re-ran events though her mind. It was her fault. She'd let Leon go with Tatton when she should have taken a firm line and made him stay behind. She'd let herself be lulled into a false sense of security, let herself believe everything was going to be all right, and now her lovely boy was dead and Tatton – darling Tatts whose child she was carrying – she would never see again.

One of the production assistants came with her in the taxi that took her home, sitting through the journey with her arm around Candy, passing her fresh Kleenexes out of a big bag. At the front door in Curzon Street there was already a bunch of sour-looking press photographers who hassled and called her name as she was helped out of the taxi. She kept her head down but they took photographs just the same, one focused on her waistline that appeared next day in the *Star* under the headline *IS SHE OR ISN'T SHE?*

A sobbing Isabella met them inside the front door and Candy was soon sitting in her drawing room, still weeping, unable to even think about the quiet, empty house. Then the front door banged and footsteps thundered on the stairs. Netta, red-eyed and unkempt, burst into the room.

'You cow!' she shrieked, grabbing Candy's hair and trying to scratch her face. 'You money-grubbing little cow! You stole him from me and now you've killed him! I hope you're satisfied! If it wasn't for you he wouldn't have been...'

Candy fought off her sister while the girl from the studio and Isabella both grabbed her from behind, then pushed her into another chair. 'You can't blame her for all this,' muttered the studio girl. 'How can you be so insensitive? After all, she's lost her child too...'

Still trying to restrain Netta, Isabella half-turned in surprise. 'Her child? Oh no, does she still think..?'

She let go of Netta, who sank back quietly, and hurried across to Candy. Taking her damp, white face between her two capable brown hands, Isabella looked her in the eyes. 'I am so sorry, Mrs Candy. I never thought. I did send you a message and I never thought you wouldn't get it... Leon was doing an exam in school and the headmaster wouldn't let him leave. His lordship went without him. The child is safe upstairs.'

The Earl sent her a handwritten letter inviting her to what he termed 'a quiet family funeral' in the estate church in Yorkshire.

'I want to be sure that you don't feel excluded simply because no marriage has taken place,' he wrote. 'I know how highly my son regarded you and I would like to meet you.'

Candy wept afresh at his sentiments but wondered whether he knew about the baby. Might that not change things? Would he still want to meet her?

Leaving Leon in London she took a train to Yorkshire exactly one week after the dreadful day of the plane crash. It hadn't been an easy week. She had tried to comfort Leon without letting him know how blessed she felt that he hadn't been on the plane. He wasn't even aware that he might have been and she had managed to keep it that way until his school headmaster had told him what a lucky boy he was to be alive. The effect had been devastating for Leon who had collapsed in hysterics and she'd had to fetch him home. After that he was not only mourning a newly found favourite adult but bearing a burden of guilt that he was alive and not Tatton. She had wanted to take a week off work but on the Thursday she had been summoned to the studio where the make-up assistants worked overtime to restore her complexion and the producer gave her a long, private dressing down about getting pregnant. He wasn't too pleased about her taking time off to go to Yorkshire but when she showed him the Earl's letter he decided it would be worth the delay for the free publicity.

'And when you get back,' said the producer, 'We'll have to talk about what we're going to do about that baby.' Candy shuddered. A studio creche would be nice but she didn't think that was what they had in mind.

Back at home she barely had time to pack before catching the train. Isabella had laid out two stylish black suits and a dress on the bed, together with a hat and coat. 'Will they be all right?'

'I'll only need one. Which one?'

'The dress is...but will it fit?'

'I want to look right, respectful but not like a flashy mistress. But I haven't time to try them on now. You'd better pack them all.'

'You weren't his lordship's mistress. You were his fiancee.'

'Who's going to believe that?' She sniffed into her hanky, then caught sight of the embroidered flowers on its corner. 'Flowers! I haven't got any flowers to take!'

'You don't take flowers, you send them. I've already phoned Harrods. They'll be delivered to the undertaker in the morning.'

'Oh, Isabella, what would I...'

'Please Madam, hurry, or you'll miss the train. They won't hold it, even for you.'

But Candy's doubts were growing. 'Perhaps I should miss the train. Perhaps that would be better than having to face all those upper-class people who'll only make me feel small.'

'Madam...' Isabella stopped folding the dress she was packing and came forward and took Candy's shoulders...'Dear Madam, did his lordship ever make you feel small? No, he loved you. And it's his family you'll be meeting. You must go, to show them that you loved him.'

Candy slept for most of the journey and by the time the train pulled into the station at Thirsk, where she had reserved a hotel room for the night, it was dark and a fine rain was falling. She had intended to hire a taxi to take her on to Northelm House the next morning but as she booked into the hotel she was handed a stiff cream envelope with an impressive monogram embossed on the flap. Inside was a handwritten note saying that a car would be at the hotel at nine the next morning to drive her to the funeral. It was signed simply 'Penmore'.

She was grateful but at the same time startled and intrigued. How did the Earl know her travel plans or where she would be staying? Did he have a network of sleuths at his disposal? What else did he know? Not looking forward one bit to the following day she called Leon from the public phone in the hotel lobby, ate a miserable dinner in the ill-heated dining room and settled down for the night in a damp bed.

She didn't sleep well and the following morning it took all her will power to wash and dress in her Hardy Amies suit, which she decided was the most conventional, and her neat black hat. The car arrived on time, the elderly chauffeur greeted her respectfully but with unmistakable curiosity in his eyes and she was driven in solitary state away from the little town and through farmland and moorland. It took over an hour to reach the house itself, the house she had thought she would be visiting as Tatton's fiancee. It was hidden deep in a park, bounded by a high yellowish stone wall, approached by a long, curved driveway. As though by prior arrangement, when the house itself came into sight the rain clouds parted and a shaft of morning sunlight shone on the wet stone, emphasising the fact that many of the long, narrow mullioned windows were shuttered. Overgrown rhodedendron and magnolia shrubs crept right up to the walls of the ground floor terraces, as though providing a protective shield.

The car didn't stop at the house but took her down a steep slope to a small church that nestled amongst a few stone cottages about half a mile further on. As the car drew up at the church gate and the chauffeur came around and held open the door for her, a little group of people pressed forward to catch a glimpse of her. There was nobody to greet her and once she had made her way into the church she saw why. The elderly Earl was already sitting in the front row of pews, his back ramrod straight, and at his side sat a young woman with dark, permed hair.

But as Candy hesitated at the back of the church a morning-suited usher leaned over and spoke to the Earl. Immediately he rose to his feet, turned and walked back to where she stood and came to a halt before her, all eyes following his every movement. He was tall, taller than Tatton had been, and better looking too, with a leaner, more craggy face. He had to bend forwards to speak to Candy quietly enough so that only she could hear.

'My dear, thank you for doing us the honour. You're a brave lady.' And he held out an arm to her and led her to his pew, where he sat her between himself and the permed lady. The lady turned with a half smile and Candy recognised the profile of Princess Margaret. As she settled in her place, the Princess withdrew one elegant black leather glove and reached out a beautifully manicured had that closed on hers in a private gesture of sympathy.

As the church continued to fill up Candy's eyes came to rest on the cause of this gathering, a mahogany coffin that sat on a catafalque in front of the altar, flanked by four tall white candles and covered with flowers. The coffin was closed and she remembered that Tatton had been burnt to death in an aircraft that had exploded. What would there be left for anyone to see in that big, closed coffin? Possibly nothing that even she could recognise. Better to be able to remember him the way he was.

Then there was a shuffling behind a curtain to one side and a clergyman appeared, walked across and stood in front of the coffin, clearing his throat.

'Dearly beloved...' he began.

When the praying was done and Tatton's coffin had been carried into the family vault it seemed as though the entire neighbourhood flocked to the big house for an enormous party. The Earl had obviously been expecting it because he had laid on food and cases of wine and whisky, but Candy felt too sad and desperate to join in and she soon crept into an unoccupied private sitting room where three large dogs were lying on a hearthrug in front of a meagre fire. When she came in they raised their heads and slapped their tails against the floor a few times but their demeanour was generally friendly, so she took off her hat and shoes and curled up in a huge damask armchair, pulling a fringed shawl from the back of the chair and tucking it over her legs.

How cold it was! The middle of summer and the room needed a fire! Whatever did they do in the winter? She was just drifting asleep when there came a timid knock on the door and it opened slowly. As Candy guiltily jumped to her feet a little maid crept in and closed the door behind her.

'S..so sorry madam. But I've been asked to fetch you. His lordship wants to see you in the library.'

'Now?'

'I think so. He's waiting in there now.'

Candy's spirits sank, though she wouldn't have thought it possible for them to go any lower.

This is it, she thought. This is the pay-off scene. I wonder how much they're going to offer me to get rid of my baby and disappear. She slipped on her shoes again and desperately brushed at her black suit, trying to get rid of the dog hairs. Another few moments were spent mending her makeup and combing her hair while the maid waited patiently by the door.

Candy was surprised when she was shown into the library to find only the Earl sitting there, in a brown leather armchair that had seen better days, beside a newly lit fire. She had expected a brace of lawyers at least. Sounds of music and chatter in distant rooms told her that the wake was still in full flow.

'Come in my dear.' The Earl rose from his chair to greet her and his voice sounded warm and mellow. 'Come and sit here – you must be freezing. Have you eaten? It's important that you keep up your strength. I've ordered some tea and sandwiches in here.'

'That would be nice. Thank you.' She sat down and held

out her hands to the crackling flames, waiting. She didn't feel as though she was about to be attacked.

'My son told me a lot about you. You're thinner than I expected, and much prettier. He was very much in love with you.'

'And I loved him. Not at first, but as time went on and I got to know what kind of person he is...was...'

'That's what love is supposed to be like. Not all this modern jumping into bed at first sight.'

Candy hesitated. Did the Earl imagine they hadn't done that as well? After all, they were living in the permissive society. How much did he know? 'Did Tatton tell you...about the child?' She raised her eyes and looked squarely into his.

'Yes. He was very happy that you are carrying his child.' He paused, took a deep breath and passed his outspread hand across his eyes. 'So am I.'

'You? That's not what one expects of a parent. You've got the wrong script.'

He shook his head. 'Didn't he tell you, I write my own scripts.' As he said this, he shot up twenty notches in Candy's estimation. 'What disturbs me now is that because Tatton died before you could marry, the line will pass elsewhere, unless I become a father again.'

'You could marry again.'

'I could indeed. What I really want to do, though, is legitimise Tatton's child.'

'Legitimise...? It's too late for that – he's dead.' What was he thinking of? Falsifying some marriage certificate? It could probably be done.

'he may be dead but I'm not, I'm very much alive. And I have an offer to make you. I make it in full knowledge about you – your responsibilities, your film contracts, your other children and your tendency to...lose them. Candice, I would be honoured if you would marry me and allow me to bring up Tatton's child as my own.'

A month later, having completed her work on the wartime film and bought out of her contract for the next one, Candy attended the memorial service for Tatton in Westminster Abbey as the Countess of Penmore and took on an entirely new role, one that many people described as drifting into a backwater of domesticity as the wife of an elderly aristocrat.

There were a great many things about being a countess that Candy found difficult, but being the Earl's wife wasn't one of them. She hadn't known at first what was expected of her in that direction and the facilities at Northelm House of a master-suite of rooms with a choice of sleeping arrangements gave her no hint. And there was nobody she could talk to about it. Nobody who could give her any guidance as to whether the Earl was eager to exercise his rights as a husband, or whether his relationship with her was simply to protect the family name and he would prefer a platonic relationship. He might feel there was something incestuous about having sex with the woman who was bearing his son's child. Or for all she knew, he might have a mistress tucked away somewhere – that's what aristocrats were famous for, wasn't it? He might even despise her because of her past.

She watched him for signs. He was scrupulously polite, making suggestions for suitable daytime activities that wouldn't be too strenuous, filling her in on the complicated family trees of the neighbourhood, easing her into the routines of planning menus with the housekeeper, giving her notice of times when he would have to go to London on Parliamentary business, asking her if she wanted to go along with him, which she did for a while until Jeremy was born and Leon was sent to a school near to Northelm, so that all her time was taken up in Yorkshire. But at the end of every day he took his glass of whisky and an armful of reading matter, bade her good night, and shut himself in the bedroom beyond his dressing room.

At first Candy was relieved but after a few weeks she began to feel rejected. She was growing to like Robert and she had stopped thinking of him as Tatton's father and began to see him as a dignified, kindly person with a body that was well-honed for his years, probably because of the endless miles he seemed to walk over the hills with his dogs. From thinking, I don't expect he wants to have sex, she progressed to, I suppose it's easier if he doesn't want sex, to Why doesn't he want sex? What's the matter with me?

So she took a trip to Harrogate and bought herself some new underwear and a sexy silk and lace nightgown and that evening, after Robert had shut himself in his room, she put on the new gown. The mirror told her that her bulge hardly showed while her breasts were swollen to a ripe roundness that she didn't usually have. She remembered all the times Luigi had coached her in how to be irresistible to men and crossed the room with the swaying walk he had taught her. She decided against knocking on Robert's door but simply opened it slowly and silently, finding him sitting in an armchair, back to her, already dressed in his old-fashioned striped pyjamas, sipping his drink and engrossed in his reading.

He heard her and twisted around, and half his papers slipped from his lap onto the floor. His features were startled. 'My dear...' He had taken to calling her that when they were together.

She forgot her carefully prepared lines and felt herself blushing. 'I was wondering...'

'Yes?'

'I was wondering if you wanted...you know...' What she wanted to say was, I was wondering if you wanted me in your bed, but after more hesitation it came out as, 'I was wondering if you wanted to make love.' Then another quick rush of words. 'I was wondering why you've been neglecting me.'

He was on his feet in an instant, spilling the remainder of his papers onto the floor, coming to stand in front of her. 'Neglecting you? How's that? I though I was being the soul of solicitousness. Haven't I looked after you morning, noon and night?'

'The morning and noon bits have been okay but the nights...' She reached up a hesitant finger and flicked gently at the buttons of his pyjama jacket. 'You see, you haven't made it clear what you want our – arrangements – to be. Do you want me to be a proper wife or a genealogical convenience...'

'Oh, I'll take the proper wife option any day.' He smiled and his eyes screwed up in the corners and gave Candy a hint of the kind of man Tatton would have become. 'I am a man, after all, and you are a very desirable woman and I have been in love with you for longer than you know. I was desperately jealous when I heard Tatton had met you. I didn't marry you because I felt sorry for you, you know. I must admit my first instinct after Tatton died was to buy you off but when I actually met you, I couldn't do that. All I could think of was to find a way to keep you safe. I only left you alone because I thought, in the circumstances...I thought you must want some space.'

'What I want,' she said, realising it herself for the first time, 'Is a husband who will love me and look after me and not steal my children or run off with other women.'

With that, the new Countess started the happiest part of her life. And five months later, in a discreet Harrogate clinic, she gave birth to an heir to the title, Jeremy Tatton James. The Earl was reported to be overjoyed.

Pippa stared out of the train window, hardly able to conceal her excitement as the crammed, dirty houses and grey factories slid by, gradually giving way to fields and comfortable-sized red brick houses where people might want to live. This, at last, was their summer holiday week with Mummy, and instead of spending it in the London house as they had the weekends before the court case, they were going to Northelm, the 'country place'. Pippa wasn't so sure just what was so special about the country place, except that it was large. Daddy's school was large too, and in the country, but it was obviously different if you belonged to an Earl's family. Picnics had been mentioned, and a boating lake, and pony riding.

Pippa wanted to share her excitement with someone, talk about what they were going to do for that short week of fun, but she was forced to keep it to herself. Across the carriage from her, in the corresponding corner of the parallel bench seat, Danny sat in moody silence, staring out of the same window but looking back at where they had been instead of forward towards their destination. Danny hadn't said a word since Daddy and Eleanor had seen them onto the train at Kings Cross. She wasn't looking forward to her holiday at all.

Danny was often like that these days; difficult to talk to, living inside some private world. The only person she ever listened to was Eleanor, when Eleanor went on about God and what might happen to their immortal souls if they committed the sin of pride and thought they were anything special because their mummy had married an earl. Eleanor had a way of talking about that as though Mummy had done something really wicked instead of just getting married and having a baby.

Pippa loved the baby. She hoped she'd be allowed to help bath it, and give it a bottle, the way she had years ago with Leon. She'd loved little Leon and she was sorry he wouldn't be there for this holiday, she would have liked to get to know him again. But she knew he had gone to California to stay with his father for the summer, which would make him happy. Pippa fell into a little dream, remembering how lovely it had been in America with Rupert as their daddy. What fun it had been with a swimming pool on the terrace and lots of pretty clothes to wear, and someone always there to play with them. It had always been a lovely day then.

The train went through a tunnel and suddenly Pippa was looking at her reflection. Her Panama hat with the school ribbon was still wedged onto her head, flattening her hair and making the two stubby plaits that Eleanor still insisted upon stick out at odd angles. There was a little oval mirror set into the panelling above the row of seats and she got up, took off her hat and began to unravel her plaits. Fishing in the small shoulder bag that Eleanor had given her to carry the tickets and taxi money, she found a brown tortoiseshell comb with several teeth missing. Briskly, she combed out her hair, raising it towards the crown at the back as she bunched it into her left hand. Then she held the comb between her teeth as she felt in her blazer pocket for a rubber band she had hidden there. With her hand raised above her head she could see the rounded outline of her breasts pushing against the thin cotton of her dress, making the button gape in front. She was worried about having breasts because she knew they had something to do with sex, which she knew nothing about and didn't dare to ask Eleanor. It was the same with the blood that had stained her knickers a couple of years back, frightening her into thinking there was something wrong with her insides. Eleanor had finally found the dirty garments in the laundry and had come to her bedroom holding them in her hands.

'Why didn't you tell me you'd started menstruating?'

'W...what's that?'

'The monthly curse.'

'Curse?' She was even more frightened. Why had she been cursed? Who by?

'Yes. All women get it, every month. You bleed for a few days, then it goes away.'

Pippa had tried to imagine going to school and playing games while she was bleeding into her knickers. Perhaps... 'Do I have to stay in bed while it's happening?'

Eleanor had given a short laugh. 'No, of course not. You just wear a pad and a belt and get on with things. I'll give you what you need and show you how to use it.'

Pippa had felt a little better, knowing that this happened to all women, but why hadn't anyone told her about it? 'Why does it happen?'

'It's just one of those things. We don't talk about it.'

But the girls at school had talked about it. Pippa hadn't understood before what they meant by their 'monthlies' and 'the curse' but she did now and it made more sense. But still nobody had been sure why they had to endure such an imposition on their freedom. Only one of the girls had thought it might have something to do with having babies. 'You know you're pregnant when the monthlies stop.' After that Pippa was terrified every month that the bleeding might not come and she would find herself to be pregnant. She had thought it only happened to married women, that only they could have babies, but apparently not. This holiday, Pippa was determined to find out the truth from the one person she felt she could talk to about it. Candy would be sure to know. She'd had four babies now. Pippa would wait for a quiet time when they were alone together and she would ask her.

Balancing herself as the carriage swayed, still holding the bunch of hair at the top of her head, she made several turns around the stem of the bunch with the rubber band so that she had a bouncing pony tail. It wasn't very long but she flicked it back and forth a few times, admiring it in the little mirror.

Danny eyed her balefully. 'Vanity is a sin,' she said.

Pippa flicked her pony tail again as she began to flatten the hat so that she could stuff it into her pocket. 'So is being grumpy. If you can't say something nice, don't say anything at all.' That was one of Eleanor's sayings so it made Danny subside into an even more grumpy silence. She turned her pinched face away and stared out of the window. Pippa knew she was wishing she was back in Brisewood with Daddy and Eleanor, so that she could be sure she wouldn't be tempted into sinning.

'Here we are, darlings! Northelm House!' Sitting in the back of the station wagon, crammed into the back seat with one of her mother's warm, clinging arms around her, the other gripping Danny's shoulders, Pippa craned her head to take in the formal vista before them. It wasn't a disappointment, except that it was just a big house really, not a castle, but it was dispiriting. Many of the windows were shuttered, especially the big reception rooms at the front, and instead of sweeping up the driveway to the imposing curved steps at the front door the driver brought the car to a halt before a side door. 'We don't live in the main part of the house – it's far too big. We have an apartment in the west wing.' And she said to a middle aged man with a stoop who came forward to take their bags out of the car, 'This is Miss Philippa and Miss Daniella, Samuels.' The man inclined his head and Pippa only just remembered not to hold out her hand. Somewhere she had read that one didn't with servants. Danny didn't know that but it was obviously part of her campaign not to be polite to anyone and she said nothing, which Pippa found to be both a relief and an embarrassment at the same time.

In the west wing apartment the decor was clean and the windows sparkled. They looked out onto a large formal garden that was, by contrast, barely cared for; the lawns were uncut and the plants straggled out of their beds and across the paths.

'Why is it like that?' Pippa asked, gazing out of the window while her mother helped them to unpack in the spacious bedroom she was to share with Danny, next door to baby Jeremy's nursery. 'Why isn't it properly looked after?' She was tempted to compare the surroundings with the school, where Eleanor would never tolerate an untidy garden, but she held her tongue, deciding that would be unfair.

Instead, Danny said it. 'Eleanor would go mad if she saw that mess.'

With an air of distraction Candy said, 'There's lots of parts of this place not well looked after – it's not like the London house. It's all very expensive to run, you see, and hard to come by enough servants to do the work.'

'I thought earls were fabulously rich,' muttered Danny, folding a jumper. 'What's he done with his fortune, gambled it away?'

Pippa was shocked at Danny's bad manners in talking about other people's money. Candy turned and gripped Danny's arms to her sides, making her crumple the carefully folded jumper. 'Please, darling, you mustn't say things like that. It's all far more complicated than you can possibly understand. We just try not to waste money unnecessarily.'

Danny shook off her mother's hands and turned her face away. 'When will you realise that I am not your darling?'

Pippa caught the look of pain that flashed across Candy' face and she quickly crossed the room and gave her mother a hug. 'I love you, Mummy,' she whispered, 'And I'm jolly pleased to be here.' And she glared at Danny, daring her to say something else hurtful. They carried on unpacking in silence, then Candy found a layer of books in the bottom of Danny's case.

'No wonder this was so heavy. Whatever did you bring all these for?'

'To read, of course. So that I'll have something to do.'

'But there's plenty to do. We shall go for walks, and we've

borrowed a couple of ponies so that you can ride, and there's a big picnic planned for Sunday, with neighbours coming, and they're sure to invite you back...'

'Ponies? I don't know how to ride a pony.' Danny was lining up her books on the bedside table. Pippa thought the plans sounded lovely and wondered if a week was going to be long enough.

'I know you don't know how to ride, but there's a groom who'll take you out and teach you what to do.'

'Do we have to?'

'Robert has been to a lot of trouble to arrange it. I want you to give it a try. All girls like ponies.'

Pippa certainly did, and she went riding every day, and helped to look after the ponies as well. She did enjoy brushing and feeding them, and after the initial stiffness had worn off she enjoyed the feeling of the live, muscled animal between her legs. But most of all she was interested in the young man, one of the Earl's employees, who was acting as groom and riding instructor for the week. He was about eighteen, Pippa guessed, with a tanned, cheerful face only slightly marred by a row of protruding top teeth. He wasn't tall but because of the physical work he did he already had the broad shoulders and muscular thighs of a grown man. His name was Tom Bright and, because of him Pippa couldn't wait to get down to the stables each morning.

Danny was still adamant that she didn't want to ride, so instead of leading them at a walking pace round the meadow, Tom rode the second pony, which was only just large enough for him. That way they could go further, along bridle paths and tracks through the estate. Because she knew Tom's eyes were always on her, Pippa concentrated on what she was doing and was rewarded by hearing him tell her she was a natural.

'Main thing is, yer mount trusts yer. She likes yer cos you're good to her. You make a mistake, she'll put yer right you see.'

At the end of the ride on the third day, helping her to unsaddle her pony, he came very close and brushed his arm against hers by accident. Pippa felt a spark of excitement running from the place where their skin had made contact, fizzling out somewhere in the middle of her chest. The next day it happened again while they were brushing the animal's flanks. Tom was closer to her than he had been yesterday and their arms touched again, and the effect was the same. Pippa realised then that this was no accident. With a mounting sense of excitement she understood that Tom really liked her. And as she half-ran, half-skipped out of the stable yard towards the west wing and lunch, she told herself she had fallen in love with him.

As she helped Candy bathing and feeding Jeremy in the nursery on the very same afternoon that she had made this deep discovery, Pippa framed a question that had been creeping up on her ever since they'd had a guided tour of the house on the first day of their visit. 'Do you *like* it here?'

It was obvious that her mother was absorbed in looking after her new baby and was waited on hand and foot, but although the countryside was beautiful, it can't have been as interesting for her as being in London. For instance, there were no friends popping in and out, no Isabella to talk to. And apart from these few rooms they lived in, the place was so shabby and gloomy.

'I mean,' continued Pippa, trying to cover her mother's silence, 'It's like living in a museum, isn't it? And a not very well-looked-after one at that. Look at those curtains in the ballroom. They must be fifty years old and they'd fall to pieces if anyone took the trouble to wash them.'

'Yes, there's a lot that needs doing. It's like a mausoleum and I don't know why it's been allowed to get into this state.' Candy signalled that she was ready to lift the gurgling baby out of the enamel bath that stood in a folding frame alongside her chair. Pippa picked up the fluffy towel that lay on another chair and held it out. Between them they wrapped the baby up and Pippa ended up holding it in her arms. She bent her head and laid a cheek against the peach soft skin, smelling soap and a fresh new scent that she'd never come across anywhere else. Her heart swelled with love for the tiny creature.

'You little darling,' she cooed. 'You are so lucky, Mummy, having him.'

Candy smiled, laying out a clean nightdress and nappies. 'I'm lucky having you all. Don't you want to come and hold him, Danny?'

Pippa was sure Danny would say no, just to be disagreeable. But she looked up from her book in her place on the window seat and saw Pippa cuddling him and said, 'Yes, that would be nice.' She set aside her book and got up and came across and Pippa had no option but to pass her the squirming bundle and her moment of happiness evaporated.

'Actually,' Danny said, 'I don't think you're lucky having us all. Eleanor says it's just carelessness.'

Candy flushed. 'Eleanor has no right to comment. She's never been a mother. I doubt she's ever...' The sentence was left unfinished and Pippa wondered what her mother had been about to say. Jiggling Jeremy in her arms, Danny took a turn around the room and the baby, suddenly insecure, began to cry. She quickly thrust him into her mother's arms.

'There you are. I think he's rather horrid, actually. Can I go and read in our own room?'

'You can go and get washed and change into something clean for dinner.'

'I haven't got anything clean to wear.'

'You'll find some new dresses in the closet in your room.'

'They're not mine.'

'I bought them for you. I told you yesterday. You go and help her, Pippa.'

'Can't I stay and help you?' Pippa was passing tiny garments to her mother. She wanted to restore the happiness she had felt earlier. And the talk of babies had reminded her that she wanted to have a few minutes with Candy, without Danny's presence - something she had almost forgotten about with the fun of riding. For once Danny's awkwardness played into her hands. 'I can manage,' she said, picking up her book and flouncing off.

Once the baby was dressed Candy settled him on her lap and Pippa took the feeding bottle from the warmer and efficiently tested the liquid on her hand before passing it to Candy. Then, drawing breath to give herself courage, she asked, 'Mummy, how do you know when you're going to have a baby?'

She noticed, for the second time, a flush in her mother's cheeks and guessed he subject wasn't one she was comfortable with.

'Well...For one thing, your periods stop. You know about periods, do you?'

'Yes, mine started ages ago.'

'Oh, I see.'

'Does that mean I could start a baby?'

'No darling, of course not. You have to have sexual intercourse first. With a man.'

'That's what the girls at school say. But nobody's sure what happens.'

Candy's blush deepened and she gazed a the baby's head rather than look up at Pippa. Oh dear, thought Pippa. I'm making her very unhappy.

'It's down below, darling, where we're different. If you like someone you let them join up with you and that makes a baby.'

It was Pippa's turn to blush. She'd had a feeling it was to do with that private part of a man that she'd never seen other than on her little brothers. How disgusting! She couldn't imagine letting that thing anywhere near to her body. The only way it could be endured would be to close your eyes and keep very still and pretend it wasn't really happening. She could see how you'd only do that if you really wanted a baby. It couldn't at all be carelessness, like Eleanor had said. So it was fascinating as well as disgusting. 'What does it feel like? When you join up?'

'It can be quite horrid,' Candy said with a frankness that confused Pippa even further. 'But if you do it with someone you really love it's just...heavenly.'

At dinner every evening the man who Pippa could only think of as THE EARL, though she was supposed to call him Uncle Robert, questioned her politely about where she had been riding, and then how she was getting on at school studying for her Higher School Certificate.

'We don't do School Certificate any more. It's called the General Certificate of Education at Ordinary and Advanced level and we get separate grades in every subject we take.'

'I see. Things are always changing. And how well are you expected to do?'

His voice sounds as though he's really interested, thought Pippa and she said, 'Oh, I passed last year in everything, except French. That's very hard to understand. I'm only doing English and History this year."

'Latin?'

'I can do Latin. I liked it – all that stuff Caesar wrote about the British. But we don't do it in the sixth form'

All the while they were talking Pippa couldn't keep out of her mind a disturbing picture of him joined at the genitals to her mother, making Jeremy. Would they have done it standing up or lying down? And would they have had to take their clothes off? She supposed yes, down there anyway. Had he been one of the horrid experiences or one of the heavenly ones? And why were they different anyway? Surely it all felt the same whoever you did it with?

Then, just as Danny was beginning to shift impatiently in her seat because she wasn't getting enough attention, The Earl turned to her. 'And, you, my dear. What is your favourite subject at school?'

'Religious Study. I like learning about sins and the way God punishes people.'

The next day, Saturday, it was raining and Tom Bright was quite surprised when Pippa appeared at the usual time, ready to ride. In his experience toffee-nosed girls weren't usually so keen when it meant getting wet. He felt a surge of admiration for her but he wasn't best pleased. Rain wasn't his favourite weather and he'd been hoping to get away with giving the ponies half an hour's exercise around the yard.

Then he wondered if it was the ponies she'd come to see, or him. He'd certainly got her jumping and fluttering her eyelashes at him and he'd like to go further, but this girl was an unknown quantity and he'd have to be careful. No sense in frightening her off or getting himself into trouble. Play it cool, give her the signs and leave it up to her. A bit of petting would be fun but if he held off till she was gagging for it, he might get lucky and she'd go all the way.

So he smiled when he saw her and suggested a short ride through the woodland. While they were saddling up he didn't wait for her to move out of the way before stepping forward to check she had the girth right, and his whole body pushed against hers. She didn't draw back and as he worked he could feel through their clothes the soft rounding of her left breast against his shoulder. When he straightened up and looked at her face he saw a tell-tale red stain spreading up her neck to her cheeks. Their eyes met and she smiled uncertainly.

Got her, he thought. 'Right', he said. 'Let's be off. Make sure you button up your mac well.' Perhaps tomorrow, a kiss and a fumble.

Pippa couldn't get Tom out of her mind and she didn't dare to talk to anyone about this unfamiliar obsession. She even dreamed about him when she finally fell asleep. That he hadn't made any advances to her beyond being close only added to the strength of her feelings. She believed he was too good, too nice to take it any further. She was hazy about what 'taking it further' might actually mean. Perhaps he would ask her to go for walks in the evening, he might put his arms around her and give her some passionate kisses. Perhaps he would want to touch her breasts, a prospect that excited her deeply as soon as she thought of it. Would she let him? Probably not. It would definitely be beyond the bounds of decency.

And afterwards...what? In three more days she would be on the train back to Lincolnshire. They could write each other letters, then. They could arrange to meet during her next weekend with Mummy, either here or in London. And after she'd taken her exams and left school they could get engaged and marry and live in one of those nice little houses on the estate that Tom had told her were for servants and tenants.

Sunday's ride was cut short by preparations for the picnic party. At twelve thirty Pippa knew she had to be dressed up smartly and waiting with her mother and Uncle Robert to welcome some people called the Conways and the Sheffords who had been invited because, it seemed, they had children about the same age as Pippa and Danny. There was also a young man called Trasker who, explained Candy, was Uncle Robert's Parliamentary Secretary, but he had stayed overnight and spent hours in the study with Uncle Robert working on papers. Pippa was disappointed to find that the picnic wasn't a proper picnic with rugs and sandwiches on the lawn. It was an array of cold buffet dishes served on a long table on the terrace and in the fresh breeze that followed yesterday's rain it was quite uncomfortable, with napkins and carefully set hair blowing about at random.

Pippa helped herself to food and went to sit on a small chair near the wall of the house. She would have liked to sit near to her mother but Candy was hemmed in by the adults who were chattering and laughing. Danny was sitting on the terrace steps, another little girl beside her and not a word passed between them as they tucked in to sausage rolls and chicken pie.

One of the 'children', a boy who might have been about Pippa's age, drew up a chair beside her. 'Hello,' he said in a friendly way. 'You're Philippa aren't you? The Earl's new stepdaughter? So pleased to meet you. I'm Geoffrey Shefford. I say, this is jolly, isn't it?'

If only, thought Pippa, you were Tom, it would be extremely jolly. She tried hard to make polite conversation to the boy but all he wanted to talk about was his school sporting teams. He didn't seem to know anything about films and books and he thought London was dirty and boring. But he did fetch her a plate of jelly for pudding and because he was trying to be nice, she smiled at him and pretended to be interested. After lunch the young people were sent off to play French cricket on the lawn and after a while Trasker came to join them, then the rest of the men, while the ladies cooed over Jeremy and passed him around from lap to lap.

Then a dreadful thing happened. In a break in the game, when everyone was drinking lemonade, Pippa heard Candy calling her over. Obediently she went to find out what was wanted. 'Darling,' Candy said, indicating the blonde-haired woman who sat beside her, 'Lady Conway has invited you over tomorrow to ride with Felicity and Jane. Won't that be lovely? You'll have some company at last – you've been so good about riding on your own.'

'But...' Pippa's face fell and she began to blush furiously. 'I haven't been alone. What about Tom and the ponies here?'

'You don't have to worry about that, darling. We'll send you over in a car after breakfast...'

'Yes, and why doesn't she stay to lunch? All right, Pippa? We'll expect you tomorrow.'

Pippa mumbled her thanks as graciously as she could and just about managed to return their smiles before she escaped back to the game that now seemed a merciful relief rather than a boring irrelevance.

There was no way she could get out of the invitation for tomorrow, she could see that immediately. Not without causing her mother considerable embarrassment, anyway. But whatever was she going to do if she couldn't see Tom tomorrow? She would just die. She just *had* to talk to him or she might never, ever get to see him again. But it was afternoon now, he would be at home and with all the things he had told her about the place, he hadn't mentioned where he lived. She tried to keep cheerful and choke back her tears during the rest of the visit but it wasn't easy. Finally, after a cup of tea all round, the visitors piled into their cars and waved goodbye. 'See you tomorrow!' called Felicity and Jane in turn, and Pippa raised a leaden hand and matching smile in acknowledgement. Afterwards, while helping to carry the chairs indoors, she couldn't bear the pain any longer and she slipped away and ran to he stables, half-blinded by tears. Inside Frisky's stall she put her arms around the pony's shining neck and buried her face in its mane, breathing in the warm animal scent. The pony shifted its weight and tossed its head, reached round to try to nibble at her back.

'Oh Frisky,'she wept. 'I love you too, but not nearly as much as I love him. And I have to go home the day after tomorrow. Why, oh why can't I stay here for ever?'

The contact with the pony quietened her tears. She even thought of saddling up and going for a ride there and then but she wasn't dressed for it, and she was a little afraid of what would happen if something went wrong. After all, it wasn't her pony. She was suddenly startled by the swish of bicycle tyres on the cobbles outside, followed by the squeaking of brakes, then footsteps accompanied by a merry whistling. Her heart leapt as she recognised the sounds and it was a though the sun had burst forth from behind a black cloud.

'Tom!' Of course, he'd come to feed and water the ponies.

'Surprise, surprise!' He grinned, then saw her face. 'What's up?'

She turned from the pony and flung herself against him so that he had no choice but to put his arms around her or he would have overbalanced. 'Oh Tom! I've been invited to ride with the Sheffords tomorrow and I thought I'd never see you again to explain why I didn't turn up.'

'Most young ladies wouldn't have bothered about that.'

'Yes but...I...' She felt a blush rising from her throat. 'I love you Tom.'

'Yes, I know.' His voice was gentle and he closed his lips over hers in what was her first sexual kiss.

At first it felt strange, hot and prickly and she almost drew back. But he kissed her again and again, on her cheeks, her temples, her neck, then back to her lips, and she began to feel a rush of excitement. She responded with pressure from her own mouth and even let him push her lips apart and touch her tongue with his. Then she felt his hands clutching her buttocks, fingers exploring the cleft through the cotton of her dress. At the same time a hard lump in his trousers began to press against her stomach. A pulse began to beat between her legs and it was as though a fire was spreading through her body.

So this was why people joined together to make babies! And now, far from finding the idea disgusting of him touching her with his thingy, she actually *wanted* him to do it.

Candy had been aware of the upset that the riding invitation had caused Pippa and as soon as the guests had gone she meant to take her to one side and find out what the problem was. If Pippa didn't want to go, she wasn't going to force her. But by the time she'd put Jeremy in his pram, Pippa was nowhere too be seen. Only Danny was still helping to carry stuff in from the terrace.

'I expect she went to meet her lover,' said Danny when Candy asked if she'd seen her sister.

'Her lover?' A jolt shot through Candy. Surely...? But Pippa was not much older than she'd been when... Unwelcome memories came flooding back and a kind of terror gripped her heart. She mustn't let Pippa suffer as she had done.

'Yes.' Danny was obviously pleased with the effect of her words. 'That Tom. Who looks after the ponies. Pippa's in love with him. I've been watching them,' she added with dark glee.

Candy didn't wait to comment. Her heart pounding, she ran along the pebbled paths that led to the stable block. At the door of the ponies' stable she paused, looking around, knowing she wasn't alone. Then she saw them, locked together in a passionate embrace, and immediately registered relief that they were still on their feet and still had their clothes on. But it was a near thing. Tom's hand was up her skirt and Pippa had a look of bliss on her face. Feeling awful about interrupting but desperate to rescue Pippa from what would inevitably happen next, Candy leaned on the door post for a moment. Then she cleared her throat. 'Pippa! Stop that at once, both of you.'

They sprang apart as though they'd been stung, hastily trying to smooth their clothing and Candy gathered courage. 'You should know better,' she directed at Tom.

Tom jumped back and raised his hands, as though to convince her they were clean. 'I ain't done nothing to her, Yer Grace. Nothing at all except a few kisses and it were her that...'

'Yes, yes.' She knew, only too well. She stepped forward and clasped Pippa's hand and pulled her outside, into the yard and along the path. 'How could you?'she hissed as they stumbled along. 'You're asking for trouble, and with a stable lad too!'

'But we love each other, Mummy!' wailed Pippa, pulling her hand away.

Candy slowed down and led the way to a little arbor off the main path where someone had once installed a marble seat for people to rest on as they walked around the huge garden. 'Darling, it's out of the question, you know that. A lad like that would never make a decent husband. You'll get over this feeling you have for him, I promise you, and someone really nice and suitable will come along.'

She tried to put an arm around Pippa's shoulders but it was shaken off as Pippa carried on sniffing and sobbing. In her heart Candy knew that it would be a long time before Pippa forgave her. But she had done the right thing, she knew she had. It would have been a disaster to have history repeating itself. Or would it? Should she have left the child – she could still only think of her as that – to enjoy her first sexual experience, then helped her to pick up the pieces afterwards? Should she? Then she thought of Peter and Eleanor, how they would pounce on any reason to keep the girls away from her, how they would point their fingers and say 'I told you so!'

Pippa crept into the house at her mother's side, trying to keep her face in the shadows, and she went straight up to her bed and continued to weep quietly and helplessly into her pillow. Again and again Candy tried to talk to her, comfort her, again and again Pippa shrugged her off. What did she want with her mother's arms when it was Tom she was crying for? A tray of supper was brought, she never saw who by, but she ignored it. How could she be expected to eat? She was aware that Danny came into the room and sat on the window seat with her book for a while, then went away again.

She woke up later with a terrible headache and it was dark and she wanted to go to the toilet. Danny was asleep in her own bed so she was quiet as she changed into her nightdress, then made her way along the corridor. She saw the soft glow of a nightlight in the baby's room and on her way back from the bathroom she crept in and looked down at her little brother, asleep in his cradle.

So sweet, so perfect.

She reached out to stroke the back of one of his tiny hands, then uncurled his fingers and let them grip one of hers. How she would love a baby of her own! She leaned forward and brushed his downy head with her lips. Of course, she wasn't old enough yet but the time would come. She would see Tom when she could and as soon as she was old enough to marry they could make their own baby. At least she now knew that it wouldn't be a distasteful experience, it would be sheer heaven.

She didn't go to the Sheffords' the next day. She felt really tired and she looked awful with red puffy eyes and a sore nose. Candy phoned after breakfast and said she was ill, and instead she spent the morning alone in her room writing the first of many long letters to Tom. He never answered a single one of them and next time she visited Northelm a girl groom was looking after the ponies and they told her that Tom had gone off to join the army.

*   *   *

All through the service Leon supported the old lady near the back of the church, trying to ignore the heavy sherry fumes she was breathing into the damp air, and trying to help her to avoid tripping over the hem of the blue dress that trailed haplessly along the ground where it dipped out of shape because her figure was several sizes smaller than the one the dress was designed for. She patted his arm, linked through hers, and smiled and called him 'dear boy' and he was sure she didn't remember which dear boy he actually was. But he was remembering her, all right. It was the blue dress that brought it all tumbling back, the evening that Isabella had clucked in annoyance because his mother and Aunt Netta were squabbling about the dress which made Candy late for dinner, which annoyed Isabella even more. He had hidden on a bend in the stairs and seen Tatton arrive. That was the first time he had seen Tatton, who was really kind to him after that and who carelessly crashed his little plane which made their lives suddenly change again. After that his mother got married to the Earl and began to pack up the house in London, and Isabella and Carlo went back to California. Then his father came over from Hollywood and took him back for the summer holiday. That was all Leon had wanted in the world, to be with Rupert in the place he regarded as home, and after arguing about it for what seemed like for ever, his mother let him go. It didn't seem to matter that the summer holiday somehow never came to an end and he only came back again when he was a grown man, for the rock concert.

And as he remembered, he knew he'd got things all wrong. It suddenly became clear what had happened and why his mother had changed her life and married the Earl, and he knew who Jeremy's real father was. Then the important questions came into his mind.

Does Jeremy know?

And what about Aunt Netta?

9
LEILA

'I want to go up to the house.'

Netta's voice was cracked and wavering, yet still not to be argued with. The family from the front row had shuffled, heads bowed, towards the crypt but most of the guests were emptying out into the churchyard and beyond, many already strolling the half-mile up to the big house. Leon wanted to follow Jeremy and his family into the crypt but as the old lady clung to his arm he took the line of least resistance. What did it matter if he was there or not? It wouldn't make one jot of difference to the proceedings. The little fat nun had already stepped out towards the house and Pippa – where was Pippa? In a sudden panic he swept his eyes around the church lest she be close to him without him knowing. Then he saw that she was one of the black-clad figures following the coffin towards the entrance to the crypt. He desperately wanted to follow her, to abandon this bizarre scene that was developing around him and to walk at her side, eyes lowered, behind their mother's coffin. There was sin to atone for, the terrible shadow of her parting words so long ago.

'Over my dead body…'

Could that ever be erased?

And yet something important was happening here as well. He couldn't quite work out what but it was as though he was having one of those nightmares when they had started on the wrong backing for the song he had to sing.

Aunt Netta was tugging at his arm. 'I'll need a car,' she was saying. 'I can't walk up there.'

Several cars had been ordered to provide for this eventuality, big black Daimlers with suitably sombre drivers, and Leon led Netta towards the road and waved one of them forwards. As he did so, an equally big Mercedes, made sinister by tinted glass, crept up the road from the village and parked directly in front of them. As it drew to a halt a brisk and expensively suited young man jumped out, hardly concealing the gun he carried under his dark jacket. He stood for a moment, back to the car, eyeing the slowly moving groups of people. Then a second man alighted from the car, slightly portly, well dressed, grey-haired, clean shaven, an olive tinge to his complexion. He glanced around, stepped forward and held out a hand to Leon, and said in slightly accented English, 'Excuse me, is this where they are holding the funeral service for the Dowager Countess of Penmore?'

This isn't happening, thought Leon. We're in Yorkshire, not Hollywood. He was sure that Jeremy and Meggie were not expecting any visitation from foreign royals or Middle Eastern terrorists. Yet the manner of his mother's death swept once again to the forefront of his mind and he thought, car bombs! He glanced wildly around and took an instinctive step back. Then he recovered his composure and shook the stranger's hand and said, 'You've missed the actual service but not the reception at the house. I'm Leon Taylor.'

'Delighted to meet you. I am Naseem Fahy. I believe we share a mother in common. I am sorry I am late, but ...' He was interrupted by a small shriek and groan from Netta who seemed to have fainted on Leon's arm.

More than anything, Leon wanted to sit down and talk with this urbane stranger who, he realised, must be the baby his mother had left in Jaffa. It made all other considerations seem unimportant, the funereal music that was weaving melodies and counter-melodies in his head, even his need to talk to Pippa. But he was stuck with having to help Netta into one of the cars and ride up to the house with her, then help the old lady up to a bedroom where she could lie down and, hopefully, recover her senses. If she ever had any in the first place, Leon thought unkindly.

Ahead of the family party, sombre groups of guests were beginning to arrive from the church and catering staff were hovering around with trays of drinks to greet them as they came through the door. Leon helped himself to a large Scotch from Jeremy's private decanter, then found Naseem Fahy standing alone on the terrace, regarding the view with an almost proprietorial air. He also held a glass of Scotch in his hand and Leon thought, 'Not a practising Muslim, then.'

Composing himself, he approached Naseem, extending a hand. No need to make the fellow feel uncomfortable. 'Is this your first visit to Yorkshire?' he asked, feeling a pang of recognition at the long, tapering fingers that rested in his, and the large dark eyes that were turned towards him with a quizzical smile.

'No. I have been a guest here many times. Our mother and her aristocratic husband were welcoming towards me in recent years. I must admit, though, that since his death we tended to meet up in London or my house in Surrey.'

Christ! thought Leon, why didn't I know about you? And he felt a rising anger at a two-faced nun who had coolly lied to him, then accepted his money. She must have known about a child being born to the terrified English girl. Then he understood that he might have known more if he had been a more frequent visitor in his mother's life. But after Pippa...

'And Palestine? Did you meet her in Palestine?' He was unearthing a whole new side of his mother's life. Was he also coming close to the reason for her death?

'No. Never. I advised her never to go to Palestine, and it gives me no pleasure to have been right.'

'So you must know who killed her?'

'Indeed I do.'

'And...'

'The matter is in hand. Unfortunately it isn't simple.'

'Is that all you've got to say?' Leon raised his voice. The turmoil of his emotions was coming to a head. He felt guilt at all the happy years he had passed with Rupert in Hollywood, never giving his mother's feelings a thought. And at the same time he felt anger with her for having a life that didn't include him. And an enormous sense of desolation at the knowledge that he was an outsider here, a bit player on a stage where he might have been a star.

Naseem Fahy, the insider, looked at him almost tenderly. 'No, it is not all I have to say, but I would prefer to speak to the whole family together, then there will be no misunderstandings.'

'Does Jeremy know?'

'A meeting has been arranged for later.'

'He didn't tell me.'

'I wasn't sure that I could get here. I had another funeral to attend in Tel Aviv yesterday. He'll tell you when he knows. As soon as they arrive back at the house.'

Which wouldn't be long now. And that would mean Pippa would be there too, no escaping it. The part of his body and soul that longed to see her again thrust him forward in anticipation. The part that told him there would be nothing there, it had been too long ago and only disaster and disappointment would come from this day, held him firmly back and told him to find somewhere to hide. Shaking his head in confusion, he stepped away from his newly-found brother just too late to avoid the whirlwind that was Aunt Netta, now fully recovered and nursing a glass of what looked like gin and tonic but smelled like neat gin. She tottered past Leon, right up to Naseem, and gripped his arm, peering up into his face with a mixture of anger and hauteur.

'Naseem Fahy!' Her cry was almost a screech. 'What do you think you are doing here? You weren't invited! You're nothing but a jumped-up houseboy!'

Naseem smiled, unabashed, and spoke to Leon over her head. 'She thinks I'm my father.' He patted Netta's arm. 'I'm Leila Fahy's grandson, the boy your sister gave birth to after my father was murdered by your father.' It came out in such a pleasant, conversational tone that the groups of people circulating nearby never guessed they were talking about anything more intense than the weather.

'That's not true.' Some of the aggression fell away from Netta and she faltered as she looked into Naseem's eyes and saw something there that she recognised. 'Is it? She didn't have a baby. We all went to England, then to America because of the war...'

'She didn't go with you,' Leon said. 'She was left behind in the convent in Jaffa.'

'I'm sure...' Netta shook her head. She let her hand fall from Naseem's arm and stepped back, taking a comforting swallow from her glass. 'I was sure...but it's all such a long time ago. Just like her, though, always flinging herself at men. Pretending to be something she wasn't...' She raised her glass and her voice began to carry further than the two men she was standing with. 'Here's to Candy, Countess of Fairyland. Give her a few more years and she'd have made herself queen!'

One or two people standing nearby smiled indulgently, some turned away in embarrassment. Leon wondered if he should take some responsibility and steer his aunt somewhere quiet and discreet but he had already left her once in a darkened bedroom. If she was so determined to join the function, there was no way she would be kept out other than putting her under lock and key, and he didn't see that as something he could make a decision about. Just then Jeremy strode out onto the terrace, clearly looking for someone. Nodding to right and left and shaking a few hands as he came forward, he crossed the flagstones and stopped in front of Naseem.

With a warm handshake he said, 'So pleased you could get here.' Then he turned to take Leon into the conversation but Leon was already making his escape, knowing that Pippa wouldn't be far behind, probably upstairs taking off her hat and powdering her nose, or whatever women did these days. He panicked, turned and made his way through the rapidly increasing press of people, through the door that led to the kitchens, and into the gun room, where the banished dogs were delighted to have some company. There he flung himself down onto the old armchair that the dogs slept on and pondered on why Naseem and Jeremy, the oldest and youngest of his siblings, born into two different worlds, could possibly know each other so well.

* * *

In the year after Candy became a countess and Pippa, like hundreds of other English girls, nearly lost her virginity to a stable lad, the young Naseem Fahy graduated from Beirut university and chose to exercise some form of defiance against the wishes of his family. They wanted him to do two things that he wasn't happy about. The first concerned whom he should marry, the second what he should do with the next stage of his life.

He learned about the marriage plans by accident, overhearing a telephone conversation between his Aunt Fawzia, Hanif's wife, and her cousin Yasmina. He quickly realised they were doing what elderly ladies liked to do best, discussing the marriage prospects of the younger generation and at first he was amused.

'Yes, I know about her teeth, but she will bring a good dowry and what's a few protruding teeth compared to a lifetime of happiness.' Pause. 'No, I don't think he has.' Pause. 'No, he's not that sort.' Pause. 'He will soon get settled down now and find a job...yes, he's clever enough...probably in Hanif's business.' Pause. 'Well, I'm sure in view of the teeth, they will overlook the unfortunate matter of his mother ...'

It suddenly occurred to Naseem that they were talking about him and some girl he had never met, with buck teeth and a rich father. What was it they thought he hadn't done? Slept with girls? Well Aunt Fawzia, I have news for you, but I better not tell it to you. A lot of that goes on in Beirut, it's that sort of city. Full of beautiful girls, many of them not that fussy.

Naseem crept away from the old lady's telephone conversation and sat on the verandah, pretending to read a book but in fact thinking about a girl he had first seen in the university library. For weeks now he had been taking his books to the table opposite her every afternoon and waiting for her to look up, as she always did, and meet his eyes and smile at him. When that happened his heart fluttered and the blood pounded in his veins and he thought to himself, Am I falling in love? Is this *the* one?

Not being a timid young man, he began passing her notes and soon discovered that she was Armenian and her name was Marianne, and that she would be happy to meet him for coffee some time. That 'some time' became every day, after lectures were over. Marianne was studying languages with a view to becoming a teacher and their shared background as refugees from their homelands increased the attraction between them. He even confided the truth about his strange English mother and his murdered father, and she told him how her mother had been smuggled out of northern Iraq wrapped in a carpet, like Cleopatra. By the time he overheard his aunt's plans Naseem had become obsessed with Marianne's wide brown eyes, her rich reddish hair, her quick smile. They had shared kisses but no sex, simply because neither of them could think of anywhere to go in private. As the weeks passed and Naseem felt the tensions rising within him every time he walked or talked with her, he became more and more certain that he wanted to marry Marianne. The only problem he could see was how to introduce her to his family in such a way that they would understand that a dowry was not an acceptable recompense for buck teeth and a girl he didn't love. He would have to be sure, first, that he had a decent job that didn't depend on the family's help.

It took a while, but he finally summoned the courage to broach the subject with his Uncle Hanif. They were sitting together in the cooling evening on the verandah of the apartment, where Hanif was always banished after dinner to smoke a cigar. Naseem had always liked these companionable times. The smell of cigar smoke and his uncle's soft voice telling him stories, explaining to him things he didn't fully understand about his studies, were part of the man's world that the women inside had no knowledge of as they talked of clothes and parties. Hanif, who by now ran one of the biggest stationery businesses in Beirut, knew all about the real world and Naseem believed he would get an honest answer to the problem that was vexing him.

He asked, 'Uncle, is it true that you want me to marry some girl with buck teeth?'

Hanif puffed several times on his smelly cigar and regarded his nephew through narrowed eyes. 'What gives you that idea?'

'I overheard Aunt Fawzia…'

Hanif waved a dismissive hand. 'Don't take any notice. Women like that sort of gossip…'

'Then I can marry who I like?'

'I didn't say that. Have you met someone?'

'There is a girl…'

'And you are madly in love?'

'I suppose you might say…'

'It's what *you* might say, not me.'

'I love her, yes.'

'And you must marry her?'

'Not 'must'. I want to.'

Hanif paused, a long pause while he puffed some more at his cigar. 'This marriage, it should wait a while. '

Naseem's heart screwed up with longing and disappointment. Even to be told to wait until next week distressed him. 'I know her family is not wealthy, Uncle, but she is clever, she is to be a teacher, and she is beautiful and together we can make a happy family, I'm sure.'

'I'm sure you can, but life is not primarily about making happy families with beautiful girls. Have you forgotten that we are exiles? Have you forgotten what happened to my brothers?'

'Of course I haven't forgotten, but what can I do about that?'

'You can do what many of your compatriots do, Naseem. You can join the liberation army and fight for your homeland.'

'Me?' This was something new, something Naseem hadn't anticipated, and he didn't know how to respond. It had never crossed his mind that Hanif would expect him to become a soldier. He felt a choking nausea rise in his throat.

'Why not you?'

Naseem closed his eyes tightly and felt himself being sucked into the nightmare that still woke him some nights. He heard screams and saw Rashid and Jamal spilling their blood on the dust of their farm before they could save the girls. What if that happened to him, to Marianne? 'You want me to go back to Israel?' His voice stumbled with fear.

'Not immediately. But you are an engineer and, unless I am very much mistaken, I have not paid for your education for nothing. I want you to go now to Algeria for a few months. Several of your cousins are already there. They have training camps set up where you will be turned into an efficient soldier and then we will decide whether to keep you here or send you to the West Bank.'

'You want me to kill people?'

Hanif nodded. 'As few as possible, of course, but yes. It is the only way. Civilised negotiations have broken down. We must fight – well, you young people must fight. And I want the name of Fahy to continue to mean something in Palestine.'

'It's called Israel now, Uncle.'

'That's what I mean. Now, you can see that it would be wrong to commit yourself to any young girl as a husband while we are engaged in an *intifada*. In fact, it would be better if you don't see your girl again – make it less painful all round. Let her think you have deserted her. I was going to offer you a little holiday first, but perhaps it would be better if you go to Algeria right away?'

Naseem nodded, but in his heart he felt anything but complaisant. No need to wonder why Hanif had kept these plans from him until now. It was clear that the whole family was still involved in the web of secrecy that his uncle Jamal had started all those years ago. He probably hadn't been told because students talked carelessly and they would not entirely trust him. But once he had gone to the training camp he would automatically be suspect to the authorities, and could be relied upon to keep his mouth shut.

That evening and the following night his emotions wavered between fear and anger. By what right did his family think they could just take over his life, simply because they had looked after him all those years? Once it began there would be no way out, no chance of happiness, just a cruel, lonely death. He wanted no part of it and there was only one way to escape. Now he understood why his grandmother had left the scrapbooks for him. It was time for him to go to England.

Would Marianne understand? Would she come with him? Would either of them be able to get out of the country? He had a passport because of a study trip his class had made to Germany last year, but what about Marianne? Then he remembered she was a language student – she would be bound to have travelled to other countries.

First thing the following morning he met Marianne at 'their' café and told her what was happening. To his utter relief she grasped his hands in hers and tried to calm him. 'Of course I will come with you. I have a little money. We can marry next week, then fly to London and claim refugee status.'

'Did you say marry?'

'Of course. You don't think I have any other plans for you, do you?'

Gazing into her eyes, feeling her firm grasp on his hands, he suddenly felt secure again. All right, so what he was about to do would anger Hanif and the whole Fahy clan, but they would soon forget, and he knew in his heart that marrying Marianne and going to England was the right thing to do because that plan crushed his despair and made him feel happy. Their wedding was quick and quiet, attended by a few of their student friends, who admired them for being modern and taking matters into their own hands instead of bowing to their family's wishes. They spent their wedding night in the bed of one of their friends, who moved out with pretences of grumbling that hid his envy of Naseem. They coupled with a sense of complete joy and adventure – they had each other safely at last and there was no going back.

It wasn't as easy as Naseem had expected to get settled in England and find his mother. It didn't take long to find out where Candy lived but he wasn't at all sure of exactly where Yorkshire was, or the best way to approach her. After all, he had nothing except his name to prove who he was and the worst thing would be for her to think he was simply looking for money. So he concentrated on finding work and looking after Marianne. They were admitted into England on tourist visas easily enough and soon managed to hide themselves from the authorities and find work - Naseem in a music shop in the Tottenham Court Road, Marianne in a café nearby. But Naseem wasn't content with just getting by, feeding themselves and paying the rent for an ugly bed-sitter. He soon noticed that London was full of people wearing outlandish clothing from a place called Carnaby Street and he bought Marianne a sewing machine and persuaded her to make Arab-style garments that pleased the fashionable younger generation and which he sold at a good price on a market stall. Before long they had their own factory and a shop in Covent Garden and the *'Famous Fahy Fashion'* label was becoming well known amongst the flower children.

Which was why Pippa, on one of her visits to her mother in London, one day dragged Candy to the shop to buy some cool gear. She knew her father would never let her wear those kind of clothes but she thought that Candy would like them, even though her tastes were becoming a little old-fashioned as she grew older. As Pippa struggled in and out of one garment after another and Candy patiently picked up and folded the discarded dresses, Candy's only thought was how pretty her daughter was becoming. Then, as Pippa struck poses in front of the mirror, Candy's eye caught the label in one of the garments and she became so absorbed in what it said that Pippa had to prompt her to admire the next outfit.

'What's the matter, Mummy? Don't you like this one?'

'Of course. They're all lovely.' But Candy continued to frown over the words *'Famous Fahy Fashions'* and she turned to the shop assistant and asked where the clothes came from. 'Do you import this stuff from abroad?'

'Oh no, Mrs Fahy designs them and they're sewn in a little factory just off the Mile End Road.'

Candy felt her heartbeat increase and she sat down sharply on a chair just outside the fitting room. She knew it was a co-incidence but she couldn't stop her heart pounding as memories flooded back of a desolate girl starting work sewing rough cloth for soldiers' uniforms. Was there really still a factory in the same street, now turning out these pretty clothes? She thought the whole area had been bombed.

Then Pippa came out of the fitting room and did a turn to show off how the gauzy material clung to her body. 'What do you think of this one?'

'Whatever you like, darling. You look lovely in all of them.'

The next day Pippa went back to Lincolnshire, but she took care to leave her Fahy outfits in the wardrobe in the small apartment that had taken the place of the Curzon Street House as Candy's pied a terre in London. The house had been sold for a small fortune and the money been used to start renovations at Northelm. Candy had another day of shopping planned, looking for light fittings for the breakfast room at Northelm, then she was to meet Robert for dinner and an evening reception. But as she dashed from shop to shop she couldn't throw off the feeling of being haunted by the strange co-incidence of the Fahy clothes and a factory in the East End. By lunchtime it had become too much for her. She flagged down a taxi and told the driver where she wanted to go. He was surly and unfriendly and Candy knew London well enough to recognise that he deliberately took her a long route to Mile End. But finally she was there, standing on the wide pavement outside the underground station, looking around for some sign of *Famous Fahy Fashions.* Nothing was as she remembered it. Twice she asked directions from young women who didn't seem to speak any English. Finally an elderly Sikh gentleman sent her to the right street and she found her self standing outside a blank-walled building with *Fahy* painted on a board over the entrance door.

'What am I doing here?' She said it out loud as she stood on the opposite pavement. Who was she looking for? Even if there was a connection between the owners of this factory and her first lover long ago in Palestine, it meant nothing to her any more. Naseem had been killed, her baby had died. God only knew what had happened to the rest of the family.

Then a van drew up outside the factory entrance. The driver jumped down from his cab and knocked on the factory door, then opened the back of the van and began to unload rolls of cloth. A moment later a second young man came out of the factory to help him with the work and as she watched strong arms lifting the packages and heard snatches of Arabic conversation, Candy knew she was dreaming. She must be, because this was a ghost in front of her.

Then Naseem turned and looked at her and their eyes met.

He recognised her because, even though she was ageing, with greying hair and the beginning of lines around her eyes and the corners of her mouth, she still looked like the film star photos he kept in the box his grandmother had left for him. For her part, she recognised a likeness to the boy she had loved so startling that the first thought that washed over her was that Leila had lied to him, and Naseem hadn't been murdered after all. But then she realised the man she was looking at was far too young to be her Naseem – he must be some younger relative of the family. Slowly he came across the road towards her, holding out his right hand, and when he was close enough he said, 'Excuse me, but you are Countess Candy, aren't you?'

She nodded and extended her own hand to grip his. As she touched him she seemed to freeze and she had to try three times before she could say, 'Yes...but who are you?'

Finally it got through to her that he was saying, 'I am Naseem Fahy.'

'No, you can't be. Naseem died. I saw him dead...'

'But you had his child. My grandmother Leila told me you had his child.'

'No.' She was still standing shaking her head. Her knees were shaking so much that but for his firm hand gripping her arm, she might have collapsed right there on the pavement. 'No. My baby died.'

'No, I am very much not dead. My grandmother Leila brought me up in the West Bank and Beirut. Now I have this business in England and a little daughter of my own. But I lack a mother. Please, please say that is you and you still want me.'

'Of course I still want you! I've always wanted you!' Tears poured down her face as she realised what she had missed, what had been stolen from her when they took him away and told her he had died. Whose idea had that been? Leila's? Her father's?

Naseem folded his arms around her and gave a spontaneous whoop of joy. The passers-by and most of the staff of *Famous Fahy Fashions* were then treated to the unexpected sight of an almost hysterical young Arab lifting a middle aged English lady off her feet and whirling her round and round.

* * *

'Watch me, Grandma! Watch me!'

Candy acknowledged the cry by getting up from her lounger on the terrace and shielding her eyes with her hands. The teenager on the pony was obviously very proud of what she was about to do and Candy knew that she would be expected to ask her some intelligent questions about it.

Leila spurred the overweight pony round the outside of the paddock, gathering speed as it approached the four jumps that the girl had spent the last half hour arranging. It didn't seem to Candy that the pony was being very much challenged by the height of the jumps but after it had heaved itself over the last one, Leila leaned forward and patted its neck effusively, so Candy took her cue and applauded and cried 'Bravo! Well done!' Then she felt she could sit down again while the girl galloped the pony around the paddock a couple of times.

The scene was almost perfect. She was sitting on the back terrace of Naseem's large Surrey house, on a beautiful early English summer afternoon. Scents of flowers and new mown grass mingled into a heady perfume, while the birdsong wasn't quite drowned out by the purring of the motor mower and the distant hum of the motorway traffic. She was waiting for Naseem to finish a lengthy phone call somewhere inside the house but in the meantime she was thoroughly enjoying the role of grandmother to his beautiful dark-haired daughter.

Candy liked being here. The elegant house, the pony, the very exclusive girls' boarding school for Leila, were all part of

Naseem's project of using his business profits to turn himself into an English gentleman. Since Marianne had died four years ago, he had even been selecting possible second wives with honey blonde hair and creamy skin. So far he had refrained from proposing marriage because he could see that Leila hadn't liked any of them very much. Naseem didn't mind. He wasn't in a hurry. He could have his pick of elegant women at any time. When his daughter had grown up and left home, then he would choose another wife to comfort him in his old age.

Leila dismounted and led her pony over to Candy. 'He's tired now,' she said. 'I'm going to feed and water him. Are you coming?'

Together they walked the pony towards the stable on the far side of the paddock. After a short silence, Leila said, 'Gran, if I wanted to be an actress like you were, would you be able to introduce me to people who would give me parts?'

'What's brought that idea on?'

'Oh, we were talking about careers and suchlike in school. Some of the girls in my year have parents in show business and the teacher was saying that talent alone often isn't enough.'

'I think talent will usually get you where you want to be. The idea that it's not enough is a theory put about by those who have very little of it, or don't want to work hard. You wouldn't want to feel that you didn't deserve your success, would you?'

'No... I suppose...'

'But why do you want to go into show business? You've got the looks, to be sure, but you've got brains as well. You could be a lawyer, or a writer. '

'Yes. I could. I've thought about that, too. I could be a civil rights lawyer and represent political refugees.'

'You only say that because it's the cool thing to do. You don't even know what it means. '

'Oh, but I do. We had some speakers from the Law Society in school and they explained to us what all the different branches of law are about. They told us some case study stories of people who fled from persecution. And I thought, that's us, me and my parents, they came here first off as refugees, didn't they? I could help Palestinians, couldn't I? When my cousins from Beirut were over here at Easter they were telling me about the way refugees' rights are often violated. After all, Gran, it's all very well enjoying all this...' with a sweep of her hand ... 'but how long can I just accept it and pretend England is my true home? I don't know how Papa...'

'You don't know, darling, that's just it. You don't know what it was like for him and you certainly don't know what it's like for Palestinians in Israel. Don't be so ready to criticise.'

But Leila shot her a look that said she was being a stuffy adult and Candy felt a dark shudder disturb her hard-won contentment. This was the first time Leila had expressed these views but it sounded as though she had been pondering them for some time. Because she was a clever girl she was thinking and asking questions of her world. Candy knew it wouldn't stop there and she made a mental note to speak to Naseem about it – perhaps suggest that he keep an eye on Leila's contacts with their more militant cousins from Beirut, to whom Naseem was quietly and excessively generous.

But that was the last time that summer that she could spend any time with Leila. That same evening the phone rang during dinner and a frightened Jeremy came on the line and said that his father had fallen whilst out with the dogs that afternoon and struck his head on a rock. He would have recovered from the fall but there was a deep puddle at the foot of the slope he had rolled down and he had drowned before he recovered consciousness. Candy was driven home through the night in one of Naseem's big cars knowing that Jeremy and his little wife Meggie would need her support, but unsure of what she was going to do with the rest of her life without Robert's solid, loving presence. It was a long time before things were settled at Northelm, before Meggie and Jeremy were sure of their roles as Earl and Countess, and during that time she hardly saw Leila. She hardly noticed the way Leila's face hardened and her pretty smile gave way to an expression of permanent contempt for the world around her.

‘Sit! Sit! Sit!’ The chanting rose in volume and the press of people swirled across the road, blocking the traffic.

‘Sit! Sit!’ Rashid pulled Leila’s arm sharply downwards so that she had no choice but to join him in the barrier of bodies that was forming at the feet of the riot police.

Leila was terrified. ‘Suppose they shoot us?’

‘This is London, sister, not Tel Aviv,’ said one of Rashid’s other companions with a smile and Rashid said, ‘Can you see any guns?’

‘No, but...’ She was still frightened. She didn’t think Rashid would let anything happen to her – there’d be hell to pay from her father if he did – but suppose he was powerless to prevent it? Suppose she got arrested? She was still a student. She wasn’t ready to be a martyr yet.

There was another mass movement, as half a dozen big black police vans pulled up on the other side of the cordon of policemen. The back doors burst open and more police poured out. Working in pairs, they began at one end of the line of demonstrators, lifting them one by one and throwing them into the vans. Leila didn’t like the look of that at all. She scrambled to her feet, closely followed by Rashid, and the line broke. As one the demonstrators turned and ran, dispersing amongst the fountains and down side streets. Their protest was over.

Leila tore off the *burkah* she had worn in case there were newsreel cameras - the last thing she wanted was to be recognised by her father getting involved in something as mindless as a demonstration – and stuffed it into the shoulder bag she was carrying. She noticed that she had a cut hand and remembered one of her follow demonstrators stepping on it in their hurry to get to their feet. She didn’t make a fuss about it but when Rashid saw it he stopped and wrapped some tissues round it. ‘You must get that seen to.’

They walked fast through the streets until they came to the squat where Rashid lived and he took her inside so that she could wash her hand and bandage it properly. He took Leila's arm and guided her through darkened, ill-furnished rooms where young faces looked at her suspiciously. There was a lot of movement up and down the stairs because many of the people here had just returned from the demonstration. In one room where they passed an open door she heard the low murmuring of male voices, in another room the voices were raised in argument. In the kitchen, where she was taken to sit while somebody looked for a bandage, a dozen young women were cooking large pans of rice and meat. She felt hungry but they didn't invite her to stay. She guessed they knew who she was and that she wasn't really one of them. A feeling of discomfort and isolation took hold of her, made worse by the realisation that most of the conversation around her was being conducted in Arabic and she only had few words of the language. That made her ashamed.

As soon as she could she thanked the girl who had bandaged her hand and began to make her way to the door. She couldn't see where Rashid had gone. 'Please tell my cousin I have gone home,' she said over her shoulder.

One of the girls nodded, then said to another, in English to make it clear she intended Leila to hear, 'She is lucky to have a home to go to.'

Leila knew that. She made her way the few blocks to the underground garage where she had parked the TR7 her father had given her for her twenty-first birthday. She knew she was lucky, being able to get into a flashy car and drive to a comfortable home at the end of the day. Yet she was beginning to resent that luck, beginning to understand that however clever she became, she would never understand the feelings of the dispossessed people she wanted to work for unless she became as one with them. How could she make them accept her?

'It's no good just saying you are Palestinian,' Rashid told her. 'It isn't possible to live like an English princess, doing nothing, living on your father's bounty, and still to understand what it feels like to be dispossessed of your country.'

'I am doing something. I am studying law.'

'And when you are qualified? What will you do then? Make more money?'

'You don't know what I am thinking of doing,' Leila said sulkily. She wasn't sure that she liked Rashid being so ready to criticise her father when he took full advantage of his hospitality whenever it was convenient. Yet in a way he was right, what he said echoed what Leila had thought for a long time. She had long since admitted that she had never felt entirely comfortable in her school, one amongst an international group of girls pretending to be English. She had always been aware of a great gulf between herself and her funny fond English grandmother. In fact, when she was younger she had found it difficult to believe they belonged in the same family and had asked Naseem if he had been adopted as a baby. And as for this house her father lived in – nothing was further removed from the stories Rashid and her other cousins would tell her about Beirut and Israel, where they seemed to visit regularly. Wasn't there something faintly pathetic about the way her father surrounded himself deliberately with all the trappings of Englishness that money could buy? It wasn't as though anyone was fooled. Whatever he did, he remained a WOG, a Westernised Oriental Gentleman – someone had unkindly explained the term to her at school. He was somebody pretending to be something he wasn't.

Was that what she was? A female WOG? Was that what she would always be as long as she stayed in England?

Next time she saw Rashid she asked him to take her to Beirut as soon as she graduated.

'Your father would kill me!' He looked genuinely afraid.

'My father won't know. I will simply disappear.'

Rashid shook his head. 'It isn't that easy. I can travel light as a single man. With you I would be more of a target. I mean, people would ask questions to see a single Muslim girl travelling with a single man.'

'We could marry.'

'We could,' said Rashid with a cynical smile at her

naivety. 'But weddings usually involve arrangements between families at the very least, and at best some kind of sexual feeling between the couple involved. It would be very hard to achieve all this without your father knowing and I assure you, he would not be pleased. Beside, what would be the purpose? What could you do?'

'I could work for the refugees. Or the Palestinian Government.'

'There is no such thing.'

'Then we must create one. You and I together. After all, what do you do when you go on your trips to Palestine?'

He hesitated a moment. 'I teach young men to be soldiers.'

'There!' she exclaimed. 'Perfect! We complement each other perfectly! You will be a fighter and I will be a politician and together we will establish a new Palestine.'

Rashid laughed, but he could see that this was not a joke. Leila was serious. Her heart had already been recruited to their cause with only the minimum of encouragement from him. She would be a force to be reckoned with and it was up to him to make sure she was used effectively by the organisation he served.

*　　*　　*

Throughout the church service and the interment in the vault, Pippa kept expecting to feel some twinges of grief for her mother's passing, and she was surprised to have no emotional reaction at all. She was aware of one or two sad sighs from Jeremy, in front of her, and Meggie was sniffling quietly into her handkerchief. Nothing from Danny except the irritating clicking of rosary beads but that was to be expected. Ever since the kidnapping Danny had been closed in and cold, any sign of grief would be surprising. From her position in the second pew Pippa had been acutely aware of Leon being at the back of the church and had wondered why he didn't come forward to join the rest of the family. But she didn't dare to look around because he might be hanging back to try to avoid her, and he might be watching her, and there was no knowing what would happen if their eyes met over the heads of others. She was prepared for anything, from a shudder of loathing to a spark of recognition that annihilated the years between them, years that she was sure had dealt more kindly with him than with her.

Pippa wondered if Leon would linger in the churchyard and as the family group stepped out of the church into the warm sunlight she looked quickly around. But he wasn't there and she took her pang of disappointment as a warning that she was already attaching too much importance to this meeting. Most likely he wasn't thinking about her at all, hadn't thought about her very much since that last, terrible day when they had decided to part. Why should he have? He who had the world at his feet with all the adoration and sex any young man could want.

So she walked up to the house with Jeremy and his family and when they were inside, she let them go their separate, prearranged ways to look after their guests while she gazed around uneasily. It was a long time since she had been there and nothing had changed, yet everything had changed. As she made her way around the ground floor, looking for a cloakroom, she could see the differences. For one thing, the place was no longer neglected and gloomy. Everything had been refurbished. The fifty year old curtains in the drawing room had been replaced, the floors were carpeted or polished, the portraits were clean and the walls were papered with stuff that must have cost more for each roll than most people paid to decorate an entire room. Somehow, in the years since she'd last been here, fortunes had changed without her knowing it.

But then, why should she have known? She had been on the other side of the world, living her own pretence. The other thing that struck her, with almost physical force, was that her mother was no longer there to censure her. She could walk into any room and know for certain that Candy wouldn't be in there, waiting to tell her what to do. At last she could call herself a free woman. But doubt still lurked. 'Over my dead body,' Candy had said. And over her dead body it was, but would that be enough?

Pippa ignored the food and helped herself to a large whisky from the drinks tray on the next table. But she didn't stand still for long because after the fairly lengthy proceedings in the church, followed by the walk back to the house, what she most needed was a toilet. She could remember that somewhere on the rambling ground floor there had been a sort of cloakroom where she and her sister had often gone to wash their hands before a meal, but after so many years she was no longer certain where it was. Was it part of the front section of the house or was it concealed behind the big hall, along the corridors behind the baize door where the kitchens and service rooms were hidden? There had never been any distinction between 'upstairs' and 'downstairs' when her mother had ruled the house, which was why Pippa was confused now. They had been just as likely to eat a supper prepared by the Countess around the big kitchen table, as to be told their evening meal would be in the grand dining room because someone important was coming to visit.

Pippa was solving the problem now by opening every closed door she came to and looking inside. She didn't need to worry about the main reception rooms because they were already open, but the next door was closed and when she put her head round she found it was quite a small room, probably an office. She was met by the startled eyes of two elderly gentlemen who were sitting side by side at the central table, heads together, poring over an impressive looking pile of documents.

She apologised and withdrew even before they needed to explain who they were. In the next room, which she quickly remembered as the library, she found Jeremy and some arab-looking gentleman and she quickly raised a hand and backed out. She would have liked to talk to Jeremy but her memories of bathing and cuddling him would probably embarrass him. After all, he was quite an important man now.

There was a breakfast room on the far side of the hall but that, too, was open and echoed with the forced conversation of people who didn't really want to be talking to each other. So Pippa's only other option was through the door to the back of the big staircase, where she found herself in a wide flagged corridor and suddenly remembered that if she went through the door to her right she would be in the room they had always called the gun room – though she could never remember there being any guns in there - that led through to the hand-washing place. She pushed it open and was met with the sight of a small, shabby room with an armchair piled with old sweaters. Along one wall ranged a dozen hooks laden with old coats, scarves, and hats of various materials and fashions. Half a dozen umbrellas leaned against the coats in various attitudes of disarray. Two portly Labradors pulled themselves to their feet from the floor and snuffled across the room towards her. She was just reaching down to pat them and try to keep them away from her black coat when a tall lean figure unfolded from the armchair and turned to face her.

'Leon!' It was as though she froze in time and space, was transported back to that morning when she had wept so much she thought she would die, and then wept some more and wished she was dead, and then realised she wasn't going to die, she was going to live for ever with the pain of loving the one man she couldn't have. Now, in this one moment, she knew the answer to the question that had been nagging at her for the last few days. The spark was still alive, and it did matter, it mattered very much.

She knew Leon must feel it too. His face was white and he tried twice before he could speak or move. Then it was a whispered 'Pippa!' as he came forward and closed his arms around her. She didn't resist him and they stood, locked together, swaying slightly, each transported back across the years towards something they had lost, never to be recovered.

'Pippa, my darling!'

'My love...'

'Am I still...?'

'Always and only. After you left...' A silence.

'But you decreed our parting...' He was stroking her hair now, leaning away from her and looking into her eyes.

Yes, she remembered, she had said they must part, because of the threats that were made. 'It seemed like the best thing at the time, didn't it?'

'Not to me.'

He stepped back and she was aware that he was studying her closely. She felt ashamed of the lines she knew she had sitting in the corners of her eyes and on her neck. Leon had lines on his face too but they seemed good humoured, distinguished, not the inevitable sculpting of advancing years. She reached up and removed her funeral hat and tossed her hair to tidy it, knowing it would still fall thickly to her shoulders, the way it used to. Leon's eyes lit up. 'You haven't changed a bit.'

'Neither have you.'

He kissed her then and she didn't try to stop him. She hadn't expected it, hadn't expected him to still want her, hadn't expected, either, that she would want him. But there it was, as though it was yesterday they had first made love that night at the festival so many years ago.

As she emerged from his kiss she said, 'You know, I never meant you to take it seriously, when I said we shouldn't meet again…I thought you would follow me, find me...That's what they do in stories, isn't it? Lovers' quests and all that?'

'Oh God, Pippa, I wanted to so much, but I thought I had to do what you said…'

He was leading her by the hand, out through the side door of the gun room, across the stone flags, up the back stairs.

'Where are we…?'

'Where we should always have been. Together.'

He gave her a little pull and she followed him up the stairs and into the bedroom where he had slept last night. She didn't try to resist as he kissed her and gently pulled her black dress over her head. But as he took her in his arms again it was slowly, hesitantly and she thought about her sixty-year-old body and knew that what she had to offer wouldn't be enough.

'I'm sorry.' His head rested on her shoulder. 'I can't do this.'

'I knew it.' She stroked his hair. 'I'm too old, aren't I?'

'No, of course you're not.' He raised his head and looked into her eyes again. 'But once we've done it we can't hide it. Everyone will know and what will they say? Will they punish us all over again?' A pause, shuddering. 'Will it always be like this?'

'Perhaps somewhere else, on some other day. '

'I love you Pippa.'

'I know.' She stroked his hair, gentling him along.

'But I can't do this.'

'I know.'

'It's too late, isn't it.' He still clung to her, but it was as a child to its mother, not as a lover. 'Don't leave me, Pippa.'

'No, of course not.' But in the end mightn't that be her only option? Even if the sex was as wonderful as they remembered, they could only make a life together if she could keep up with his energy, his talent, his aptly named *Hounds of Hell* lifestyle. Somewhere deep in her heart she knew she might have been alone too long to be able to share all that. It would be better if the love between them remained a memory.

Downstairs in the library, Jeremy listened in horror to the details of Naseem's trip to Israel. He didn't know what to say. He didn't know whether to be a sympathetic brother or a potential government minister with a stake in national security. He knew there were steps he should take, official and legal responses he should make, but somehow all that seemed to be sidelined by the central facts of the matter. He was being asked to accept that his mother had been systematically and illegally supplying money to the Palestinian Authority through channels controlled by her grand-daughter Leila. That government agents knew about this and when the Countess was finally drawn into making an unwise visit to see her grand-daughter, they decided to rid themselves of both women by targetting a bomb on their first known meeting and attributing the crime to the Palestinians.

The two men sat in the comfortable studded leather chairs on each side of the reading table, facing each other but not looking at each other. Naseem held a large white handkerchief in one hand and every now and again he coughed into it and dabbed his eyes. Jeremy was dry-eyed but he could feel that tell-tale tightening of the throat. 'No, surely not,' he kept muttering as one fact followed another. But he knew from his peripheral dealing with Middle Eastern politics that however far-fetched the story sounded, it was quite likely to be true. He listened while Naseem talked on.

'They didn't tell me at first that Leila had been targeted too. I thought she was going to walk into the room at any moment, then they broke the news that she had been the woman walking towards Mother as the bomb went off...' Naseem paused for another cough, an excuse to pass his handkerchief across his face again. 'I knew Leila was an idealist and I should have listened to her more – I somehow thought that an English education would be enough to turn her into a sensible person…'

Jeremy made a silent vow to make sure he knew what his two boys were thinking, not to leave it to Meggie.

'Mother used to talk to her a lot and I suppose that was how she got the idea of going to Israel – you know Mother was always talking about going back …'

'She used to think of it as a holiday…'

'Yes, indeed, but I managed to dissuade her – or I thought I did. When Leila took off without letting me know where she was, I left it as long as possible before telling Mother, thinking how shocked she would be, because she had become very close to the girl. Now it seems as though I needn't have bothered, she knew all along what was happening. She was part of the plot.'

'I wonder how we never knew?'

'You never had the slightest suspicion?'

Jeremy shook his head. 'I suppose that's what comes of taking dear little old ladies for granted. We tend to forget that they weren't always old ladies. Chances are there's always the remains of a revolutionary hiding in there somewhere. Now I wonder if we've got the whole story.'

'Unlikely. We'll probably find she was acting as banker for a whole Hamas cell. Have you checked out her emails since she died?'

'Emails? Never thought of it.' Jeremy glanced towards the computer that sat quietly in a corner of the library and Naseem followed his gaze. 'Might shed some light…'

Jeremy went over to the terminal and switched on. 'I'm not sure of her passwords, though.' He clicked away on the keys, then gave a satisfactory 'Ah! Not very subtle.' Then after a couple of minutes, 'Come and look at this, Naseem.'

Naseem crossed the room and together, with a growing sense of amazement, they scrolled through nearly fifty saved emails from Leila, sent over the past year and half. Some were no more than shopping lists, asking for make up or clothing. Others were diaries of meetings with politicians. 'You see. They were in touch all the time...'

'Yes, and a lot of this could have been intercepted. Look, here's where she makes her travel arrangements, and arranges to meet Leila at that cafe. No wonder they knew how to arrange for the bomb. The pair of them must have walked straight into it.'

'Bloody hell!' Jeremy had tried to remain calm but this was almost too much to listen to without showing his shock and anger. 'And you say you know who was responsible for this bomb?'

'I am afraid I do.'

'And there's nothing you can do about it?'

Naseem recalled the hot room, the craking of the insects, Jamal's heavy-lidded, contemptuous eyes as he suggested that if Naseem wanted to take the struggle personally he should be in Gaza with them, planning revenge attacks. Around the table they all looked at him expectantly, but he didn't miss a sense of lies and corruption in the air. He didn't miss the possibility that he was being drawn into a trap. He even knew why – it was all part of the propaganda war. If he didn't accept the explanation that had been put to him that the Israelis had organised the bombing to blacken the name of Hamas, what would remain? The conclusion that Hamas, those very men he sat with around the table, had arranged the assassination to blacken the Israelis. It could go on for ever, round and around in vicious circles of death.

Jeremy went on, ‘So, you just walked away?’

‘I don’t even know how to fire a gun. If I had thought in terms of retribution at the time I would not be sitting here telling you all this. And I think it is important that you should know.’

‘Yes? Why? What can I do about it?’

‘You, nothing. It’s up to me now.’

‘What can you do from here?’

‘From here?’ Naseem had been thinking about it very carefully. From the moment Jamal had finished speaking and the rage had erupted in his brain, he had found it very hard to restrain himself from jumping across the table and punching his cousin. He had to work hard to remember that he was a man of peace. ‘I have a meeting tomorrow with a man from your security services. I’ll see what he wants of me and make my plans accordingly.’

‘Bloody hell!’ Jeremy gasped again as he sank his head forward, hands over his ears. He suddenly realised why he had been getting discreet invitations from one of his old school friends working in MI6 to meet up for a drink one evening. ‘You start talking and they’ll murder you, for Chrissake.’

Once she had made her way back up to the house Danny found that nobody took much notice of her. Her brothers and sisters seemed to be deliberately avoiding her and none of the other guests had any idea who she was and showed no interest in finding out. After giving her vague smiles, as though it might be bad luck to frown at a nun, they all hurried on their way towards the food and drink where they could relax and talk amongst themselves about things they understood.

She didn’t expect much civility from Pippa, not after their exchanges during the time Danny had announced she wanted to go to the convent, when Pippa had been full of contempt for what she called escapism and intellectual laziness.

But she did think that her half-brother Jeremy might have the good manners to pass the time of day, instead of which he was nowhere to be seen.

She helped herself to a plate of snacks and a glass of lemonade, and sat for a while in a wicker chair on the enclosed terrace, remembering when she had been a lonely little girl, forced to visit her mother and hating every minute of a time she was supposed to enjoy. She had never realised, when she flatly refused to come to Yorkshire that last time, that her next visit would be to see her mother into her grave. Now it was done and she could be on her way back to the convent – she knew she had only to ask for a car to take her to the station. But, as though a great cloak of shadow had been removed from the landscape, she found she rather liked being here, at the centre of things. Then she decided she was falling prey to the sin of envy. There was nothing this great house could offer that she couldn't find in her convent. Except perhaps more of those delicious little chicken vol-au-vents. She went back into the dining room and put half a dozen more pastries on her plate, exchanged her lemonade glass for what looked like a glass of ginger ale, then went and sat herself on the window seat beside one of the young men she had seen sitting in the front pew with Jeremy.

'So many people,' she muttered as she looked around, at the same time popping a cheese straw into her mouth, 'And none of them I remember. Except that elderly aunt person – she used to be around a lot.'

Charlie looked at her with something approaching interest. 'You must be my father's sister. Not the one who went to Australia, the other one.'

'You know about us?'

'Gran used to tell us about you all. And Uncle Leon. He's here somewhere too. You know, we've got all his albums on tapes upstairs in the attic and we've never been allowed to play any of them.'

'Quite right too!' Danny leaned towards her nephew and grabbed his arm. 'He's an evil, strutting peacock!'

Charlie tried to pull away. There was something in the

nun's eyes that was frightening him, some poisonous intensity in the gaze that seemed to pierce right through him.

'He's only a rock star,' protested Charlie.

Danny leaned even closer to her nephew and lowered her voice. 'He's much worse than that. He's an incestuous, bastard spawn of the devil. You keep away from him!'

Charlie laughed outright. 'Aren't you being a bit over the top? He seems to be a perfectly regular guy to me.'

'Then where is he now? And where's his whore, Pippa? They're probably together right now, fornicating over our mother's grave.'

Charlie sprang to his feet to escape from this diatribe, almost knocking Danny's plate and glass to the floor. He decided that his aunt was stark raving mad, but that's what too much religion probably did for you.

Meggie was upset. In spite of her careful planning, things were not going well at all. Guests were starting to leave and Jeremy, who should have been on the doorstep with her bidding farewell and murmuring thanks to important people like the Lord Lieutenant and various members of parliament was closeted in the library with Naseem, whose conspicuous bodyguard insisted on standing outside the library windows. Leon, to whom she felt she could have turned for some moral support, had disappeared somewhere quiet, no doubt with a bottle. That awful hag Aunt Netta, tripping around in that totally unsuitable and ill-fitting fifties-style dress, was getting steadily more drunk and buttonholing anybody who would tolerate her for more than a few minutes to regale them with salacious stories about her sister, the Dowager Countess. The fat nun was sitting on the dining room window-seat, eating a prodigious amount of vol-au-vents and stuffed eggs and watching the remainder of the food on the table as thought she was a starving Biafran. The stunningly beautiful woman who didn't look a day over forty but who must be well over fifty and was probably

Pippa was wandering around looking at the furnishings of the house as though she had a proprietorial interest in them, which made Meggie nervous. After all, Pippa had been there before she had and although she had been cut off from the family for over twenty-five years, probably knew more about the early days than anybody.

To make it worse, it had started to rain.

In a pause between the departure of two groups of guests, she spied out of the corner of her eye her sons Tatton and Charlie, sneaking towards the door that led to the kitchen quarters. With a spritely sideways shuffle followed by two long strides forward, she intercepted them, took their arms and hissed, 'Tatts, go and see if you can find Johnson and tell him to bring some umbrellas to the front door. And Charlie, go and talk to the fat nun and see if you can drag her away from the food.'

'I have tried to talk to her, and she doesn't want to say anything sensible.'

'Go and find out if she intends to stay overnight. I've made up a bed for her but she doesn't seem to have brought a bag.'

'She smells horrid, as though she doesn't wash.'

'She may need a taxi if she's going...' Meggie caught sight of another sombrely-clad couple making their way towards the front door and sidled back in that direction. She should have asked one of the boys to fetch Jeremy. The trouble was, with her mother-in-law's strangely-assorted family, one never knew where one was. There was something so potentially vulgar and suspect about them all. They weren't the sort of people one would expect to have at a place like Northelm. That had been a problem all along with the old lady – she didn't share one's outlook. Very pretty and charming but unpredictable. Meggie had never been able to understand what had possessed the old Earl to fall in love and marry her. Probably because he was in his dotage or lonely after his first wife died. After the death of his heir, couldn't he have found someone normal to provide the spare instead of a fading film star? Silly old man.

Meggie couldn't remember a time when she hadn't

known Jeremy. She and her two brothers had grown up on the neighbouring estate and, as far as anyone had been friends with the new Countess, their mother was, so the four children formed the nucleus of a group that played together in the early days. Later they went on holidays together, sailing little boats in the Lake District and trooping around museums and art galleries in London. From the age of fourteen, Meggie had made up for her homely looks by practising sex with Jeremy on every possible occasion. Her mother, a Lady rather than a Countess, and keenly aware of the distinction, had been well aware of the growing sexual promiscuity and had positively encouraged it, because in her view it was the surest and most time-honoured way of securing the position of Jeremy's future wife and ensuring that Meggie inherited the mantle of Countess of Penmore. Because they grew careless and she became pregnant, this happened quite quickly and they married when both she and Jeremy were little more than eighteen. Ever since, she had lived at Northelm without really knowing much about how the estate was run, or where the money came from that the Dowager Countess had used to refurbish the place so that it looked like a modern stately home instead of Dracula's castle.

That was why she felt both bewildered and inadequate when the guests had finally left and the family began to assemble in the library where, according to a message sent out by Jeremy via the butler, Candy's will was to be read. Why were there two lawyers there – John Fairclough the estate lawyer and a portly, very elderly solicitor from London who Jeremy introduced as Bob? Why had Aunt Netta, hiccupping gently, assumed a prominent place as though she expected to be a beneficiary – surely she had money to look after herself? And why did Jeremy look so tired and resigned when Leon and Pippa appeared and sat down close together on one of the sofas?

Meggie watched them with close interest. What was it with those two? They can't have seen each other for years, not since the first rock concert, and she only had vague memories of that event. Her mother had considered it totally unsuitable for any girl to attend who wanted to keep her reputation and had made her stay away, though of course she had sneaked over on her bicycle one night to hear the Stones. Jeremy had been preoccupied and distant throughout the weekend, feeling the responsibility of managing the event. The morning after the festival was over she had ridden her pony over to Northelm and been an unwitting eavesdropper to the most terrible row going on in the library – this very room. It wasn't the kind of row she had ever heard in her own family, where everything was softly spoken and understated. It was a total, one-hundred-octane row, with everyone shouting and crying together, Candy screaming louder than anyone, doing her actress bit with 'If you do, I shall never speak to you again!' and 'Don't you realise the harm it will do to you both?' Even the gentle old Earl was joining in with 'How dare you upset your mother so!'

And Pippa cried and screamed things like, 'You've always been a hypocryte! One rule for yourself and one for me! You can't bear to think of me having sex at all, can you?'

And later, Leon and Pippa walking away down the drive, hand in hand, carrying small back packs, not even waiting for the car that took everyone normal to the station.

Meggie leaned across to Jeremy and asked, 'What is it with those two?'

He gave a wry smile that made him look even more tired than his earlier frown. 'Could it be love?'

'*That* kind of love?' Meggie blinked. 'It's illegal, isn't it?'

'Are you going to tell them or shall I?' Jeremy rejoined, then regretted adding sarcasm to the equation. 'Listen Megs, it's their business and we know nothing about it, okay?'

'I think it's disgusting. '

'Just think of them as two elderly people who've met up again after years apart.'

In Meggie's view that made it even more disgusting – old as well as incestuous. But she could see that Jeremy didn't want to discuss the matter any further and she thought perhaps he was right. In an hour or so they would just go away and she wouldn't have to think anything about them at all.

When everyone had quietened down, Jeremy began to speak and Meggie noticed that he was shaking and he had to cough and try twice to make his voice sound normal. 'Thank you all for coming,' he started, and Leon laid himself open to his brother's wrathful glance by murmuring, 'Wild horses wouldn't have kept us away...'

Ignoring him, Jeremy continued. 'As this is the first time ever we have all met together, and will probably be the last, I thought it would be a good idea, before we all go our separate ways, to take the opportunity to hear about the arrangements our dear departed mutual mother made for the distribution of her estate...her not inconsiderable assets. It's not very complicated, but I think you should all hear from the legal profession exactly what she intended.'

He coughed again and nodded towards the portly old London solicitor who rattled his papers nervously before proceeding and looked around the assembled family group with the anxiety of an antelope facing a pack of lions. 'Candy...the Countess...your mother... you may know or you may not... she amassed a considerable amount of personal wealth after her marriage to the Earl...'

'How?' piped up Netta, who had been sitting back in a leather armchair, her eyes half-closed. 'It can't have been honest.'

'I assure you it was completely above board,' the solicitor said, a trifle testily. 'I looked after her affairs from the time she left Hollywood. She had alimony from her marriage to Rupert Taylor, she had her own earnings, which were considerable from her last few films, she had prime property in London. Through the eighties and nineties she played the stockmarket and increased all this capital a hundredfold....'

And I thought she played bridge and went to the theatre, mused Meggie.

'She can't have done,' said Netta again. 'She didn't know anything about money. She left me to look after our mother and the old lady died in poverty.'

The solicitor was even more irritated by this. 'I assure

you, she knew a great deal about money. She even became a Lloyds name. You see, once she married the Earl and gave up acting, she needed a new project in her life and she soon had her husband's agreement to completely refurbish this house. But she not only refurbished the house, she refurbished the way the estate was run, the way the capital was invested. In other words, she dragged the whole system from the middle ages into the twenty-first century. And as for her mother, over the years she paid thousands into Mrs Hargreaves' account, and met her funeral expenses.'

'Okay, suppose we buy all that,' said Leon. 'How did she learn these financial skills? Who helped her to find her way around the world of high finance? I'm stacked, and I wouldn't know where to begin.'

'I did,' said Naseem Fahy, drawing attention to himself for the first time. 'I grew up in Beirut. After I graduated from university there I came to England and started my own business. I made contact with my mother and the Earl and, I must say, we got on rather well together. In fact, after the war in Lebanon ended we went into business together shipping out construction materials and developed a multi-million-pound hardware business.'

'Then you're not a terrorist?' Leon said. 'When you arrived in that big black car I thought....'

'No, no. I saw enough violence in my youth not to follow that path. I decided to live in the world as it is, not as I would wish it to be.'

'Like making money out of wars?'

'Leon...' murmured Jeremy, as Naseem made a small, dismissive gesture. 'This is straying off the point. Could we continue?'

'Very well.' The old solicitor coughed again and coloured nervously as the pack turned their gaze back in his direction. 'Well, this is what your mother had to say about her personal wealth. Nothing is to go to the Earl, because he and his family are well provided for by the entails of the estate trust – Mr Fairclough here has the details of that. I believe you knew that, your Lordship.' Jeremy nodded. 'Neither of her daughters have been given any bequests because they have already inherited half shares in the school their father owned and neither seem to need any further capital, particularly Sister Daniella, also known as Sister Mary James, who would give it all to her convent anyway. Nothing is to go to Leon Taylor because he is already a wealthy man by his own efforts and he will inherit a considerable amount from his own father. The eldest son, Mr Fahy, is not in need of money, either.' The solicitor paused in his reading and looked around into their stunned faces. 'Three million pounds has already been put into separate trust funds for her three grandchildren – Viscount Northelm, Charles Northelm and Leila Fahy....'

Suddenly several people talked at once.

Jeremy said to Naseem, 'Of course, that will have to be unravelled – you say Leila had no family?'

'Not that I know of.' Naseem shook his head helplessly, acknowledging that he might be wrong on that.

'What about me?' screeched Netta.

'You, madam, have been left her clothes, including all her couturier models from her films, and her fur coats. You may not want to wear them all, but several items have considerable value. Her jewellery is to remain in the Northelm family. Finally, all her remaining personal estate is to go into a trust fund to help the children of Palestinian refugees, to be administered by Naseem Fahy's family. All her interests in the Penmore estate revert to the Earl and his heirs.'

'That's not fair!' Netta was on her feet, gesticulating towards Jeremy, fulfilling Meggie's worst fears about her mother-in-law's family. 'That should have been me. She stole it all from me. I was your father's girlfriend first off and she stole him. You should have been my son!'

That would have made her my mother-in-law, Meggie thought as she raised her eyes in silent gratitude for small mercies and Jeremy flushed with anger and rose to his feet to confront this apparently mad old lady before she actually attacked him. For the first time, the nun joined in the verbal melee. 'You never came here, Auntie Netta,' she said. 'None of us came here before Mummy had Jeremy. You can't have ever met the old Earl. You couldn't have been his girlfriend.'

'I don't mean the old man – he's not your father!' She was so angry that spittle was spraying from her over-rouged lips all over the legal documents on the table. 'I mean Tatton.'

'Who is Tatton?' asked Meggie faintly.

Jeremy said, 'Tatton was my eldest brother, who died before I was born...a plane crash...'

'Tatton is your father, not your brother,' insisted Netta. 'The old Earl was your grandfather, not your father...'

Jeremy hesitated, working it out. 'I don't believe that,' he said. 'They had such a very happy marriage. It can't have been just a convenience.'

But Leon lowered his face into his hands as he remembered. A promise of a plane trip up to Scotland with Tatton, bitter anger at a headmaster who wouldn't let him out of school because of some Latin test, his mother lying in a darkened room weeping and vomiting in turns, Isabella muttering about her not needing another baby to look after. Jeremy had certainly been on the way before she ever met Robert.

The estate solicitor raised his voice. 'Madam! I must ask you to restrain yourself or I shall have to seek an injunction to stop you repeating such a calumny! Viscount Tatton's death was a terrible tragedy but there is no doubt of the legitimacy of the line. I was present when the previous Earl registered his second son's birth and he certainly had no doubts as to his paternity.'

'Just a little hiccup,' murmured Leon.

Netta continued to splutter but she said no more because she was being upstaged by another discussion developing between Naseem and the London solicitor.

'Are you sure it was her?' Bob was asking.

'The authorities have presented me with pretty convincing evidence.' He drew out a wallet from his inner jacket pocket and extracted a small folded document which he passed across. 'Her death certificate, written in Hebrew, I'm afraid. She would have regarded that as the ultimate insult.'

The solicitor took the document, glanced at it, then handed it back. 'We shall need a translation and copy of that in due course. My commiserations.'

'Excuse me,' said Meggie, 'But who are we talking about now?'

'My daughter, Leila Fahy. She was with her grandmother when the bomb went off in that café and she died too.'

'But the bomb,' said Pippa. 'Who…?

'We have evidence,' said Naseem quietly, 'That it was a terrorist organisation. One of the many that seek to represent the interests of Palestinians.'

In the silence that followed Naseem's statement all eyes were on him and tension mounted as everyone struggled to make sense of what they had just heard. He prayed silently that nobody would ask why because that would make necessary lengthy explanations that he preferred at this moment to leave with Jeremy.

If that's what they were talking about earlier, Meggie thought, no wonder Jeremy was looking so uptight when he came into the room. Leon remembered the tensions and secretiveness of the visit to Israel to collect his mother's remains, and began to understand a little of what Naseem – who he still couldn't think of as his eldest brother – had been going through. Danny stared in pop-eyed disbelief at each of them in turn, then pulled her rosary out and began to finger the beads obsessively. Netta, reseated in her armchair, looked from one to the other of them, then burst into tears.

Prompted by Jeremy, Meggie looked at her watch. It was time to end this scene before anything else alarming came to light. 'If any of you want to catch this evening's train to London, you'll have to get your skates on. A car will be leaving for the station in twenty minutes. Of course, anyone who would rather stay the night is welcome...'

'What about it?' said Leon, speaking softly to Pippa.

'What about what?'

'Are we going or staying?'

'We...? I didn't think there were any plans for "we".'

'I'm not leaving without you, whether you want me or not.'

Pippa wasn't at all sure at that moment what she wanted. What if Leon came to London with her and they made out successfully in some anonymous hotel room? She was beginning to understand that would just lead to a whole new set of problems. But desert him, now?

'You'd better get your stuff then, because I'm catching that train.' She watched him hurry up the stairs, then went to find Meggie and Jeremy to say goodbye. Then, seeing that Leon didn't reappear she went up to his room, but he wasn't there. She felt a sudden dread, as though she had challenged fate and fate had taken it seriously and was punishing her by spiriting him away at the last minute. She decided he must be waiting for her in the library. But he wasn't there. Danny saw her coming through the door and turned to smile at her, a mirthless, evil smile.

'Looking for Leon?' asked Danny. Then, without waiting for Pippa's reply, she said, 'He left a few minutes ago. Said to tell you he's changed his mind and not to wait for him. But I don't suppose you care, do you?'

10
DEPARTURES

With a cry of rage, Pippa swung round and hit Danny squarely on her nose. Danny was felled to the floor where she lay, motionless, as blood spurted from her mouth and her broken nose. Naseem stepped forward and grabbed Pippa from behind, as though to prevent her from a further attack, while Jeremy bent over the stricken nun. Jeremy's two sons stared at one another in open mouthed disbelief.

Megan wailed, 'For God's sake don't get blood on the carpet!' as she rushed for the door to fetch some towels.

Jeremy lifted Danny's prostrate form and laid her on one of the sofas. Charlie came forward and told him how to arrange her in the recovery position, which he had just learned about on a first aid course at school.

'Recovery?' Naseem said, still holding onto Pippa. 'I think you may have killed her,'

'If I have, it's only what she deserves, the pious little cow. I should have done it years ago!' Then her rage turned into a paroxysm of sobs and she buried her face in Naseem's shoulder. 'I must find Leon!'

Jeremy said, 'I'm sure he went off in one of the station cars.'

'I must stop him.'

'She's still breathing,' said Charlie, who had been bending over Danny. 'But shouldn't we phone for an ambulance?'

'Yes...yes.' Jeremy was trying to stretch his attention in three directions at the same time. 'Perhaps you could organise that, Tatts?'

Megan came back into the room with an armful of clean towels which she handed to Naseem, who was trying to get a connection on his cellphone. Not knowing what to do with the towels, Naseem passed them to Netta, who was hopping around like a demented bird. Netta promptly began to wrap one of them around Danny's head and face, making her look like a mummy and in danger of suffocating her.

'Ambulance will be here in half an hour,' Naseem announced.

'I must get to the station,' wailed Pippa.

'Don't worry about it,' Naseem said. 'My car will be driving me to London shortly. I can give you a lift.'

'No, no. You don't understand.' If he got on the train without her and reached London ahead of her, he could disappear anywhere. Danny had said he had changed his mind. Why?

Jeremy understood. He turned to Pippa and said, 'If we go through that door now, I can get you to the station before the train gets there.'

'You can?'

'If we go now.'

The journey to the station was bumpy. The driving rain had covered the lanes with a thick coating of mud and the vehicle slithered from side to side. Darkness had fallen by the time they got there and a single platform light shone onto a figure who sat hunched over on the wooden platform seat. Pippa breathed a sigh of relief and both she and Jeremy scrambled out of the vehicle.

'Leon!' called Pippa, but her voice was drowned by a shrill electronic whistle announcing the imminent arrival of the train. The figure didn't respond and Pippa stopped in her tracks, overtaken by a terrible vision of a distracted Leon throwing himself under the approaching train, just to get away from her. Then she realised that she was standing in darkness so he couldn't see her and she ran forwards again as the train appeared round a bend in the tracks and began to slow.

He stood up, picked up a bag, then moved towards the edge of the platform, waiting to board the train. Pippa shouted again – would he ever hear her? Was he deliberately ignoring her? Was he going to jump?

She was just contemplating the possibility that she couldn't reach him in time and would never see him again when the train stopped and he turned his face in her direction. A moment later he was coming towards her and as he flung his arms around her she couldn't tell where the tears ended and the drenching rain began.

'Oh Pippa! I thought I was going to have to spend the rest of my life without you!'

'No, no. It's all right. You didn't wait.'

'You went without me…'

She knew then that Danny had lied to them both to try to keep them apart. The train was growling expectantly, a light was waving along the platform, the train guard was talking to Jeremy, then coming towards them. 'Are you travelling, sir?'

'Yes. Sorry to delay you.'

'And the lady?'

'Yes, both of us.'

Jeremy drove back to the house a good deal more slowly than he had driven to the station. His head was beginning to ache, his mind a blur. All those people! He felt as though they were standing around in a circle shouting at him personally. He hadn't expected the day of his mother's funeral to be a good day but it had been worse than anything he had dreamed of, and he suspected it wasn't over yet.

He approached Northelm just in time to see an ambulance drawing away and Nasseem standing on the front steps looking uneasily at his watch. 'Thanks for dealing with that, old boy,' he said, putting a friendly hand on Nasseem's shoulder. 'Are you going to come in and have a drink? How is the old girl?'

'Concussed, broken nose. No more damage than any rugby player can expect on a Saturday afternoon, but then she's probably not so used to violence as they are.'

The ambulance rattled its way from the country road and onto the main dual carriageway that led to the nearest Accident and Emergency department. Danny lay shivering under a rough blanket, drifting in and out of consciousness. The neck brace they had put on her and the straps holding her onto the stretcher made it impossible for her to find her rosary even though she struggled feebly to locate it with her fingers. The paramedic sitting with her mistook her efforts for panic and tried to soothe her. 'You're doing fine, Sister Danny. You're doing fine.'

If I'm doing fine, thought Danny, why is the siren going and the blue light flashing?

She longed to be back in her little room in the convent, all on her own, reading her Bible. What a mistake it had been to go to the funeral! All those people who had driven her into the convent in the first place – she had forgotten how selfish and misguided they were. What had she ever done to deserve a family like that, when from being a small child all she had tried to do was be good, please Jesus and her father? And why was God punishing her now? Was it her fault her brothers and sister were sinners? All she had done was tell the truth.

Which was more than Pippa had ever done. She couldn't contain the tears that rose and tried to choke her when she thought how Pippa had bullied her when they were children, how she had told lies to get her own way, how badly she had behaved when Jeremy was a baby and Mummy had been busy looking after him. She had always hated Pippa, but she never thought it would come to this. She never thought Pippa would try to kill her.

She began to cry again. Her nose hurt and she felt dreadfully sick. Then there was another pain, searing up her left arm. Please God don't hurt me any more! The paramedic at her side stopped trying to soothe her and moved urgently forward, calling through to the driver, 'We're losing her! She's tachycardic, poor old dear!' And as the ambulance swayed to a stop on the hard shoulder of the road, the paramedic began to pull at Danny's clothing, baring her chest.

'He's trying to rape me!' Danny tried to push the

invasive hands away. She tried to scream but no sound would come. What had they been taught? That even if their bodies were defiled, Jesus would save their souls. The pain in her arm was spreading through her chest, then everything was going black and the pain faded. In its place was a bright light and in the middle of the light she could see a figure coming towards her. At first she thought it was Jesus or one of the saints but as the figure came closer, smiling and holding her arms open, she saw that it was her mother.

After Nasseem had collected up his chauffeur and his bodyguard and the big black car had crept away into the darkness, Jeremy made his way through the drawing room and into the library, straightening chairs and side tables as he did so. The caterers were still going back and forth, picking up glasses, but apart from their soft footsteps and occasional quiet word, everything seemed orderly once again.

On the library table he found a neat set of papers, copies of the will and supporting certificates as proof of identity, left there by the solicitors. Jeremy sat and looked through them, curious. It was the first time he had ever had all the family certificates together and he was tempted to open them all up and lay them out, to see if what Aunt Netta had said was true. Was he really Tatton's son and Robert was his grandfather? And did the solicitors know?

He picked up the certificates and turned them over. It only mattered if the inheritance of the title was in doubt, and his birth certificate clearly said he was Robert's son. The solicitor had said so too, therefore he must be legitimate. He supposed that the modern obsession with DNA testing might have turned up something interesting but Robert had been in his coffin in the vault for years now. Jeremy was the Earl, young Tatton was his heir and nobody wanted to challenge the status quo.

Better keep an eye on Aunt Netta, though.

And that reminded him – where was Aunt Netta? He had

totally forgotten about her. She must be lurking around the house somewhere. After the way she had been drinking, she could have collapsed in any of a dozen bedrooms, or she could have taken one of the hire cars to the station. But there had been no sign of her on the platform.

Jeremy gathered up the papers he had been looking at and took them through into his study and shoved them untidily into the safe that stood in one corner. He would look at them more carefully tomorrow but he was already sure they would reveal nothing new, or they wouldn't have been available for inspection. Just then Johnston walked past the door with a tray of cups and saucers.

'Has everyone gone?' asked Jeremy.

Johnston paused. 'The caterers have just finished.'

'I mean the guests. What about the old lady in the blue dress, my aunt?'

The butler hestitated. 'I'm not sure, sir. There is a light on in her ladyship's quarters over the stables – the ladyship that's deceased, I mean. I was going to check on it in a minute.'

'Don't worry, I'll go.'

'Very good, sir.'

He wasn't surprised to find Netta in the dowager apartments. She must have been there for some time. She had opened the huge wardrobes, pulled out hanger after hanger of couturier clothes and flung them all around the place, on the floor, on chairs, on the bed. She lay unconscious in the middle of them all like some parody of the sleeping beauty, snoring loudly. She must have tried on some of the clothes because she was stripped of the blue Balmain gown and was wearing a grubby peach silk slip that had twisted this way and that and barely covered her body.

Even as he regarded the chaotic desecration of his mother's rooms, Jeremy couldn't help feeling sorry for Aunt Netta.. Was it true that but for a quirk of fate, she might have been his mother? He didn't even know where she lived, though deep in his heart he felt a growing fear that, for the time being, this was going to be her home.

As carefully as he could he cleared clothes off the bed and lifted the old lady so that she was snug under the eiderdown. She weighed almost nothing. As he turned out the light she turned over and muttered in her sleep, 'Wait for me, Candy!'

Nasseem settled into the comfortable upholstery of the Daimler and slotted his favourite *Hounds of Hell* disc into the car's passenger stereo. He listened to the raw energy of Leon's voice delivering the words at screaming pitch:

'Here I dwell, At the gates of hell, With a heart that's cold, And a soul I sold....Lo-o-o-ng ago-o-o-o...'

As a younger man Nasseem had identified with the heavy themes of his brother's music but only now did he hear the words as though they had been written for himself.

I really have sold my soul, he thought. What else? I've turned my back on my own people and tried to be something I never really understood or felt comfortable with. Jeremy and Leon are not like that. They are both what they were born to be. But I was afraid so I took another way out.

And now he was afraid again, because his anger over what had happened to Leila had made him agree to name the people she had been working with and the reprisals for doing that would be as swift and brutal as the conflict that had clouded his childhood. Furthermore, he would be a traitor, not a hero. A man who betrayed his cousins and nephews as well as his country's independence. Whatever he had said to the authorities in Tel Aviv, whatever he had said to Jeremy, he could not make himself follow that path. His grandmother Leila, his Uncle Hanif, they had made it possible for him to get an education, his mother had helped him to amass a fortune, now he could use it all to help Palestine, carry on the work his daughter had tried to do. He saw how it might be done. Not by violence but by negotiation, working with those who were trying to establish a viable government. There were people in power who would listen to him and who needed his money.

As the car sped through the night down the wet motorway, passing the occasional truck or other night travellers, he turned over the options again and again in his mind. Go and talk to the MI6 officer who had approached him when he returned from Tel Aviv and who would be waiting for him in his faceless office tomorrow morning? Or go back to Israel and make contact with his cousins, thereby working towards the future of his country and putting himself in considerable personal danger for the rest of his life?

They were on the M25 and the car had just passed the first of the warning exit signs for the A24 towards Surrey when he made his decision. He leaned forward and pressed the switch that connected him via the intercom to the driver and the bodyguard who sat beside him in the front.

'I'm sorry to do this,' he said, 'But I've changed my mind. Turn round at the next junction and take me to Heathrow please.'

'Not going home, sir?'

'That's just what I am doing.'

After putting the old lady to bed, Jeremy went in search of his family. He found Megan sitting at the kitchen table, crying quietly. From somewhere upstairs he heard loud rock music that told him where his sons were. With a start he recognised the heavy beat of one of the *Hounds of Hell* numbers that had taken the world by storm more than twenty years ago.

'Where did I lose you? Where did you go? Was I not watching? Was I too slow? Too slow? Tooooo slow?'

Had Charlie and Tatton bought one of Leon's CDs themselves or was it an old tape or vinyl from some dusty drawer? If so, who had kept it all these years? Who had cared enough about Leon's doings to hoard his music?

He put the kettle on and sat down alongside Megan. 'That's it' he said. 'It's over. Everyone's gone.' He decided not to say anything about Aunt Netta until tomorrow. 'Think we can get back to normal now?'

She sniffed and blew her nose. 'You tell me,' she snapped.

'Hey.' He moved closer and laid an arm round her shoulders. 'I know it hasn't been an easy day but you've done amazingly well to keep control of everything.'

'Don't patronise me. And don't tell lies. Nothing's been under control at all. Everybody's been behaving as though they were barking mad. And it's rubbing off on the boys – they've found my old record collection and they're working their way through all Leon's hits. All the ones I hid when your mother forbade us to have them in the house. And now he's run off without a word of goodbye.'

'He had other things on his mind...'

'I know that.' She began to cry again.

It occurred to Jeremy that he had absolutely no idea why she was upset. After twenty-five years of being together, he still couldn't even begin to guess whether this was a marital crisis or if she was just tired. He supposed he could ask her but what would he do if it did turn out to be something awful like she didn't love him any more? He couldn't bear that. He wanted his life to stay the way it had been last week, last month. The way his mother had taught him it should be. Smooth and ...yes...boring. Something he understood.

The kettle began to whistle. 'Cup of tea?' he suggested.